D0718907

Dear Reader,

A lot of you will, I'm sure, be thinking about your summer vacation now. So whether you're planning to sit in the sun by a pool, have a sporting holiday or just laze around at home (*my* favourite form of relaxation!) I hope reading *Scarlet* will be part of your holiday fun.

This month we are proud to offer you: the first award-winning novel by Julia Wild; critically acclaimed author Jill Sheldon's third *Scarlet* romance; a peep into the glitz and glam world of international tennis from talented new author Kathryn Bellamy; and a skilfully woven second novel, with a delightful Scottish background, by Danielle Shaw. As ever, we hope there are stories to suit every mood and taste in this month's *Scarlet* selection.

I always seem to be asking you questions – and here is another! Are four *Scarlet* books a month enough? Would you like to buy more?

I am very grateful to all those readers who have taken the trouble to complete our questionnaires and/or write to me. We are very grateful for your comments and we *do* act upon them.

Till next month,

Sally Cooper

SALLY COOPER,
Editor-in-Chief – *Scarlet*

JULIA WILD

DARK CANVAS

SCARLET

Enquiries to:
Robinson Publishing Ltd
7 Kensington Church Court
London W8 4SP

First published in the UK by Scarlet, 1997

A copy of the British Library Cataloguing in
Publication data is available from the British Library

ISBN 1-85487-961-8

Printed and bound in the EC

10 9 8 7 6 5 4 3 2 1

PROLOGUE

Never, even in her wildest dreams, had Abbey imagined success like this. Neither had she ever imagined she could be this happy, could soar above the shadows. It was a dream, her dream and it was coming true.

'Hey, Abbey – ' She turned in response to the call. 'How about a pose beside the Woodland scene for my album?'

'Sure.' Abbey raised her glass, bubbles rushing upward in a joyful bid for freedom, just the way she felt inside.

She tried not to squint at the flashlights. 'No need to ask you to smile tonight, is there, Abb?' Her closest friend, Lynn, laughed, raised her glass for filling to a hunky-looking waiter, then joined Abbey, slinging her compact camera on to a wrought-iron table before slumping, sighing, on to a hard chair.

'I could do him some damage.' Lynn followed the waiter's progress with her eyes as he moved amongst the thirsty crowd, mostly friends now the press were slipping away to file their reviews and print their pictures. 'Where did you find these guys?'

Abbey shrugged, laughing. 'Rick arranged everything, they come with the package. Why don't you ask him what he's doing when he finishes here?'

Laughing, Lynn rolled her eyes heavenwards, but they didn't quite go – too much champagne. 'Trouble is, I'd sleep through my fantasy – I've been up since dawn.' She looked at her watch. 'I've an early start tomorrow, too. I'm going to hitch a lift as far as London with your father when he leaves, Abb, do you mind?'

'No. I wouldn't mind slipping away either.' Abbey lowered her voice. 'It's been like a dream today, but I'm knackered now.'

'You can't leave till the end.' Lynn yawned. 'I wish I could stick around, but I had to swap shifts so I could come today.'

'What time's your flight?'

'I'll be checking in at five a.m.' At Abbey's horrified expression, Lynn added, 'Don't worry, I spent yesterday sleeping in preparation for today.'

Abbey leant back in her chair and stretched languidly. 'Miles is joining me at the beach house for a few days.'

'You won't be getting much rest, then!'

'Abigail?'

'Hello, Father.' She twisted round in her chair, caught the slight look of disapproval in Nedwell Roberts's bright blue eyes and asked, 'Is something up?'

'You can talk with Lynn any time. Shouldn't you be mingling with your guests?'

Any other time, Abbey might have taken offence, but she was too elated, too happy to argue. 'Don't worry, I'm an artist, no one expects me to be the perfect hostess a hundred per cent of the time.' She scanned the thinning crowd. 'Besides, I don't get to see Lynn much, not now she's off on long-hauls.'

To Abbey's surprise, Nedwell accepted her words

with a slight nod. He set his drink and catalogue down on their glass-and-handbag cluttered table. 'I haven't seen you look this happy in a long time, Abigail.' He smiled solicitously at the young woman, intense eyes following Abbey's movement as she pushed thick, strawberry blonde hair behind her ear. 'If only your mother was well enough to join us – '

Abbey paled visibly, held up her palm, determined that nothing was going to affect her mood. 'Not tonight, Father.' She stood, smiled down at Lynn, 'Let's go and say hello to Rick. He's the one who set all this up. Coming, Father?'

But the damage had been done. The effervescent edge had gone from Abbey's mood. She knew some measure of relief when her father collected his stack of belongings from the table and shook his head. 'Another time. I really must go, darling, it's a long drive home and I'm travelling a great deal over the next few weeks. Have a wonderful rest.'

'Thanks – ' she squeezed his forearm as he kissed her cheek ' – and thanks for making the time to drive all this way. It meant a lot to me.'

'I wouldn't have missed it for the world. Sorry to drag you away, Lynn, but are you ready?'

'Ring me, Abb – ' Lynn hugged her friend '– I'm home four days next week.' She turned to Nedwell Roberts, put her arm through the crook of his. 'Your dad's promised me a demo of his new CD player.'

Abbey lingered in the soft night air to wave her father and Lynn on their way, turned, almost collided –

'I'm leaving now, Miss Roberts.' A press photographer shook her hand. 'Where do you want the proofs sending?'

3

'Rick?' Abbey guided the photographer towards her agent, gave him a smile. 'Would you pick the best proofs?'

'That's what you pay me for.' Rick pulled a slender silver box from inside his light wool jacket, took out a business card and handed it to the photographer. 'Look forward to hearing from you.'

'It's been a great party, Miss Roberts – ' the photographer smiled at her '– thank you.'

'Think he fancies you,' Rick chuckled as the photographer strode out of earshot, then turned to Abbey. 'No Miles yet, Abbey?' He shoved his hands into his pleat-fronted trousers. 'Hey, don't look so worried, Miles'll have a good reason for being late.'

'I was just thinking about him.' Abbey glanced down at her delicate gold watch. 'Maybe he got held up – Friday traffic and all that?' But even whilst she spoke, Abbey didn't believe her own words; even on a Friday, it shouldn't take from close of work until almost midnight for her boyfriend to make it across town. On the other hand, Rick was right – Miles always had a good reason for anything he did. There would be a good reason for his lateness.

Abbey knew a niggle of conscience; she should have thought about Miles before this, but the exhibition, the party, her own wave of excitement had carried her along in a timeless vacuum – she hadn't even looked at her watch since noon. Guiltily, she thought she hadn't even missed Miles. Until now.

'I'm going to make a call, back soon.' Abbey slipped away from the bar to the opposite end of the room, to the hooded telephone booth beneath the spiral staircase.

'Miles?'

4

But it was his ansaphone. 'It's Abbey, I just want to know if you're okay, Miles, I've missed you tonight.' She crossed her fingers. 'If I don't hear from you, I'll see you at the beach house later – ' She paused. There was something very difficult about having a one-sided conversation with a machine, but gamely, she continued, 'I want to say thanks for the flowers, all your patience – ' the machine bleeped then ' – guess that's goodbye'. She replaced the receiver and moved beneath the shadow of the spiral staircase, more than a little aware that she hadn't been entirely fair to Miles, or their relationship, over the past six months. She'd never really given him the time he wanted, always her painting came first. Well, Miles, she glanced at the telephone, for the next few days I'll make such a fuss of you, you won't know whether you're in heaven or paradise! But despite the thought, Abbey didn't really know if she could be somewhere as inspirational as her home, the house they loosely referred to as the 'beach' house, and ignore the need to paint.

'Which is your favourite painting, Miss Roberts?' A reporter waylaid her *en route* to the bar.

'Oh, hi.' For a second she was wrong-footed. 'I'm sorry, I thought the press had all gone.'

'I was just hoping for something exclusive, you know, something no one else has come up with.' The woman was young, eager for something to get her teeth into. It showed in her gleaming eyes.

'It's been an exciting day for me, er – '

'Laura Glover, the *Weekly Treasure*.'

Abbey nodded. That was where they all started. 'Well, like I said, it's been exciting for me, but I'm sure you've been bored out of your brains!'

5

'No – ' Laura sighed ' – you know how it is? I was hoping if I hung out till the last, one of your friends would be dreadfully outrageous and strip off or something.'

Laughing, Abbey shook her head. 'I'm afraid we're all in our "mid-twenties sedate stage" at the moment. Give it a year or so, one of us might do something scandalous!'

'Has anyone asked you how you feel when you sell a painting?' Laura frowned, tapped her bottom lip with her pencil, dislodging some of the 'supermodel' red lip-gloss on to the small pink rubber.

'Yes.' Abbey couldn't help liking Laura Glover, her enthusiasm, 'But no one's asked me how I feel when I've just finished a painting.'

'Go on – '

'Finishing a painting – it's like the best and the worst part – '

The lights flickered, hummed. Abbey fought a shudder of unease to continue saying, 'The best because I've put all I have into the work; the worst because I always feel I might never do that well again.'

The lights buzzed loudly, flashed off and on.

An inexplicable chill gripped Abbey. Strobing lights struck hard, cold moving shadows. The lights died, buzzing louder, acrid burning smells invading the room.

She froze. Air rushed from her lungs, a blow to her cheek distorted sounds, splintered time. Screams froze in her throat. Long-buried, disjointed, recollective flashes of herself as a child fighting, like now, to escape – fighting against the hand over her mouth, to breathe . . .

CHAPTER 1

'Jake Westaway.' Jake rubbed his sleepy blue eyes, blinked to try and clear them so he could see the clock, groaned when he saw the time. 5.43 a.m. 'Is this some kind of joke? Do you know what time it is?'

'Jake, I need your help, old pal.'

'Miles?' He swung his legs out of the bed, pushed his fingers back through dark hair; it immediately flopped back on to his forehead. 'Miles?' He stood, rolled his shoulders to rid the tension two short hours of sleep had done nothing to shift. Miles was talking, but Jake couldn't pull the words around. He was mentally and physically exhausted. That was why he needed a break. Why he was going to have a break.

'Jake? Did you hear me?'

'Let me get some caffeine inside me, Miles, I'll call you back.' He was halfway to replacing the receiver.

'No!'

'Okay,' he muttered, 'I'm still here.'

'Take this number. I'm not at home, I'm in hospital.'

'What?' Shock or coffee – either one did the trick.

'Got a pen?' Miles asked. 'Ring me back, Jake – ' the voice wavered ' – money will run out soon.'

'Fire away.'

* * *

7

'Okay, Miles – ' Jake's second cup of coffee and the shock that his mate was in hospital had both gone a long way toward waking him up ' – do you need a ride home?'

'No. I'm here for some time. I need something a lot more than a lift home, I'm afraid.'

'Ask away, so long as it doesn't take all day.' Jake itched to board his motor launch, take off for a complete break. A six-month stint watching the back of an unpopular Eastern gentleman had left him ragged.

At Jake's response, Miles fell silent, if you didn't count the curse under his breath.

'Come on, Miles, you don't wake me up at 5.43, then hold out.'

'I need you to check on Abbey for me.'

'I'll need more than that. Abbey who?'

'Abbey Roberts.'

'The artist?'

'Yes, my girlfriend.'

Impressed, Jake let out a low whistle. 'What else have I missed out on in the last six months? What do you want? Details of her account?'

'Jake, I – damn, I can't talk over the phone. Drive over and see me, will you?'

Half an hour later, showered and dressed in jeans and a white T-shirt, Jake inserted his favourite soft-rock cassette and gunned his way toward St Michael's Hospital. Whatever was on Miles's mind shouldn't take long to sort out; the boat was already loaded and ready to go. A small smile curved his mouth at the thought. Holly was probably loaded and ready to go, too.

'Miles Pendleton-Smythe?' The nursing sister

smiled appreciatively at Jake; he smiled back. It was the tan, he thought, got 'em every time. 'I'm about to check his obs if you want to come along.' She treated him to another smile before swishing off up the wide corridor. 'Are you a relative?'

'Friend.'

The nurse straightened the sheet around Miles's traction-weighted leg, eased the head of the bed flat. 'Mister Pendleton-Smythe may be drowsy because he's had a pre-med; the consultant has scheduled surgery to reset his shattered femur.' She hovered, straightened the 'Nil by Mouth' card hanging on Miles's metal tube bedhead. 'Your friend may need a pin inserted. If you have any questions, I won't be far away.'

'Thanks, you've been very helpful – ' Jake smiled again ' – but this is a flying visit.' He waited until the nurse had gone before pulling a chair up to Miles's bedside. 'So, what is it, Miles?' And when Miles roused, 'What is it you want me to find out about Abbey Roberts?'

'I was supposed to be joining Abbey at the beach house at Fasthead last night.' Miles winced with pain, his eyes glazed with the effects of medication.

'And you want me to drop by with a message that you won't be coming?' Jake pre-empted him, to save Miles the effort of speaking. 'No probs, it's close to the marina, I can drop a note in on my way to the boat if you give me the address.' Jake glanced at his watch. Plenty of time.

'No!'

'Miles, you'll have to help me out. Just what is it you want me to do?'

'Tell her personally, Jake – ' Miles struggled against

closing lids ' – I've been softening her up for six bloody months – don't want to wreck everything.'

Jake frowned. But what the hell? Just so long as he didn't miss the midday tide. 'What do you want me to tell her?'

'To visit me – ' Miles was fighting the drug-induced lethargy sucking at him. 'I – I love her.'

His raised brow went unnoticed by Miles. 'Okay.' Jake rubbed his shadowed chin with the palm of his hand. 'I'll check up on her and telephone you before I sail? If you're asleep, I'll leave a message with your nurse that Abbey Roberts's fine. Okay?'

Miles grunted, losing his fight against the drug.

'Abbey'll probably be sitting right here when you wake up.'

Before he left St Michael's, Jake sought out the nursing sister and explained that he would be calling with a message: would she pass it on to Miles? Then he telephoned Holly from the lobby.

'What do you mean expect "me when you see me"?' she shrilled. 'You should'a been here by now! It'll take ages to load all my gear in your crate! You promised you'd be on time – '

Jake held the phone away from his ear until Holly's sharp tone stopped. 'Holly,' he responded calmly, 'we could still make the noon tide. I'll deliver a message for Miles, then swing by and pick you up.'

'Why you, Jake? Why does it have to be you playing messenger?'

'We go back a long way, sweetheart. I owe him, okay?'

'Just so long as you're not going cold on me, sweet-buns.' Her voice as velvet as it had been sharp.

The change amused Jake, who laughed. 'No, I'm not going cold, darlin'.' For a moment, he let his thoughts ride on Holly's mind-blowing shapeliness, her red lips, the way her jewellery rattled with every move. 'Sooner I get going . . .'

Still early morning, Jake made short shrift of the journey to the Fasthead beach house. He parked in the rough, behind the cliff-top house fence, disturbing dust as he hurried down the slight incline to the Spanish-style two-storey building.

The door opened with fingertip pressure. Jake shouted, 'Anyone home?' The door caught on a local newspaper, a letter and some circulars. His trainers squeaked on the highly polished wooden floor as he carried the papers toward the kitchen, looking for any sign of the occupant. 'Miss Roberts?' he called. 'Abbey Roberts? I have a message for you.'

There was no response and Jake sighed loudly. Maybe she wasn't here? He threw the folded paper on to the pinewood breakfast bar. Maybe he ought to leave a note, telling her to go to St Michael's Hospital to see Miles and leave it at that. He glanced at his watch, scanned the pristine kitchen to check for signs of life. The work tops were clear, the toaster cool to the touch. The kettle warm. 'So you are around.' He called again, 'Miss Roberts!' Heavy sleeper, maybe? But a fast circuit of the Jacuzzi-cum-bathroom, sprawling lounge and two bedrooms found no sleeping Miss Roberts.

He picked up the large envelope he'd brought into the kitchen and uncovered the front-page headline of the *Weekly Treasure*. Prickles rose on the back of his neck as his eyes first scanned, then read properly: Local Artist,

11

Abbey Roberts, Ordered To Rest After Collapsing With Exhaustion. The piece went on to describe the phenomenal success of Abbey's exhibition – paintings that sold whilst they were being hung on the walls for the exhibition preview. At the end of the piece extolling Abbey's work, her genius, the reporter, Laura Glover, added with refreshing honesty: Miss Roberts seemed perfectly happy up until the power cut. We had been discussing different angles for an interview together. There was some noisy confusion. When the lights came back on, Miss Roberts was unconscious at my feet. A visiting doctor said she was suffering from exhaustion and needed uninterrupted rest, and that Miss Roberts should make a complete recovery.

Arrangements were made for her to be taken to a secret location, after a thorough check-up at St Michael's Hospital confirmed the doctor's diagnosis. All of us at the *Weekly Treasure* congratulate Miss Roberts on a brilliant exhibition and wish her a speedy recovery.

'Probably a publicity stunt.' Jake flung the paper down, glanced at the time and swore. 'Why in hell paint for money?' The house reeked of silver-spoon wealth.

Abbey's long walk helped diminish the woolly-brained effect of tranquillizers administered at the hospital the previous night. Her limbs, though, were heavy as she climbed the steep chalky path from the beach. A shiver raced over her skin – neither the walk nor the tranquillizers had done anything to quiet the fear last night's attack had exposed.

Her heart pumped erratically at the fragmented

memory. The heat under the stairs, the tall form looming in front of her; the brutal fist hitting her cheek, powerful hands slinging her to the floor and squeezing the breath from her. Worse – much worse – the disordered flashes of recollection rising from all those years ago . . . Pop grasping her upper arms, distraught, demanding, 'Who was it?' Sounds of people in the background, someone laughing, an obscene counterpoint to the grief-twisted form of her mother. She'd tried to speak then, to respond to Pop's question. But no sound had come out of her. Last night she couldn't scream for help either. When she'd been small, though, her voice had returned in minutes, whatever she'd witnessed sunk away – forever, she thought. 'I didn't see anyone, Daddy, I was hiding.' When it happened, hiding on the stairs in the shadow of the coat stand in the hall – the grown-ups' party too much of a curiosity for her to simply lie in bed and hear all that laughter and music.

But now, this time, disjointed images, scenes she had managed to displace, subconsciously tucked away because they were too harrowing for her young mind; this time, those recollections had stolen her voice. Her pace slowed as she took the last few steps to the beach house. She tried again to make some sound, but it was just air. What would Miles say? Words he'd spoken not so long ago taunted her now, 'At least we communicate well, Abbey. If you didn't make me feel so good when we do talk, I don't think our relationship would stand a chance.' It didn't seem very long – a little under six months. Miles, ex-public school, ex-army officer Miles, introduced to Abbey by her father, became her financial advisor, then charmed her into becoming his girlfriend.

13

Her thoughts tripped back to the previous night, to her absolute happiness, the friends, the warmth emanating from everyone at the exhibition. The devastating knowledge that someone there wanted to harm her. That looming, all-powerful form that had stolen her happiness and breached the dam behind which those confused, terrible recollections had been held. On a surge of frustration, she tried to make a sound. But there was nothing, only the beat of her own terror when she saw her front door flapping open.

Here? Her stalker was here? In the grasp of anger, Abbey weighed a sturdy piece of broken fencepost in her hands, frantic to be freed from her silence, certain that the answer to regaining the power of speech lay with the identity of the stalker. Her bare feet moved silently up the wooden steps, then she stood to one side of the flapping door.

Abbey could hear a deep male voice muttering, swearing, growing louder as it approached the door. Her hands trembled, she couldn't breathe as the door was deliberately slammed open.

'Where the hell is – ?' Abbey swung the fencepost at his head with all her might. Shock registered in his eyes as he half-turned before dropping to the deck. Whoever said surprise was the greatest ally was right. The absurd thought gave her the guts to prod the man from his side and on to his back with the lump of wood.

But he didn't look familiar. He didn't look even vaguely familiar. Disappointment brought tears to her eyes because there was nothing when she tried to make a sound; there was no great pouring back of the gaps in her memory. No return of her voice. She stared down at the man's supine form, frustration knotting her stomach. If this man was her stalker, why didn't his presence feel familiar? Sinister?

A deep groan escaped him. Abbey's mouth dried and her heart pumped fiercely as she lurched to move past him down the wooden steps. His eyes opened unexpectedly, locked with hers for an instant before he jerked the wood from her hands. Her lungs hurt as she fled down the worn chalk path to the beach, feet barely touching the sand. The caves! She focused on Bluff Cove, she could hide there – but her feet were knocked out from beneath her.

Winded, she fell face down in the soft, dry sand, saltiness on her lips. Before she could kneel and run, she was flipped unceremoniously on to her back, straddled, hands pinned at the side of her head.

Anger fairly sparked in the man's dark blue eyes. His breathing was ragged, and there was a worm of blood on his forehead where she'd struck him. 'Miles never told me you were a crazy woman.'

Ineffectually Abbey struggled, trying to dislodge her stalker. But he increased the pressure on her wrists. 'Wriggle all you like, Miss Roberts, but you're not going anywhere until I've delivered a message from Miles.'

She stilled, green eyes growing wider. Miles?

'Do you greet all your visitors this way?'

At the mention of Miles's name, Abbey's panic began to recede. Who was this man? What was he doing here? How did he know where to find her? Unless Miles had told him? Maybe this man wasn't a threat to her. But what right had he to poke his nose in her home? At that thought, she started to struggle and buck in a mammoth effort to topple him.

'Look, Miss Roberts – ' frustration joined the anger in dark blue eyes ' – that publicity stunt you pulled last night doesn't hold any water with me. I'm here to tell you Miles is concerned about you.' His breathing had returned to normal, Abbey's hadn't quite. Publicity stunt? The creep! 'He can't join you, he's in St Michael's Hospital with his leg in traction.'

Her mouth fell open; grains of sand from her lip fell onto her tongue. Green eyes begged for more information, but 'the creep' just seemed disgusted with her lack of verbal response.

'What is it with you? Don't you care?'

Suddenly, he released her wrists and rose agilely to his feet. 'If I had the time, I'd tell you exactly what I think of you, Miss Roberts. As it is, I'll use your bathroom to clean the blood off, and be on my way. You know where to find Miles when you tire of your melodra-bloody-matics.' Abbey caught the muttered, 'Damned spoilt rich bitch,' carried on the soft sea breeze as his long legs strode easily up the path toward the house. She followed slowly.

'Where's your cotton wool?' Jake shouted from the bathroom, 'This damn cut won't stop bleeding.'

Automatically, Abbey pulled the first-aid kit from beneath the kitchen sink, padded barefoot into the bathroom and shoved it toward him. He took the box, his eyes catching Abbey's for the briefest second, then dropping to her cheek. He caught her chin between his finger and thumb and turned her head slightly to one side to study the tight, shiny bruising, the small cut.

'Looks like somebody said hello right back – with a baseball bat.' A light frown knotted his brow, fleeting concern flickering in his dark blue eyes.

Blood trickled thickly down Jake's cheek, mingled in his five o'clock shadow. She popped the lid from the first-aid kit and pulled out a wad of cotton wool, wiped upward from his chin where a blob had been ready to drop on to his sand-dusted white T-shirt.

For a long moment, puzzlement glittered in Jake's eyes, but then they were angry again. 'I can manage.' He plucked the cloud of cotton from her fingertips, then glanced at his watch before cursing. 'Can I use your phone?'

One of the joys of this haven was the lack of a telephone. It was close enough for Rick to drop by and see her if he needed to relay any messages; anyone who knew her well enough came by to see her. Going in search of a pencil to write the cursing man a note, Abbey left him to tend his cut.

'Sorry, no telephone,' she wrote on the large envelope lying on the breakfast bar. Then she cringed, hoped that this arrogant pig of a man wouldn't tell anyone she had lost her voice.

Rick had known, and in his wisdom decided it was better if the outside world remained uninformed. 'It's temporary, sweet pea,' he'd reassured her when he'd dropped her off at the beach house in the early hours of the morning. 'I don't want to see you go through having your past raked over if this comes out. I'll stay until Miles gets here, should be easy enough to cancel my breakfast meeting.'

No, she'd shaken her head and hugged him with relief. Miles would be on his way – he wouldn't be happy if Rick was here. Not at all happy. Abbey was well aware that some agents might capitalize on the novelty value of having their primary source of income

17

struck speechless by shock. Rick, though, was always concerned for her need to keep on an emotional even keel. The past was her weakness; he was one of a close circle who knew that. Thankfully, the world at large had never been privy to what had happened that dreadful night. Whilst she inwardly acknowledged Rick's concern, his friendship, Abbey opened the letter, pulled out a plain manila sheet and propped the envelope against the wooden salt-and-pepper pot where Miles's messenger would see it, flipped open the folded sheet and padded toward her studio. She had no wish to face the creep's cynicism again. A publicity stunt? If only it was. Once he left, she would walk to the nearest phone box and order a taxi to take her to St Michael's Hospital. Phone box? Damn! I can't speak – how can I order a taxi! She started to crumple the thin paper out of pure frustration, realized what she was doing, stopped herself and unfolded the letter. Walk, it's only a few miles.

Then thoughts of visiting Miles flew out of her mind as the ugly, thick writing shot off the page. Its impact made her stagger to the front door for air.

Now I know where you are, I can come and get you any time – again. Her world tilted, darkened. *I could have taken you from under everyone's noses last night, Abbey Roberts. Tell your father to cash his assets. He'll need a lot more to get you back this time. Involve the police if you like, but they will only protect you for a while. I have all the time in the world.*

'What do you mean, there's no bloody phone?' the 'creep' boomed from her kitchen. 'Where the hell are you?'

'Go away and leave me alone!' Abbey would have

18

shouted if she could. She fought the dancing lights in front of her eyes. Her legs trembled so badly, she staggered to the top step outside and gasped silently. Keep it together until the man leaves – get to Miles. Miles was the only one who could help her. Or he'd know someone who could.

'Where – ?' The door banged behind her, the note fluttered from her fingers and caught against Jake's leg.

'Where'd this come from?' Jake frowned down at the paper, the ugly writing, the uglier message.

'Miss Roberts?' Another publicity stunt? 'Miss Roberts?' He reached toward her, fingers touching the shockingly cold skin of her shoulder. 'Did you just open this?'

She nodded in response, hair tumbling untidily around her face.

'Miss Roberts!' Jake moved to a step below Abbey, so his face was level with hers; at her total lack of response, he put a hand to her jaw and raised her face. 'Will you please tell me what happened? Did you just open this?'

Jake frowned as Abbey nodded. Pure fear screamed in her wet green eyes. Yet she didn't make a sound. If this was a publicity stunt, someone had forgotten to enlighten her.

More gently, he tried, murmuring, 'Can you tell me what's going on?' His large hand rested on her upper arm. He was shocked again at her chilled skin. She was trembling so badly, he allowed that she probably wouldn't be able to string two words together. Not for a while.

Jake sighed. He didn't need to look at his watch to know he'd miss the noon tide now, didn't need to be a clairvoyant to know that Holly would be shrieking mad with him. He'd make it up to her – let her make it up to him.

'Okay – ' he settled on the step beside Abbey, rested his elbows on his jeans-clad knees ' – tell me when you're ready.'

She shook her head, hair wild, tear-drowned eyes trying to communicate, prompting him to grasp one of her hands to keep it from trembling. 'What is it? I can't help you unless you tell me what's going on.'

Abbey snatched her hand from his, would have screamed with tension if she could, but instead took a deep breath, tried to think logically.

'I'm not a qualified doctor, Miss Roberts, but I'd hazard a guess you're suffering from shock.' Jake pushed his fingers back through his dark hair. 'Look, I don't mean to be rude, but is there someone I can contact to come here and stay with you? I'm supposed to be going away for a couple of weeks.' Jake stood, squinted down at the woman and sighed again. 'I'll get you some sweet coffee, maybe that'll help.' He disappeared indoors.

Suddenly, Abbey was alone, feeling tremendously vulnerable; at least for a couple of minutes Miles's friend had stood between her and the stalker. She fought the urge to follow him inside and find comfort in company. What good was he? He thought this whole nightmare was a publicity stunt.

Jake pushed open the door with his leg, set a coffee mug down beside Abbey Roberts, who hadn't moved, if you didn't count her trembling, whilst he'd been inside. Despite the fact that all he wanted to do was speed away and collect Holly, enjoy a couple of weeks of uncomplicated sex and sea, Jake couldn't help his mounting

20

concern for Miles's girlfriend. She was so quiet it was weird. If Holly had a massive black eye and a crank letter, she'd be very noisy. He'd have to kiss her to keep her quiet!

'Any better?' Jake asked as she put down the empty mug. He leant down beside her to rescue it.

But the heart-wrenching expression in Abbey's green eyes said everything. Her mouth opened, then she grasped his forearm when a loud, shattering discord of breaking glass splintered the silent summer morning.

Instinctively, Jake pulled Abbey to her feet, held her against his side, absorbed some of the shockwaves coursing through her. 'Okay, it's okay.' He pulled her to a chair beside the door. 'Wait here, it's probably a car throwing up a stone from the road.'

But Abbey shook her head, following him inside. 'I guess you're coming with me.' His tone wry as they entered the house.

She shoved her shaking hands into her baggy sundress pockets whilst Jake rescued the orange-sized rock from amongst the shards of glass scattered all over Abbey's patchwork-quilted bed. He snatched the rubber bands away and uncrumpled the sheet of thin, cream writing paper. His feet crunched on the glass as he moved toward Abbey, uncertain whether or not to show her the message: *As soon as you are alone, expect me.*

'This guy's a crackpot.' He tried to lessen the impact of the grim message. 'Get some shoes on, we're going to the police.'

Abbey hugged herself, tried to speak, force something out, but nothing came.

'It's okay.' Jake put an arm around her. 'I've gathered

21

you can't talk, so I'll explain some crank's threatening you.'

Relief surged unexpectedly through Abbey. She took a deep breath, put her hand against Jake's shoulder and leant her forehead against his hard, cotton-covered chest.

For a long time, Jake held the woman, her untidy hair catching on his shadowed chin. 'You'll be all right,' he found himself saying, wondering what Miles saw in this silent, strange mess of a woman. 'I promised Miles I'd make sure you were okay. We'll take these letters to the police, they'll deal with everything.' She felt different to Holly, more mentally different than physically; Jake was surprised that Abbey's shapeliness, every bit as luscious as Holly's, was much less blatant; the sack-shaped sundress covered attributes Holly would've died rather than hide.

Abbey's trembling lessened in his arms. He felt good about that; it made him feel intensely powerful to be needed. Holly never got this close without ripping her clothes off. Without even realizing he was doing it, Jake's hands moved in a comforting motion over Abbey's untidy hair, over the soft, chilled skin of her shoulders.

'Are you feeling any better, Miss Roberts?' Jake's deep whisper flitted easily into Abbey's relaxing state.

She nodded against the soft cotton T-shirt, closed her eyes, absorbed his warmth. For a while, she had forgotten this man was a stranger, that she'd first thought him the 'stalker'. He'd only come here to deliver a message from Miles, got hit with a lump of wood for his trouble and ended up having to calm her down. She couldn't explain the warm ease she felt when he held her. It was as if he'd thrown a protective quilt around her. And it worried her, because if it had been Miles holding her, Abbey wasn't sure she would feel this safe.

Then she remembered, a little guiltily, that this man had to be somewhere. He was going on holiday. Despite the fact that she'd rather stay right where she was until he mentioned moving, Abbey thought she'd better find some way to communicate with him, tell him she was ready to go to the police station. He might miss his flight – that was no way to repay someone who'd helped her.

Taking a deep breath, she pushed gently against his hard chest, looked up into deep blue eyes and pointed to the breakfast bar.

'You're hungry?'

She shook her head.

'Surely you don't want me to throw you on there and make love to you?' The question shocked Jake as much as it brought laughter to transform Abbey's features. Silent laughter. So unexpected, he was strangely gutted. Because in that single moment of transformation, Jake glimpsed exactly what Miles saw in wild-haired, bruised-faced Abbey Roberts.

She pulled a pen and note pad from a kitchen drawer, settled on a high stool, and wrote: *Police, then you can catch your flight?*

Jake sat on a stool beside her. 'It's not a flight, Miss Roberts, I own a motor launch. I'm due to sail out with a girlfriend.'

What's your name? she wrote quickly.

'Jake – ' his mien serious as he offered his hand ' – Jake Westaway. I'd have introduced myself earlier, but you weren't in the mood.' Amusement flickered in his dark blue eyes and Abbey smiled.

I'm sorry, she wrote, *I thought you were the man who attacked me last night.*

'At your exhibition?' Frowning, Jake passed Abbey the newspaper. 'There's nothing about an attack here.'

She read the article, recalled Laura Glover and the story she'd wanted so badly. Ironic. She'd missed the most frightening part. Whilst she read, Abbey's fingers touched the tender skin around her eye.

'Didn't you tell the police . . .?' His voice trailed. 'Ah – you couldn't tell anyone because you lost your voice.'

'It mentions the lights going out.' Jake scanned the story. 'Is that when you were hurt?'

Abbey nodded.

'Does anyone know you've lost your voice?'

Only my agent, Rick, she wrote.

'Did he see anyone near you?' There was a suspicion at the back of Jake's mind that Abbey Roberts had imagined the attack, that her injury was caused by falling to the floor. But a niggle responded that surely she would have put her hands out to save herself – it was a reflex action.

Abbey shook her head; dreadful fear creeping back into her luminous green eyes.

No one saw. Her writing irregular, fingers trembling, Jake slid the pen from her fingers and covered her hand with his own.

'Would you rather not do this?' He cursed Miles for sending him on this errand.

Abbey glanced at him.

That was all it was, a glance, but Jake instinctively knew what she wanted to say. He knew what she would write before she wrote it, and it was so uncanny, a cold trickle slid down his spine.

If I don't tell you, who can I tell?

The police, Jake thought, but maybe he ought to find out all he could and help her relate the details. But he didn't have much time. And Miles – damn it! There would be no simple 'Abbey's fine' message to ease his mind. He wouldn't be getting away today if he got any further caught up in this mess. The thought drove a curse from him.

'Could you tell Miles?'

Abbey could sense Jake's growing impatience with her, his restive need to be out of this mess and off on his motor launch. She hesitated, a little too long, then nodded.

'Yes – ' Jake ran his palm around the back of his neck ' – you could tell him, Miss Roberts, but he couldn't do anything about it – he could hardly keep his eyes open when I saw him. Reckon he'll be that way for a few days.'

Abbey rescued the pen. *I need to get my window fixed.*

'You can't stay here, Miss Roberts.' Jake frowned. 'The police'll want to look the place over.'

Call me Abbey. We'd better be going. I AM staying.

'Okay, Abbey.' He frowned again at her. 'Are you sure you're up to this? You don't look too hot.' Correction, she made the wild woman of Borneo look well groomed.

I'm fine, she scribbled quickly. *I can write notes to the police, you don't have to stick around.*

Tempting, very tempting, Jake thought. But he caught the brief flash of panic in Abbey's eyes and instead said, 'Let's play it by ear.'

During a bumpy ride to the police station, Jake inserted his rock-music cassette, it saved talking. Why should he feel mean for planning to dump Abbey and her problems in someone else's lap? Because, damn it, she wasn't his problem.

At the narrow crossroads, he glanced across at her. She looked tiny, frail, the huge tinted glasses doing little to disguise the bruising on her cheek. Jake gripped the wheel tighter to vent the ridiculous surge of protectiveness tearing through him. Not my problem, he kept on reminding himself.

Abbey smiled at Jake; he wished she hadn't. Miles's girlfriend was just too damned addictive when she smiled. That's it. Take her to see Miles.

'I'll run you to the hospital to see Miles once we've done with the police, Abbey.' He pulled out into the long road to town and missed Abbey's response.

What would Miles say, Abbey wondered, when he saw her bruised face? When he found she couldn't speak? He was a wonderful, charming man, but she knew that part of her attraction to Miles was her ability to get along with most people, to say the 'right' thing. And to look glamorous when the need arose. It mattered to him. Miles had made no secret of the way he felt – or that Abbey owed him some time. After all, he'd put few demands on her since the beginning of their relationship.

But how could she begin to explain all that to Jake? She turned to look at the undulating countryside; heat rose from the hills against the skyline. Miles would have a pink fit if he knew she'd found comfort in the arms of his friend – a red fit if he knew how much she would have liked to stay there. Miles was one of those ex-army

26

officers with 'Don't mess with me' tattooed somewhere beneath his charming, fifty-pounds-a-time hair cut and well-spoken veneer. So far, she hadn't disturbed that veneer and Miles remained affable, charming, dependable.

'Got your note pad?' Jake held the passenger door wide for Abbey, steadied her elbow as she made to jump from the high Land Rover step. 'You're still frozen,' He frowned, reached into the back seat and unearthed a denim jacket. 'Borrow this.'

The garment drowned Abbey. I shouldn't have done that, Jake thought, pushing the door closed and locking it, now she looks even more pathetic.

As they entered the front door of the police station, two response vehicles blurted out from the rear carpark, sirens blaring.

The desk man was burly, sweating, didn't look at all impressed as Jake explained the situation.

'So you want these checked out?' He wiped his wrist across his sweat-beaded forehead, held the corners of the cream sheets of paper between pudgy fingers, 'Shouldn't think we'll get much in the way of fingerprints off these – ' he pulled a face ' – and there's a broken window?'

'Yes,' Jake pointed to the more crumpled note of the two. 'That one was fastened round a rock.'

'So what this amounts to is one threatening letter and one rock through a front window with another threatening letter attached?'

'It's enough, isn't it?' Jake shot back angrily. What did the guy want? A round of applause? 'Miss Roberts needs someone at her home to keep watch for this crank.'

27

'Mr – '

'Westaway,' Jake supplied.

'Mr Westaway, I appreciate your friend has had a shock, but we don't have the manpower to keep a permanent watch on Miss Roberts.'

'Chrissakes!!' Jake banged the counter. 'She was attacked last night!' Roughly, he pulled the glasses from Abbey's face and glared at the apathetic desk sergeant. 'What has to happen before you'll take some notice?'

'Was a report filed?' He dabbed his cheeks with a dog-eared handkerchief, flipped through a large stiff-paged book. 'Where did the attack take place?' Eventually he looked up at Abbey. 'I'm sorry, miss, but there's no mention of an assault last night. Do you want to give me details now?'

Silence. Abbey looked to Jake and grimaced.

'She's too shocked to talk about it,' he put in hastily.

'We're a sub-station, Mr Westaway, we don't have huge resources, not like the old days. I'll have a GPV drop by and examine the damage at Miss Robert's home. It'll probably be late afternoon, but he'll take a statement from you whilst he's there.' He looked at Abbey, his manner softening visibly, 'At least you can arrange to have your window fixed.' He flattened his palms on the desk, smiled. 'How does that sound?'

Dark colour stained Jake's cheeks; Abbey could feel the anger in him. 'We'll do the statement now.'

'I'm sorry, sir, I can't leave the desk.'

'We'll do it here, then.' Jake fumed. 'We'll both sign it. Okay?'

Abbey left Jake's side to get some coffee from the drinks machine; she missed the desk sergeant's exchange with Jake.

28

'Abigail Farraday-Roberts?' He scratched his head. 'Name rings a bell.'

'Artist,' Jake responded, writing out his version of events on the rough sheet the man had furnished. 'She had an exhibition last night.'

'No, I mean from years back –' he scratched his head as though stirring the memories to the surface, whilst Abbey selected a coffee for herself and one for Jake ' – when the family first moved to the district.' He scratched his head again. 'That's it!' He looked pleased with himself. 'Heard a rumour from an old sweat in the Met – they'd moved down this way to get over their daughter's kidnap.'

That cold, unwelcome prickle whispered down Jake's spine again; he stopped writing and gave the man his full attention. 'Abbey?' He lowered his voice.

The sergeant leant toward Jake. Talking he didn't mind. Filling out reports he minded. 'Rumour has it she was taken from some swish party her parents threw. They must have paid up to keep it quiet.' He tapped the side of his nose. 'Family's loaded, her father was a self-made millionaire; the whole business was hushed up. That's if it was true, mind you.'

'Guess you'll never know.' Jake frowned, 'Thing is, she's alone at Fasthead – the guy that was due to join her isn't able to.' Jake nodded his thanks as Abbey set down a plastic cup of coffee at his elbow.

Jake continued writing as Abbey smiled at the police-man. No one understood what they were dealing with. Someone who could slip into an art exhibition, attack her and leave unnoticed, his attack unreported. Someone who was so clever, no one would believe her – Jake Westaway hadn't – when she claimed she had been

29

assaulted. Someone who made *her* seem like the crazy one. No one had seen him and there had been people all around, people she trusted.

Colour ran from her cheeks; she sank on to the hard bench seat. Someone who could steal into her parents' house at the height of a party and take her to hell. Someone without a face, but with the power to take her to the edge of sanity with the fear he created in her.

Someone she had buried away in a bid for survival, for a normal life; this someone back again to take everything. Now he had her voice. Soon he'd have everything. There was nowhere to hide, no one clever enough to protect her.

'Thank you for your help.' Jake had Abbey sign the report and handed it to the sergeant. 'If you could have your man swing by soon as possible, it'd be good.' Then I can get to Holly . . .

'Sorry I can't do more – ' he came out from behind his desk, walked them to the heavy front doors ' – the visiting PC will assess the situation.'

Abbey smiled, shook the man's hand. Jake's hand rested at the base of her spine as they walked in the heat to his Land Rover.

'We'll pick up a mobile phone.'

Abbey frowned. Was he mad? How was she supposed to use it?

'I'll make a tape, you can play it back.' Damn it, he was doing all he could think of. Why didn't it feel like enough?

With a small phone and a neat, portable tape recorder and a couple of tapes, they made their way to St Michael's Hospital to see Miles. Abbey scribbled furiously before they got out of the Land Rover, handed Jake a note.

Don't tell Miles what's going on, he'll worry. There's nothing he can do.

'What about your voice?' Jake frowned. 'He's not exactly going to overlook that.'

Laryngitis? Abbey scribbled, raised her brows hopefully in Jake's direction.

He shook his head. 'Give it a try. I'd agree, there's not a lot Miles can do.'

Miles was groggy after his surgery, but a sleepy smile lit his features at the sight of Abbey. Jake hung back at the door, yesterday's nurse hovering and smiling at him.

'What happened to your face, Abbey?' Miles's smile faded when she moved closer. He might be sleepy, Abbey thought, but he never missed a thing. Especially when it was connected with appearance. 'You look bloody – terrible.'

'She fell.' Jake was going to leave them to it, but now didn't seem like the time. He shoved his hands deep into jeans' pockets and leant against the door frame.

'I love you dearly, Abbey – ' Miles caught hold of her fingers and pulled her closer ' – but you could have made a bit of an effort to cheer me up. You look awful, darling.'

From his position by the door, Jake watched with interest as Abbey leant across and kissed Miles's cheek, smiled and settled into the chair close to his shoulder.

'How was the exhibition, darling?' He yawned. 'Were you a roaring success?'

Abbey glanced at Jake. 'There was a power cut.'

'Can't you answer for yourself?' Miles said, irritated. Abbey put it down to the painkillers.

She shook her head.

31

'Laryngitis,' Jake threw in, smiling at the nurse.

'I was hoping you'd spend time in here talking to me.' Miles yawned again. 'I get so bored.'

Abbey took one of Miles's hands in both hers, put his palm against her cheek and kissed it. Miles's manner softened. 'I had plans, Abbey.' He toyed with a strand of her hair. 'They've hit the pan, I'm afraid, between my failing brakes and your laryngitis. We've messed up, haven't we?' His eyes were drooping sleepily. 'At least stay and keep me company, darling.' His voice trailed as Abbey stroked a finger down his cheek; it was softer than Jake's, less severe.

She stayed at Miles's side whilst his physiotherapist adjusted the traction and fiddled with a drip at the top of a slender steel pole. 'I'm afraid it'll be a good three months before your boyfriend's back to strength.' In answer to Abbey's concerned look, the nurse explained, 'What he said about being bored, I shouldn't worry too much, he's been sleeping and not much else. He's just being a baby.'

Jake cleared his throat at the door.

'In other words, nurse – ' Jake pushed his fingers around the back of his neck ' – Miles isn't going to know whether Abbey's here or not for the next few days?'

'Loosely speaking.' She smiled at Jake. 'You'll be welcome any time.' She spoke to Jake, glanced at Abbey.

Abbey grinned to herself. Knock 'em dead, Jake, she thought. The man was a walking hormone – he just couldn't help himself. Why didn't he leave and go off on his holiday?

'If you've done your stint for today, then, Abbey,' Jake said, 'we've got some tapes to take care of. And you need to be at home – for your caller,' he added pointedly.

She scowled at Jake. He'd been trying to get rid of her all day, why didn't he just go? The tapes – so she could use the phone, of course.

'I hope your throat improves soon, dear.' Abbey thought the nurse was talking to Jake until, belatedly, she switched her attention to Abbey. 'Resting your voice will do as much good as anything.'

'To save time – ' Jake revved his Land Rover, then roared out of the hospital car-park ' – make a list of things like, "taxi, please" and your address, same for a distress call to the police – anything you can think of.' He jerked a thumb toward the phone and tape recorder. 'I'll knock that out, then as soon as the police have been, I can leave you to it.' He drew a disgusted look from Abbey when he added, 'You could even put in your favourite pizza order.'

Gamely, Abbey began the list. There was no point whatsoever in trying to explain to this walking hormone that she wouldn't need the phone. She was being tormented, trifled with, there were different levels to go through with her stalker before she needed to call the police. He'd toy with her until she spun on the outside edge of sanity, frighten her by being invisible to everyone but her; clever, he was clever. What she was really fighting for was her mind. That was what she had to keep in focus. It warmed her slightly to realize she had managed to keep her mind when she'd been seven years old. She'd won then. She could win again.

When she'd been seven, trapped in that dark, airless hell, fear and panic had disabled Abbey for a time. Until she had let her mind slip into a parallel world – a kind of automatic self-preservation, she realized now.

In her mind, she painted pictures, beautiful, detailed, exquisitely escapist pictures; and somehow, by using the technique of building the painting slowly, imagining every brush stroke, every mix of colour on the palette, she had kept her mind, burying the dreadful, terrifying reality deep within. Escaping into the paintings.

And afterward, all through school and the art college beyond that, her conscious mind had been set on acquiring the skills to make those beautiful paintings a reality. The ordeal forgotten, its legacy her driving need to paint. It was a gift she had developed during that indeterminable period of time, to envision, focus beyond the reality and rise above unbearable angst. To block out hammering madness so it became a weak, ineffectual tap.

'Have you finished your list?' Jake cut into her thoughts, parked above the beach house.

She handed him the note pad, which he scanned quickly. 'Okay, let's go inside and do it.'

Whilst Jake made the tape in Abbey's sea-view lounge, measured the broken window and contacted a local glazier to come late in the day, Abbey made him lunch. 'I really need to get going.' Jake frowned, looked at his watch again. 'Where are the police?' Distracted, he plucked the plate from Abbey's fingers. 'Thanks.'

Abbey played the tape back whilst Jake ate; he cringed, shoved the fluffy egg into his cheek. 'Lord, I hate hearing myself on those things, can't you wait till I've gone?'

Abbey laughed silently and turned up the volume.

Irked, Jake lunged from the stool and yanked the tape

player from her fingers, pressed the 'stop' button. 'I said wait till I've gone!' As Abbey reached for it, he swung it around his back. She grabbed for it, their legs tangling. Abbey almost had it from his fingers when his free hand clamped around her waist. 'I said wait!'

Jake looked down into laughter-sparkling eyes, became acutely aware of Abbey's feminine softness too close to him. It was a shock to his senses, electrifying, exciting, enticing. He wouldn't mind . . .

'I'd love to play around – ' he let his hand drop away before looking pointedly at his watch '– but my girl-friend is likely to be tearing my head off all our photos right now. I'm about six hours late. Where are the police?'

Jake's words were interrupted by a loud rapping at the front door.

After going through the earlier statement and inspecting the bedroom where the rock had shattered the window, the police constable offered, 'I'm going to recommend to the DCI that you have a panic button installed, Miss Roberts. I'm sure you won't need it, but it'll give you a feeling of security.' As he pocketed his notebook, he reassured her, 'We aim to attend all flash-graded calls within ten minutes in urban areas.'

Jake and Abbey flanked the officer on his way to the front door. 'This ain't urban,' Jake shot back dryly.

'Twenty minutes' response time in rural areas. The closest patrol vehicle comes straight away – it can be quicker.

'The CPO will explain everything. I need to hurry up, or there won't be time to get this authorized today. Can't you call your parents? Have them come stay the night?'

Jake couldn't answer that one for her, so he leant against the doorframe, stared down at the grassy-edged cliff and the sea beyond, wondered how much longer this whole mess would take.

Grimacing, Abbey wrote quickly, *My father's abroad on business, my mother's in Misty Hills Hospital.*

'Ah – I see.' The officer looked mildly uncomfortable and Abbey wondered whether he imagined that she belonged in Misty Hills Psychiatric Hospital too. 'Like I said, I'll do my best to get this pushed through before the day's out.'

Turning to a clean sheet, Abbey wrote, *Thanks for everything. I mean, really, thank you.* And shoved the note into the pocket of Jake's denim jacket. As they moved out into the late afternoon heat, Abbey thought Jake didn't even notice she was following him to his car to wave him on his way.

But he had. He turned, feeling strange as Abbey slipped out of the denim jacket she had trailed around in since he leant it to her and took it from her fingers.

'The crime prevention guy'll be here soon. Will you manage?'

Abbey nodded, rolled her eyes as if he was daft for even asking.

'Yeah, I know, you've lost your voice, not your mind.'

Not yet, she thought. That's the next thing to go.

He was awkward for a moment, pushed his fingers back through his dark hair. 'Okay, this is it, then.' He opened the car door. When he turned around, he was surprised to find Abbey's extended hand. Quaint. And cold – she was still so cold. 'Maybe I'll call in and see you when I get back?' Damn! He didn't even know why he'd said that. If Holly thought he was creeping off to see another female – it would be curtains.

Abbey's lovely smile made him regret his 'maybe' even more. She'd walloped him around the head, she'd made him late, she'd started his insides twisting and turning somersaults. And here he was, saying maybe he'd come back for more. Not bloody likely.

'Okay, then – ' he couldn't very well take the words back ' – take care, Abbey Roberts.'

She touched his forearm lightly and smiled, lop-sided, cute. 'Yeah, I'll take care, too.'

He climbed in his jeep and fought the urge to wind down the window and ask if she was sure she'd be all right. But he might as well have, for all the hesitation he was showing. He wound down the window. 'You know, Abbey, if we'd spent any longer together, I don't think you'd need that note pad of yours.'

She smiled, a big, generous smile and shook her head, pointed along the narrow road in the direction of the marina.

Jake gave a solitary wave to the solitary figure at the crest of the hill. Yep! Problem solved. Freedom at last! Two weeks on the water, Holly as eager to get her hands on him as he was on her.

CHAPTER 2

The glazier stood back and extolled cheerfully, 'This 'ere's shatterproof and double-glazed, with two large, locking openers.' He demonstrated the openers, then handed her the tiny window keys. No sooner did the glazier depart, then the CPO arrived.

'I'll run through everything, Miss Roberts.' He tapped the shoe-box-sized radio alarm, which he tucked away and plugged in a corner of her bedroom. 'Leave this plugged in, then you can forget about it.' He passed Abbey a small, cigarette-packet-sized box. 'This is a wireless panic button, carry it in your pocket all the time. Keep it close at night. When you hit this button, there's no sound, but the signal is relayed through the plugged-in UHF radio alarm. The closest patrol vehicle responds.'

How do the police know who's pressed a panic button? Abbey wrote.

'Every alarm has a different sequence of bleeps. The officers familiarize themselves with each before their shift.' He hesitated. 'Don't worry, these systems are used regularly for witness protection – they are effective.'

After checking the system, the man left. Abbey waved, yawned and reflected that, at least with the activities of the last few hours, she hadn't had time to dwell on matters. Or Jake the Hormone Westaway.

He'd made her laugh on a day when she would have sworn there was no laughter. And every time she brought his parting words back into her mind, they had a strangely warming effect. 'You know, Abbey, if we'd spent any longer together, I don't think you'd need that note pad of yours.' Maybe the walking hormone had a heart. Whatever Abbey thought of Jake, he had made her feel safe. Miles would never bang on the counter in a police station in anger. Miles wouldn't want to go in there with her in the first place – in case anyone thought he'd been up to something dodgy. He'd send someone else to do his dirty business. And she doubted, too, whether Miles would seriously consider taking up mind reading or exchanging notes to keep the lines of communication open. Maybe she was being unfair. He had wanted her to stay with him today. Stay with him and talk to him. She cringed inwardly.

I'll sketch until I fall asleep; normal thoughts helped to keep lurking shadows at bay. She planned to use Jake's tape and get a taxi to see Miles first thing in the morning. I'll write to Lynn, too, tell her what's been going on.

As it was, Abbey took her sketch pad to bed, propped pillows behind her and let the pencil move freely over the sheet. It was therapeutic to see what developed on the paper. And she smiled a lop-sided little smile. The tall figure in the centre of the sheet could really be anyone stood against a boat – a 'motor launch', he'd called it. But it wasn't anyone. It was Jake Westaway, the man who'd tried to put her world to rights, who had made no effort to hide that he didn't want to get involved. And right now, she thought, refining his lean, muscular form, he's probably well under way with his girlfriend . . . Holly? His girlfriend Holly helping to mop the decks, or whatever it was girlfriends did when they were on a motor launch with someone like Jake.

'All day!' Holly thrust her arm out, bangles rattling. 'All day I've been sat here like a lemon waiting for you, Jake Westaway!'

Jake winced. Sometimes, Holly's tone could really strike a nerve. She could induce a migraine at ten paces – make that twenty, he thought as she shrieked and swung overstuffed scatter cushions at his head.

'I'm sorry.' He fielded the cushions, grasped Holly's elbow. 'I'm here now. Do you want to come, or don't you?'

Shaking Jake's hand free, she planted her hands akimbo, glared at him. 'You know, you really cheese me off.'

'I kind of gathered that.'

'And don't smile at me when I'm mad, you jerk!'

Oh, Lord, Jake couldn't help himself, it always got him into trouble, but it wasn't just Holly's bangles jangling, her whole body was joining in now. 'I'm sorry – you just look so – ' He was going to say 'wild' but that flashed up a vision of Abbey, so he said, 'Sexy,' and watched as Holly began to melt.

'All the same, you should have phoned me.' She stuffed her make-up into a giant bag and zipped it up. 'You've got just two weeks, Westaway – ' she walked her fingers up Jake's chest ' – to make it up to me.'

He grinned. 'No problem.' Just so long as she stayed off that nerve-jarring note.

Abbey Roberts – pathetic though she might be, didn't have any jarring notes. She didn't have any 'notes' at all.

40

'Do you really need all this stuff, Holly?' Jake pictured the small cabin bursting with Holly's luggage. 'We're going on a thirty-six-foot launch, not a cruise liner. There isn't room for all this – '

Holly shrieked, Jake closed his eyes.

'Holly, I'm serious, two bags, the rest stays.'

Eight suitcases for two weeks? The woman had a serious problem, but he refrained from telling her that.

Angrily, moaning the whole time, Holly repacked her things, and by the bulkiness of the suitcases she finally produced, Jake had his suspicions that she'd emptied the eight into two.

'Are you happy now?' She pulled on her furry jacket and slipped her feet into patent-black high heels, 'You can't blame me for *this* hold up.'

'Fine.' Jake wouldn't chose the word 'happy' to describe how he felt right at that moment. His head was in a permanent wince from Holly's high-pitched protests. And right now, he didn't have the resources to go over – yet again – the impracticality of high heels on a launch. He pushed down the image of Abbey Roberts's shoeless feet, their perfect shapeliness dusted with sand.

Jake enjoyed the sharp salty tang in the air as he unloaded Holly's belongings on to the boat.

'Yo! Jake!' Todd, the manager of the marina, raised his hand and sauntered over to them. 'You guys making a late start?' His eyes flicked appreciatively over Holly, who smiled and rattled her bangles with equal appreciation. Jake grinned, at ease with the effect Holly had on the masculine libido. He set down one of Holly's heavy cases as Todd asked, 'Do you need the keys for diesel or water? I'm about to go off for the night.'

'No.' Jake grabbed the handle of the heavy case. 'We're all set, 'cept for Holly's luggage.'

'Have fun, then.' Todd palmed the huge bunch of keys, shot an envious glance in Holly's direction, and said with a deliberate conspiratorial note, 'Don't rock the boat.'

Waving to Todd, Jake reached inside the Land Rover to hook out his denim jacket and shrugged into it. Abbey's fragrance rose from the garment, unsettled him. He wondered if her window had been fixed, if she had used his tape yet to communicate with the outside world? If the CPO had visited . . .?

'Jake!' Holly gasped. 'This bloody plank is stuck on my shoe.'

He helped wriggle Holly's high heel from the gap in the planking on the jetty. 'You'd better take these off, Holly. Do you have any flat shoes?'

'Of course.'

Well, that was something. 'Come on, then, get your delicious body on board.'

Holly loved that. She smiled and her bangles rattled. 'Aren't you going to carry me?' She pouted.

'What are you, woman, helpless?' He laughed, lifted Holly into his arms, depositing her over the side and into the launch.

'Are we going to eat? I'll get sick otherwise.' Holly's voice held a slight whine. 'What time are we sailing?'

'There's a tide in just under an hour. Do you want to throw something together while I get ready to go?'

'I'm not going to spend all my time in that kitchen.' Holly jerked her taloned finger at the galley.

'No, you're not.' Jake gave her a sexy smile, hoped it'd be enough for now to keep her quiet.

He checked his top pocket for a small screwdriver to make some minor adjustments, and his fingers met with a small piece of paper. Frowning, he pulled it out, turned on the navigation light to read, *Thanks for everything. I mean, really, thank you.*

Quaint. He smiled and looked across the cliffs to where her house was, although he couldn't see it at this distance. At that moment, he was rocked by the memory of holding her, the way she'd really needed him. The way it felt good, the power it gave him to have her panic recede in his arms. He forced his thoughts back to tweaking the engine, but that dazzling smile of hers, the transformation when she laughed – silently – hung in there at the edge of his mind. And as though to compound his thoughts, Abbey's fragrance hung on tightly to his jacket and tantalized him every time he tried to concentrate.

'Stop it,' he checked himself, 'I did all I could.'

But Abbey's potent scent was freed by the heat of his body inside the jacket. 'You're not my responsibility!' he said grittily.

'Who're you talking to?' Holly swayed up the galley steps, an untidy jam sandwich on a paper plate. 'Here, this'll keep you going.'

'Thanks.' When he'd asked her to 'throw something together', he hadn't meant literally.

'So, tell me what the big deal was today, then?' She leant against the padded seat.

'Just a minute, Holly, I've nearly done, love.'

In other words, he thought darkly, let's get going before my conscience grows a conscience.

'You said that twenty minutes ago!'

Twenty minutes? The response time to a flash-graded call. A lot could happen in twenty minutes.

43

He swore and twisted out of the jacket that insisted on evoking illusions of those green eyes and cold, soft, shocked skin, flinging it to the deck in a gesture meant to fling her out of his mind.

Within the half hour, the twin diesel engines fired into life.

'So?' Holly sprang, wrapped her arms round his middle whilst he negotiated the way out of the floodlit marina. 'What happened today? What was this message business?'

Okay, now he could do it, they would be free and clear into the open sea in less than ten minutes. 'You've heard me mention Miles? The ex-army financier friend of mine?'

'Uh-huh.' She blew warmth through his T-shirt. 'Posh geezer you went to college together, you trained him and some of his mates in the army?' She wrinkled her nose. 'What's that smell? Why do you smell of a rich woman, Westaway?' Her arms dropped from his middle.

Jake didn't have to turn around to know that Holly's eyes would be flashing with rage. And he was as cheesed off as Holly that Abbey's evocative fragrance infused not only the jacket at his feet, but his T-shirt too. 'Miles was supposed to be joining his girlfriend, but he broke his leg badly, couldn't make it. I went to tell her.'

'So you went to the hospital?' Holly's tone was waspish. 'Then you spent the whole day with Miles's girlfriend?'

'It wasn't that simple.'

'Knowing you, Jake Westaway, I'll just bet it wasn't that simple.'

'Look, Holly, it wasn't that simple because she'd had some trouble, I had to take her to the police station and sort some things out for her.'

'So what is she? Helpless? Helpless and under thirty-five, I'll bet.' She strutted away from him, then spun around. 'Why do you smell like you've been climbing all over her?'

Jake sighed, but not at Holly's jealousy – he'd expected that. 'She was shook up; I held her for a bit.' No, he sighed because of the screaming inadequacy of a twenty-minute response time – what protection was that against someone who could infiltrate Abbey's exhibition, presumably when she was surrounded by people she knew? He slid the control levers slightly, trying to blow the niggle from his mind, leave it behind. *Free Spirit* answered his touch, sped clear of other masts, the engines powerful, perfect. Any moment now, the aspiration of raw diesel would sink the rich bitch without trace. I'm going to enjoy this holiday. He concentrated, steered *Free Spirit* straight at the mouth of the marina.

'You didn't have to hold her!' Holly was pacing, hands on hips, really letting fly. 'And you held her for a "bit"? What do you mean, a "bit"? A bit of what?'

Just two hundred yards and Jake would be outside those concrete marina walls, break into the sea, where the moon lit the water without interruption. 'I held her because she was afraid. End of story.' Straight ahead, nothing between him and freedom.

'So you say. Afraid of what? You leaving without trying it on?'

Eyes forward, Jake pushed the speed lever a notch higher, the heightened engine noise helping to dull out

Holly's ear-cracking tone. 'You're having a joke – she's Miles Pendleton-Smythe's woman. Our tastes don't coincide.'

'Do you love me then, Jakey?' Her arms were round his middle again.

'Mmm.'

Nearly there, fifty yards to go.

But Abbey's image, her delicate wave of farewell, that wave he'd been so relieved to see, altered in his mind to flailing arms, terror-stricken green eyes, no sound coming out of her mouth.

You're not my responsibility! Get out of my head!

In the large open space of the bay, Jake spun the wheel around, tilting the boat, sending up a circular wash. It was no good. Like it or not – Abbey would have to come along with them. There was just no other way to ensure her safety.

'No way, Jake!' Holly threw a fit. 'I am not sharing you with some bimbo who can't even get to a police station on her own!'

'Holly, I'm not asking you to share me with anyone. I want you. But this woman, she can't speak – she's not safe – some jerk is after her.' He tried to explain, but Holly wouldn't stop screeching, hanging on that note he couldn't stand. She thumped his chest until Jake caught hold of her hands. 'Enough, Holly. I've had enough.' Blue eyes glittered with restrained anger. 'I need you with me to help me out, I can't look after her on my own.'

'Tough! Unload my things.' Jake could tell from the look in Holly's eyes that she was calling his bluff, her anger erupting again when he merely shrugged and dragged her obscenely full cases on to the jetty. Word-

46

lessly, he slung them into the Land Rover, cursing himself for caring whether Abbey was all right, cursing himself for not losing himself in Holly's gentler side.

'Are you really going to pick up that – that dumb twit?' Holly, gasping, couldn't believe what was happening.

'Sweetheart, I'd rather have you along, but if you won't believe that nothing went on today – '

'Damn right I don't believe you.' Holly climbed off the launch and rocked the Land Rover as she climbed in and sat down. 'Take me home. If she means more to you than I do – '

'No, she doesn't, Holly, don't you understand?'

'No! Take me home,' she repeated, still calling his bluff.

Reluctantly, Jake did just that.

The sketch pad dropped on to the patchwork quilt as incredible sleepiness dragged at Abbey. Somewhere in her mind rose the suggestion that this wasn't natural sleep, but it couldn't be fought against. It's exhausted sleep, she answered the suspicion.

It was as dark as night could be near Abbey's house. No street lamps, no other house lights; just a single track of light from the moon as it played across the sea.

As Jake drove along the winding cliff road, he was overwhelmed with regret at the memory of Holly's tears. Right to the last he'd tried to cajole Holly into coming along. 'One look at her, Holly, you'd know Abbey Roberts does nothing for me,' he'd tried, 'she's a mess.'

'She's a woman, isn't she?' Holly tossed that at him,

but he hadn't taken the bait. She had had tears in her eyes.

'Come on, Holly, her life could be in danger.' But all the while, he could hear the PC saying they aimed to respond within twenty minutes, and each time, it sounded more inadequate. 'If nothing else, Holly, remember that Miss Roberts is Miles's girlfriend – even if she wasn't a mess, I wouldn't touch her for that reason alone.' So long as you define 'touch' pretty loosely, he admitted silently. Holding someone when they clung to you, terror screaming in their eyes, didn't count. 'Holly, I'll make it up to you.' He had kissed her, too briefly to satisfy either of them, the recollection of Abbey's fear-filled green eyes somehow throwing urgency into play.

Jake turned the bend into the cove where Fasthead nestled on the grassy cliff edge. How he would make it up to her? A security light flashed on outside Abbey's house, sending a wide funnel of white light across the massive band of grass between the house and the cliff edge. So Abbey was still wandering about? Or the police had responded to her panic alarm. Or – ? 'Christ!' He slammed down the accelerator, the road moving too slowly beneath him.

Dust sprayed as he juddered to a halt. Jake reached into the passenger well for a torch and ran, slid, down the incline to Abbey's home. The sweet smell of burning wood mingled with dust in his nostrils, searing his lungs. The decking at the front of the house was fogged by smoke, the front door wedged closed by a heavy lump of wood. Jake heaved it aside, burst into clouded air inside, dropped his arm from his mouth, eyes smarting, ran to Abbey's bedroom, flicked on his torch, terror spiking him at what he might find.

Lassitude, heaviness, a hot weight across her mouth. Abbey tried to raise her hands against the pressure; she had to breathe – but there were no bones in her body to stiffen the flesh. Like water, she flowed beneath the hand, cheated its effort to smother her. And she sank, down, away, where no one could harm her. Something smelt wrong, but it helped her escape, slip away from the memories.

'Christ!' Jake shouted hoarsely, curls of smoke rising like demons around Abbey. A note secured with long thin nails to her pillow. Eerie in the torchlight; Jake couldn't read it, the effects of smoke making his eyes stream and itch. He lifted Abbey from the patchwork cover, went to grab the note, changed his mind. Flashing the torch quickly around thickening smoke, light glinted dully on the handle of the newly installed window. Throwing Abbey over one arm, Jake wrenched at the handle, swearing when it didn't move. Beaming the torch light around for a key, Jake fought to clear his eyes of water. 'Where, Abbey?' His voice was gravelly, as he considered that he might have to leave the way he came in – something, instinctively he didn't want to do – but the smoke was denser outside her bedroom. Cursing, he threw Abbey back on the bed, turned up her pillows, emptied a bedside pot of trinkets. Wiping his fingers across his stinging eyes, Jake focused long enough – yes! Fitted the key and flung open the window, then pushed Abbey out, cringing as she slapped on to the wide pathway at the front of the house, quickly following her.

Stopping to shove his torch in his pocket and sling Abbey over one shoulder, Jake slipped and scrambled up the incline to his Land Rover. He placed the slumbering Abbey on the front passenger seat, and ran swiftly back to the house. First things first, he decided and dashed inside to fetch water to douse the still-smouldering deck. Luckily, whoever had set the fire hadn't made a very good job of it, for the flames hadn't taken serious hold. When the fire was out, Jake surveyed the damage. Apart from a scorched front door and a few charred spots on the floor, the house, and Abbey, thank heavens, had got off lightly.

Jake stalked back into the house, to check thoroughly that no sparks had touched the interior. All was well, but, as he wandered from room to room, a thought struck him. Returning to the sitting room, he looked through Abbey's desk drawers. Sure enough, her passport was there and he quickly pocketed it.

Leaving the house, he walked swiftly back to the car and climbed behind the steering wheel. The wheels scudded on the dust and the old engine protested when Jake floored the accelerator, making the Land Rover fly off bumps along the coast road, checking feverishly that no one followed.

Cursing, barely able to see for the stinging in his eyes, Jake slewed the Land Rover into the marina car park and halted more by luck than judgment in his parking bay.

Only then did he heave a sigh of relief.

Twisting in his seat, he shone the torch on Abbey, felt the pulse at her neck. Compared to his own quickened pulse, Abbey's was slow, weak.

Carting Holly aboard *Free Spirit* had been hard enough, but Abbey, although lighter, was a dead weight, completely unconscious. She couldn't hold on, she just flopped. 'Sorry about this, Miss Roberts,' Jake said as he unceremoniously slung her over his shoulder. Kneeling on the gang plank, he hauled her on to the cushioned seating in the well of the boat.

Fighting his most immediate need, sleep, Jake cleaned up the cuts on Abbey's face, arms and legs, mostly caused by his need to make theirs a speedy getaway. He checked her pulse again. It was stronger. He wrapped her in a warm quilted sleeping bag, put her in the galley cabin and opened a sliding window close to her, then, too exhausted to set sail, slumped down on the berth opposite Abbey.

'Yo! Jake!' A loud summons dragged him from deep sleep. He splashed his face and rolled his shoulders, opened the cabin door and went to greet Todd.

'That little raver of yours keep you from casting off last night, Jake?' Todd squinted against the risen sun.

Wiping his palm down his still damp face, Jake responded automatically, 'You could say that. She's not going to stop me this morning, though.'

'Still asleep?' Todd arched slightly, trying to catch a glimpse of Holly through the open cabin door.

'Now that's not gentlemanly,' Jake grinned, blocking the doorway with his frame.

'You'd best get underway, then – ' Todd chuckled ' – 'fore she wakes up and gets busy again.' He shoved his hands into his back pockets and rolled back on his heels in true mariner fashion, scanning the horizon. 'Tide's about right.'

'Cheers. Throw me the rope?'

Obliging, Todd repeated yesterday's words, 'Don't rock the boat!'

'Not much chance of that,' Jake muttered once the twin diesel engines throbbed into life. He made careful, then swift progress from the marina and out of the bay across open sea.

The tangy sea air smoothed the ragged edges from Jake. He slowly relaxed, thoughts drifting back to the conversation with Todd. He wasn't sure why he'd let Todd believe it was Holly bunched up in a quilt in the galley cabin.

Maybe because anything concerning Abbey was so weird that he didn't fully understand it himself. Face it, Westaway, he acknowledged the regret leaving Holly behind caused him, you're just plain crazy. Why else bring Abbey Roberts and all her problems on board *Free Spirit*?

Abbey's skin prickled with dread as she broke free of deep sleep. A deep, throbbing noise disoriented her; weakly she pushed herself upright, swayed and blinked into the dimness. Terror charged her like an electric shock; overrode the thumping in her head, the water weakness of her limbs. Droning engine noise increased; Abbey's terror increased. He had her – ! No!

She yanked aside the curtain. At sea – she was at sea! Lurching across the cabin, she repeated the action. Shook her head against the proof of her eyes. Began to tremble with rage, with fear. At sea. But how? When? Abbey tried to make a sound – nothing happened.

A strange odour rose from her silk nightshirt; summoned recollections of the previous night, the same unnatural odour penetrating her senses; unable to fight, unable to stay awake. Unable to press her alarm button.

Panic splintered through Abbey. The stalker had her. The vessel bounced, tilted slightly; she clutched the kitchen work surface. Got to get away – got to get away. The words chanted in her pounding head. Sweat chilled her skin. No choice. Had to get away.

Silently, Abbey eased open the cabin door. Blinding sunshine intensified the throbbing pain between her eyes. She had to get away. Or lose her mind.

She grasped the side rail, blinked against blinding flashes before her eyes, tried to focus on the boat's wash, ignore the sluggishness of her limbs. If he turned around – he would stop her – take her to the hell she had known as a child.

She leapt, a second's freedom before she hit cold water. A funnel of bubbles above her, blood pumping in her ears, salt water rushing up her nose, into her mouth.

As Abbey broke the surface, she forced arms barely strong enough to keep her afloat into movement, grew chillingly aware there was no engine noise. But his shout, 'Abbey!' compelled her to redouble her efforts, realizing too late that whatever saw her sleep so deeply also rendered her weak beyond belief.

She could hear him cursing. Abbey flung her arms forward, 'got to get away – can't go through that again', drumming in her ears. But greyness pulled at her; she fought her way back up to the air, spluttering, weighted, knew that soon the third time would come and she would escape her stalker forever. Grey and blacker.

Sunshine, bright light, childish giggles filled her ears. She chased a butterfly toward the large house; and as she neared, Pop roared with deep, masculine laughter, held his arms open – 'Come to your Dad, princess' – then he whirled her around and she flew, elated, heavy sandals weighting her feet so they raised right up in the air.

But she broke from his grip, flew backwards, away from him. 'Pop!' She spun away, further, further, heart aching. 'You can't die yet' – his words elongated, down a tunnel of time; he waved to her, smiling, sent her back to the greyness.

'Breathe!' Jake checked for a pulse again. There was nothing. He straddled her, pushing down with the heel of his palm, counted, breathed air into her oxygen-starved mouth. Her chest raised, but there was still no pulse.

'Woman – ' Jake counted, depressed her chest, breathed air into her lungs 'damn – I'm not kidding, you can't die on my boat.' A trickle of water escaped the corner of her mouth. 'Breathe!' He repeated the process, swore when projectile salt water hit his chest. He turned Abbey on her side, pulling her arm and leg into the recovery position; she coughed, retched, dragged air into her lungs.

Jake felt like throwing Abbey Roberts straight back over the side for her stupidity, had to quell his anger as he knelt at her side, pushed the bedraggled hair back from her face. 'It's okay, you'll be all right.' What the hell was she playing at?

Once he was certain she'd be okay, Jake knelt and raised Abbey into his arms. 'You need to rest for a day or two before you go swimming.' He shouldered open the cabin door. He almost dropped her when she began to wriggle.

'What is it with you?' Jake growled, arms tightening around her.

Water trapped in her ears and distorting Jake's voice, Abbey flailed against his hold. The air left her when he dumped her on the cushioned bench seating; her hand flew upward and caught his crooked nose; she struggled to sit, but his eyes blazed with anger as he pushed her firmly back down. 'What's the matter with you?'

Salt-brightened eyes stared back at him. They were filled with fear and hatred. He caught hold of her forearms and held them at her side, stared down into eyes that damned him. 'What?' Anger flashed through him. 'You think I – ?' He digested the horrible truth. 'Hell! You don't think it's me? You think I'm your bad guy?'

Yes, she was certain. That voice – distorted.

He stood, repelled, pushed his fingers back through dripping hair, took a step away. 'You're doing my head in, woman!' He turned. 'I turned my boat back last night because I was worried about you!' A muscle twitched in his jaw, eyes pinned her, penetrated. 'It's a bloody good job I did – you were practically comatose from some smoke!' He stuck a hand straight out. 'I came back, but I'm beginning to wish I'd let you take your chances.' Rage surged through Jake, but he checked it, his tone lower. 'I don't know who your bad guy is, Miss Roberts, but it sure as hell ain't me. I ain't that desperate.' He slammed the palm of his hand against the shower-closet wall, disappeared inside and turned on the water.

Abbey pulled away from Jake when he yanked her to her feet, but his strong arms easily thwarted her. 'Now let's get something straight.' He lifted her just off her feet and carted her toward the shower room, 'Try that again, I'll leave you to drown.'

Silently, Jake stood beneath the rods of hot water, holding Abbey against his stomach until the awful chill left her. She could feel the tension in his taut frame, vaguely aware that she had put that tension there.

'The prop could've torn you to shreds.' His tone as harsh as his grip, he tipped shower gel on to her head. 'I can't believe I was dumb enough to come back for you, I don't believe it.' Hard-ended fingertips rubbed against her scalp, thin ropes of lather trickled down her tattered silk nightshirt, and Abbey thought he said, 'I could've been screwing Holly. Instead, I'm stuck with you', but his voice was fluctuating in volume.

Warmth for Abbey brought with it a return of the consuming weakness; too many shocks in too little time, too much anguish uncovered.

Jake swore as Abbey slumped in his arms. He hauled her into the cabin, tore the wrecked nightshirt from her and pulled a thick quilted sleeping bag over her wetness. Finding Abbey's pulse reasonably steady, her skin warmer, Jake peeled off his own wet jeans, dried hurriedly and pulled on a pair of worn green army fatigues. 'You're going straight back where you came from, Roberts,' he ground out, 'just as soon as I can leave you on your own long enough to take you there.'

The strangeness of events though, had taken their toll on Jake,' he longed to throw anchor and sleep. 'So why don't I?' He pulled down a chart from an overhead locker and confirmed their position was well away from the shipping lanes, then let the anchor go.

Hours later, Jake woke suddenly; his resting mind had served him a sickening scenario. He'd returned Abbey to her beach house. The headline the following morning bellowed: Artist In Brutal Kidnap. The dream was one of those that clung, seemed real even after he'd splashed his face with water.

Disgusted at the mess he'd got himself into, Jake stared down at Abbey. She was resting, so he went above board and fired the engines, needing to clear his head and put more distance between himself and the conflicting urges to return Abbey home, or take her with him.

It was late evening when Jake returned below deck. Abbey thrashed at the cover, strands of hair clung to her forehead and cheeks. Instinctively, he put his hand on her forehead. Burning. 'Great.' Now he had to nurse a woman who thought he'd kidnapped her.

Abbey stirred, immediately aware of Jake's presence slumped in sleep at her feet. She had no inkling that almost twenty-four hours had elapsed since her bid for freedom. Jake's chin was shadowed, his head dropped forward, a white flannel in his hand. Instinctively, she drew her feet away from his thigh – Jake responded instantly, sleep-darkened eyes fixed on her face.

'You're back in the land of the living then, Miss Roberts?' Lord, she was pale, the ugly bruising on her cheek so dark in contrast. Anger clenched Jake's stomach as Abbey scuttled to the far end of the padded bench, sleeping bag clutched around her, green eyes defiant.

Gritting his teeth in silent anger, Jake filled the kettle and lit the gas ring. So she still thought he'd kidnapped her? 'I've done some pretty unsavoury things for money, Miss Roberts, but I'm not so freaking stupid I'd kidnap anyone!' Spinning round – 'Do you think Miles would've sent me if he didn't trust me?' His blue eyes challenged her then. 'Y'know, you trusted me yesterday, you were like a freaking barnacle!'

Confusion thickened in Abbey's mind. This wasn't her stalker's voice she was hearing now . . . not like yesterday. This was Jake Westaway's voice – the man who'd made her laugh yesterday, the man she'd sketched before sinking into unnatural sleep. The man in whose arms she'd known a strange sense of safety. And, yes, she had trusted him.

Whilst Jake made coffee, leaving hers on the small table before going on deck, Abbey pulled the facts through her mind. When she'd taken that foolhardy dive over the side of the boat, she hadn't known whose boat she was on – only that she had to get away. And because of her close encounter with death – water-logged, barely conscious – it was feasible that her fear-drenched mind and seawater-filled ears worked together to produce the horrendous distorted mono-tone voice from her past.

And like Jake said, he had come from Miles in the first place – taken her to visit him, then stayed whilst the PC visited . . . Knots of fear unravelled as Abbey sipped the bitter coffee, wondered how on earth she could begin to explain her blunder to Jake. It was understandable, yes, but in Jake's eyes it was likely to be unforgivable after all the trouble he'd gone to on her account. To try and explain by scribbled notes would only make matters worse. If she had her voice, she would attempt to put her case; without it, it was hopeless. In her confusion, Abbey had overlooked the most obvious fact of all. Jake was five, at most ten, years her senior. Presuming the spectre haunting her now was the same figure from the past – she knew he'd been old. A cold shiver crept over her skin; old, then – ancient, more cruel, now.

A soft moan of revulsion escaped her, surprised her. She tried her voice. 'Jake?' she whispered huskily, gasped with delight, convinced Jake Westaway had returned her power of speech, and driven back the walls of silent insanity.

'Jake – ?' She wriggled from the sleeping bag and pulled a sheet around her nakedness, tied it beneath her arms, tried the door to the deck.

'Jake, I can speak.'

'Mmm, good.' He didn't even turn from his stance at the rail. '*What*?' Jake spun around.

Abbey laughed, put her hand on his shoulder and stared into his dark blue eyes. 'I can talk, Jake. Isn't it great?'

Jake was momentarily elated that her voice was soft, deliciously husky, then he was angry because she had suspected him. Last time I help a female in distress, he thought darkly. Never again. 'You're practically naked.' He snapped because she was too close, 'Kidnappers indulge in other vile sport.' He slung her a disgusted look and moved to the opposite rail.

'Jake – !' Abbey clutched the crumpled sheet and moved after him. He had his back to her, staring out over the inky-black sea, tension written in every moon-lit muscle.

'I know it's not you,' she said simply, a lifetime's practice of dealing with difficult moods making her certain she could convince Jake. 'I – I know it's not you because I feel safe with you.'

Still, he didn't move, save for a muscle in his cheek.

'Thanks – ' she touched his upper arm ' – thanks for turning back when you didn't have to.' And when that had no effect, 'And for fishing me out of the sea – I wasn't thinking straight, I woke up in a flat panic.'

For a reason he couldn't explain, the husky tones of Abbey's voice angered Jake all the more. He spun around. 'First – you shouldn't feel safe with me.' Her

59

eyes met his steadily, unflinching, as he erupted. 'And second, I didn't turn back for your sake, but for Miles's,' he ground out, 'and if I'd been thinking straight, I wouldn't have fished you out of the bloody sea.'

'You're still angry with me,' was Abbey's unexpected response.

'Damn right I'm angry!' Jake wished he hadn't let his eyes drop to the breasts pushing against the cotton material tied carelessly around them; it destroyed his flow. 'Would you get out of my face?'

Undaunted, Abbey rested her cool fingers on his warmer forearm. 'Will you tell me what happened at the beach house?' She didn't blame him for his anger, but whatever it took, Abbey could be civil for longer than Jake could be pig-headed.

He frowned at her like she was crazy, dropped his arm so her hand fell away and snarled, 'Don't you understand English?'

'You should try seeing this from my side.' Abbey's husky tones practically stole Jake's anger; but he hung on tight to the remnants as she clarified, 'I woke up in a strange boat and panicked. It's not unreasonable after everything else that happened to assume I'd been kidnapped again.'

'I don't feel like being reasonable right now, Miss Roberts. I'm too ticked off.'

'Call me Abbey.'

'Abbey, I'm severely ticked off.'

'I probably would be too.' She moved to his side, leant against the rail, facing him. 'Where's your girlfriend?'

'Well now, I'm glad you reminded me,' Jake took savage pleasure in growling at her, 'she refused to come along when I told her we'd have a passenger.'

60

'That won't do your hormones any good.' She folded her arms. 'No wonder you're "ticked off" with Holly.'

For a second, Abbey thought Jake Westaway was going to grab her and throw her overboard, so intense was the anger flashing in his eyes. 'I'm not ticked off with Holly. I'm ticked off with you.'

'Will you tell me what happened at the beach house?'

'In a few years, when I've cooled off.'

'No, now.' Abbey raised her chin as a night breeze caught her hair and released its fragrance, her eyes challenging. 'Please?'

He caught her chin between finger and thumb. 'Lady, I've no doubt you can twist Miles around your little finger, just don't push it with me.'

'Ah,' she said, as if something very important dawned on her, 'you're not used to having conversations with women.'

Jake frowned at the gall of the woman. 'What's that supposed to mean?'

'You're one of those macho sex-machines who only says enough to have a woman quiver with delight and roll on her back.'

His frown deepened as Jake honestly wondered if he was hearing things. 'Maybe I don't go in for deep and meaningful any more, Miss Roberts – '

'Abbey.'

He paused. 'Miss Roberts,' and glowering, 'but you don't know me well enough to come out with crap like that.'

'Okay.' Abbey shrugged lightly. 'Prove me wrong.'

Jake shoved his fingers back through his fringe and sighed. 'You've lost me again.'

'I want you to tell me what happened at the beach

house, Jake. It's the least you can do since you have me practically "captive" on your boat.'

'The least I can do?' Jake grasped the aluminium rail instead of Abbey's neck. 'The least – ? Woman, since I delivered that message to you four days ago, I've lost my girlfriend, I've rescued you not only from a smoke-filled building, but from drowning, and been accused of kidnapping!' He had to shake her, had to. 'And – ' his knuckles turned white against the rail, he daren't let go ' – I spent the last twelve hours nursing you like a goddamned baby because you had a temperature.' Low menace laced his tone. 'And do you know what? I'm too ticked off to talk to you about what happened at the beach house, okay?'

'Mr Westaway . . .' Abbey paused, refused to be browbeaten by Miles's friend '. . . I think we have a problem.'

'Tell me about it.'

'We are stuck on this boat, together.'

'That's something I'll fix just as soon as I can.'

'In the meantime – ?'

'In the meantime, Miss Roberts, stay out of my face.'

Abbey sighed. She was losing this battle, but couldn't quite give up. 'After everything you've done for me, Mr Westaway, it would be rather nice if we could try and get along.' At the sheer incredulity in Jake's eyes, she offered, 'First names would be a good start.'

Jake shook his head. He just couldn't believe this woman. 'What are you on? Rather nice to get along? After you accuse me of kidnapping you?'

What bothered him more than anything right at that moment was the sheet that Abbey had tied around herself had flapped open in the breeze, revealed a shapely thigh.

'Are you deliberately flashing your legs?'

She hadn't been; the accusation stung. 'No, of course not.' It stung until she realised it bugged Jake, then she felt the warm power of femininity drop into play. 'I've been brought up not to preen once I'm dressed.'

'I wouldn't call that dressed.'

'Perhaps you could lend me something to wear, Mr Westaway?'

'Will you quit calling me "Mr Westaway"?'

'Of course, if you'll call me Abbey.'

Jake gripped the rail again. 'Did anyone ever tell you how infuriating you are?'

'No,' she lied with great aplomb. 'You look exhausted, Jake. Why don't you have a lie down?'

He closed his eyes and counted to a hundred and thirty. Jake was a quick counter. He'd never dealt with a woman like this – in all his experience. 'Just how does Miles cope with you?'

'Generally – ' she pulled the gaping sheet together ' – he tells me what I want to know, so we don't have these fracas.'

Any more, and Jake would buckle the hand rail. He stared across the moon's path, took a deep breath against the gut-deep tension riding him. The waves lapped against the side of *Free Spirit*, tried their best to soothe his dark mood.

The water pump hummed loudly into the silence.

Abbey gasped, shivered, and when he glanced at her, he saw something he didn't want to see. He saw pure fear and vulnerability shining in her eyes. 'What is it now?' His tone was testy to cover the strange lurch of concern in his stomach. 'The water pump can't harm you.' Jake sighed and shook his head.

63

'No, I know – ' she sank to the bench seat ' – it's that noise, it's like the sound before the lights go out.'

'When the lights go out? Like at your exhibition?'

She nodded, shuddered, 'It brings it all back, the fear, I mean.' Her voice huskier than ever when she added, 'I can't control the fear, Jake; it controls me.'

His anger sank without trace. Jake sat beside Abbey, covered the hand that clutched the two sides of crumpled sheet together with his own large hand. 'Hey, you got your voice back, it's a place to start.'

'I wouldn't have it back if it wasn't for you.'

'Maybe, maybe not.' He didn't want to take the credit – who was he trying to kid, of course he did. 'If it helps, Abbey, you're one place no one can get to you.' When she nodded, kept her eyes downward, Jake tried again. 'In a couple of days, you'll be so used to the water pump, you won't even notice it.'

'I know you're right.' She did look up then; wetness sat in her eyes and Jake held her cold hand. 'It's the knots in here' – delicate fingers brushed her chest – 'sometimes I think they'll suffocate me.' She gave a little grimace. 'You won't tell Miles how pathetic I am, will you?'

'I think he'd understand a touch of pathetic after everything you've been through.' But somewhere deep inside, that didn't feel like the truth to Jake. Miles's women were always flawless mannequins, with little emotion.

'Do you want to talk it out – what happened at the exhibition?'

The breeze caught a strand of Abbey's hair and snagged it on Jake's shadowed chin. He stood, held out his hand, 'It's too cold out here for sheets, come on.'

A smile curved his lips, 'I'll dig out something warm for you.'

Lost inside Jake's deliciously warm rugby shirt and overlong track-suit trousers, Abbey drew her feet up to her bottom and rested a mug of warm soup on her knee. 'Do you mind if I tell you about it? What happened?'

He pulled a white T-shirt over his head, finger combed his hair. 'No, Miss Roberts, I don't mind.'

Abbey gave a small, husky laugh at the reminder of their clash, let her eyes close for a second on the mercurial male sitting opposite her, elbow propped on his raised knee, for all the world as casual as if they were discussing the weather. Maybe that's what made it so easy.

'The most frightening thing is that everything must have been planned down to the smallest detail.'

'Go on?'

'I was kidnapped as a child. There was that awful loud buzzing noise just before this hand covered my mouth and I couldn't breathe.' She faltered, then continued, 'It was a party – at a party my parents were throwing. I should have been up in bed, but you know how it is when there's music and laughter – ?'

'And you're seven years old?' Jake threw in.

'Yes.' Abbey's cup shook in her hands when the loud pump started up unexpectedly.

'You'll get used to it.' Jake took the cup from her fingers and set it on the table within easy reach. 'Go on.'

'As a child I buried the memories away. The details, they lay there forgotten until the other night at the exhibition.'

'If something's too tough to cope with,' Jake offered, 'it's a safety valve shutting down, else you wouldn't cope.'

'You're right.' She rubbed her arms, enjoying the comfort of Jake's rugby shirt. 'I think it was to protect my parents, too.' She sighed, 'The more things come back to me, Jake, the more I realize I couldn't have managed if I had remembered everything.'

'Do you remember everything now?' Jake asked gently.

'No.' Abbey shook her head, 'Mostly the intimidation, the games he played with my mind, the helplessness.' She wanted to be in Jake's powerful arms, feel the warmth she had found there when he'd held her at the beach house.

As though drawn, Abbey crossed the cabin, sat beside Jake. 'Will you hold me?' It never occurred to her he would refuse as she leant her head against his shoulder and rested her hand on his jeans-clad thigh.

Briefly, Jake entertained misgivings, mostly concerning Miles. Then he reminded himself, holding someone when they're canning it doesn't count. But – and there was a big but – Abbey felt far too good to encourage this kind of easiness. He almost began reassuring her that everything would be all right, but didn't honestly know that it would, so he stayed quiet, put one arm around her and purposely kept his coffee mug in the other.

Oddly, he wondered who had held her when she'd been a child after her abduction. Had she needed holding? Or had her total shutdown as far as memory went made everything okay? What was it like now – now she knew constant fear? Fighting, training, sifting intelligence, watching people's backs were things he'd trained for; but how did a young woman wrapped in money and privilege, talented, closeted, not beautiful, but with eyes that spoke and a voice that bordered on sexy – how was she supposed to cope?

Yawning, Jake slid his cup on to the work top, aware that Abbey seemed to have nodded off, caught himself about to wrap his other arm around her and stopped himself. Miles would only 'understand' so much. Easing her from his side to the bench, Jake covered her, searched out a bottle of whisky and had a good double slug before climbing on to the opposite berth. Maybe he could teach her a few self-defence moves. It wouldn't do much good, but at least he'd feel as if he was doing something.

Waking to the sound of quiet, off-key singing and the spit and sizzle of burnt cooking when he'd been dreaming about Holly – or someone like her – didn't start Jake's day too well.

'Abbey!' Jake reached in front of her and turned off the grill control. 'Don't use the grill, it doesn't light properly.'

'I opened the window.' Abbey jerked a fork at the opening.

'Methane sinks to the bottom of the boat and lays there, that's why you've got to be careful. It could ignite.' Quite why he was acting so bolshy, Jake didn't know. Yes, he did. If there was one thing he found hard to resist, it was a sleep-dishevelled female wearing his rugby shirt and not a lot else, and one that could cook. 'Finish it on top in a frying pan.' He padded toward the shower. The colder the better.

CHAPTER 3

'Self-defence?' Abbey almost choked on her coffee.

'Yeah. Forget it, it was just an idea.'

'No, it's a good one – but I'm really out of shape. I haven't done anything but paint for months.'

Abbey's enthusiasm surprised Jake, 'From what you've told me, for the air to leave you, the jerk must come up on you from behind – in which case I might be able to help you. Or he gets to you when you're asleep – I can't do a damned thing about that.'

'I appreciate the offer, Jake.'

'It'll have to wait until night time, I want to cover some miles today.' And shortly afterwards, when Jake fired up the engines and Abbey sang off-key and made short work of tidying up, he seriously began to consider whether it was a good idea to plan on grappling around on the well-deck with Miles's girlfriend.

Unearthing a Biro and a note pad, Abbey settled herself on the well-deck seating behind Jake, rolled up the gorilla-length sleeves of his rugby shirt and began a detailed study of Jake's musculature. She was fascinated by the play of sunlight on sweat-sheened skin, the dark hair that split and clung to his neck. Back in her art-school days, weeks were spent on

68

the human form, but none of the models had inspired her so much as Jake.

'What are you doing?' Jake put the throttle into neutral so they could relax and eat.

'Just sketching.' Abbey handed him the pad. 'It'll look better when it's finished.'

'Mmm.' It looked amazing already. Detailed, shaded, pretty much finished, he would have thought. He'd never admit it, but he couldn't help feeling flattered that Abbey had spent all morning drawing him.

'You have a beautiful muscle structure, Jake.' Abbey spoke purely from an artist's point of view. She continued eating and so missed Jake's startled look, the way he had to force down a mouthful of sandwich. He bit down the instinct to return the compliment and ate in silence. But he nearly choked again when Abbey said casually, 'I'd like to sketch you without your T-shirt, do an in-depth study of your torso.'

He laughed, strangely uncomfortable. 'Hell, I ain't posin' around for no one.' Perversely, his mind served him the difficulties of posing naked for a woman. If he was supposed to keep still . . .

'What's the problem?' Abbey glimpsed the shock in Jake's dark eyes. 'You've got a fantastic body.'

To his horror, Jake began to feel embarrassed. This was Miles's woman, for Chrissakes! 'Are you hitting on me?'

She shook her head, 'There's nothing carnal about my interest in your physique.' Laughter danced in her eyes, which annoyed the hell out of Jake. 'It's like a photographer wanting to photograph a beautiful scene.'

Jake frowned slightly. 'Yeah, well, Miles might have something to say about that. Wait till you see him and sketch him.'

'I sketch who and what I want, Miles has no influence there.'

'If you were my girlfriend, I wouldn't feel too happy about you sketching a nude "macho sex-machine".'

It was Abbey's turn to have trouble swallowing. 'I can't believe I said that.' Warmth rose to her cheeks. 'It wasn't very nice, was it?'

Jake's laughter was infectious as he shook his head, 'It was – ' he paused ' – a surprising description for an upper-crust artist.'

'I'd like to sketch you.' Abbey tucked a stray strand of hair behind her ear. 'And I didn't say anything about you being naked.'

Jake studied Abbey for a moment. 'Miles would have someone blow me out of the water if he thought you'd spent time drooling over my bod.'

'Miles doesn't get violent.' She shielded her eyes against the sun. 'Jake, you have a beautiful body, but I'm afraid I don't drool.'

His ego was instantly deflated. 'So I'm a set of pecs you enjoy looking at?'

'No, you're a man with a fascinating physique.' A sparkle entered her eyes then. 'I'm going to sketch you anyway, whatever you say.'

'You don't give up easy, Roberts, I'll say that for you.' Jake recognized Abbey's tenacious streak. When she had tried everything to get him to tell her about the night he'd brought her on board, he'd seriously wanted to strangle her.

She gave him a smile then, a delicious, lop-sided smile and took the plate from Jake's hands. 'I like a man who knows how to give in graciously,' she whispered about a foot from his ear in that husky voice of hers.

70

That almost-sexy, all-woman whisper that she probably used on Miles to get all her own way. If he'd known her better, if she wasn't involved with Miles, Jake would have snapped a rag at her rear end.

The water pump started up as Abbey disappeared into the cabin. Instinctively, he watched for her reaction. But there was nothing; she didn't even flinch.

'Swimming?' Abbey raised the hair from her neck. 'I thought you were going to teach me self-defence.'

'You said you weren't fit.' All afternoon and into the early evening, Jake had been increasingly aware of Abbey's presence. Of her sketching him in her completely 'non-sexual' way. And the more he thought about it, the wiser it seemed not to start anything physical – even self-defence training.

'The water's a lot warmer here. There's some things in the locker Holly forgot to take.'

'Are you going in?' She shaded her eyes, set down the pad on the bench seat.

'In a minute.'

Abbey grimaced, wriggling into the white, crocheted bathing suit Holly had left hanging in the locker and snapping off the shop tag. Either there was more of her than there was of Holly, or else Holly intended to spill out of the strapless costume. Judging by the high-cut leg and non-existent back, Abbey decided the 'spill out' theory was likely the right one. 'Very subtle,' she muttered, leaving the cabin and bumping straight into Jake.

His hand brushed the top of Abbey's thigh, briefly, but his touch lingered strangely after he jerked his hand away. 'Thought you'd fallen asleep,' he snapped testily.

71

'No. I've been using your razor, this – ' she plucked at the middle of the skimpy costume ' – has less fabric than a handkerchief.'

'Yeah, well, I'm sorry if it's not to your ladyship's taste.'

Abbey planted her fists at her waist. 'There's no need to be sarcastic.'

Ignoring her remark, Jake indicated the small ladder over the side. 'Go in off the ladder.'

'Moody.' Abbey scowled at Jake as he let the cabin door slap closed behind him. She ignored the ladder and jumped into the turquoise water, defiant, angry. She swallowed a mouthful of sea water before she broke the surface to be met by Jake's glowering features – he was beside her in the water.

'I said use the ladder.'

Spouting the water from her mouth, Abbey lurched toward him. 'Stop telling me what to do.'

He caught her wrist, brought her hard against him beneath the water. Her senses leapt uneasily at the contact. 'I said use the ladder.'

'I heard you.' She jerked her wrist from his, but he caught it again as Abbey said, 'You make me angry.'

'I make you angry, so you ignore the fact that there might be rocks beneath the surface?'

'You wouldn't have parked here if there were any rocks.' Her eyes flashed with challenge.

Exasperated, Jake threw her wrist away, 'Fine, maim yourself if you want to. Just wait till I've dumped you at Marianne's.' His intense, dark eyes burned before he flipped over and swam with strong, easy strokes away from the boat.

Abbey kicked after him. 'What do you mean?' She

didn't stand a chance of catching him, so she shouted, 'What do you mean "dump me at Marianne's"?' She, too, became exasperated as Jake continued swimming, but then, with no hope of catching him, Abbey paddled about near the boat.

She swam around the other side, floated on her back, let the early evening sunshine and the gentle swell of the sea relax her.

Jake swam until his tension lessened. Abbey spilling out of Holly's swimsuit bugged him. It reminded him that Holly would've been with him – not Abbey – if things had been different. Damn, she was stuck-up! What kind of woman said things like 'you've got a fantastic body', whilst remaining so detached it made him want to yell? And where did she get off having such a sexy voice? And Miles? When did he ever show any interest in the 'Wild Woman of Borneo' type? The woman was all contradictions: frightened and sassy, an incredible mess – yet undeniably sexy. But stuck up. She was definitely stuck up. What did she mean picking holes in Holly's costume with 'more fabric in a handkerchief'? What would she chose? A wet suit? And just what did Miles see in her?

He spun about in the water, scanning the area around the boat. Where was she? He swam back to the boat quickly.

'Abbey!'

She had been swimming around on the far side of the boat and, tired, held on to a rope. 'Yes?'

'Why didn't you stay where I could see you?' Jake thundered, then swam around to her grabbing her arm and pulling her from the rope. 'I thought you were trying to drown yourself again!' He pushed her toward the steps. 'You are seriously doing my head in, Roberts.'

Smarting, Abbey climbed the steps, then spun around as Jake immediately followed. 'Do you have to be so rude?' She had the greatest urge to shove Jake right back into the water, but was distracted by the droplets of water running down his tanned skin, his dark hair. 'There's no need to manhandle me that way!' She rubbed her arm where he'd yanked her from the rope.

'You should've stayed where I could see you!'

'You shouldn't have swum off so fast – I couldn't keep up!'

Swiping the water-logged fringe back from his forehead, Jake let go of an exasperated sound. 'Will you move? Or do I carry you out of the way?' He was still balanced on the top ladder step, one hand laid casually on the rail.

'You'll do no such thing!' Abbey shoved him, hard, but his fingers clamped around her wrist and, as he fell backward, he took Abbey with him.

Sinking beneath the surface in slow motion, bubbles shooting from her surprised mouth, Abbey clutched around for support. Jake's arm clamped around her waist, sped her to the surface.

Spluttering, her legs tangling with Jake's, she grasped at his upper arms, let go briefly to push the curtain of wet hair from her face. 'You sod!' Abbey coughed. 'You rotten sod!' She wriggled against him, punched at his shoulders so ineffectively that Jake began to laugh.

'This really must stop, your ladyship,' he teased, 'your tantrums are getting out of control.'

Green water-brightened eyes looked up at him. 'If I was having a tantrum, Westaway, you'd have my knee in your groin.'

Somehow, he spun her around and she was halfway up the ladder without having made any effort.

'Thanks for the warning,' he retorted drily.

Abbey seethed anew then, as he pulled himself on to the deck, Jake's eyes travelled slowly down her wet form, up again, amusement glittering in them when his dark gaze met with hers. He'd seen something funny and she'd missed it – that was the sensation she had.

'What now?' She put her fists on her waist again. 'Are you deliberately trying to annoy me?'

Jake laughed and shook his head; drops of water spun in the air. 'Nope.' He finger-combed his hair, folded his arms, mouth curving into a grin.

'You make me feel capable of incredible physical violence!' Abbey gritted. 'I could slap you with your Speedos.'

'You're gonna be mad enough with yourself.' His mouth twitched, as if he was having trouble keeping his laughter smothered. 'That costume you borrowed off Holly, I don't think it was meant for getting wet.'

Transparent as wet net curtain. Abbey's eyes widened as she looked down. 'It was probably intended to turn you on.' Abbey felt more naked than if she was naked, but resisted the urge to cover herself and dash for the cabin, tried saying calmly, 'It'll be decent again when it dries.'

'Yeah, on Holly maybe.' The heat in Jake's eyes jolted her stomach; staunchly, she kept her arms at her side. 'You wanna get the salt water showered out of that, or it'll fall to bits.'

75

Unexpected heat spread through Abbey's entire body beneath Jake's sultry gaze.

She levelled an equally sensual gaze at Jake, his own body betraying him. 'I suggest you do the same – ' she let her eyes drop pointedly, briefly '– and make it a cold one.'

'It's got nothing to do with you, Roberts.' Jake had the almighty urge to strangle her again. 'I was imagining Holly in that get-up.'

'Well, I'm sorry to disappoint you, Westaway.' Shaken at the effect Jake had on her, Abbey turned from him, moved to the bench and picked up the pad and pen. Without looking at him, she said, 'It'd be best for both of us if you "dump me at Marianne's" – whoever she is – just as soon as you can.' Probably some ex-girlfriend with three hundred of his children, she thought snidely.

'Yeah. Damn right.' Jake slammed into the cabin, the water pump starting up as he turned on the shower, his mood deteriorating further when the water began to splutter, a sure sign the tank needed filling. He flicked a switch for the reserve tank.

'We'll have to stop tomorrow, we used a lot of water.' He turned his back on Abbey's raw sensuality. Miles's woman, he ground silently, not on the agenda. 'Then I want to make it in one hop to Marianne's place. I'm running behind schedule.' Jake grew infuriated when Abbey glanced up at him and continued sketching. 'Will you get dressed!'

'In a minute.' Already, she was sketching again.

'Get something on.'

Abbey laughed in the face of Jake's growing irritation with her. 'I was wrong about you, Westaway – ' she set down the pad and pen ' – you're a prude.'

'No.' Very slowly, very deliberately, Jake turned around to face her. 'You are my mate's girlfriend and if he thought for one minute you were flashing your body at me, he'd have one of our ex-army mates trash this boat and me.'

'Are you afraid of Miles?' Abbey stood in front of him. He wanted her to clear off. But he stared straight into Abbey's clear eyes. 'I'm not afraid of him. We just don't make moves on each other's women.'

'I don't want you to make a move on me, I want to draw you.' Her gaze was as steady as his. 'Anyway . . .' she shrugged and Jake wished she hadn't '. . . he'll be grateful to you for taking me out of danger.'

Blowing out an exasperated breath, Jake scowled, 'Do you reckon?'

She rolled her eyes heavenward, 'Yes, of course!'

'Just how well do you know Miles?' Jake squinted his eyes. 'Because I ain't too sure we're talking about the same person.'

'Are you asking me if I've slept with him?'

'Hell, no! I don't want to know what you've done with him, I said how well do you know him? About how he earns his money?'

'That's his affair.' Abbey frowned, unwilling to admit she probably didn't know Miles very well at all. Miles was her financial advisor-lately-boyfriend.

'Just so long as he has enough dosh to keep you interested, you don't care, right?'

'My father introduced us, Jake, so I presume he's kosher.' Defensively, because she didn't want to answer any questions about Miles, she said, 'And I don't think I want to hear anything you want to tell me about him.'

'You are so prejudiced!' Jake shouted.

'I am not!'

'You are, Roberts – you presume anything I'd tell you would be bad.'

Sheepishly, she admitted, 'Yes, I did.'

'Listen, mutual friends said when they were up against it in Beirut, in the Falklands, Ireland – there was no one they'd rather have in their team. Miles is one hell of a strategist.'

'But . . .?' Abbey prompted. 'Are you going to tell me he has some deeply buried perverse characteristics?'

'Are you on drugs? No, I'm not!' Jake turned away. 'I only freaking asked you if you knew what he did for a living.'

'He's a financier.'

'That's all I asked you.' Jake rubbed his hand around the back of his neck. 'Let's drop this – I'm turning in.'

'What about my self-defence lesson?'

'Forget it.'

'But you said – '

'I said forget it!'

'Typical. You're all talk and no action.' She folded her arms and looked across at the sunset as Jake disappeared through the cabin door. Then Abbey cringed as he banged around in the cabin.

What was it with Jake Westaway? It was as though he deliberately found reasons to anger her – as if his moments of gentleness had to be negated in case she got too close to him.

He appeared seconds later, carrying the padded bench seat covers, then tossing them down on to the deck. He disappeared again, returned, threw the track-suit bottoms at her. 'Put these on.'

'You're obsessed with covering me up,' Abbey muttered, as she pulled on the huge tracks, 'you just want me to keel over from heat exhaustion. Or are you afraid I'll excite you?'

'No, lady,' he ground out, 'you're not my type.'

Abbey laughed. Jake's head snapped up. 'What?'

'No, it's nothing.'

'So tell me.' He took hold of her upper arms, stood her in the centre of the mattresses, with her back to him.

'I had this strange sensation – ' she laughed again, a sweet, husky sound ' – that you couldn't take your eyes off my breasts.'

'Yeah, right.' Where I come from, we call them boobs. 'He's coming at you from behind, what do you do?'

'Nothing usually?' She shivered despite the heat of the early evening. 'I don't get any warning.'

'Okay, how does he usually get hold of you?'

Frowning, Abbey turned to face Jake. 'Shall I show you?'

He shrugged and turned around.

'You'll have to kneel down – ' she sighed ' – you're too tall to play me.'

'Okay.' Anything – anything for a quiet life.

She stood a few paces away from Jake, frowned, looked, tried to assimilate in her mind how her attacker had successfully disabled her. The air left her lungs, so there was force; her mouth was covered.

'Any time you're ready.' Jake blew out between pursed lips.

Unexpectedly, Abbey flung herself at his back, hooked one arm beneath one of his, yanked it round his back; slapped her hand over his mouth and hung on. It wasn't quite right, but her hands wouldn't reach his mouth if she did it properly.

'That wasn't right.' She slid down his back, landed on her rump on the mattress. 'Jake?'

He was laughing, pushing himself to his feet.

'What's so funny?'

'I don't think you'll ever be a combatant, Miss Roberts.' Death by cuddle.

'I don't want to be a trained killer, thank you, I just want a chance to put up a fight!'

'Right.' Trying to keep the grin from his face, Jake turned her around in front of him. 'The only way we can do this is if you put me in the attacker's place.'

Glancing over her shoulder at him, Abbey grimaced. 'I'll try.' She closed her eyes to better visualize, took one of Jake's hands and tugged it. 'You'll have to come right up against me.' She took his other hand and arranged his fingers at her neck. 'He sort of tries to strangle me – ' she arranged long, strong fingers and clamped them over her mouth ' – then smother me – ' she jerked his fingers back to speak.

'Okay, what's this hand doing?' He drummed his fingers on her shoulder. Her cool, creamy, flawless shoulder.

'I'm trying to think – you have to remember, he's just knocked all the air out of me.'

'Yeah, I'd like to – ' he said derisively.

'Sort of this – ' she pulled his arm right across her front, banding both hers ' – then he – I think he jerks me off my feet.'

Jake obliged.

Abbey's head spun. His movement was so swift, it exactly mimicked the attacker's. Panic rose. But it still wasn't quite right.

'Now what?'

'Ah – ' Nothing else would come out.

'Abbey?'

She shook her head, gasped, 'That was almost it.' Her words tremulous.

'You need a gun.' Jake returned her to her feet, caught her elbow when she staggered slightly. 'There's no way out of that manoeuvre.' Not for someone Abbey's size, not without a black-belt fourth dan.

White-faced, Abbey turned to face him. 'There's nothing at all I can do?'

'Nope,' he spoke grimly. 'I'm presuming his first move is a shoulder to the centre of your back?'

'Yes, I think it must be. I'm not sure – '

'That takes care of most of the air in your lungs – if he didn't stop you falling at that point, you'd hit the ground – hard.'

Abbey rubbed her arms, nodded. 'I see.'

'The hand over your mouth, the other at your throat starves the oxygen just long enough to disorient you. He probably traps your arms at your side with his?'

She nodded, looked very, very vulnerable. 'Yes.'

'The one thing you could do is stamp down hard on his foot.'

'He lifts me – '

'Yeah, so that takes care of that.' Jake frowned, 'You probably wouldn't be able to think straight enough in any case, it's a very effective move.'

'Jake – there must be something you can teach me.' That small hope that she would learn to defend herself had been extinguished and the helplessness in its wake was worse than ever.

Immediately, Jake recognized the desperation in

81

Abbey's eyes. He couldn't just wipe her out. 'Okay, try this.' He put his arms around her front. 'Jab back with your elbow. Harder. Harder!'

'I'll hurt you!'

'You won't.'

She did. 'I'm sorry – ' She turned around, reached a hand toward him.

He raised his palm. 'No, that's great.' He rubbed his ribs, exaggerated a grimace to make her feel good. 'Shins, now that's something else to go for. Unless he has you face down on the floor, he can't trap your legs.'

Picking Abbey up from behind, he said, 'Kick back. Harder!'

'I am!'

'You're tickling me.'

With a growl, Abbey struck back with her bare heel.

'That's better,' he laughed, dropping her to her feet.

Hope was back in her eyes when he turned her to face him. Jake suddenly wanted to arm her with more moves. 'Okay, the next thing you could try is jerking your head back on his nose. That hurts.'

She laughed at that. 'I don't want to try that on you.'

'No, I think we'll give that one a miss. Don't do it, but I'll lift you up just to show you.'

'Like this?'

'Yeah.' Quick learner.

'If you ever are still on your feet, a good move is to drop to the floor, take him with you. If you can fall on your side, you can get out from under.'

Abbey blew her fringe upward on her forehead. 'That sounds a bit advanced.'

'Not really.' He turned her around by the shoulders and the second he had his arms around her front,

82

squeezing her arms to her side, he directed, 'Okay, drop.'

Abbey's knees bent, she tried to fall sideways, but landed in a flattened heap beneath Jake.

Undeterred, Jake pulled her to her feet. 'That was good, this time, drop and roll.'

'You're too heavy, I can't roll away.'

'Try.'

For half an hour, Abbey tried to master the move. 'I can't do it!'

'Get mad and try again.'

'I don't want to do this any more!'

'Do you think he cares about that?'

'No!'

'Okay, look, do it this way.' He adjusted her position, so she side-stepped slightly before dropping to the ground.

'If you'd rolled quicker then, you'd have got away!' Jake clamped his hand at her waist as Abbey made a belated attempt to 'get out from under'.

'Would I?' Abbey rolled on to her back, smiled up at him. 'Would I have got away?'

'You'd have had a chance.' A minuscule one. Teach her how to shoot. 'You'd have an element of surprise on your side.'

But his words of encouragement zapped Abbey's enthusiasm. She was on her feet first – for the first time since they'd begun, Abbey was standing, holding her hand down to him. 'Can I try again?'

'Yeah, then we'll call it a day.'

'What is it?' Jake asked when Abbey hesitated.

'That's it! At the exhibition, I think he hit me in the face from the front – ' she frowned ' – I think.'

Dodgy, Westaway. He turned her around. 'When you drop, stick your knee in his groin.'

'I can't do that to you!'

'I said *his* groin, not mine; there's a limit to how far I'm prepared to go, Roberts.'

'Right.' Immediately Jake clamped his arms around her, she dropped, taking him with her, but couldn't roll.

'I've kneed you in the groin,' she gasped, laughing because she couldn't move with Jake's weight square on top of her.

For a second, with Jake's elbows resting at the side of her head, Abbey thought he was going to kiss her. She felt his hard body reacting to her closeness; something primeval moved inside her, shocked her, because in that brief moment, she wanted Jake Westaway like she needed air – to survive.

'I – ah – I don't think we ought to do this any more today.' Abbey whispered huskily, her body on fire.

Dark blue eyes challenged for a second. 'You've had enough?'

'Yes.' She sat up as Jake sprang to his feet, offered her a hand.

'Maybe you're getting nervous because I turn you on?' He laughed to himself, mortifying Abbey.

Instead of being angry, Abbey laughed.

There was amusement in his dark eyes as he glanced at her before turning toward the cabin. 'I need to adjust something in the shower.'

Abbey settled for a wash in the kitchen sink and borrowed his toothbrush. Whilst rooting through Holly's things for something to wear, a box fell from the wooden locker to the floor. Her eyes saucered. It was the biggest box of condoms she'd ever seen in her life;

the lid opened and millions of foil wrappers shot everywhere. Every imaginable flavour and colour, some with added extras.

'Oh, damn!' She palmed them back into the box; prayed Jake would take longer in the shower. The click of a slide bolt sounded as she pushed down the lid on the condom mountain and flung it back into the locker.

Abbey sprang guiltily to her feet, wriggled into a yellow, button-fronted jersey short dress and stood in front of the locker as Jake stepped from the shower cubicle.

'You found something, then.' He combed his fingers back through slick dark hair. The towel tucked around his waist drew her eyes.

'Yes,' Abbey choked. More than she'd bargained for.

Her back flat against the locker, Abbey thought for a moment that Jake was thinking about Holly again – how much better she'd look in this excuse for a dress than she did.

'Anything wrong?' she asked sweetly, still leaning against the locker door as if the condoms would start hammering at the back of it at any moment, shouting, 'Hey, Jake! She found us!'

He frowned quizzically. 'I was going to ask you the same thing.'

'No, no, I'm fine.' Hot with embarrassment, but fine, she added silently.

'Good.' He was still frowning at her.

Abbey still leant against the locker door, wondering whether Holly would've suffered from rubber fatigue if she'd come along.

'Do you want something?' Jake folded his arms and Abbey hoped his towel would stay where it was.

'Mmm? No.' She could feel an uncharacteristic blush rising from her neck.

'I thought you'd be sketching,' he said.

'No, I need a rubber – ' Lord! Why did I say that?

'Can't help you there.'

He must really like what I'm wearing, Abbey thought, he hasn't stopped looking yet.

'Could you move?' Water dripped from his lightly furred, powerful forearms as he gestured toward the locker. 'I need some gear.'

'Mmm – ah – yes.' She prayed the condoms had tucked themselves in neat little rows in the box, that they had gone quiet again. 'I'm going to sketch – !' Abbey practically bolted from the cabin.

Jake shook his head. 'Basket case,' he muttered as he swung open the locker door, pulled out a pair of faded black jeans and T-shirt, shucked them on, leaving his feet bare.

Something stuck to his damp foot and he peeled it off. Chuckling to himself, he slid it into his pocket. He pulled a casserole dish from the fridge and put it in the oven, made himself and Abbey a cup of coffee and wandered up on to the well-deck. She sat beneath the navigation light, working in the dusk. And he noticed she'd dragged the mattresses to one side of the deck.

'Hey, Abbey – ' she looked up as he pulled something from his hip pocket ' – I found you a rubber.'

Instinctively, she reached up to field the flying object, caught it and flung it straight back at him. 'Wrong flavour,' she muttered.

Laughing, Jake set the mug down close to her.

'So what do you and Miles do?'

For birth control? Stunned, Abbey's mouth fell open. That was none of his damn business!

At her silence, Jake tried his coffee. 'Does he still play rugby? When I went to the Far East, he was trying out for the first fifteen.'

'It's been all tennis just recently.' Abbey couldn't believe her own thoughts. 'His broken leg will put a stop to his athletics for a while, I should imagine.'

'You'll have one frustrated man on your hands.' Jake chuckled. 'I believe he caught one in the shoulder in the Falklands, he was like a bear with a sore backside.'

'I never asked him how the crash happened.' Abbey grimaced guiltily. 'Did you?'

'You couldn't speak. I had other things on my mind.'

'Yes, I noticed.' Abbey smirked. 'She was carrying a bedpan at the time.'

'I was doing your talking for you, if you remember,' Jake drawled lazily.

'Do you want me to cook?'

'It's already in the oven, thanks.'

'Can I do anything to help, then?'

There was a popping sound and the navigation light went out. Abbey gasped and dropped her pad to the floor.

'Can you grab the torch from the cabin?' he said. 'The fuse has blown.'

Taking a deep breath, Abbey steadied the lurch of panic, which receded as her eyes adjusted to the dark. 'Yes, sure', but her voice still sounded afraid, husky.

'It's just inside my locker on the floor.'

Flicking on the torch to light her way back, Abbey swished it in Jake's direction.

'Could you shine it down on this panel?' He'd

unearthed a screwdriver to open the panel, deftly unscrewed the brass countersunk screws, then crouched down to look inside. 'Yep – ' he wiggled out a small cylindrical fuse ' – it's the fuse.'

Abbey shone the torch into the open panel whilst Jake pulled a spare fuse from a small box on the inside of the panel. She wobbled the light when Jake's head brushed against the sensitized skin of her thigh.

'Could you keep it still?'

Why? Abbey held the torch in two hands. Why do I suddenly feel like a nymphomaniac? This man's hair brushes against my leg and I could quite happily push him on the deck and jump on him! She shook her head. Typical. It's a reaction, that's it. If someone tells you you can't have something – human nature wants it all the more. As she held the torch, Abbey managed to convince herself that, if there was no Miles, no Holly, there was no way she would want Jake.

That conviction lasted about half a minute, until Jake twisted around and snarled, 'Will you keep still?' And his breath broke against the tormented, sensitive skin of her inner thigh.

Concentrating, lowering the beam, Abbey muttered something inaudible.

Jake dropped the new fuse to the deck. His finger and thumb had pinched too tight when he turned around and found his face almost in Abbey's shapely thigh.

'Fu-dge!' He had the almighty urge to shock Holly's dress off her, to slam her down on the deck and show her something more interesting than how to fend off an attacker. This couldn't go on much longer, he had to dump her somewhere – out of harm's way. No – out of his way.

He took another fuse from the box. 'That should do it.' He tried the light switch and it came on.

'Shall I look for the one you dropped?' Abbey offered, relieved when Jake moved out of her 'grab him and make love to him' zone.

'I'll find it tomorrow in the light.'

Yes! She was fine again. Fine just so long as Jake wasn't crushing her into the deck and smiling down at her; fine just so long as his hair wasn't tickling her sensitive skin. Some animalistic thing, she reassured herself, quite certain that if she kept her distance from Jake, there need be no more of these body-shattering urges.

Funny though, she reflected whilst they served up the casserole, Miles never gave her those 'take me, take me, I'm all yours!' urges.

'This is delicious.' Abbey, quite recovered from her lapses, endeavoured to strike up a benign conversation.

'Uh-huh.' He barely spared her a glance.

Thank goodness! Everything was as it should be. He was Miles's friend, she was a nuisance to him. The sooner I get back to the beach house and normality, the better.

'Where are you stopping for water tomorrow?'

He told her.

'I'll make my way back home from there, then.' Her mind was made up. Rick, her father, even Mr Helpful Sweat-a-Lot, might have noticed her gone – be concerned.

She thought Jake hadn't heard because he continued to eat, and upended his can of beer.

'I think it'd be for the best.' She pushed a succulent piece of chicken around her bowl. 'You could have

Holly fly out and join you and I can go home and we'll both be happy.' She sighed, stabbed the chicken and ate it. 'Now I have my voice back, I don't have any excuse to stay on board.'

'You can go home from Marianne's.' He finished his beer – 'S'cuse me' – rose to his feet, dumped the empty plate in the sink, his beer can in the rubbish bin, then he folded his arms.

Genuinely confused, Abbey frowned up at him. 'Why not tomorrow? It's obvious you don't like me, Jake. The sooner we go our different ways, the better.'

'Where we're stopping, there's no facilities to travel home. From Marianne's it's simple; there's an airfield close by.'

Am I crazy? Jake shook his head. He'd just squashed the chance to get rid of Abbey Roberts and bring Holly hot-footing over to him.

Jake leant into the small fridge, pulled out two more beers and raised one toward her. He was certain she'd say something like, 'Don't you have any wine? Dry? Expensive?'

'Thanks – ' she took the proffered beer ' – I didn't like to ask.' She missed his surprise, wrenching open the ring-pull with a practised movement.

'A beer-drinking, toffee-nosed painter. Can't be bad.' Jake laughed at the way she guzzled the drink.

'I'd better add beer to that shopping list, I don't see my stash lasting a week if you like the stuff that much.'

Beer! Abbey wrote, and underlined it twice.

'You'd better add some underwear to your list, too, I won't last a week if you keep on flashing your bo–' He stopped himself. 'Breasts.'

'Call them what you like, Jake.' Abbey's mouth

curved in a delicious lop-sided smile. 'Miles calls them all kinds of names.' Quite why she said that, she wasn't certain.

To his embarrassment, Jake blushed. He turned his back, looked out across the ocean, took a long swig of his beer. Christ! I haven't blushed since – I don't think I ever have.

'How long will it take to reach Marianne's?'

'Five or six days. I've got to be there for Friday, my brother-in-law Monty wants to discuss business and there's a bash in the evening for Marianne's birthday.'

'Ah, right.' Abbey added paper and pencils to their shopping list – there would be plenty of time to sketch. 'So Marianne's your sister?'

'Yeah.'

'Won't she be expecting Holly to be with you?'

'That's not your problem.' Jake's reply was harsher than he intended. 'I'll sort it.'

He expected her to fall silent, to sulk, but when he turned around, Abbey was still thoughtfully making the list. He couldn't help but laugh. 'There ain't any superstores where we're stopping.' Jake was so sure she'd crumple with disappointment. A woman like her – she probably spent half her life in glitzy stores.

'Good.'

Jake frowned quizzically. 'You don't like to shop?'

'I don't like crowds.' Laughter and challenge sparkled in her eyes. 'You've decided you know all about me, haven't you?'

'What do you mean?' Drawn, Jake sat opposite her.

'Because my family's rich, you think I shop till I drop, and I should paint as a hobby – I mean – why would I need the money, right?' A delicious, husky laugh escaped

91

her. 'You think I'm a spoilt, shallow bitch.'

'Hey, I'd never make assumptions about the shallow bit.'

'You shouldn't make any assumptions.'

'Like you didn't?' Jake passed her another beer. 'According to you, I'm a macho sex-machine!' The strong beer and Abbey's laughing green eyes saw Jake relax like he hadn't in a long time.

'I think we're both talking first impressions.'

'Okay. What was yours of me?' She tipped her can to his, then drank. 'I mean very first impressions.' The challenge in her eyes left Jake no room for manoeuvre.

'I thought you were the Wild Woman of Borneo's ugly sister.'

'I thought you were my creepy stalker.'

'I couldn't imagine what Miles saw in you.' Jake found Abbey's laughter so infectious, he wanted more.

'It's my trust fund – ' she shrugged, rippled with laughter ' – must be. My friend, Lynn, says I'm useless in relationships.' She hiccoughed. 'She's probably right – I forget to return calls, turn up for dates. I start a painting and nothing else matters.'

'Yeah, that could be a problem.' A grin curled his sculptured lips. 'Miles bibbed and tuckered and raring to go – and you're covered in oil paint.'

'I use acrylics.'

'Whatever.' He shrugged. 'Shouldn't worry, not everyone's good at relationships.'

'Including you?'

Jake's eyes were dark, smouldering when they met Abbey's. 'No comment.'

'Let me guess.' She drained the can, hiccoughed again and leant across the narrow table towards him.

'You loved once, but it didn't work out, so you've given up. It hurt – ' hic! ' – too much.'

For a moment, Jake frowned into incredible forest-green eyes, then glanced down to her damp tempting mouth. 'Now what gives you that idea?' For two pins, he'd rip the narrow table from the hull and taste those lips; they were close enough, just full enough – her breath like a soft feather against his mouth.

Amusement shone in her eyes when she leant back. 'I'm not really an artist, I'm known as Gypsy Rose Abbey, I know these things.'

A mixture of relief and disappointment tingled through Jake; his conscience prodded: Quit this now, Westaway. You've both had too much to drink! This is Miles's woman –

'Well, Gypsy Rose Abbey, you're plastered.' He poured her a glass of water. 'Drink this and hit the hay.'

He needed to keep moving, negate the weird effect Abbey had on him. Jake made up the bench beds with unwarranted care because he could hear the rustle of clothes as Abbey rummaged through the locker for a T-shirt, the sound punctuated by hiccoughs, her slightly off-key husky singing and a tooth-brushing ritual that'd bend all the bristles on his brush.

'You can turn around – ' her laughter soft ' – I'm decent.'

'That's debatable,' Jake muttered, turned when her cool fingers touched his elbow, stiffened when she planted a hand on his shoulder and rose up on tip-toes to kiss him fully, but oddly chastely, on the lips.

'What was that for?' He couldn't help but smile. Abbey looked so dishevelled, so heedless of her appeal, and so drunk.

'You'n'me – hic!' She grasped his forearms as *Free Spirit* lifted on a swell. 'We're going to be friends forever!' She yawned, pressed her forehead against his shoulder as Jake steered her towards her bunk. 'I know these things – I can tell.'

'Yeah? So can I.' He disengaged her hand from his arm. 'Gypsy Rose Abbey –' a rich chuckle escaped him ' – I reckon you're going to have a hangover to end 'em all tomorrow.'

'Jake?' Her husky voice reached him just as he'd pulled the sheet over his head and managed to block Abbey's softness, her kiss, from his thoughts.

'Mmm?' He had turned his back to her deliberately, so he couldn't watch moonlight dancing over her curves.

'You've got a gorgeous body.'

'Damn,' was his stifled response, because parts of his 'gorgeous body' responded to that husky, sexy voice.

'Try meditation,' that helpful voice piped, 'find your inner self; it's been a while.'

CHAPTER 4

Hot and dark. Stiflingly hot – and dark like black paint.

She could hear the pounding of her own heartbeat, but nothing else.

Until he spoke.

'You'll be a good little girl for me, won't you? You don't want to upset mummy and daddy, do you? You're not crying, are you?' The tone was kind, but he wasn't kind – wasn't – the voice made her stomach mangle with dread.

Abbey couldn't move her hands to wipe the tears from her cheeks; they soaked into the gag around her mouth. If he found out she was crying, would something happen to upset her mum and dad?

'You want them to be proud of their little princess, now, don't you? Don't want to disappoint them.'

She knew her eyes were open, that it was too dark to see. Not dark like night time, but like a big pitch-black canvas.

His voice fluctuated in volume, and whilst it was too quiet to make out properly, Abbey thought of a television programme; one she had watched in awe, of an artist building a painting brushstroke by brushstroke.

'Do you think you are precious enough to mummy and daddy to give me all their money? They have too much, you know, too much.'

Stoically, Abbey fought his voice from entering her head. In her mind, she held the brush, put a pale, glistening gloss coat on the broad canvas – the black canvas – and made it light.

If she let the brush stay still, his voice grew louder; if she concentrated, she could block out most of his voice – not the hissy monotone, but the words.

Until he shouted.

When he shouted, the picture she painstakingly created slipped from her; she felt the heat. Something desperate hammered in her head, her pulse – it spoke, told her to hold the brush, hold the picture in her mind. It told her if she let the picture slip out of sight, she would be gone, would suffocate, she wouldn't see her parents again.

'Do you want to see them again?' His voice punishing, crazed. 'How much do they want to see you?'

Slipping, her picture was slipping. She played for her life to bring it back.

Then gentle again, 'I'll be gone for a while, it depends on how much your mummy and daddy want you back as to just how long I'll be.'

Drenched with sweat; like having a temperature with chicken pox – but worse. So thirsty. Don't cry. Crying made her hotter, blocked up her nose so she couldn't hardly breathe at all through the wet thing around her mouth.

She thought she heard footsteps move away; had to start the painting again, but it was different this time, a fantasy painting of waterfalls, unicorns, sunshine.

'I haven't gone yet!'

The picture she held spun away, horror like a monster swallowing her at his words:

'I'll take some of your hair, Daddy's little princess, to prove to them I have you. Or shall I take a finger? Or a pretty toe?' A horrible, deliberate pause. 'Or all three?'

Sweat froze on her skin; she froze. She heard scissors snapping open and closed. Couldn't breathe, couldn't see, couldn't speak, couldn't move . . .

'Ahh!' Abbey came awake, struggling for air, great dry gasps racking her. She shook, fought her way out of the cloying sheet.

'Jake – ?' She needed to know that was then and couldn't hurt her now. 'Jake, hold me?'

Restless in sleep, Jake turned, Abbey's words just permeating his unconsciousness state at some deep level; but it wasn't Abbey talking, it was Holly. She was asking him to hold her. What he wanted all along. He knew exactly what Holly wanted.

Still trapped in sleep, he stretched an arm towards her, drew her night-chilled form against his warmth. A soft sigh escaped Abbey as one of Jake's powerful arms closed around her.

'I'd a nightmare.' Abbey's voice was huskier than usual; she snuggled her head into Jake's shoulder, breathed the warm masculine scent rising from his naked skin. 'More memories – ' she shuddered ' – seemed so real.'

''S okay.' Jake's mind skidded over the words, his response automatic, his body more aware than his rationality. Sweet fragrance reached into his soul, soft, luscious curves pushed and warmed against his firmness, felt so good; warmth expanded in his lower belly. A husky, sexy voice murmured inaudibly.

At some abstruse level, he knew he'd be brought to wakefulness by Holly's love-making, he'd awaken inside her warmth.

It was extraordinary to soak up the warmth from Jake's muscular form – a strengthening of the sensation that just by holding her, he scared away the mind-threatening spectres. Sleep dragged at her and a soft sigh escaped against his chest as she relaxed.

But not for long.

'Holly.' Jake's limbs trapped Abbey's, his mouth found hers and swallowed her shock. Her eyes shot open, hands pushed against his shoulders, his calloused hands moulded her hips against his arousal. She twisted her mouth from beneath Jake's deliciously drugging kiss. 'Jake – no – '

'What the fu – ' Moonbeams lit Jake's shocked expression. He tore from Abbey and she tumbled out of the bunk.

Jake swung out of bed, switched on the overhead light, 'Oh, damn!'

Abbey had that Wild Woman of Borneo look again; hair everywhere, dilated pupils, skin damp with perspiration, arms rigid at her side, breathing in gulps.

'What the hell are you doing?' He reached for her elbow, but she yanked away.

'Just don't – ' she couldn't bring the frissons of electricity racing over her skin under control ' – just don't touch me!'

'What were you doing in my bed?' Jake spun her around as she lunged for the door.

All Abbey could see was anger glinting in Jake's eyes. She had to get out of the cabin, breathe some air, escape the charged atmosphere. 'Answer me.'

'I had a nightmare!' she flung back, angry herself because she could still feel the pressure of Jake's mouth against hers, his powerful fingers on her skin; angry because part of her wished she hadn't roused him from that sexy, slumberous state.

'I'm livin' in one!' Jake pulled on his jeans over the dull ache in his gut. 'Chrissakes, Roberts – do you think I'm a freaking saint?' He turned away, because despite the bruising on her cheek, the wild tumble of hair and the confused anger in Abbey's green eyes, she looked more sensual than anything he'd ever laid eyes on. 'I thought you were Holly.' Christ! Had he dreamt the softness of her skin?

'It was a mistake.' Abbey backed up to the door. 'My mistake thinking you could just hold me – yours thinking I was Holly.'

'That doesn't alter the fact, another couple of seconds, Roberts, I'd have been takin' you for a ride.'

'You're so crude!' Abbey fought back, balled her fists because she wanted to hit Jake – and kiss him all at the same time.

'I'll tell you something that's worse than crude – ' Jake's facial muscles tensed. 'I'd have betrayed a mate because you had a bad dream!'

'You wouldn't have got that close, Westaway.' Abbey reached behind her for the door handle, yanked it open and darted on to the night-damp deck. The memory – the childhood torment uncovered for the first time in detail – so vivid, so raw, it could have happened the day before. It could have happened a minute before. She lay on the well-deck seating, too shaky to stand, and stared at the sky. Have to keep my eyes open, have to. Don't want to remember any more.

Her skin tingled where Jake had caressed her, she shuddered; she'd wanted his warmth, damn it! She'd wanted holding – not sex!

'Freaking hell!' Jake pulled a whisky bottle from his locker, took a long slug and stared at the cabin door. He splashed his face in the sink. 'You dog, Westaway, that's Miles's woman!' A string of expletives tore from him. Frustrated, he kicked the locker door. She'd never believe he'd made an honest mistake. 'Not in this bloody lifetime. Not Miss "the world is my dia-mond-studded oyster" Roberts.'

It wouldn't matter to her that he'd been doing so well; that she was the only consenting-age woman he'd spent this amount of time with and hadn't screwed.

He fought the tentacles of regret rising through him, fought them with the thought, Hell, I put myself out for her – I dumped Holly for her. Fool!

He grabbed Abbey's sleeping bag, stormed out through the cabin door and stopped short.

Abbey stared up at the sky, his white T-shirt drown-ing her. She was so still, so white, he thought she could be dead.

'Abbey.' He approached her slowly, his voice low, but she didn't respond.

The fingers at her arterial pulse sprang Abbey from her trance. She blinked, frowned at Jake leaning over her. Tears of shock, at the recollections, at her almost overwhelming need for physical comfort were so close, but she drove them back, stiffened her arms at her side because the need was so powerful.

He put the sleeping bag over her. 'If you want the cabin, I'll sleep out here.'

Too susceptible, too vulnerable to any kindness,

Abbey shook her head. But she couldn't speak yet; well, she didn't think she could. Because if she did, it would come out in a disordered jumble of sounds. He'd know just how close to the edge she was. That greatest of all fears.

He hesitated, didn't know what to do. He couldn't hold her now; she wouldn't trust him. He wasn't sure he trusted himself right at this moment in time.

'Can I get you something?'

Abbey shook her head, stared back at the sky.

Jake rubbed a hand around the back of his neck, paused, then shrugged. 'Okay.' He almost said, you know where I am if you want company – but given Abbey's freaked state, he bit that one back down.

As soon as the door closed behind Jake, Abbey let the tears flow down her cheeks, blurring the star-spangled sky into a kaleidoscope. Aloneness settled around her because there was no one she could share the intense fear with, no one she could describe the feelings to – the realization that, although the nightmare happened so many years ago, now she had to begin to face it. Worse still, face the threat that it was going to happen again. For the first time, Abbey considered it might be easier to let herself begin to go slowly insane than to fight; let the suffocating dark of madness close around her; let the paintings, the light, the fragile grip on sanity slip away. As her mother had . . .

There would be nothing then. No! She was disgusted at her own thoughts. No! Never! He wants your mind. She sat up, pulled the sleeping bag around her. No – it's mine!

Somehow, the horror that she'd even entertained those dark thoughts helped to bring her fear to an almost manageable level. Something normal, she needed something ordinary to engross her. Drawing Jake? Planning the exquisite details of her next picture held her terror in check until dawn broke, and with the light, Abbey sank away to sleep.

'Abbey?' Jake shook her shoulder. He'd come to a decision. Strictly business, so long as he kept his distance from her, he could handle this thing with Abbey. Miles's woman, he corrected himself. Get her as far as Marianne's and 'bon voyage, sweetheart', they'd be out of one another's lives and free to live their own. Just think of this as another job. Hell, he never played around with the people he minded – he didn't know why he hadn't thought of that angle before.

'Hi.' She shaded her eyes from the watery, early-morning sunshine, a small smile playing around her lips.

'Breakfast's on the table.' He turned from her. 'I've filled up the water tanks.'

'You look like you're in a sack race.' Jake's eyes glittered with amusement as Abbey entered the cabin, walking inside the sleeping bag. Hell! She was a mess. Like one of those string-haired mops he used on the deck.

He thought she'd pick at the cholesterol-fix breakfast, shoot him moody looks because he'd tried it on last night, but she didn't.

Abbey had woken with the certain knowledge that she was going to survive. Memories couldn't kill her; they'd only destroy her life now if she let them. The great, greasy breakfast was something so endearingly normal, the reminder she needed that this was her life and if someone threatened her, abducted her again, it wouldn't happen whilst she was with Jake. She pushed down the fear that it could be today, tomorrow, and decided she owed it to herself to keep the shadow of torment from clouding every living moment until it did happen. She knew it would. The only question was when.

She pushed down the voice that reminded her she was as brave as she needed to be – until night time.

'Thanks.' She rose to her feet. 'Will you still take me to Marianne's? Or did I upset you last night?'

'We made a deal, Miss Roberts. There's no facilities here.'

'Right. Do you have to shop at all?'

'Already done it. I want to give the engine a quick seeing to before we leave here.' He rose to his feet, took the plates.

'Pass me that spanner?' The breeze caught the edge of the borrowed, minuscule yellow dress and revealed the whole sexy length of Abbey's legs. Jake felt the now familiar tightness in his lower belly and snapped. 'Look, go and get yourself a coffee or something, get that list of stuff you made. I'll be a couple of hours with this.'

'I don't have any money.' She folded her arms beneath her breasts as Jake rose to his feet.

'My wallet's in the locker, help yourself.'

'Thanks.'

Uncertain how much she would need, Abbey eased all the notes from Jake's wallet and rolled them in her palm. 'Can I get you anything, Jake?'

'No.' He had his face pushed up against the engine cover, but raised a black, greasy hand in farewell.

Abbey bought boxes of pencils, soft rubbers and sketching paper; as she strolled, looking in the tiny, marina shop-windows, a rack of postcards caught her eye. Miles – she picked one out; and her father, another – and what about Lynn? And her aunts? She should thank them for attending her exhibition. Without even counting them, Abbey picked up a handful of cards showing the sunset over the small boatyard, bought stamps and settled at a dark green wrought-iron table out front of the nearby coffee shop. Shielded from the hot sun by the umbrella, Abbey wrote first to Miles, helpless in his hospital bed.

Dear Miles, I hope you haven't been worried; your friend Jake is taking good care of me. She paused, sipped the strong reviving coffee. *So there's no need to worry. Jake's taking me as far as his sister's and I'll make my way home from there. I'll explain everything when I see you, but I'm not quite sure when that will be. Thinking of you constantly and hoping your leg is improving. All my love, Abbey.* She wrinkled her nose after re-reading the card, it sounded so formal; but after littering the writing with kisses and little doodles, it didn't look so 'stiff'.

On the other cards, Abbey made her unplanned escape from British shores sound like an impromptu break – the general tone one of, *Decided to take a break. Having a lovely time – be in touch when I return.* And to the aunts, two of them, who had stayed at her exhibition for the first hour, eaten all the truffles and caviar, downed copious amounts of champagne, the aunts in whom Abbey sensed jealousy and antagonism – she merely thanked them for attending. They attempted to camouflage their emotions in a blanket of fawning comments, but those twin, piercing eyes held animosity no amount of smiling could disguise. Never able to rid herself of that 'done something wrong' feeling when she was with her aunts Rosemary and Cynthia, Abbey responded by skating over her confusion with them, kept her distance, remained polite.

'Oh, my God, I look like a witch!' Abbey caught sight of herself in the mirror glass of a small salon, her palm shot to her face in horror. Violet smudges beneath her eyes, hair sticking up – out – everywhere; and it was dry from the salt and sea – Jake didn't run to hair conditioner, didn't need it, she thought wryly, well, I do. She pushed open the glass door, the perm-flavoured warmth of the salon greeting her.

Some wonderfully rich, tropical-scented shampoo and conditioner and a meticulous trim saw her hair fall in soft, gentle strawberry blonde waves; a luxurious moisturizer tried its best to replace the natural softness in her skin.

Armed with a newly purchased wash bag stuffed with cosmetics, moisturizers and sun cream, Abbey took herself to the loo and applied a little mascara. The bruising on her cheek had faded to a yellow and she looked more like herself again.

Pulling the postcards from her bag, Abbey dropped them in the marina post box, made her way back toward the jetty. Tempted by the aroma of fresh bread, she bought a crusty loaf with the change she had left.

What if Jake had taken off without her? The thought jolted her, she knew a moment's panic before she saw his familiar form moving on the deck of *Free Spirit*.

A strange thrill ran through her as she wondered what kind of terms they would be on today if she hadn't stopped his sleepy advances? If she hadn't pulled back and reminded him she wasn't Holly?

He'd have been mad as hell because, despite Jake's sexuality, he'd never lay a finger on 'Miles's woman'. For him, the sooner they made Marianne's and he could fly Holly out to join him, the better life would look. A smile played on her lips. Jake had such a beautiful body, the sketches would be fantastic. She could feel the excitement in her veins, that charged, adrenaline-like rush that hit her and stayed with her through moments of planning, that kept her awake, that made art her driving force, her love.

The passion that would see her fight for sanity.

Footfalls on the jetty broke Jake's concentration. 'Abb – ?' The rest of her name got stuck somewhere in Jake's chest. This wasn't the wild woman who'd left his launch this morning. Neither was she the terrified, comfort-seeking scrap who'd shot from his bed last night.

'I didn't recognize you.' He held the rail, looking down at her as she made her way across the gangplank. Gorgeous legs – gorgeous.

But that wasn't all. Something hit him straight in the solar plexus when she smiled at him.

'Have you finished your engine?'

'Uh-huh. Just.' He held up black-to-the-elbows arms.

She smiled that lop-sided, delicious smile and Jake thought if it was any other woman smiling like that, he'd think he was on to a good thing. Abbey just smiled like that because that was the way she smiled.

'This smells lovely.' She broke off a piece of crusty bread with a delicate twist of her wrist, held it out for him to bite. 'I hoped you weren't a "frog-legs" man.'

At the moment, he thought, chewing the bread, I'm an Abbey Roberts 'leg man'.

He watched her as she studied him for a reaction, her eyes so big he could've fallen in them. ''S good.'

'I'll clean up, then we're ready to go. Grab a beer?' If she drank enough beer, Jake thought hopefully, maybe she'd get a pot belly and he could stop fancying her.

They'd been underway for a couple of hours, Abbey in her favourite position at the back of the well-deck, sketching, eyes shaded by a white peak cap she'd bought, Jake concentrating on making as much ground as he could before nightfall.

'I wish you'd quit that.' Jake had pushed the controls into neutral; his shadow fell across Abbey's sketch.

'Most men would be flattered.' Abbey shrugged; Jake noticed she hadn't spent any of his money on underwear.

'I'm not most men.'

'I know.' Their eyes met, for one, charged moment, then Abbey smiled unexpectedly. 'Don't worry, Jake, five or six days isn't forever – it'll soon be over.'

'Yeah. D'you want to make yourself useful? I could use a coffee.'

'Me too.' She left the sketch on the bench, knowing Jake would pick it up and study it the minute her back was turned.

What she didn't expect was that he'd still be looking through the sketches when she returned with their drinks.

'You haven't drawn my face.' He flicked through the anatomically detailed drawings again.

'No.'

Jake frowned at her quizzically, took a mug from her fingers. 'Why not?'

She settled beside him, wrapped her arms around her raised knee. 'Your physique is a gift for all to admire, Jake, but I couldn't draw your face.'

'Why not?'

'It's difficult to explain – '

'Try.'

How could she explain? She didn't know herself. Anyone else, she would have done masses of facial sketches, expressions by now. The breeze caught her hair, snagged a strand on Jake's shadowed chin.

'It's too personal.'

Unexpectedly, Jake laughed while the wind freed Abbey's hair from his chin. 'So's my butt.' He jerked a thumb at the jeans-clad sketch. 'Didn't stop you sketching that.'

'It's nothing like that.' Abbey shook her head. 'One thing I think we have in common, Jake – we both show the world what we want them to see – no more.'

Jake frowned, grew uneasy as she continued, 'I know I wouldn't want just anyone to see beneath the surface. I'm just guessing you wouldn't either.'

'You're too freaking deep for me. Draw my face if you want.' He'd risen from her side, fired the engines, didn't speak again for a long time; and Abbey knew she was right. There was a lot more beneath Jake's knock-'em-dead veneer than he ever wanted anyone to see. He didn't even want to look for himself.

Christ! I'm cracking up! Miles, you jerk, why'd you have to break your bloody leg?

At the marina, Jake had restocked the cupboards, refuelled his diesel tanks, tweaked the engine and topped up the water tank. If he pushed, they could be at Marianne and Monty's in four, maybe five days.

The sooner the better. This Abbey Roberts was making him uneasy. Not just because she had a body a man could die in, not even because her smile hit him in the guts and her voice moved things inside him that wanted to stay still. None of that. She saw straight through him – and he could live without that. Snapping at her to keep her distance wouldn't do any good at all if she could see through him. But it was all he could do. What, he realized, he'd been doing all along.

Jake's face was just so easy to sketch; he had something Miles's patrician features didn't. Jake had eyes that burned with anger, glistened with laughter, smouldered with male sensuality. Miles was a handsome man, sensationally so; but Jake's whole visage was a more earthy, masculine one; there was more emotion to portray.

'Come on and eat, Roberts.' He'd thrown the anchor for the night, but Abbey still sketched beneath the navigation light. 'Or I'll toss that pad over the side.'

'Try it, Westaway – ' she did look up briefly ' – and I'll kick you in the groin.' Her eyes were back on the sketch before she'd finished talking.

Jake raised a brow, muttered, 'Knew I shouldn't have taught you that self-defence stuff,' and turned into the cabin. He stopped dead when she responded, 'You know as well as I do you were only humouring me. There's no way I can take him on.'

'Yeah.' He shrugged. 'You looked like you needed humouring.'

'I did.' She met his eyes then. 'All done, and if you don't like how I've drawn your face – tough.'

He laughed at that. 'Getting abrasive now, Roberts?'

'Got a good teacher.' She pushed the sketch pad towards him.

He took the pad to the table, studied the pencil sketches. They really were him, all four of them. On one, he was frowning, the play of light on the sea reflected in his eyes, leaning on the rail, as though he had something on his mind. It wasn't just how Abbey saw him, it was how he really looked. How he really felt.

The second, he stood, hip rested on the pilot's high seat, his whole manner completely relaxed, the wind blowing his dark hair back from his face, a hungry, determined expression in his eyes.

Thirdly, she had sketched him fishing, casting the line, his entire body involved in the manoeuvre, anticipation in his eyes, written in his features. He could almost feel the deck moving beneath his feet by looking at the sketch.

It was the last rough that was the biggest surprise, up to his elbows in engine grease, hair sticking up where he'd run his hands through in concentration, beer can perched on the pilot's seat, tools everywhere. And a big 'I've finally fixed it' grin on his face.

Flicking back through the sketches, each on their own sheet, Jake noticed his eyes were telling a completely different story in each one. Abbey had drawn him reflective, determined, anticipatory, and just down-right satisfied. But she had each subtle mood exactly right. In them all, he was dressed in black jeans and T-shirt, the clothes he favoured, his feet bare – the way he preferred them.

It was strange, like Abbey knew him without having to know him – she'd picked up on details of his personality he wasn't even aware he displayed.

'If I'm any good, one of the sketches should leap out at you and shout, "That's me!"'

'Mmm.' He rubbed his chin with his palm, looked through them again. 'They all do.'

'I do sketches like that before I begin a painting.'

'Are you going to paint me?'

Shrugging, Abbey said, 'Not at the moment, I don't have all I need.'

'Do you want a beer?'

'Yes, please. Do you have any music?'

'Be my guest, Miss Roberts.' He pulled down a beautifully finished wooden flap, displaying CDs, tapes – and a player for both. 'I'm afraid I don't have any Mantovani or Vivaldi.'

She screwed up her nose. Jake noticed three faint freckles and smiled. 'This is perfect – ' she pulled out a soft-rock compilation ' – I play this at home.' Abbey soon discovered that her own and Jake's taste in music almost exactly coincided. 'I have this one – and this one!'

She made a funny 'eeking' noise at one of his CDs. 'Oh, yuk!'

He snatched it off her. It wasn't his. Holly had left it behind. 'Don't say another word.'

'Jake, if I was to paint one of those in the future, which one would you prefer me to do?'

'The first one.' He didn't hesitate, but he didn't know why he'd picked it either. 'But – '

'Stick with it.' She smiled. 'It's the right one.'

'How come?'

'It'd fetch the best price.'

'How do you know?'

'I just know.'

He smiled, shook his head. 'You're the expert.'

Something really strange began to happen – a first for Jake; he found he genuinely enjoyed Abbey's company. Not just as a woman, but as a friend.

Music and beer relaxed them both as they ate. 'Is Marianne your only sister?'

'Yeah. Jake finished the last of the fresh bread. 'No brothers.'

'Do you have any nieces or nephews?'

Without conscious thought, Jake collected their plates, dropped them in the sink and threw Abbey an apple. 'Two of each.'

'Thanks.' Abbey bit the crisp fruit, visualized Jake playing with 'two of each': being sat on, pinned down and play-punched; delighted shrieks of 'Uncle Jake!' filling the air when he tickled them into submission.

'Leave that, I'll do it in a minute.' She waved her apple at the sink. 'You should have another beer, relax a bit.'

' 'S okay.' He shrugged, kept his back to her, his inner voice smug. That's good, Jake. Keep your distance. Don't bother trying to relax, it's too dangerous.

But in an instant, she was at his side, tea-towel drying the plates; Jake couldn't help laughing at the comic sight: Abbey, his rugby top drowning her, bare legs and feet, vibrant hair completely wild, and an apple trapped in white teeth.

'You don't look anything like a rich woman, Roberts.'

She flung him a disgusted look, the apple shot out of her teeth, landed in the soapy water. 'Well, my tiara's at the jewellers, it does make a difference.'

'Damn, that thing must be a size.' He shook his head pityingly.

Abbey raised a soapy salad spoon, threatened him. 'Are you saying I have a big head?'

'Not your head.' His dark blue eyes darted with feigned nervousness to the soap-laden spoon. 'It's all that hair,' he laughed, 'it's one big mess!'

Abbey pulled back the top of the spoon, aimed the suds at Jake's face, squealed when it hit him square on the nose and Jake scooped a handful of foam.

'This is war, Roberts.'

'No!' Her palms towards him, she backed toward the cabin door. 'No!'

'Yes!' The suds sailed, splattered on Abbey's cheek. 'You've had it now, mister.'

Jake's laughter caught when Abbey jerked open the shower-room door and grabbed his shaving foam, sent a thick squirt to land on his cheek, drip on to his T-shirt, then slap to the pale floor.

'Take it back!' She aimed the nozzle at his face, her voice barely audible through laughter. 'Say, "You don't look a mess, Miss Roberts!"' Whilst she spoke, she advanced towards him. 'Say it!' She let another fat worm of foam expand from the can, but it splattered on to the floor between them. Undeterred, she moved towards him.

'Abbey – don't – ' Jake tried to stop her 'it's slip – '

Abbey skidded on the foam, landed on her backside, still clutching the can.

'Bet that hurt.' He held out his hand, shook with amusement, pulled her to her feet and got a face full of shaving foam for his trouble. One sweep of his hand cleared his eyes; he hooked the can from her fingers. 'Learn when you're beaten, Roberts, I ain't goin' to lie.'

She rubbed her bottom, flicked some foam from

Jake's upper lip. 'I'm not beaten, I just have a battle injury.'

'Yeah, well I ain't goin' to offer to rub it better.' His eyes lingered on the swaying hem of his rugby shirt as Abbey inadvertently revealed more thigh, laughter still rippling through her.

'You'd better not!'

His inner voice choked, Stop looking!

Cool down, Jake flashed back, you haven't touched her.

The thought of Jake 'rubbing her better' sent hot colour to Abbey's cheeks. The air between them crackled when she glanced up at his smoky blue eyes, tore her gaze away and deliberately grimaced at the mess on the floor. 'Have you got any rags?'

'Sure – ' he jerked a thumb at the locker ' – right down at the back on the floor.' He wiped the rest of the foam away whilst Abbey plunged into the locker, a smile playing around his lips.

Trying to reach to the back was hopeless. Abbey wriggled into the confined space, grabbed a handful of rags, cringed as her elbow knocked something solid to the floor. A framed photograph.

Abbey backed out of the locker with both rags and photo frame, only intending to check for damage. But the faces in the photograph grabbed her, held her spellbound. Behind the shielding locker door, she studied the picture. It was Jake, a little younger, a completely unguarded smile, and warmth, real warmth, shining in his sexy blue eyes. The woman with him had short, dark hair, a lovely kind face; her army uniform accentuated a trim figure. She looked like she couldn't take her eyes from Jake long enough to look at the camera, the emotion between them so – tangible. A tiny notation in the corner pledged, 'I love you, Jake, from me.'

'Are you sulking in there?' Amusement laced his words, which snapped Abbey's attention from the photograph.

'No,' she whispered. 'Jake, who's this?'

'Who's what?' His hand dropped on to the top of the locker door, then an audible gasp escaped him. When Abbey looked up, his expression darkened . . . Anger? Pain? Before her eyes, Jake's features hardened – she could read nothing in his countenance. He took the photo from her.

'What's her name, Jake?'

For a moment, he stared down at the photograph, then said, with a rough catch in his voice, 'Are you cleaning that floor, or am I?'

'Ah – I'll do it.' Abbey stepped around him, sensing now would be a good time to shut up.

As she cleaned the foam away, Abbey wondered about the photo. Some instinct told her it wasn't Holly with him. And when she'd finished, she found him out on deck, deep in some kind of trance, still, cross-legged. Perfect for sketching.

'Abbey, get some sleep.' He pushed his fingers back through his hair. 'Don't you ever stop that?' He gestured to her sketch pad.

'I'll sleep later.' She was so inspired, it was amazing. Each drawing was better than the last. The better she got to know Jake, the more stunningly correct her portrayals became.

She switched on the battery 'daylight' lamp and stopped work long enough to look up. 'Goodnight, Westaway.'

'Yeah.' He raised his hand.

For a while, Jake lay awake, waiting for Abbey to turn in. In a few days, he'd got used to her presence in the opposite berth; the sleeping bag just didn't look right without her in it. 'Damn, I'm going soft,' he muttered, pulling the sheet over his shoulder to go to sleep. Yeah, I know, he humoured the voice in his head, Miles's woman.

The night air cooled and Abbey slipped silently into the cabin to retrieve the sleeping bag. Time had ceased to exist, tiredness held at bay by the developing outline.

If Abbey had to sleep, it would be during the day, when those choking terrors couldn't reach her; when she wouldn't waken up in the dark, alone, so terrified it defied depiction. Even with her portable 'daylight' lamp, Abbey shivered at the darkness beyond the boat.

As dawn approached, her eyelids drooped – she couldn't give in to sleep yet. But she was so exhausted, she began to tremble. Had to put the pencil down, force herself to her feet. 'Darkest before the dawn,' she shivered as she repeated the words heard somewhere. At that moment, desperate for sleep, desperate to stay awake, Abbey actually considered going in the cabin and telling Jake to 'budge over'.

She hugged the sleeping bag around her and hovered close to the pool of light.

'What the freak are you doing?' Jake burst out of the cabin at the same time the light broke free of greyness. 'Have you been awake all night?'

'Mmm.' She felt numb all over, that slow, couldn't-care-less type of numb. She'd won though, she'd escaped the terrors . . .

116

'Right.' He picked her up, sleeping bag and all, and shouldered open the cabin door. 'Stay put till you waken up, right?'

'Uh-huh.' She'd won!

'And when you wake up, you eat. Right?'

'Yessir . . .' She was asleep before she'd finished the word.

'Oh, boy – ' Jake scratched his head ' – if you carry on like this, Roberts, you'll be a ghost by the time Miles sees you again.'

After a deep, refreshing sleep, Abbey showered and dressed in a short yellow swing skirt and a white vest T-shirt.

There hadn't been any horrific recollections awaiting her in slumber and Abbey had the sense of escaping, of winning another round of the battle. She was getting stronger.

She took coffee out to Jake, breathed in the delicious salt air. 'Hi.' She set down the cup.

'I want to talk to you.' He pulled the throttle into neutral.

'Good morning to you, too.'

'Cut the crap.'

Abbey frowned. 'What do you – ?'

'You don't have to prove anything to me. You don't have to put in so many hours sketching you start wandering around half-comatose; it's not worth it. So long as you stay out of my bed when I'm sleepin', I ain't gonna jump you.'

'You're ticked off again.'

'Yeah.'

'Why?'

117

'Why? Because Miles won't think you've been up all night painting, if you have bags the size of melons under your eyes when he sees you.'

At that moment in time, Abbey didn't care what Miles thought about anything. 'I'll get started, if you don't mind.'

'I mind.'

'What?'

'You'll eat first.'

'All right, I am hungry, I just didn't think about it.'

'Right. What are you trying to prove?' Jake asked as they sat down to eat.

'It's not that simple, Jake.' She couldn't say, 'Look, I had a nightmare and I don't want another.'

'Try me.'

'You won't understand.'

Jake imagined the 'worse-case scenario', trying to imagine it from Abbey's point of view. 'Are you pregnant?'

'No. It's nothing that tangible.' Maybe she ought to be straight with him, but to bring up the recollection now, when she was feeling stronger, would risk bringing it all back.

Jake leant back on his seat, spread his hands. 'What have you got to lose? I'm not going to repeat it to anyone.'

What had she got to lose? Her mind, basically. But where to begin?

Holding the hot coffee cup between her palms, Abbey tried. 'The nightmare . . . I remembered part of my kidnap as a child; not just some vague, flitting memory, but every heartbeat.'

She waited for his response: 'So? It's only a memory!'

118

But to her surprise, he remained silent. She looked up from her coffee. 'It was like visiting hell, Jake.'

'You should have told me.'

'Did something bad ever happen to you, and you just couldn't talk about it?'

'Yeah, like, leave it till it's a few days old, then take another look?'

'That's exactly it.' She glanced down at her cup, back at his dark blue eyes, 'Trouble is, it's not over. I fought sleeping last night because the fear of remembering more is unimaginable.'

'In the day, it can't hurt you.' Jake glanced out of the window as Abbey glimpsed the deeply understanding Jake Westaway she'd known existed.

'I don't want to go crazy.' She shook her head, blinked hard, didn't look up again until she was under control. 'I know there's more and I don't know if I can take it.'

Jake saw the sparkle of unshed tears in Abbey's eyes and prayed she wouldn't. If there was one thing he couldn't deal with . . .

'Tell me about it.'

'The memory?' She shuddered, shook her head.

'Talking about it won't make it any worse, Abbey.'

She wanted to believe him, he could tell from the look in her eyes.

'If you had remembered all this as a child, you would have told someone, wouldn't you?'

'I don't know who.' She pulled at her bottom lip with her teeth. 'I lost my voice as a child for a short while – it was a relief because if I'd told Mum and Pop, they'd have been desperate. I almost think they couldn't have faced me.' She expanded quietly, 'When my voice returned, the memory had gone.'

119

'So you all carried on as if it never happened?'

'It was easier. I knew I'd been abducted, but there was nothing to remember so I let it go.'

'You're paying for it now. Tell me, I don't get desperate.'

A sad-sounding, husky laugh escaped her, 'You mean you don't know me well enough to get desperate, Jake. I'm not your seven-year-old child.'

'True.' He paused. 'Tell me this, then. If you'd been at the beach house and remembered, who would you have told?'

'I couldn't tell anyone. They're happier not knowing.'

'Right – so break the pattern.'

'I might fall apart.'

Jake rose to his feet, grabbed the whisky bottle from his locker, added a generous measure to their coffees, then set it on the table by the window; he put Abbey's favourite soft-rock CD on the player.

'You won't fall apart.'

'I'm more afraid I'll look to you for comfort, Jake – the fear – it – ' she grimaced guiltily ' – it sort of fades when you hold me.'

Leaning back in his seat, Jake studied her. There she was, making him feel good again, needed. It was as if he couldn't get enough of her belief in him, in his ability to remain what they'd become: friends – from the ground up. Yet there was something dangerously potent between them, and Jake needed to prove to himself he could control their situation and help Abbey at the same time.

Unexpectedly, he tugged Abbey to her feet.

Abbey let Jake pull her into his arms, knew that

120

wonderful secure sensation she had known there before.

'I'm a stranger. You can tell me anything because we won't see one another after this dance.'

She leant her head against Jake's chest, listened to the solid, regular thump of his heartbeat, breathed his male scent. 'It was hot, hot and dark . . .'

Whilst she spoke, Jake held her close. Hey – we're only dancing, he shot down the voice that reminded him again that this was Miles's woman. It doesn't count. When she faltered, he held her tighter. A warning voice blared because his body hadn't stopped reacting to her luscious closeness since he started this. Yet Abbey's husky, emotive voice kept everything except the 'protect' hormones in check. She was trembling. 'He can't hurt you here,' Jake reassured her.

She looked up. Jake smiled because, although she was white and trembling, she was holding on hard to those tears. 'I heard him opening and closing the scissors – ' Abbey closed her eyes, sank against Jake again, her relief as enormous as the relived horror.

It was a slow track or two later when Abbey asked, 'Would you tell me about the night you rescued me?'

Hey! Put her down! Jake's inner voice yelled, she doesn't need holding any longer!

Yes, she does, he threw back, when she hears what I've got to tell her, she'll need another hour – at least.

'Why did you come back?' she urged him.

He couldn't very well say, 'Because your eyes wouldn't get out of my mind' or 'Your perfume was all over my jacket.'

No, you can't, the voice agreed.

'Didn't seem that anyone you already knew could do anything to protect you.'

121

'What made you think you could?' Abbey frowned faintly, looked up at him.

'I'm in the business of looking out for people.'

'Oh?'

'Yeah, I watch backs, work with the security services. Monty runs the operation.'

Suddenly, Abbey felt even safer. Maybe he had this effect on all his clients. Only she wasn't a client, she was someone he hadn't been able to leave unprotected.

'This has turned out to be a busman's holiday for you.' Keeping her arms around his waist, she smiled up at him, grimaced comically. 'I'm sorry.'

He just shrugged, the way he did. 'It's not like there's a threat close by.' His eyes fell on her delicious mouth. Miles wouldn't know – he could just –

You're pushing it, Westaway! That bloody voice again. You owe Miles.

I'll do this my own way, he returned. 'Are you feeling better?'

He thought she'd shrug out of his arms, announce joyfully, 'Oh, yes, fantastic!' But then, he should have known.

'Mmm.' Lazy, sensual green eyes looked his way, sent strange darts through him, and she rested her cheek against his chest again.

Hey! Now you're really pushing it, Westaway!

Will you just shut up! I know what I'm doing.

Before you know it, you'll be convincing yourself, so what if she is Miles's woman? Give her one anyway. Low-life.

'Ready to get back to work?'

Abbey thought she would rather stay right where she

was, hold him rather than draw him. But that wasn't part of their script. 'Sure.' But she made no move. 'In a minute.'

He grinned at that, squeezed her. Told you I know what I'm doing, he sneered at the voice. Even if I wasn't – Abbey's completely in control.

Yeah, right.

The CD ended and Abbey sighed, stepped away from him. 'Thanks.'

'If you have any more recollections . . .' Jake held his hands wide.

'You'll be my stranger?' Her lop-sided smile twisted his insides. He knew it shouldn't – but it did.

'Yeah.'

Fine! Don't listen to me!

Hey! Jake retorted, shut your face, I can handle it, jerk!

It was different from then on between them, not earth-shatteringly different – but subtly so.

A lightness settled around Abbey after talking to Jake; and Jake, he was well pleased with himself – because he knew he'd put that lightness there.

And apart from, Don't get carried away, the voice let him be, most of the time.

Every sketch gave Abbey that shivery, nervous sensation that this was going to be one of her finest-ever works.

They covered a good bit of coastline, stopped to eat, then Jake fired up the engines again and the journey continued.

Conversation was easy between them, laughter and music made the atmosphere an infectious, happy one.

Only when dusk came did Abbey show any sign of tension.

'Tonight, you sleep, Roberts,' he said firmly. 'No arguments.'

'But – '

'No arguments.'

It was a deliciously balmy evening. Abbey was warm and tired, didn't feel like arguing.

'Fancy a dip?' Jake asked unexpectedly. 'It'll help you relax.'

'Yes – yes, I do!' Suddenly, the approaching night didn't seem so bad. 'I'll get changed.'

When Abbey emerged from the cabin in Holly's white costume, Jake was already in the water, swimming towards a buoy a couple of hundred yards away; his crawl stroke powerful, easy. If only Miles were more like Jake, she thought, if only Miles made me feel this alive. She cringed, thinking she should feel more guilty than she did at the thought – never mind the thought – she should feel more guilty at enjoying his friend's company so much.

Miles would never hold her, dance with her the way Jake had – given her what she needed by pretending to be a stranger. Miles and she had only danced when he was wearing a brand new tux and she wore a magnificent evening gown. And if she tried to talk to him about her memories, he'd say something like, 'Visit your shrink, darling, he'll sort you out double quick!' and step back from the overwhelming emotion inside her. It was Miles's way to delegate in every situation. Even emotionally, she thought a touch sadly.

Jake, though. His brusqueness she found reassuring, for a reason she couldn't explain. There was something

124

so elementally honest about him; she couldn't imagine him lying just to please someone; couldn't imagine him pretending to be anything just because someone else wanted him to be.

As she swam toward the buoy, she compared the two men. Jake, she thought, is built from the ground up, reckless but solid, honest, a man who loved women and wasn't ashamed of it, wasn't ashamed of anything about himself or afraid to work for what he wanted. He was a man other men felt comfortable with, she imagined – a man women adored. Miles? Miles had been handed his army commission, accolades, sporting medals on a plate – even his car was a gift from his father. His swish Docklands apartment was part of a business deal. And women were attracted to Miles's confidence, his high opinion of himself. He was good-looking, rolling in money, relatively even-tempered – but always, he talked about his deals, about this one and that owing him large amounts of money. And when something went wrong, deviated from his plan, he grew stressed with the fervour of a child. And something else that had bothered her about Miles, but she had overlooked because he seemed to enjoy her company so much – everything had a price tag. It wasn't his fault, his father was entirely the same way; but Abbey found herself imagining not going out with Miles. She regretted sending him the postcard, suggesting how much she couldn't wait to see him again. Didn't even know why she'd written that. But then she realized. She had written it because Miles would want to read it. His appetite for attention rivalled that of a child.

Her breathing was laboured by the time she reached the buoy, where Jake floated on his back. He came upright, caught at a rope when she gasped for breath. 'I'm terribly out of shape.'

'I can see that.' Jake laughed when she splashed him, pretending indignation. 'Nice costume,' he tormented her, 'I can see right through it.'

She pushed herself towards him, legs tangling with his when she tried to duck him. Laughing, he resisted effortlessly, then suddenly went under the water easily, too easily. Unperturbed, Abbey swam back to the buoy, hooked her fingers around a rope.

'All right, you've proved you can stay underwater for a long time, buster, come on up now, enough's enough.'

But Abbey grew uneasy when Jake didn't reappear quickly. 'Come on, Jake . . . Jake, don't mess around!' Clinging to the buoy rope, she twisted to look for him. '*Jake!*'

The water was clear in daylight, but in the dusk, opaque. 'Jake, don't do this to me!' She shook her head. Time expanded, seconds seemed like minutes. 'Jake – no! What've I done?' She took a deep breath and forced herself to go beneath the surface, some irrational part of her mind presuming that, because she wanted to see in the dusk beneath the water to find him, she would be able to.

But, unaccustomed to underwater swimming, she soon popped to the surface. 'Jake, I'm sorry,' the heartfelt words sobbed from her, 'I'm sorry!'

'Hey, don't be sorry!' He broke the surface close to her, a big grin on his dripping features; and Abbey freaked. Her fists pounded his shoulders.

'You rotten pig!' She flailed out at him. 'I thought I'd *drowned* you!'

He was laughing; she was practically crying. 'I never

knew you cared, Roberts.' He caught hold of her wrists.

'I don't!' she shot back defensively.

'I'm sorry.'

'No, you're not – you're laughing. You're heartless!'

The sky had pulled on its full night-time regalia. The moon trailed a broken path over the sea, the lights from Jake's launch spread in their direction.

'I'm sorry,' he repeated. 'I didn't expect you to freak like that.' He tried to wipe the smile from his face.

Abbey just glared at him.

'C'mon, let's get back, you can beat me up if it makes me feel better.'

'Damn right I will.'

He quelled the urge to laugh at her idle threat and swam back to the boat with the same effortless stroke, Abbey in his wake, her own swimming technique as jerky and unbeautiful as Jake's was flowing. 'I'll bloody well kill you,' she threatened and earned a mouthful of salty water, which made her angrier still.

He gave her a hand on board, completely unprepared when, as soon as she found her footing, Abbey grabbed a fender and whacked him around the shoulder with it.

But in a millisecond he had it from her and threw it across the deck. 'Grow up! I was swimming, for heaven's sake!'

Not content, Abbey picked up her sketch pad, would have whacked it across his shoulder. 'Not that!' He dodged behind her, gripped her around the waist. 'Abbey, put it down.' And prised it from her fingers. 'Not that.'

She frowned, realized what she had been about to do and gasped, shook her head.

'You're a bloody fruitcake.' Jake dropped her to her

127

feet. 'You spend hours on something and try and wreck it in a second.' He shot her a disgusted look and stowed the pad in his locker.

When Abbey turned around, he flung a towel at her.

'You prat!' Abbey pulled the towel around her shoulders. 'I thought I'd drowned you.'

'What were you worried about? Being alone?'

'No!'

'What then?'

'You!' She bit her bottom lip, turned away from him, because something was happening to her. Abbey sank to the bench and stared out at the moonlit ocean. Tears gathered in her throat. She kept them there until she heard the cabin door close behind Jake, then she let them consume her, held the rail against the sobs racking her body. They were tears held inside too long, for the return of some memories, for the fears constantly prodding her like the points of sharp sticks; for the way she felt about the beautiful man who had made her angrier than she had ever been in her life. Angrier and happier.

Fear made her lose control – that was understandable.

But Jake horsing around? That wasn't understandable.

Jake took a slug from his whisky bottle, recapped it, glanced through the door window at Abbey and cringed. She was crying like it was going out of style. Anything but that. Just keep your tears outside, away from me, he thought, because I can't hack 'em. He showered off the salt water and dressed.

Then he made her a coffee and drank it himself, made her another.

'I said I'm sorry.' He stepped back quick in case she started whacking him again, did a double-take when she stood and wiped her cheeks, turned to face him.

'I don't know what happened.' She frowned up at him as if he had all the answers. 'I have never in my life "freaked out" like that.'

Jake shrugged, handed her the coffee. 'Happens.'

'No, it doesn't just "happen", Jake, not to me.'

'Maybe nobody laughed at you when you got mad before.'

'Jake, it's not that. You're the only person I've confided in and I thought I'd – '

'Hey – ' he took hold of her fingertips, pulled her toward him '– I don't die that easy.'

His whole body stiffened when she wrapped her arms around his waist and clung to him.

Jake clenched his teeth, looked to the stars; her towel fell to the deck, his arms at his side, itching to crush her to him, but that damned voice shouting, Miles! Miles! just wouldn't let him be.

'Jake, I know you don't find me attractive, but would you kiss me?'

She was all needy eyes and sensual lips, hair drying in soft little curls – and what the hell was she talking about?

'No.' He kept his arms stiff at his side, thought about Miles sending a hitman with a machine gun, thought about all the money Miles had, that the man had comforted him when . . . Dredged up one turn-off after another. It didn't help his hot reaction to Abbey's costume-clad closeness. He felt as if she was being absorbed into him. Say something! his ever-helpful, inner voice suggested, Like, hey – draw me all you like, but it ends there.

He rolled his eyes heavenwards at the voice. Try again, jerk, he countered, it isn't that easy. In fact, if she snuggles those beautiful curves any closer – I've had it.

'Roberts, just because you're one rich lady, doesn't mean you can have everything you want.'

Those big green eyes that jumped his pulse looked up at him, questioning for a moment, then she smiled. 'You're right, I'm being silly.' Her arms fell away. 'I'd better shower off.'

Are you satisfied? he ground at the voice. Are you bloody well satisfied now? Because I'm freakin' not!

Unlike a deeply frustrated Jake, Abbey, emotionally and physically spent, slept soundly, rose with the dawn and began drawing.

She had sketched the sky and sea surrounding the launch, knew a delicious nervous anticipation as she began the foreground. Jake.

The black jeans and T-shirt first, shaded subtly with dark grey pencil and dense black, so that his clothed body had the appearance of being just as well-honed and masculine as it really was. One set of shoulder muscles flexed as he leant against the rail, the other relaxed, his palm resting on the rail. Every pencil stroke brought his image to life. It was practically drawing itself. Abbey was beginning to wonder whether other artists actually fell in love with the image they created.

So involved, she barely noticed as Jake put on the CD player and fired up the engines. She looked his way, but he didn't even spare her a glance. He didn't even nag her to stop to eat.

A small smile curved her lips. Ticked off because he wants Holly, not a mixed-up artist. Lucky Holly. The thought surprised her. The sooner we get to Marianne's, the better. We'll both be happier. Well, she corrected, Jake will be.

Determined to live for the day, Abbey thought it prudent to pretend her lapse in manners the previous night was best forgotten about. As far as Jake was concerned, that is. She was quickly discovering something within herself that was so drawn to him, it defied all logic. Jake Westaway was as far removed from her ideal man as he could possibly be; yet she had never in her life lost her temper that way, and she had certainly never before asked a man to kiss her – never would again. A moment of madness, she told herself, not for one minute believing it. It felt like infatuation, or something stronger that she couldn't even begin to examine.

Abbey was relieved when the ease between them returned after several hours. She worked from dawn till sundown, then they swam, played cards and music, then talked and drank beer. But Abbey didn't allow herself the luxury of dancing with him, or getting closer than she had to.

'Wonder how Miles's leg's coming on.' Jake brought up the subject often, in order to remind himself that he and this gorgeous woman could only ever be friends. And not even that when Miles was around. 'Maybe you ought to telephone him when we reach Marianne's.'

'Maybe,' was her husky response. 'How about Holly, did you phone her when we stopped for water?'

'Meant to.' Jake grimaced. 'Didn't get round to it.'

'Might be best to contact her when you've arranged her ticket to fly out,' Abbey suggested. 'She'll love that.' I would.

'Maybe.' He wondered how Holly's voice would sound to him now, after days of Abbey's drop-dead sexy tones. Like a cinder under a door, fingernails screeching on a blackboard. Abbey didn't rattle every time she moved, she didn't wear bracelets; she was as ungraceful as a clockwork frog in water, but out of it, Lord, he could watch her and not get tired. He had fantasies about kissing her smooth golden thighs, nibbling them till she begged for something more; fantasies about suffocating in her delicious curves. Abbey Roberts had got to him in a big way. But there was no way he was going to do anything about it. Apart from his inner voice reminding him Miles was a player in Abbey's life, he actually liked Abbey too much to use her, then drop her for Holly. And there was now another voice in him, too, one that knew – if he made love to Abbey, he might not want to drop her for Holly. Too dangerous . . .

'Do you want to see it?' Abbey signed her name, rubbed her eyes, then the small of her back, stood and stretched. 'If I do paint you, I'll use this one as a reference.'

It was the finest study she had ever done. Abbey's developing emotions for Jake had been poured into the work, every single facet of his personality shone in the reflective eyes, every element of shape individually shaded.

Jake put the control levers into neutral, their destination in his sights. He'd been cruising slower than he needed, to give Abbey more time. To give himself more time to be ready to let go. Despite that he'd held right back, done all the 'right' things, he wasn't feeling too hot. 'Yeah.'

She propped the sketch on a clean sheet of paper and moved over to stand beside him.

'What do you feel about it?'

'Like somebody kicked me in the guts.'

'Yeah, right.' She mimicked the words he used often, yet when she looked up at him, his expression was the exact same one as the drawing.

He rubbed his hand around the back of his neck. Abbey hadn't painted the illusion he portrayed to the world, the 'get 'em off, darlin' – Jake's here' image. She had gone way beyond what he thought himself capable of. Abbey Roberts portrayed him with emotions deeper than an oil well. And a perfect physique. He could look at himself and know that one more person in his life had seen past the surface, believed in the real man. It didn't bother him any longer, it comforted him.

'Fancy a beer to celebrate, Westaway?'

'Mmm. Yeah.' He could hardly speak, couldn't understand why he actually felt moved. Didn't try to understand.

Abbey tapped her can against his. 'Cheers. So how far are we from your sister's?' She followed his finger as he pointed to the land beyond the rag-taggle of mast-and-fishing-boat-cluttered coastline.

'The low white building.' Jake brought the boat into the jetty and tied her off. 'Did Holly leave anything fancy to wear? You should come to the bash tonight, Abbey. I've got to get straight off and meet Monty now.' Jake's eyes were unusually warm as he added, 'You could follow me there in a couple of hours.'

Even sensing it was unwise, Abbey responded, 'We ought to celebrate not killing each other. What kind of "fancy" did you have in mind?'

133

'Kind of informal fancy.' He leant into the locker, pulled out his wallet and swore at the lack of cash.

'I spent it.'

'What – all of it?'

'There wasn't much there in the first place.'

'What isn't much to you, Abbey, is a bloody fortune to me.' He realized he'd been in danger of forgetting they lived in completely different worlds. Hers had plenty of money in it.

'I'm sorry. I'll pay you back.'

'Yeah. Right.' Jake stuffed the wallet in his jeans' back pocket. He pulled a file of papers from an overhead locked compartment. 'If you want an evening with a freaking pauper, I'll be at the white building. If you'd rather make your own way home – there's a travel shop tucked away two streets inland on the left. They reopen around three.'

Jake's harsh tone hurt because they'd become friends. But he'd gone from the boat before she could respond.

'Damn!' Abbey fumed. 'You're not getting rid of me that easily. You're trying to take the quick way out and finish this on a sour note – I'm not letting you get away with that!' Piling her hair into a top-knot and pulling on a peak cap to keep it in place, a pair of sunglasses from the locker, and dressed in Jake's rugby shirt and giant tracks, Abbey ventured on to the crooked jetty, spent an age locating a bank, even longer waiting whilst faxes moved between her British bank and the Spanish one, verifying her signature. Then she withdrew an obscene amount of money.

And something perverse moved inside Abbey when she returned to Jake's launch, rummaged through the locker and unearthed a deliciously tempting dress on a hanger right at the back; and a small black handbag full of costume jewellery.

The dress was red silk with a black laced over-corset, strapless, and had a short swing skirt. Red strappy shoes perched crookedly on a shelf right at the back and a small black shoulder bag helped Abbey create the image she instinctively knew Jake wouldn't be able to resist. That is, if Holly's revealing clothes were any measure of his tastes.

Before dressing, Abbey took a thick wad of money from the borrowed track-suit bottoms and tucked it inside Jake's denim jacket pocket, a note alongside. *There should be enough here for your inconvenience and to fly Holly out. If I don't get chance to thank you for everything – thanks. It's been an experience. Your friend, Abbey.*

There was enough money to fly Holly around the world and to fill Jake's boat with diesel for months – but to Abbey, a thick fold of cash was just that.

She fluffed her hair so it tumbled around her shoulders, applied the newly purchased mascara, put on red dangling earrings and finally wriggled into the dress. 'You might be on to something with this "rig out", Holly.' She smiled at the siren's image in the full-length shower-compartment mirror. 'This looks like a lot of fun.'

CHAPTER 5

'Splendid!' Miles boomed down his mobile telephone. 'I'll contact the bank and have them transfer funds!' He waved his hesitant private nurse into the room. 'I'll be in touch when it's all finalized.' With that, he switched the phone off. 'What I really need is a fax machine in here. Could you arrange it?'

'I really need to straighten up your bed and tidy away all these papers, Mister Pendleton-Smythe, before the consultant arrives this afternoon.'

'I've told you before, call me Miles, my dear.' He spoke softly. 'Now, about that fax machine? I can have one delivered from my office *tout de suite!*'

The nurse propped her hands on her hips. 'This room is more like an office than a hospital room already, Mister Pendleton-Smythe – ' she gathered up papers, passed them to Miles whilst she spoke ' – I don't know what you'll be asking for next!'

He took hold of the nurse's hand as she passed him another sheath of papers, drew her towards the bed. 'There is something you can do for me, my dear.'

Her manner softened. 'Again? Mister Pendleton-Smythe, there's barely time before the consultant arrives.'

'Pull the blinds, darling, we don't want to shock anyone, now do we, aye?'

The nurse had barely buttoned up before the consultant's bark resounded along the vast, airy corridor.

'I'll be in trouble – ' the nurse put her hand to her mouth ' – I haven't recorded your obs. Mr Simpkins is red-hot about recording obs!'

'Panic not, my dear! I'll tell him you were indulging me!'

'Oh, no!' She giggled.

'Oh, don't worry, I know the man – I'll sort it.'

'Ah, Geoffrey!' Miles boomed when the orthopaedic consultant entered his room, 'I was just telling dear Nurse Trellany here not to panic – I've had her assisting me with papers and such and kept her from doing my obs.' His tone of voice left no doubt as to what they had been doing.

'Is this true, Nurse Trellany?' The stern-looking consultant caught sight of a discarded stocking under Miles's bed and cleared his throat. 'And did you have to undress to help him?'

The nurse turned beetroot red. Her mouth dropped open as she looked from 'Geoffrey' to Miles, desperate, mortified.

'Go along, my dear.' Miles wafted his hand. 'That's all for now.'

'Really, Miles, you are a bounder.' Geoffrey settled in the chair at his patient's side. 'Are you sure all this activity is a good thing with your bad leg?'

'Don't deny me my pleasures, Geoffrey, it's hard enough trying to run my business from this place.' He tapped his cheek with a long, white finger, 'I'm going to contact my office and have my facsimile machine installed here temporarily. What do you think?'

'It will be another three to four weeks before you can walk with crutches, old boy.' Geoffrey rubbed his chin. 'And since you are paying over the odds for the privilege of this room, I don't see why you shouldn't bring it in.' The consultant stood then, checked over Miles's charts, his leg and pain control. 'Anything else we can do for you? Your father is coming to visit you tomorrow – I'd like him to know we've made you as comfortable as possible.'

'Once I have the fax machine and the mail delivered here daily, Geoffrey, I'll be just fine and dandy.'

'The pins are doing their job.' The consultant pushed the X-rays into a clip at the top of a lighted white facia. 'It is going to take time though, Miles, to completely recover. Bones can take a while to fuse, especially after a break like this.'

'I shall recover here much faster, surrounded by my work, Geoffrey – ' Miles gave the consultant a broad smile ' – and the night-time nurse is an absolute inventive genius. I'm arranging to take her home with me when I leave here.'

Geoffrey Simpkins raised a brow. 'Really?'

'Don't worry, Geoffrey, she's an agency nurse. I brought her in myself to take good care of me, you know.'

'Ah, well, me boy, that's all right, then.' He laughed. 'But you really should spend some time resting. All these aerobics could slow up your recovery.'

After spending half an hour with Miles, the consultant left. He shook his head at Miles's exploits; an indulged young gentleman indeed he was. But his father was one of the richest, most influential chaps he'd ever known. 'One of these days,' Geoffrey muttered to himself as he left the Plumegate Private Hospital, 'someone will say no to that young man and there'll be hell to pay.'

'Miles?' The stunning dark-haired nurse slipped into his room. 'I collected your mail from your home like you asked. There's some things redirected from St Michael's.'

Rising from a snooze, Miles held out his hand to the woman. 'Pull the blinds and come here, sweetheart, I'll look at them in a while.'

It was the following morning, as Miles's night nurse dressed to leave that Miles stretched and indolently flipped over the postcard, a lazy, satisfied smile on his face.

The smile froze at Abbey's message, 'Your friend Jake is taking good care of me so there's no need to worry – '

'Westaway!' Miles's expression was thunderous. 'What the hell are you playing at?'

The nurse fastened her shoes, gave Miles a little wave of farewell that he ignored, then she slipped out to hand over to Miles's early shift nurse – a no-nonsense matron type – and vaguely wondered what had happened to the regular, pretty nurse.

Miles's mood grew fouler, more agitated. 'Bloody Westaway!' He gritted his teeth. 'You won't get away with nicking my woman, old boy! You can't have her! She's mine!' he ranted, shaking his traction-hung leg. 'If you think you can seduce Abbey Roberts, let me tell you, you're wrong!' Barely pausing for breath, he

139

reached for his telephone, punched out a number, teeth clenched, fingers drumming, as he waited for a response at the end of the line. 'You'll pay for this, Westaway – you'll pay! I thought Abbey hadn't visited me because of her bloody sore throat – and all the time, she's with *you!*'

'Ah, good morning' – his tone smooth, slick – 'I need someone sought out and reported on. Spain. Yes, I have the exact location.' Miles squinted at the date on the postcard. 'He'll be arriving tomorrow or the following day – yes, start with a fishing village called . . .'

Rick sifted through his morning mail. He'd picked it up himself on his way into the gallery office. Cheques, in the main, for Abbey's paintings. 'Abbey – ' he made one pile of cheques for banking, another of the requests for commissions by Abbey Roberts ' – Abbey, you are a gold mine. I think we'll up the ante, babe.' His brows raised at the telephone-number amount offered by a hopeful client for one of her detailed scenic fantasy paintings. 'Je-sus! If you died, Abb, your paintings would be priceless.' He buzzed his secretary. 'Sue, has there been any word from Abbey?'

'She's not at home, Richard,' came back the response through the intercom. 'I called around the beach house on my way here today.'

'Thanks.' It wasn't like Abbey to just take off – in the years he'd represented her, Richard had always known just exactly where he could reach her, even when no one else did.

A bright postcard slid from between a couple of still-unopened envelopes. He flicked it over, gasped with surprise at the hastily written: *Rick, taken off for a few*

*days with a friend, will contact you when I return. Love,
Abbey.*

He pressed the intercom. ''S okay, Sue, I've heard
from Abbey. If anyone asks, she's taking a break.'

'Er – there's someone here to see you, Richard.'

'Not yet, Sue, I'm still – '

The door banged open. Rick winced as the brass
door-knob hit the bookcase with a whack.

'Where is she?' Nedwell Roberts demanded. 'Is this
some kind of publicity stunt to put up the price of her
paintings?'

'I'm sorry, Mr Roberts, you've lost me.'

'Days! For days I've been trying to raise my daughter
at that blessed hermit home of hers! Where is she? I've
business to discuss with her!'

Richard took a deep breath to stem his annoyance with
Abbey's father. 'Here, I got this in the morning mail.'

'Is this it?' He pulled an identical card from his
pocket. 'I want an explanation, Richard, and I want
it now! Why wasn't I told she'd been taken ill? Why did
I have to read about it in this!' He threw down the
neatly trimmed newspaper article from the *Weekly
Treasure*. 'You could at least have put a letter in with it!'

'You were abroad, sir,' Richard said respectfully,
wishing Nedwell Roberts would sling his hook. 'And
with all due respect, I'm Abbey's agent, not her keeper.
Besides, I didn't send you that – ' he gestured with his
solid gold pen at the press cutting ' – it's not my style.'

'This – ' Nedwell flicked his own postcard ' – isn't
Abbey's style. She doesn't just "go off" with her
friends. At the very least, she would have left me a
message with my answering service.'

Nedwell's eyes caught and lingered on the pile of

cheques neatly stashed inside Richard's paying-in book.

'I know Abbey, Richard, she would have left me a message. She hates people worrying about her.'

'Sue, could you bring in some coffee, please?' Richard released the intercom button, turned his full attention to the agitated Nedwell Roberts. 'Abbey didn't want to worry anyone, so we deliberately kept it quiet, Mister Roberts . . .' Richard paused whilst Sue brought in the tray with his morning coffee, along with an extra coffee cup. 'Thank you, Sue. Would you do the banking for me now, please? Switch on the ansaphone before you nip out.'

'Yes, Richard, I've a personal errand, too. Do you mind? I'll work through lunch?'

'That's fine, Sue.'

'Kept what quiet?' Nedwell demanded.

'The night of her exhibition, Abbey lost her voice.'

'Lost – her voice?'

'The duty doctor put it all down to exhaustion and laryngitis, told her to rest for a couple of weeks. She obviously thought about it and decided to take off.'

'What happened to make her lose her voice?' Nedwell sipped his coffee, his eyes speculative. 'There's something in that article about the lights going out – about her collapsing on the floor.'

'Exhaustion, pure and simple, so the doc said.'

'She looked sensational, Richard, when I saw her at the exhibition – not a trace of tiredness.'

'She was thoroughly checked out, I took her home and Miles was due, so I didn't stick around.'

'Why not?'

'Because Miles has a jealous streak a mile wide, Mr Roberts.'

'I presume, then, that Miles is with Abbey?'

'Guess so.'

Nedwell's eyes narrowed strangely. 'I'll leave you to your business, Richard.' He dropped a business card on to Richard's desk. 'If you hear from her, do let me know.'

'Sure.' As soon as the door closed behind Nedwell Roberts, Richard heaved a sigh of relief.

The man gave him the creeps.

Abbey's co-habiting, twin aunts passed the postcard between them over breakfast. 'Didn't know she had a holiday planned, did you, Cynthia?'

'She's not likely to tell us, is she, Rosemary?'

'Fancy. She's jet-setting around the world and her poor mother – ' Rosemary scowled ' – our beloved sister-in-law is tucked away in that psychiatric hospital. You'd think the girl would spend her holiday visiting Rebecca, wouldn't you?'

'Too wrapped up in her own affairs by half. Her fault, all of it. If Nedwell hadn't urged us into going to that showy exhibition of Abbey's, I'd really rather not have gone.'

'So you keep saying.' Rosemary buttered her toast with an ornate silver knife. 'At least he visits Rebecca every few days. No matter how much travelling he does, God love him. Which is more than I can say for Abbey. That family fell apart at the seams after – ' She drifted into silence; some things were just to painful to say out loud.

'Mmm. More tea?' Cynthia ripped up the postcard. 'Of course, I knew she was bad the minute I laid eyes on her.'

The twins nodded, one agreeing mind between them formed two score and ten years ago in the womb, drifted

143

simultaneously for a spell, their thoughts identical.

The child had sympathy, understanding, a trust fund the size of a small bank; and she had freedom to do as she wished – to jet-set around the world at a whim. It was a hard pill to swallow when they looked at all they had lost.

Like a slickly rehearsed tragedy, Cynthia poured Rosemary another cup of stewed tea. 'Abbey was the only one to gain – '

'I've said it before and I'll say it again – ' Rosemary nodded, then their voices were as one, indistinguishable, 'We lost so much more than a fortune . . .'

They raised their cups to drink in synchronized perfection, the time faded, fussy surroundings somehow at odds with their mournful mood.

That mood altered yet again as they set down their cups in elaborate, chipped, china saucers. 'It's my turn to work today, Rosemary. There's time for one of your delicious rock-cakes before I catch the bus.'

'You really are a marvellous cook, Cynthia.'

'Thank you, dear. I simply long for the day when I don't have to spend every hour baking for a bunch of unappreciative idiots. Now don't forget to make those chocolates how I showed you? You've got everything you need.'

'I won't. It won't be long, Cynthia, then we can retire.'

A smile crossed two matching faces, eyes meeting as they ate the legendary rock cakes, expressions a touch dreamy.

Lynn yawned, relieved to be home after the gruelling long-haul flights. The postcard from Abbey caught her attention amongst the freebie newspapers and brown envelopes waiting to welcome her on her brown, hairy door mat.

'Good on you, Abb!' She chuckled at the brief message and the promise to telephone when she returned home. 'Hope you and Miles are really living it up.'

Lynn dropped her flight bag to the floor and then cringed. Her ever-present camera was at the bottom; quickly, she rooted it out and checked for damage. It was fine. She flipped open the back and removed the used film and put it alongside the others on the hall shelf awaiting developing. 'I'll get you copies of this one,' Lynn spoke to the postcard, propped it at the back of the shelf, the film she'd used at the exhibition first in the queue. She kissed her chunky little camera. 'You've nine lives – like a cat! You've been lost, left, dropped and half-drowned – and you still come up trumps!

CHAPTER 6

Strolling slowly in the oppressive early evening air, Abbey caught sight of a reflection in a salt-misted shop window. A man across the road – he seemed to be watching her. Tall, slender, mid-brown hair and sun-glasses, his shirt white, denim cut-offs.

Abbey couldn't shake the uncomfortable sensation she was being watched, followed. Despite the heat, she shivered, let the riot of strawberry-blonde curls drop forward over her cheeks. Watched? You're being ridi-culous, Roberts, she used Jake's voice in her mind to calm her suspicions. A tourist reading a British news-paper stretched and vacated the bench he'd been occupying beneath the shade of a large tree at the edge of the pavement. Desperate for something to do with her hands, Abbey darted over to the bench and picked up the tabloid newspaper, held it up in front of her face whilst she scanned from behind dark glasses for the source of the 'uncomfortable' sensation.

Slowly, she expelled a breath of relief. There was hardly a soul about in the intense heat; leaning back on the bench she fanned herself with the newspaper – then almost launched into orbit when an accented voice shattered the peace.

'Do you have a light?'

She spun around. It was the brown-haired man, his stubble almost a beard. Irrational panic struck her in that moment. She shook her head and the newspaper spilled from her fingers. She bent down to pick it up, throat dry, heart pumping when the stranger offered, 'Allow me.'

He frowned at her when she took the jumble of papers from him and said nothing.

'Don't suppose you know the way to the Pension Lafayette?'

She shook her head. 'No.'

'Okay, thanks.'

Relieved as the man moved away, yet too shaky to join Jake and his family, Abbey set about putting the newspaper back together. A brief glance in the man's direction saw him enter a canopy-shaded shop, the owner joining him on the step to give directions.

'Get a grip, woman,' she muttered to herself as she walked slowly from the shade of the tree, 'you can't spend the rest of your life in this state.'

Abbey stared across to Jake's launch, longing for the security it represented, knowing she'd never feel that safe again. It was the boat and it was Jake. Especially Jake. If he was here now – she stanched the thought – he wouldn't be 'with her' again. Right at this moment, Holly was probably working out routes with a Kentish travel agent to join him.

Everything's going to be all right, she chanted in her mind, there's no one here who knows you. But all the fine hairs on her skin prickled when she stopped to look into a small leather-goods shop and saw the brown-haired man's reflection across the street, silhouetted against the criss-cross masts.

Abbey had to know: was he following her? She pretended she hadn't seen him, strolled casually up a narrow side street – it was a palm-lined dead end. Because the newspaper began to tremble in her fingers, she used it as a fan, turned around and made her way out of the trap.

Abbey wanted to run to Jake, but couldn't. This was her problem, hers. And she had to find a way to deal with the shadows. Perhaps if she made her way slowly toward Marianne's home, he would help her find somewhere to hide? But what would Jake say if she turned up and said, 'I'm being followed?'

Probably something like, 'Give me a break, Roberts, you're a freaking paranoid.'

There was a telephone booth in the shade of a tree. Abbey had to rest; the adrenaline dashing through her veins made her tremble. She grasped the phone, made a pretence at speaking, gibbering insensibly; breath came in short gasps. The reflection in the shiny, high temperature hood showed the man was still with her. Sweat rolled, then chilled between her shoulder blades.

As the road bent round slightly, the stout white building came into full sight, a small moss-washed fountain out front, a small kind of park in the fore; a handful of colourful tourists, cameras hanging around their necks, phrase books open, milled about.

Shielding her eyes from the sun as if scanning the people for someone she knew, she then waved and walked purposefully towards the tourists. Maybe that'll put him off. She prayed it would – he'd know she wasn't alone, think he'd missed the person waving back at her.

Keeping on the uneven footpath that led to the white building, Abbey almost cried out with relief to spot Jake talking seriously with his companion; it made her brave enough to turn around, look over her shoulder for the brown-haired man. He had gone! Maybe she had imagined the whole thing.

Monty glanced up from the table as the waiter brought them fresh coffee. 'Phillipe, tell Jake about that geezer who was asking after him.'

'He asked when you are due to arrive.' Phillipe spoke in rapid Spanish, Jake responded likewise.

'What did you tell him?'

'I tell him, come back later when Monty here and ask him.'

'Maybe it was a prospective client.' Jake took a swallow of the strong coffee, wished he hadn't been so caustic with Abbey. Distracted by the terse way he'd spoken to her, Jake began to suspect he'd done it purposely, to push her away. Well, hell, Westaway, he thought with a stab of regret, you did a damn good job – four hours gone and she's not shown up. Wouldn't now. She'd be speeding home.

'He ask if you travel with a woman called Abbey Robbins?'

Jake almost choked. 'Never heard of her.'

'I say the woman you travel with called Holly,' the waiter said proudly, wiping the edge of their table. 'Monty told me her name.'

Casually, Jake asked, 'What did this guy look like?'

'Spanish national but I haven't seen him around here before.'

'Now that's what I call a woman.' Monty gave a low

149

whistle, distracted by the flash of red and black dress moving in their direction. 'Get an eyeful of that, mate.' He jerked his thumb at the shapely figure traversing the road at the edge of the small park. 'Looks like your idea of heaven, Jake.'

Laughing, despite his low mood, Jake's eyes followed Monty's. He'd know those legs anywhere, and the rest of her, spilling out of the black-laced corset. Behind Abbey, he saw a man raise his camera, take a shot in their direction – a shot that would include Abbey.

The man hovered, made his way up the steps to the road in front of the white building. Jake scrutinized the man from behind his dark glasses; he leant against the railing, lit a cigarette, his interest still trained in their direction. If this guy was following Abbey, he wanted sacking – obvious didn't cover it.

'Holly!' Jake shot to his feet, long strides covering the space between them and without missing a beat, pulled her roughly into his arms and kissed her. 'Where've you been? Did you get lost?' Whilst he spoke in fluent Spanish, he guided Abbey to his seat, pulled her on to his lap, the firm fingers at her waist giving the clear message 'Stay put'.

'Holly, this is Monty.' Jake shot her a look from behind his sunglasses that told her to play along or else. 'Marianne's just fetching a jug of something cold. And she's insisted we have a night with them.'

Abbey had the feeling she'd walked into a soap opera and was the only one who hadn't learnt her lines. Apart from the names, she could make nothing out – her grasp of the language as basic as sticking an 'o' on the end of every word.

Even Marianne, appearing with a condensation-laden

jug of orange juice, effused, 'Great! You're here at last, Holly?'

'Mmm.' The inflection told her it was a question. Her response barely audible, she took the glass from Marianne and smiled. Whatever was going on was beyond her, but the drink was wonderful.

'Jake, what the – ?' He brought his mouth down hard on hers, his palm riding on her leg, roving higher when she frowned at him. He kissed her neck then, whispered against her ear, 'Shut up.'

'But – !'

'Shh.' He kissed her again, then gave Monty an all-male grin. 'S'bin a couple of hours.'

Monty laughed. And to Abbey's relief, Monty spoke in English, his Cockney accent music to her ears. 'So like I was telling you, this geezer said, "Has Jake Westaway turned up yet? Has he got a woman with him called Abbey Robbins?" Somethin' like that – ' He shrugged. 'I told him, mate, that's not the name of Jake's latest – when he rang and said he was coming the long route from Kent, his bird's name was Holly!' Monty shrugged again. 'Said he'd come back. Dunno what the 'ell it was about, though – wouldn't leave a message.'

'Beats me.' Jake relaxed his hold on Abbey. She twisted around to look at the railings, to see if the man with the cigarette was there. But he'd gone.

'Jake,' Abbey whispered, her lips close to his, 'what's going on?'

'Nothin'.' Dark blue eyes dropped briefly to her mouth. 'Don't worry about it, darlin'.'

Just like that? 'Nothing'? His hand was up her skirt, he'd kissed her like they did it all the time and he called

151

it 'Nothing?' Well, if he could help himself for no good reason – so could she! Maybe she hadn't learnt the lines . . .

Oozing sensuality, Abbey slid her arm around his neck, the crook of her elbow holding him still; and she saw a jolt of hot surprise in Jake's eyes when she closed the gap between their mouths. He resisted, for a second, until Abbey stroked her tongue over his firm lips, teased them apart, savoured the heat of his mouth just as greedily as he did hers. A hot, sharp thrill raced over her skin when his calloused palm squeezed her thigh and his breath quickened against her cheek, his whole body tensing.

Peripherally aware that Marianne, Monty and Phillipe chattered as though there was nothing untoward occurring, Abbey deepened their embrace, spread her fingers against Jake's scalp, wriggled her weight further up his hard thigh.

Damnation – you got that wrong, Westaway, his conscience bleated.

Uh-huh, he responded, his hand twisting in the soft riot of waves, bringing her harder against him. Hell, she felt so good, better, softer than she had a right to feel.

Put her down! This is Miles's woman!

She's kissin' me! And some . . .

And what are you doing? Fighting it?

Get real – a low moan broke in his throat as Abbey's fingers spread at his shoulder, kneaded – oh, lord, I love that . . .

Stop – now! Miles is your mate.

Shove off. But Jake knew the voice was right; okay, in a minute, it won't happen again, I'm makin' the most of –

Right now. Stop.

Jake's fingers spread at her jaw, gently, reluctantly eased their lips apart.

Then Jake realized just what he'd done. The one thing he'd avoided, Abbey had instigated – and when he couldn't do a damn thing about it.

'What are you playing at?' Jake's harsh whisper close to her ear.

That slow, crooked smile curved her lips. So only Jake could hear, she murmured, 'Tell me what's going on.'

'Later – '

'Now.'

'I'll explain later.'

'Okay.' Abbey's acquiescence made Jake uneasy.

'Holly – ' Monty glanced at their guests, smiled generously ' – how about Marianne shows you your room?'

Raising her glass, Abbey sprang to her feet, took a sip, then 'accidentally' spilt the juice over Jake's crotch. 'I'm sorry!' She grabbed a serviette and made as if she was about to 'mop up'; but Jake stayed her wrist.

''S okay. I was planning on a shower.' Only Abbey saw the flash of anger in Jake's eyes.

'You know which room, Jake.' Monty stood as Jake took Abbey's hand.

'Cheers, mate.'

'Only don't be divin' in that bed with her just yet, mate,' Monty called, 'we've got stuff to discuss.'

'Yeah, right.' Jake led Abbey through the restaurant to the living quarters up the back stairs.

Phillipe cleaned the table in the corner, the coolest

153

table with a fan wafting overhead. The fan disturbed the grey cigarette smoke curling upward; the customer, lowering his menu just enough to reveal brown hair, made notes as the couple moved quickly past.

As soon as they reached the back stairs, Abbey pulled her hand from Jake's; but she had no alternative other than follow him up the dark, narrow staircase.

Jake let Abbey enter the room before him, then closed the thick, arched wooden door.

'What's going on?' Arms akimbo, she squared up to Jake; he sidestepped into the bathroom, turned on the shower.

'I'm showering.'

Abbey sighed, moved further into the spacious room. Early evening sunshine slanted through cotton lace curtains, cast pretty shadows on plain white walls. Cool, marble tiles, their soft, pale sheen the perfect foil to the wrought-iron balcony outside, where a collection of tropical plants and cactus basked. She settled on a dark wooden chair by the window and stared down at the fountain in the street below. It was practically deserted now . . . No sign of the man in cut-offs. She shuddered. Had he followed her . . . or was she going crazy?

Beneath the rods of cool water, Jake soaped away Abbey's lingering, tantalizing fragrance – and the juice. 'She shouldn't have come on like that!' He hated the sense of betraying Miles that stuck in his guts, disgusted with himself for enjoying Abbey's luscious embrace. 'She knows how I feel 'bout that – ' It struck him then, he'd been the one who'd started the whole thing – leaping up and grabbing hold of her. He hadn't had a whole heap of choice, he tried stoking his anger,

154

Abbey had a choice. He pulled on a pair of blue jeans and towel-dried his hair. 'Just tell her why you did it, man.' He shook his head, moved out into the room.

And keep your hands to yourself while you're doing it, that inner voice chimed.

Yeah. I'll be all business and no pleasure.

'I think I was followed.' She stood by the window, turned to face him.

'You were.'

'I wanted to tell you – but you were more interested in shoving your hand up my skirt and making me look like a – like Miss Easylay-on-display! What will your sister think of me?' She strode towards him. 'That was a horrible thing to do to a friend!'

'Abbey – ' Jake spread his palms.

'It was like – look, everybody, I've got a woman who lets me do anything in public, and she'll do it with anyone!'

Anger flashed in her green eyes, her fists were balled. 'I was followed and you're more interested in groping!'

Jake shoved his hands in his jeans pockets; she was too close and that hypnotic fragrance was bugging him big time.

Turning his back on her, Jake took a deep breath. 'For someone who wanted an explanation, you're not doing much listening.' Something perverse lurched inside him as he added, 'And for someone who didn't enjoy kissing me, that was one hell of an encore.' The shower hadn't done a damn thing to shake the taste of her mouth against his – willing, open, too bloody good.

Confusion knotted in Abbey's stomach; she loved his touch . . .

'I knew you were being followed.' Jake paced to the window, looked out, anywhere but at Abbey. 'I didn't want him to know we were on to him – so I called you Holly, kissed you. I was trying to throw the guy a curve – ' his eyes did meet hers then ' – while I sussed him out.' Whilst Abbey digested this, he reinforced what he'd said. 'A half-hearted peck on the cheek wouldn't have done it, Abbey.'

Groaning, mortified, Abbey's fingers spread over her face to cover embarrassment. She shook with laughter. 'I feel such an idiot!' Her voice broke up. 'I kissed you because you called doing it to me "nothing".'

He studied her for a long moment; the cooling shadows stretched further into the room, the breeze from the open window fanned those soft curls around her shoulders, darkened her unknowingly sensual eyes. 'Nothing' hadn't been a good choice of words.

'Miles is a lucky man.'

'What did you say that for, jerk?'

The alternative was along the lines of 'I could die screwing you and not give a damn.'

'Are we friends again?' Abbey wanted at least to know that much. 'I'd hate to leave tomorrow without patching this up, Jake.'

A half-laugh escaped him, 'Yeah, Gypsy Rose Abbey, we'll always be friends, remember?' His hand rose involuntarily to touch her cheek – he stopped the movement before she noticed and jammed his fist into his pocket. 'Listen, I've got some business to finish with Monty. Will you be okay?'

'Yes. Jake, that man who followed me . . .?'

'I'll put out some feelers.' He grabbed the door-knob;

156

he'd seen the flash of panic she tried to disguise. 'Lock this when I leave.'

When Jake strolled back through the restaurant, the table beneath the fan was empty.

'Hey, Phillipe?' He propped his foot on a bar stool, raised his elbow from the white marble bar-top as Phillipe's cleaning rag swept along the expanse. 'Was there a guy over there?'

'Always it's the favourite seat in the hot weather. Many sit there.'

'Smoking, brown hair?'

'Yes. But many smoking with brown hair.'

'Yeah.' Jake thanked the youth. 'Was he the guy asking about me?'

'No, the man darker, European.'

'Thanks, Phillipe.' Jake rubbed his chin, deep in thought as he joined Monty.

'What's the story, Jake?' Monty grinned, his thinning hair speckled with moisture. 'This Holly broad ain't your usual mark. Bit on the classy side.'

Jake shrugged. 'The guy who was here, asking questions, what did he look like?'

'What's this, Jake? Some jealous lover of a girlfriend from your past?' Marianne laughed, took a mouthful of peach.

'Maybe.'

'He was a smart geezer.' Monty shrugged. 'Average, didn't stand out at all.'

'Brown hair?'

'No, mate, when I say he didn't stand out, I mean he was a Spaniard, looked it. Dark hair, nearly black. Polite. Didn't take much notice.'

157

'Would you know him if you saw him again?' Jake looked from Monty to Marianne.

'Yep,' Monty responded. 'I'll keep my eyes peeled, but I ain't seen him since.'

Marianne shrugged. 'I'm going to get ready; you two finish your business?' She moved beside Jake, put an arm along his shoulder. 'It's good to see you, brother.'

'Good to see you, Marianne.' He stood, squeezed her tight. 'This husband of yours gets uglier, you get lovelier.'

She laughed, hugged him tight and waved.

'So what do you think?' Monty pushed the paperwork toward Jake. 'A week's work in just under a week. You ask me, he's not in any bloody danger, but he wants the kudos of a minder when he does all his acquisitions. I suggested a regular security man, but he wants someone who packs.'

'Not too far from here, is it?' Jake rubbed his chin. 'How come you're not taking it?'

'I would, mate, but we're joining the rug rats at your mum's that week. Bless the old girl, she took them a couple of days ago so we could 'ave a bit of a breather.'

'Don't let my mother hear you calling her "the old girl" –' Jake laughed ' – she'd have you lynched and boxed and sent back to London.'

'Tell you the truth, mate, I wouldn't care. I 'ave dreams about good old London drizzle. Just one year to go, an' we'll be back in the smoke, just spend holidays here from then on.'

'Sounds good. Is Mum coming to Marianne's party?'

'Yep, she's bedding the critters down, then leavin' em to Grumps.'

Monty wiped his hand along his forehead. 'This job'll be a doddle, mate, reckon it'd be the quietest money you've ever earned.' Monty named a price and Jake whistled. He watched Jake closely as he added sheepishly, 'There's a couple of things – '

Jake's expression hardened. 'Now you're going to tell me half the underworld's after him.'

'You'll have to wear a suit. He fancies the idea of his muscle posing as a business strategist.'

'Sounds up Miles's street.'

'Since when did he ever have to break a sweat to earn his dosh?' Monty finished his water. 'You gonna show me the work you've done on your boat?'

'Sure.' Jake rose to his feet. 'Never thought I'd see the day, Monty.'

'Eh?'

'You. A family man.'

Jake laughed as his mate punched his arm, taunting, 'I'll still take you on any time.'

'Yeah, right,' was Jake's wry response, both men knowing Jake could make mincemeat of almost any opponent with his bare hands.

'By the way, Jake, Miles has this gorgeous babe, he brought her out here for a visit last year, stayed at the Rippoli.'

'For someone who's happily married, man, you're seriously obsessed with other women, Monty. Don't let my sister hear you talk like that.'

'Nah, I just like watching you jerks making a pig's ear of your lives. Don't know which of you's worst!' He chuckled to himself. 'There's Miles with his, "Chaps, I picked this one because she looks ornamental and is quite, quite wealthy," or you and your "If she's got big

159

tits and makes a lot of noise, it doesn't matter whether she knows how to use a knife and fork!" '

Jake laughed. Monty was straight-quoting both Miles and himself. 'It's all a matter of taste, m'boy,' Jake mimicked Miles, glanced back in the direction of the white building as they approached a slight bend in the road. Phillipe was cleaning table tops, emptying ashtrays. 'That Phillipe is serious competition for my Far Eastern au pair – talk about if it doesn't move, clean it!'

'Don't knock it, the last waiter spent all his time in front of the bloody mirror in the gent's lav. Think he ran a fan-club from the place.'

Monty squinted down the street. 'I've got to hand it to you, what I've seen of this Holly broad, she's a bit plush, ain't she? Did she fancy a bit of rough?'

'Maybe.'

'Special, is she?' Monty frowned deeply. 'You're usually ravin' on about big soft tits and how knackered you are, makin' me wonder if I've done the right thing gettin' tied down.'

'You've done the right thing.' Jake glanced back at the white building, wondered if Abbey was all right.

'You don't look like you've been at it for nearly two weeks.' Monty laughed. 'Bin holdin' out, has she? Tryin' to keep you interested?'

Jake knew Monty's interest was his own fault, he usually extolled his most recent girlfriend's virtues – all of them physical. His escapades these recent years were something Monty was proud of.

Jake wiped his fingers around the back of his neck. 'How'd it go with Maxwell Chamberlain?'

'I had more fun with him than you did with the Far

160

Eastern delight, mate, don't know how you stuck that one.'

'I felt like "sticking him", arrogant bastard.'

Monty laughed, 'Any women out there?'

'An English au pair, nothing heavy.'

'They'll write that on your gravestone, mate. Here lies Jake Westaway – mention weddings – you'll never see him again.'

Jake put Monty in a half-Nelson. 'Don't say that word, man!'

'Jeez! I'm sorry!'

Monty rubbed his neck, grimaced, caught Jake looking back again as they reached the corner. 'Tell me to mind my own if you must, but are you on the job?'

'What?'

'This Holly? Are you minding her?'

'You know I don't mind women,' Jake said evasively as they crossed the gangplank, jumped down into the boat.

'Nah!' Monty watched Jake closely. They both knew there was more to this, but Monty changed the subject. 'Next job that comes up in London – I'm takin' it. Drizzle, good British drizzle.'

'This is looking ace!' Monty entered the cabin. 'When you said you were going to fit this beauty out yourself, I didn't think you'd do it this good.'

'Want a beer before we head back?' Jake pulled two cans out of the fridge, handed Monty one.

Abbey had tidied up the cabin before leaving, stowed the sleeping bags; none of her belongings were scattered around. It was strange without her sketch pad, without reminders of her presence. He opened the locker to check where she had put her things, a smile curving his mouth to see she had put everything together in a carrier at the back of the locker, the sketch pad balanced on top.

His denim jacket wasn't where he'd left it, though, it was lying on the locker floor. Without thinking, he picked it up, noticed a bulge in the pocket.

'Mind if I use your loo?' Monty ran his hand over the varnished wooden surface of the shower room-cum-toilet door. 'This is neat, mate.'

'Yeah.' As soon as Monty closed the door, Jake pulled out the contents of the jacket pocket, Abbey's note folded around the money.

He stuffed his revitalized wallet into his back pocket as Monty joined him.

'What's up, mate?'

'Nothing.'

'You don't frown like that when there's nothing up.' Monty snapped the ring pull of his beer open.

'No.' Jake, distracted, insulted almost that Abbey had given him so much money – what did she have to do that for?

Pay him off? Forget about him? Was it his bleating about being a pauper? He'd been angry because they were from different worlds.

'C'mon, mate – give!' Monty took a long pull of his beer.

'I think I found something I wasn't meant to find until tomorrow.'

'What?' Monty eyed Jake. 'It's that gorgeous woman, ain't it? Has she given you the flick? Don't tell me she's had enough of your body, Jake – that'd be a first!'

'She's not my woman.' Jake opened his can, slid into the bench seat, rested his elbows on the table. 'I haven't laid a finger on her.'

Laughing, Monty propped himself against the sink. 'Oh – man! This is outrageous! You've had that curvy babe on this boat and you haven't – '

'No.' Jake's eyes glittered. 'I haven't.' He rose to his feet, pulled Abbey's sketch pad from the locker, tossed it on to the table in front of Monty.

'She's an artist.'

Glancing up at Jake, Monty opened the pad, turned through the sketches. 'These are fantastic. Who is she?'

'Abbey Roberts.'

'Shoot.' Monty shook his head. 'These are phenomenal, Jake.' He finished his beer, crushed the can. 'You know, I thought she wasn't quite your usual mark.' Monty's mouth moved. 'So somebody's looking for her?'

'Yeah, and it looks like they've found her.' Jake expanded, told Monty the whole story, of Abbey's kidnap as a child, of the new threat to her now. 'She's involved with Miles.'

'Hell, if you fancy her, mate, go for it.' Monty chuckled. 'You know what Miles is like, he'll find himself another ornamental chick – all the dosh he's got – anyway, he never keeps 'em for more than a few months at a time. He's probably got another one already.'

'She's not my type.'

Monty studied Jake through narrowed eyes. 'Who're you trying to kid, mate? Not me, please – I've known you too long.'

'I'm not interested.'

'So what was that snog about when she came up to us? You didn't exactly look uninterested, mate. Come to think, neither did she!'

'Abbey's being followed. I didn't want her giving the game away.'

'Well, mate, if you want my advice – '

'I don't.'

'If you want my opinion, I haven't seen you this wound up since Zav was on the scene.'

Jake crushed the can in his fist at the mention of Zav's name. 'So?'

'So you fancy her.'

He shrugged.

'Zav did that, too.'

'She's Miles's woman. I don't want to know.'

'Okay, okay!' Monty spread his palms in supplication. 'So you don't want her. All I'm saying is, Miles has had enough favours out of you – he owes you one.' Monty shrugged. 'If you did fancy her, you should make a move. That's all I'm saying.'

Jake rose to his feet. 'She's too stuck up for my palate.'

'Yeah, right.' Monty followed Jake from the cabin. 'But if you did fancy her – I mean, it's not as if Miles kept his nose clean with Zav, is it?'

'What?' Jake froze, about to climb out on to the gangplank.

Monty laughed. 'All those tricks Miles tried to get Zav off you when they were posted together in Germany. Every day, I'd to put up with his braggin'.' Amusement died in Monty's eyes and he winced. 'Shoot. You didn't know.'

Gut-punched, Jake spun around on the gangplank. 'Tricks like what?'

'I'm sorry, mate.' Monty scratched his head. 'I thought Zav would've said something.'

'Tricks like what?' Jake repeated through gritted teeth, his frame taut.

'Flowers, champagne, notes – ' Monty bitterly regretted saying anything. 'Me and my big mouth.'

'Did he – ?' Jake felt sick to the stomach, knew he shouldn't even ask the question. 'Did Miles get anywhere with Zav?'

Bleakly, Monty shook his head, couldn't meet Jake's eyes.

Seething, Jake jammed his hands in his jeans pockets. 'Zav never liked him.' Pain he had successfully buried from everyone but Monty and his sister burned in Jake's eyes.

'No, she didn't like him, but she missed you, mate.' But when Monty glanced at Jake, he could tell his friend wasn't listening, that he was rigid with anger, anger of the worst kind – impotent anger. And he was trying to convince himself that nothing had gone on between Miles and Zav.

Anything else – the favours – Miles pushing their friendship to the hilt – Jake could hack all of that. But Zav? Miles knew how he'd felt about her – she was off limits. Everyone knew how he felt about her. They were going to be married as soon as her tour was over . . . Instead, it was her funeral Jake attended. Fury raced through Jake like a white-hot knife.

All these years Jake had known indebtedness to Miles because Miles had been the one who helped him pick up the pieces after Zav's fatal accident during manoeuvres. Miles – the bloody hero, making out like he cared about Jake's grief. All the time he'd been after Zav? Jake could have been impaled on a machete and it wouldn't have hurt any more than this. And all the time he'd spent with Abbey – never touched her. Jake picked up a stone and flung it against the beach – all that time, he'd kept his distance because she was Miles's woman. Miles's woman. But to discover that a man he'd trusted had deliberately pursued Zav, and the realization that he'd never really know if anything went on between them. 'She missed you . . .' Those words tortured, sickened him.

Monty watched as anger ripped through Jake in all directions. Nothing he could say would help – he'd said enough.

'You okay?' Monty asked warily before they entered the restaurant area; an army of helpers cleared the tables to the sides, laid out food; Phillipe polished large trays of glasses, waved as the two men entered.

'No – ' Jake ordered a large whisky, downed it ' – but I will be.'

'Shoot.' Monty grimaced. 'I'm sorry, mate.'

'Don't be.' Jake slammed down the glass. The burning liquid felt good as it seared a path to his stomach. 'It's not your fault.'

'Monty!' Marianne emerged, dark hair in an elegant twist, her mid-calf-length black fitted dress understated to accentuate her natural beauty. 'You should be ready! Hurry up and change, love!'

'Wow! You look gorgeous.' Monty pulled Marianne towards him. 'I could eat you, birthday girl.'

Laughing, Marianne held Monty away. 'You and Jake should hurry up, Mother'll be here in a couple of hours.' She frowned in Jake's direction, moved to stand beside him. 'What's up, Jake? Got the blues?'

'No.' He downed another double whisky – it helped the foggy plan form in his mind. The no-holds-barred

166

plan to strike at Miles. Right where it hurt. Right in his ornamental, wealthy bloody girlfriend. But he had to get his head right first. He smiled at his blue-eyed, dark-haired sister, assured her, 'I'm okay. I'll go and get changed.'

Phillipe tilted the whisky bottle towards Jake, but Jake shook his head. 'Thanks, mate, I've had enough for now.'

The shower was running when Jake entered their room, Abbey's red and black dress laid carefully across the bottom of the bed.

'How're you doing?' He pushed open the bathroom door. The shower stopped.

'Fine.' Abbey wrapped a huge bath towel around herself, tucked it beneath her arms.

The steam and her fragrance followed her as she moved out into the room. 'Go ahead if you need the bathroom, I've finished.'

'Yeah.' He closed the door, locked it, anger spiking, striking his insides raw. No room for anything in his distraught mind except Zav – how much he'd loved her, trusted her. And Miles. It was easier to concentrate on Miles. He could strike back at Miles. But the ugly vision of betrayal kept rising in his mind, made him sweat. He was physically sickened, but that did nothing to ease the agony ripping through him.

Jake wanted to destroy, to yell with pain. Instead, he sat on the marble bathroom floor and used all those years of Aikido training, teaching and self-discipline to concentrate and gather his inner strength.

It's wrong to use highly developed skills this way to channel energy for revenge, the inner voice tried to tell

167

him. But Jake's grief was so intense, it didn't allow the voice to enter his psyche. The voice had no place now. Only revenge – there was only room for that. He didn't care, couldn't care about hurting Abbey – she was the instrument with which he'd strike at Miles. There was no other way, no other outlet for the burning, sickening grief; and no room for feelings.

Jake's sense of time sank away whilst he focused; harder, sharper, brought the agony under control and turned it into something else; something so alien to his forthright nature that he didn't like himself any more than he liked the bitter churning in his guts. He showered, every movement automatic, shock still as thick as the steam-filled bathroom.

Wiping the mirror clear of condensation, Jake studied his reflection. He looked the same, no one would know how he felt. He looked the same, but he felt completely different.

'Jake?' Abbey's husky voice permeated Jake's dream-like state. 'Are you all right?'

'Yeah. Won't be a minute.' He even sounded the same.

'Marianne just brought your tux up.' Abbey hung it on the heavy wooden wardrobe door, then leant out onto the narrow balcony, the light sea breeze lifting the hair from her shoulders, a tingle over her skin. Against the backdrop of adjacent tall terraces, a little boy chased a skinny dog, shouted in rapid Spanish – Abbey laughed, the dog had his bright new ball. 'Don't worry, little fella,' she whispered, 'he'll drop it when he realizes it's not edible.' And right on cue, the dog stopped, turned, tail wagging, and dropped the ball smartly into the lad's outstretched palms.

'Gypsy Rose Abbey strikes again.' Jake's amused voice made her jump.

'I didn't hear you.' Abbey frowned, 'I always hear you . . .' Her voice trailed because she hadn't been prepared for the sight of Jake in a tux. 'God, Jake, you look gorgeous.'

So tall, lean, yet muscular. The snow-white, pin-tucked shirt, black cummerbund and trousers, bare suntanned feet. She thought he hadn't heard her compliment because he fumbled with the bow tie in front of a small oval mirror. In a way, she was glad; it'd shot out of her, then stolen the breath from her. Lord, just the sight of him turned her to jelly. Quickly, she clutched the balcony rail, took a deep breath and studied the boat masts in the distance. Whilst Jake had showered, Abbey had begged Monty to take her to the tiny travel bureau; the ticket home for the following day nestled in Holly's borrowed trinket bag.

'Abbey, could you fasten this?'

When she turned to face him, he shrugged. 'I'm all fingers and thumbs with these.' His self-deprecating grin drew Abbey's laughter.

'You can be really cute sometimes, Westaway.' Her slender fingers looped the tie, then pulled it straight. Dissatisfied, she undid it again.

'I haven't been called cute before. Would it help if I sat down?'

'Okay.'

He sat on the bed. Abbey moved into the space between his legs, immediately aware she'd inadvertently moved into 'that' zone again. Her skin tingled. She had to fight to keep her eyes on the tie and not look into Jake's upturned features.

Jake watched her mouth slant into that crooked smile, the intense concentration in her eyes. 'You should have one of those "ready-tied" ones.' She undid it again.

'It wouldn't be this much fun.'

'Mmm, keep still.'

Accidentally, his thumb brushed her thigh. Colour shot to Abbey's cheeks, her whole body tingling at that single, simple touch. 'Jake, if you don't stop being sexy, I'm going to push you backwards and make love to you.'

He raised his palms. 'Be my guest.'

She laughed because she thought he was joking, and pulled the tie straight. Miraculously, it was perfect. 'There – you'll knock 'em dead.' Her eyes met his, sad and sensual at the same time; at odds with her unique smile. 'Shame Holly can't see you like this, Jake.'

'Why?' He caught her fingers as she stepped back, rose to his feet.

'Because you should have been here with her.'

'Yeah.' Jake couldn't dredge any regret at Holly's absence, but Abbey didn't notice; she squeezed his fingers and went into the bathroom. Since her shower, her shoulders were burning hot; she lifted her hair and tried to see why in the steamed mirror.

'Damn, I forgot to put sun cream on.' Without thinking, she called, 'Could you dig the aftersun out of that black bag, please, Jake?'

'Sure.'

'Abbey, what's this?' He had the aftersun cream in one hand, held her travel ticket towards her with his other.

She let her hair fall back to her shoulders. 'My ticket home. I'm going tomorrow.'

'When did you get it?'

'Whilst you were in the bathroom, Jake.' Part of her screamed, Ask me to stay! Just ask me . . .

'Were you planning on telling me?'

'I did, but you obviously couldn't hear me. You wouldn't let me in the bathroom. Monty said it was probably something you ate.'

He frowned. 'You went and told Monty I was sick?'

'I was worried about you. Monty said, "Don't worry, babe, he'll be fine when he's got it out of his system."' Green eyes lit with concern, she touched his jacketed arm. 'Are you all right?'

'Yeah.'

But Abbey saw a flicker of pain in Jake's deep blue eyes. She shook her head. 'You're not all right.'

Stunned, Jake stared straight back at her; shaken, because she still had the perception to read him.

'You didn't answer me, Abbey.' His voice was gentle. 'Were you going to leave without telling me?'

'No, I wouldn't do that. Maybe you should forget the party, go to bed – '

'It's Marianne's birthday.' He shook his head, raised her hands to hold her hair off her sun-warmed shoulders. 'Turn around,' and whilst his warm hands massaged cool cream on to Abbey's hot skin, he lied, 'I'm fine now it's out of my system.' Her travelling ticket found its way into Jake's trouser pocket.

'Try this for size – ' He hesitated, experienced a moment's uncertainty about what he was going to do, but thought of Zav, of Miles. 'You make me feel good, better than I have in a long time.'

She barely responded to that, her eyebrow raising imperceptibly. 'Thanks.' She dropped her hair to her shoulders and took the cream from him.

171

'You said it helped that I didn't fancy you.'

Ouch. Abbey tried to smile because it sounded like an affirmation of her words. But that honesty, wasn't that why she adored him? She did smile, but then her mouth fell open as he continued, looking almost sheepish.

'It's not true. Every time you look at me, I feel like I've been kicked in the guts, because I can't have you.'

Abbey stared up at Jake's intense blue eyes for a long, charged moment. Was he was telling the truth? It was only Miles who stood between them; but it might as well be the Great Wall of China.

Jake Westaway, the most beautiful, masculine, strangely honourable man she had ever known, wouldn't lay a finger on her because she was Miles's girlfriend. 'Maybe it's the perversity of human nature, to want what we can't have.' She smiled that crooked little grin. 'I ought to confess I – ah – I feel the same way around you.' Abbey tore her eyes from him, looked at the dark wooden clock. 'I'm only confessing because I know you won't do anything about it.'

CHAPTER 7

'Your shoulders feel cooler.' Jake dropped his hand on Abbey's shoulder as they went downstairs. He forced himself to relax, focused his thoughts on Miles's girl-friend, Miles's girlfriend, not Abbey, separating any feelings he had developed for her, visualizing her purely as his object of revenge.

'Jake! Abbey!' Monty intercepted them as they entered the full-swing party. 'You okay, mate?'

'Yeah, great.'

'Is he tellin' the truth, gal?' Monty quizzed Abbey.

'Jake's not capable of anything but.'

Relieved that his brother-in-law had visibly relaxed, Monty laughed. 'Abbey's told us her real name, Jake.' He lowered his voice. 'And Phillipe ain't seen hide nor hair of that PD.' Gesturing towards a long table, 'C'mon, everyone's waiting to start – '

'Jake!' A small, dark-haired woman leapt to her feet, was lost in her son's bear hug. ''Ow's me favourite son?' Warm brown eyes danced with life, an adorable stream of Cockney and Spanish erupted as she reached up and straightened his bow tie, shook her head, her tone slightly chiding as she spoke in pure Spanish, brought a smile to Jake's features. Abbey wished she knew what they were saying when Jake responded fluently.

Jake turned his mother by the elbow. 'Mother, this is Abbey Roberts; Abbey, this is my mother, Ana Westaway.'

Ana muttered something unintelligible about 'putters' under her breath. Brown eyes lit with suspicion – disgust? Abbey thought, confused when those brown eyes trailed downwards, then back to her eyes.

'It's a pleasure to meet you, Mrs Westaway.' Abbey all but picked up Ana's unresponsive hand and shook it. 'Your son has been a true friend to me these past weeks.'

Ana looked mildly surprised for a moment, then slid her hand from Abbey's, obviously unconvinced. She snapped out something in Jake's direction and Jake shrugged. Mild churnings of guilt moved in his stomach – Abbey had referred to him as a 'true friend' . . . He couldn't dwell on it; couldn't dwell on his mother's irritation that he always brought a different 'fancy' woman to their family celebrations. Graciously, he held out a chair for his mother and took a second to regain his focus. An image of Zav and Miles – entwined – served him well.

'Meet my cousins, Abbey.'

She frowned at him; would her reception there be as cold as his mother's? Yet Jake seemed unperturbed, rattled off names of those sitting at the long table and each in turn waved or smiled. The only name she remembered was 'Luis', and that because he was handsome in the same vein as Jake – severely handsome, with a killer smile.

The effusive chorus of introductions relaxed Abbey; but she tensed again as Jake pulled out a chair for her, opposite his mother. Whilst they ate, Abbey learned that most of the young men and women at the table were Jake's maternal cousins. They exchanged news with Jake and one another in rapid Spanish, which didn't worry Abbey at all. It allowed her to soak up the continental atmosphere; allowed her to be horrified at the amount of food and drink Jake put away when his stomach had been so bad.

'Jake – your stomach – ' She stilled his hand as he went to pour himself a large glass of red wine. 'Don't you think you should take it easy?'

'No.' He topped up his glass, certain this would all be easier if he was a bit tight.

'Don't expect me to nurse you if you're ill again, Westaway.' Abbey returned her fingers to her own glass.

She could feel Ana straining to eavesdrop on their conversation when Jake responded, 'Why not? I nursed you.' His smile was so sexy, it brought colour to Abbey's golden cheeks.

'All right – ' a husky laugh escaped her ' – I promise I'll mop your brow and wipe your cheeks, but I'm not going to sympathize.'

'You're all heart, Roberts.' He smiled again and Abbey wondered if Jake knew just how potent that smile was. Unexpectedly, he dropped his arm around her shoulder. 'I'll settle for having my cheeks wiped – ' amusement danced in his dark blue eyes ' – but you won't need to; my stomach's fine now.' Stomach's fine, he said inwardly, rest of me ain't so hot.

No sooner had the meal ended than half the diners leapt up to dance.

'How about a dance?'

'Okay.' She let Jake draw back her chair, lead her to the slow rhythm.

'Is something wrong?' Abbey frowned up at him, his arm moved around her as if he held her close all the time.

'Jake, are you drunk?'

'Nope.'

'You're being dreadfully solicitous for someone who couldn't wait to get rid of me.'

'Maybe I'm having second thoughts about that.'

Abbey breathed his familiar masculine scent; her insides lurched unexpectedly. 'Don't do that, Westaway.' She smiled, her forest green eyes holding his. 'I'm leaving tomorrow, there's no point in complicating matters.'

'Maybe I think there is.' His eyes glittered with an emotion Abbey couldn't define; before she could ask what he meant, his mouth covered hers.

Abbey fought the liquid warmth spreading through her as Jake's arms tightened, held her close. As much as she relished his closeness, she perceived some new emotion in Jake, something indefinable, and twisted her mouth away from his, needing to understand. 'Jake, what are you doing?'

A wry smile curved his mouth, 'I'm surprised you need to ask.'

It was tempting, so tempting to snuggle against Jake's hard, broad chest, whisper something arousing. But his apparent change from 'I don't touch Miles's woman' to outright seduction didn't make sense.

'There's no way you would try this if you were sober.' Abbey flattened her palms on his chest, gently held him away, watched the expression in his eyes turn to disbelief as she added, 'If anything was going to happen between us, it would have happened by now.'

She slipped from his arms, eased between the dancing couples to perch on a high stool beside the marble top bar. Quick as a flash, Phillipe served her a glass of champagne.

Marianne drew Monty to her side, gestured in Jake's direction. 'I think my brother's met his match.'

Monty frowned between Jake and Marianne. 'I don't know about that, love – '

'Ah! Men, you don't see anything! See how he watches her? It's the first time since Zav that Jake is this way.'

Monty shrugged. 'You're an incurable romantic.' But Marianne's insight was borne out when Jake pushed toward the bar to stand beside Abbey.

'Abbey and Zav – they're alike, Monty.' Marianne raised her glass in the general direction. 'Not looks, not the physical person, but on the inside.'

'Don't get too excited, babe, there's a lot going on you don't know about.'

'Rubbish!' She shot her husband a disgusted look. 'I know what I see, Monty, and Jake is having to work.' She laughed, 'it makes a nice change!' Marianne swung Monty on to the dance floor then. 'Let's listen.'

'You are a wicked woman.' Monty chuckled. 'Taking advantage 'cos it's your birthday.'

'Smile for the camera!' The peak-capped, clean-shaven, cigar-toting photographer caught Monty and Marianne in a close, laughing pose. 'Ah! Lovely!'

'Never mind what should or shouldn't have happened on the boat, why are you wearing that dress if you aren't giving me the come-on?' Jake demanded.

Anger surged through Abbey as she spun the stool,

177

her knees brushing Jake's thighs. 'For fun! Jake, you've seen me in a swimming costume that's as modest as a net curtain, you've seen me naked – for goodness' sake, I didn't honestly expect you to take one look at me in this and change your values!' She shook her head, soft, strawberry waves dancing around golden-pink shoulders, 'I wore it because I thought it'd give you pleasure – that's all.'

Jake frowned at her, his eyes still dark with anger.

'Jake, I'm sorry if I gave you the wrong impression, but you only think you want to seduce me because you've been drinking. We were never meant to be lovers. We're friends.'

'Says who?'

'The fact that Holly is your girlfriend, and I'm involved with Miles.'

The word 'Miles' triggered something dark inside Jake, something ugly. Abbey was merely using the same logic he had during their time together . . . Now he had to overcome it. But he couldn't use a crass attempt at seduction with Abbey – it wouldn't work.

'Would you do something for me?'

'If I can.' Abbey sipped the champagne. It reminded her of her exhibition, its awful ending – she set the glass down with a shudder.

'Will you stay? Spend the week here with me before you leave?'

'That's not a good idea.' Abbey smiled up at him, that lop-sided smile that hit him hard.

'Give me one good reason, Roberts.' His finger traced a line down Abbey's cheek, stopped at the edge of her lips.

'You know why.' Her eyes closed because the intensity in Jake's was too much, his fingertip against her lips too enticing.

'Tell me.' He'd moved closer, leant his elbow on the bar; his palm rested on her naked shoulder, his thighs against her knees. Those dark eyes of his that demanded the truth wouldn't release her.

'I – ' she looked down at the bar, then up at Jake ' – I've never been interested in one-night stands. It scares me, because with you, I'm tempted to break all my own rules.'

'Stay.'

'Jake, what about – ?'

'I'm not talking about anyone else, just you and me.' He ran his finger along her bottom lip. 'Stay.'

'Ask me again when you're sober.'

'You're procrastinatin', Roberts. I'm not drunk. Ask Phillipe – I'd a couple of whiskies. It takes more than that.'

'*Si.*' Phillipe refilled Abbey's glass. 'Two large whiskies – ' he winked obligingly ' – takes at least the bottle.'

Abbey shook her head. 'Perhaps some other time, Jake, I don't go in for your make-it-and-break-it style.' She stared him straight in the eyes, wanted to hold him more than she'd ever wanted to hold a man. 'I don't know why you're acting this way, but answer me this – why do you want me now? Why not before when we were on your boat?' Then came the question Jake dreaded. 'And why does it suddenly no longer bother you that Miles is my boyfriend?'

'I can't answer that.'

Missing the full implication of his reply, Abbey slid from the stool. Jake caught hold of her upper arm when

179

she would have walked away. 'But I can tell you I'm acting like this because I don't want you to walk out of my life tomorrow.'

'Jake, don't – ' She didn't want to walk out of his life, either, but Abbey couldn't let Jake make her any more vulnerable. 'I'm not like you. I can't make love with someone then "notch it up", or whatever it is you do.'

'I wouldn't do that.' He took a deep breath because he'd never expected Abbey would be so opposed, that winning her away from Miles would be so difficult.

'Yes, Jake, you would. You'd break my heart and walk away.' Pain rose in Abbey's throat, because she wanted so much from this man – but he wasn't right for her. Yet, in so many ways, he was. 'All along, I've loved your honesty, I've loved the way you've made me feel so safe – but it can't go any further between you and I, don't you understand?'

Jake frowned at her. 'No, I don't. Make me.'

'I'll bet every relationship you've ever had ends the moment a woman begins to need you, show any signs of wanting something more than sex.'

'I've never deceived a woman with promises I'd no intention of keeping.'

They were amongst the dancing couples, Jake following her as she made her way towards the open front; somehow, she slipped easily through the revellers, her pace quickening when she reached the clear space of the open air.

'Abbey – ' long strides saw him at her side in a second ' – wait.'

He was confused into silence when Abbey turned to face him, bright tears in her eyes. 'Jake, what do you want from me?'

180

'I want you, I don't want you to go back to Miles yet.'

She caught at her bottom lip with her teeth, 'Right now, I don't want to go back to him.'

'Stay with me, Abbey.' He reached out and took hold of her fingertips. 'If you want to go back to Miles at the end of the week, I won't try 'n stop you.'

'What if I start needing you?'

'Would that be so bad?'

'Yes. You'd run a mile.' She turned her back so he wouldn't see her turmoil.

'No, I won't.'

'Jake, don't lie to me.'

'I haven't – you'd see right through me.'

Abbey closed her eyes, had to pull herself together, then faced him. 'Yes, I would.'

'Spend the week with me, Abbey. If you walk away tomorrow, you'll never know – you'll wonder what might've been. We've both admitted there's something between us.'

She floundered as Jake lowered himself onto one of the wrought-iron chairs and pulled her gently onto his outstretched leg. 'I'll make you a promise.'

'Better be good.' She took the snow-white hand-kerchief he offered, blew her nose.

'It won't be me walking away from you, Abbey, you'll have to walk away from me.' A dead certainty, when she uncovered his motives. And she would – she would have the truth before this was over.

She searched his dark blue eyes, covered the large, long-fingered hand resting on her thigh, tempted into believing him, the words so at odds with the man. Something shivered deliciously through her insides. Did he really care enough about her to promise that?

'Perhaps I could paint you?' The compulsion to commit this man to canvas was overwhelming.

'Maybe you could.' His sensual eyes dropped to Abbey's lips; her insides rippled in response and a soft gasp broke in her throat when his fingers fanned against her scalp, his slow smile devastating.

Jake told himself the jolt of pleasure he experienced at Abbey's closeness was because he'd found the right words to make her stay; that it didn't matter what he had to say to keep her with him – only that she stayed. And even if Abbey didn't tell Miles about them, that clumsy excuse for a private detective was moving amongst the party guests right at this moment, playing the role of photographer, and he'd report to Miles. By the time the guy reached Abbey and himself, he was going to make certain there would be a photo that'd make Miles rattle in his traction. Because the guy was working for Miles. He was certain of that.

The dangerous, shadowy figure from Abbey's past had receded; wherever he was he – or his cohort – watched from a distance. He dealt in the slow, systematic building of fear; keeping his identity shrouded was part of the game. Two stalkers watching her – one of them he'd identified. The other might never have been.

'Smile for the camera!' A flashbulb exploded just inside the entrance and a couple laughingly obliged. Jake tugged Abbey towards him, his breath warm against her lips, eyes smouldering darkly. 'When he reaches us, let's give him something worth taking a picture of.'

Abbey's eyes sparkled, with trust, with fun, the photographer's appearance altered just enough to fool her – clean shaven now, a peaked cap over his brown

182

hair; a cigar had replaced the ever-present cigarette. It didn't fool Jake.

'What's happening?' Monty and Marianne danced close to the front of the restaurant. They had been caught up with guests for an age, but Marianne's curiosity saw her drag Monty for another dance in search of Jake.

'Dunno.' Monty shuffled, tried to steer Marianne away from Jake and Abbey. Then he grinned into the shadows, because he heard them laughing. 'Let's leave 'em to it, babe.'

'Spoilsport.' Marianne tutted.' 'I want to see what's happening.'

'I think we're being watched,' Jake whispered against Abbey's ear.

'Who by?' Her eyes rounded, she instinctively moved up Jake's firm thigh, rested her fingertips on his shoulder as one of his hands rested at her waist, holding her there.

He drew up his other leg, rested his forearm negligently across his knee, all the time aware the photographer was advancing.

'Monty and Marianne.' He jerked his suspended thumb toward them. 'They're obsessed with my love life.'

Without rancour, Abbey responded, 'Don't you mean your sex life?'

'Whether I have one of those at the moment depends on you,' he shot back wryly.

Any minute now – peripherally, Jake could see the photographer making his way towards them, so placed his hand high on her thigh, fingers spreading beneath the hem of her short dress. The provocative glow in

183

Abbey's eyes was exactly what he wanted Miles to see. To see that he'd lost Abbey.

He fumbled with the top button of his shirt, Abbey's luscious closeness driving heat everywhere beneath his tux.

'Here, let me.' Abbey pushed aside his hand and undid his bow tie, left it to straddle from beneath the collar, nimbly unfastened his top button. She blew at his exposed neck, taking Jake by surprise; as surprising as the erotic tingling racing over his skin. Just as the all-woman sensual lop-sided smile of hers curved her lips, the photographer's flash caught the erotic pose.

'Would you like a more traditional photograph?' the photographer offered.

'Yes,' from Abbey.

'No,' from Jake. He had what he wanted.

'Don't be a drag.' Abbey rolled her eyes, looped her arm around Jake's neck and put her cheek against his rough one. He felt her cheeks move as she smiled broadly.

'Oh, what the hell.' Out of camera shot, his fingers moved higher on her thigh – and he knew how Abbey's eyes would ignite.

Like everyone else, they were promised two copies of each photograph within the hour. A painful memory rose in his mind of Zav and himself, being photographed here, years ago; making plans for their wedding. Emotions knotted and confused in his stomach.

And having accomplished all he needed to sting Miles, Jake made a half-hearted effort to set Abbey aside. 'Let's go back inside.'

She laughed. 'You've got cold feet already, West-away.'

'What?'

'You – having your photo taken with me doesn't mean we have to make this permanent.' She had to let him off the hook, and quickly.

'Damn right.'

Although Abbey's manner was light, Jake's own mood took a nosedive, dived even further when she added, 'Don't worry, Jake, I still intend to leave tomorrow. There'll be people at home worrying about me.' The promise of a week with him began to sink, stealing her effervescence. She would have stayed with him, and willingly, if she hadn't glimpsed the regret in his eyes. Regret for words like, 'You'll have to be the one to walk away . . .'

He frowned. Pulled her back to his outstretched leg when she tried to get up, tried to walk away.

'You never had any intention of staying.' His tone flat.

'You never really wanted me to.' Those sensual, sad eyes caused a contraction in his guts, 'Face it, Jake, you've had time to think about it and a week has started to sound like a lifetime commitment to you.'

Had he? His hand dropped away. Jake was confused, cold when Abbey rose from his thigh. He had the awful, heavy feeling he was letting something good slip away. But he didn't know how to get it back. This was only revenge, for Pete's sake.

'Abbey.' Marianne waylaid Abbey when she would have made straight for her room, disappointment settling around her, choking her. 'Where's Jake?'

'Outside.' Abbey followed Marianne's eyes, found herself staring at Jake's towering, pacing form.

'You and he, you fight?'

185

'No.' Abbey grimaced, 'We both want different things.'

'Ah.' Marianne responded as though she understood, 'Be patient, Abbey, my brother is much deeper than he seems. He never really got over Zav. But he will.'

'Zav?'

'I thought he would have told you.' It was Marianne's turn to grimace. 'I shouldn't have said anythin'.'

'Did she leave him?' Abbey couldn't stem the driving curiosity. Was Zav the woman in the photo?

'No, sweetheart, she was killed.'

'Dear God,' Abbey gasped. 'What happened?'

'An accident on manoeuvres when she was posted abroad.'

'Poor Jake.' Abbey tried to imagine Jake's devastation, losing someone close – someone you loved. Knew too well herself what that was like.

'I'm glad he's found you, Abbey – ' Marianne's words moved her ' – it's the first time he's seemed alive in years.'

'Hey, Marry!' Monty called, making his way towards his wife. 'You seen Jake? There's a phone call for him out back.'

'Oh, would you mind telling him, darlin'?' Marianne asked Abbey. 'Mum's giving me a wave.' And with that, Marianne strode away in the opposite direction.

He leant against the park railings down in the street, his mien dark, brooding, the tux jacket catching the night breeze. Abbey slowed as she neared him, instinctively knew he was deep in deliberation. Deep in regret.

'Jake?'

He spun around, frowned questioningly at her, his expression lightening when she smiled.

186

'There's a telephone call for you "out back", Monty said.'

'Thanks.' He glanced at the party, back at Abbey. 'Come on inside with me.'

Sympathy for Jake's loss moved inside her. She'd glimpsed the deeper side of him whilst they were on the boat and now she saw it was real. He was capable of great depth, just as she'd suspected. Just as Marianne said. At that moment, she'd have gone to the moon with him if he'd asked.

'Sure.' She took his offered hand, smiled.

He guided Abbey through the revellers, through the kitchen area and into the living quarters.

'Yeah. Westaway here.' Abbey's hand still gripped in his.

'How'd you get this number, Holly?'

Holly? Abbey tried to pull away, but Jake held her hand in a death grip, shook his head.

All Abbey could think was that he'd be offering to fly Holly out here and she didn't want to listen. She tried to tug away from him again, but his eyes burned into her.

'Holly, I'm working, it's not practical.'

There was a loud, shrill response at the other end of the telephone and Jake winced. When Holly finally quieted, Jake pushed his fingers back through his hair. 'Sweetheart, I'm sorry, this isn't going anywhere, let's leave it and I'll see you when I get home.'

Abbey heard Holly's accusatory, 'Oh, no, you don't. It's *her*, isn't it? That helpless twit you went galooning off to rescue? I *knew* you'd end up giving her one.'

Jake's cheeks darkened with anger. 'I haven't touched her.'

'Oh, yeah? That's as bloody likely as me being a

virgin. What's she got that I haven't got, eh?' And before he could respond, 'If I'd known holding out was the way to trap you, Jake, I'd have done it long ago. She's clever, is she? Well, from what I've heard about Miss Abbey Snotty Roberts, she's way out of your league, Jake Westaway!'

Something moved inside Abbey when Jake looked to the floor between them. 'Yeah.'

'You'll not get anywhere with her!' Desperate, Holly yelled, 'She's one of those rich-bitch teases!'

Angry, Jake gasped, 'I haven't touched her. Holly, if you don't believe me, that's your problem. You should have trusted me.' Because from now on, you shouldn't, he thought darkly.

She said something to Jake that turned his expression to one of disgust. 'Todd's phone number? No, I don't – look it up.' With that, he set down the telephone.

Abbey was about to suggest that she telephone Miles, but right at that moment, she knew a surge of emotion for Jake that overwhelmed the intention.

'Aren't you flying Holly out here?' Abbey asked gently.

'No.' He focused his thoughts on the revenge he needed. 'I'm still hoping you'll stay.'

'Do you really want me to?'

'Yes.' A grave smile curved the corners of his lips. 'You could paint me.'

'And you really meant it when you said I'd have to be the one to walk away?'

'You will walk away, Abbey.' That much he could guarantee.

Abbey knew with certainty that she wouldn't.

'Come with me to buy some equipment tomorrow?'

'Does that mean you'll stay with me?'

She nodded. The trust in her eyes twisted his gut, so he pulled her against him, kissed her, couldn't face those eyes. 'Let's go upstairs.'

'What about the photographs?' She didn't care about them, laughed when Jake picked her up in his arms and said something obscene about the pictures.

'Make love to me, Jake,' she whispered in that husky, all-woman voice of hers when they reached their room.

Take a hike, Jake snapped at his recovering conscience, his mouth covering hers again.

Oh, God! Abbey melted against his strength, her insides trembling with pleasure, her fingers finding, unfastening the buttons of his pleat-fronted shirt, fingertips moving inside against his warm, hard stomach, up, over his lightly furred chest. Her pleasure increased when one of his hands unzipped her dress in a practised movement, let it drop in a pool at her feet. Jake pulled her hard against him, kicked the dress along the floor.

There was something unbelievably sensual about Jake's exploring hands crushing her against his fully clothed form, the rasp of cloth, buttons against her over-sensitized skin. A soft moan of pleasure broke from her lips when she realized this wasn't going to be over in a minute. Jake's palms held her waist. He set her away slightly, dark eyes meeting hers briefly before his lips closed around her nipple, teasing, weakening, drawing short gasps from her.

Instinctively her fingers ran into his hair; she held him harder against her, increased the pressure of his hot mouth. She slipped her hands inside the shoulders of his jacket, craving like she'd never done before, and slid it down his arms to drop to the floor.

Jake straightened, his mouth close to hers. 'Don't be impatient.'

She pushed aside his shirt to torment his nipple the way he had hers, flicked her tongue gently against the hardened nub; her hands explored his torso, her lips moved across, then down to his flat, hard stomach, nibbling gently; stopping as she reached the waistband of his dark trousers.

Abbey heard him gasp, thrills racing through her as he yanked her upwards, his mouth finding hers, his fingers slipping with tantalizing slowness downwards.

'Jake – ' her mouth broke from his – 'I can't stand up any longer.'

'Yes, you can.' His free hand caught her around the waist, held her firmly.

'I want you to feel this way, too – ' Her fingers found his hardness. He kissed her, jolted by the uncontrollable need Abbey set going in him, didn't fight her when she unfastened his trousers and guided them downward, her mouth moving in the same direction, leaving a trail of light, moist kisses down his torso.

'Roberts – it'll definitely be over too soon if you do that.' He gritted his teeth when her erotic tongue teased the length of him. 'Abbey . . .'

She wanted him to lose control, to be so hot he'd throw her on the bed and sink straight into her. She didn't want restraint, she wanted his powerful body in its raw, needy state. She stroked the insides of his thighs, heard him groan, saw his immediate reaction, almost laughed with pleasure when he yanked her to her feet and threw her on her back.

'Have it your way.' He drove into her, his eyes dark, intense. 'But I want more than this next time.'

Abbey bit his shoulder as he moved against her, wrapped her legs around him, rose to meet him with every delicious lunge of his hard body.

'You feel good,' Jake rasped, grasping her bottom to drive deeper inside her, glorying in the warmth in Abbey's eyes, the slight shock in their green depths, shock he felt mirrored inside himself, because it shouldn't have been this good.

His name broke from her lips; she tried to pull him down against her, to kiss her; then she gasped, trembled, began to quicken. His timing perfect, Jake covered her, matched her abandoned release with his own.

Abbey wrapped her arms around Jake, held him tight, their breathing ragged as the waves of pleasure went on and on. His body was slicked with sweat as he collapsed against her; she didn't want him to move away, didn't want him to roll over and start snoring. She wanted to hold him and remember this.

Like a sculptress, she smoothed her palms over his shoulders, down his muscled yet lean back, the instep of her foot echoing the movements down the back of his legs. Her fingertips brushed upwards through his hair, her lips brushed against his neck and slowly, Jake's breathing returned to normal.

Still inside her, he raised his weight on his elbows and looked down into Abbey's eyes. She smiled and scraped her nails gently down his back, her full breasts soft, pressing against his chest.

'Abbey.' There was a glimmer of surprise in his eyes.

'What's the matter?'

'I'm hard again.'

'Good.' She reached up, her fingers splaying at his shadowed jaw, raised her mouth so she met his lips, then Jake rolled on the bed, holding Abbey's hips so they didn't break contact, and she sat astride him, flowing, undulating, taking them both to the brink of an insatiable need, then taking them further.

She supposed it was the threat of her uncertain future making her see things differently. She wriggled to get comfortable against Jake, but this self-confessed womanizer had shown her such soaring heights; he had held back nothing of himself. And there was untold relief in her that he hadn't belittled what they'd shared by using any sweet words that could so easily have meant too much to her.

A wry smile curved her lips. She might be an artist and know about painting – what she hadn't bargained for was that Jake was a sexual genius, an artist in his own right. His knowledge of the female body put her own to shame; his understanding of pleasure and his ability to impart it generously was beyond anything in her wildest fantasy.

She turned to face him, smiled when he sleepily raised one corner of his mouth. 'Sleep, Roberts, I'll show you something really bone-shattering when I wake up.'

Jake sank like a stone toward sleep, thought he felt Abbey's mouth brush lightly against his lips. Instinctively, he put an arm around her, pulled her to lie close against him, a tell-tale ripple of pleasure spreading from her lips as they brushed his shoulder.

'Stop that, Roberts.'

She just laughed, that wholesome yet sexy laugh. Like her, she was both things. More things. Innocent in some ways, uninhibited, unashamedly sensual in others. She'd wanted so much to please him, she'd been in danger of not pleasing herself. Whatever kind of men she'd been involved with in the past, he doubted whether they'd spent much time engaged in foreplay. He could imagine the drill from Miles and the like: 'Come on, darling! Knickers off! I've only got ten minutes!'

It was an insult to Abbey's responsive, delicious body, to her willingness to explore, experiment, to give so much pleasure it almost blew his mind. He'd tried to make the pleasure all hers – but she wouldn't take from him without giving. Hell! He wished his reasons for this were different; there were so many things he could do with her. His palm flattened against the small of her back, over her bottom, down the silky skin of her thigh; he caught at her knee and pulled her leg around his hip, knowing full well what would happen the second he awoke.

But it was only when he awoke in the early hours, his system cleared of champagne and beer, that he realized he hadn't used any protection. Abbey was still completely wiped out at his side; he collected some rubbers from his jacket, put them on the narrow shelf beside the bed, before grabbing a yogurt from the fridge and pulling the sheet downward to her feet. Obligingly, she rolled on to her back.

Her skin quivered as he dropped a spoonful on her belly; she made a soft sound in her throat, but she was still asleep.

Jake smiled, knelt between her feet and dropped the creamy dessert on to each breast, then tipped up the pot and made a line, down her stomach, lower, lower. She writhed.

Abbey's eyes sprang open, confused for a second,

then they met with his in the half light and she half-smiled, half-laughed. 'Jake, hi, ah – ' Her greeting turned to an ecstatic sigh when his tongue moved up the trail, gathering, teasing, the light aroma of pineapple rising with the heat of her skin. 'Couldn't you find a bowl?' She wriggled beneath him, licked some of the dessert from the side of his mouth, needed him right away, her hand moving to put him inside, but his palm pinned her wrists at her side. 'I haven't finished yet.'

'I can't take any more.'

'Yes, you can.' His dark eyes held hers whilst his freezing cold fingers touched the heat of her, the contrast erotic.

'How – ?' She squirmed against him, thinking she'd die if he didn't do something else soon. Quick.

'Ice.' He moved inside her then, the contrast of heat even more incredibly erotic.

Whilst he kissed her, his masculine strength drawing every last iota of pleasure from her, Abbey reflected absurdly that Miles always use ice tongs to put ice in his Gin and Tonic, didn't like to get cold fingers.

They made love again in the shower, standing in the rods of lukewarm water, and again before they dressed; Jake, wearing only faded jeans, picked up a strip of cotton lace and dangled it from his forefinger. 'I don't know why you even bother wearing these.' He laughed, swung them around his back when a towel-wrapped Abbey lunged after them; he fell backwards on to the bed, taking her with him, trapping her between his legs, 'You'll have to work for them, Roberts.'

'No, I'll just torment them out of you.' Something she proved very adept at, because Jake just couldn't resist Abbey for very long at all.

She was still high on a wave of elation, of pure, unadulterated femininity, her eyes glowing, cheeks flushed when she brushed her hair before the bathroom mirror. Jake came up behind her, put his arm around her waist.

'Abbey, you know I didn't use any protection when we – '

'Had sex?'

He'd been going to say 'made love' because that's what it'd felt like. For the first time in a long time. 'Yeah.' He looked away from Abbey's curvy form, that tempting yellow skirt and her button-fronted white vest. 'Maybe we'd better find a pharmacy while we're out getting your paints?'

'Thanks, so long as you do the talking, Jake.'

'Sure.'

'That's a relief.' She put down the brush, turned in his arm. 'I don't think my *por favor* would stretch to "I got carried away last night and I need a new supply of the pill!"'

Smiling, Jake kissed her briefly. 'Think I'd better pick something up off the boat instead.'

'Oh, lord I'll get rubber fatigue if you go through that lot.'

He raised a brow, narrowed his eyes. 'Been rooting through my gear, Roberts?'

'I couldn't miss them. They leapt out.'

It was unbelievable, but his body was reacting to hers again. 'Before we get sensible, how about we put that trip to the *farmacia* off for a while?' He caressed her through her clothes, smiled when the heat in her eyes said yes.

* * *

195

'Yeah –' Monty pulled a street map from his desk ' – it's a bit of a walk, mate, but there's an art supplies shop 'bout here.'

'I'm thinkin' about taking Abbey to Uncle Ramon's vineyards for a day, mid-week, guys.' Jake pinched a strip of carrot from Marianne's growing pile and crunched it. 'If anyone comes poking around trying to find out any more about her while we're gone, could you keep tabs on them?'

'Sure, mate. Still being watched, then?'

'Yeah –' Jake grimaced ' – but the guy's a novice. I'm planning on us slipping away early one morning.'

' 'Ear that, Marry?' Monty smirked. 'Looks like you were right.'

'Right about what?' Jake frowned.

'You and Abbey. Marianne reckons she ain't seem you this wound up since Zav.'

'I ain't wound up,' Jake shot back, wandered out of the back door.

Abbey entered the kitchen then. 'Excuse me? Have you seen Jake?'

Marianne glanced up, smiled because Abbey looked so radiant and it could only mean one thing. 'He's out back' – she pointed with her knife – 'being not wound up.' Soft laughter followed Abbey from the kitchen.

'Jake?' Abbey sat down beside him on the mound of grass. 'Are you all right?'

'Just thinking.' His eyes were dark, moody as he glanced at Abbey; she knew a flutter of unease, knelt and put her arm along his shoulder.

'You're not feeling used, are you, sweetheart?' Laughter danced in her eyes, captivated Jake.

'You're a hussy. Don't torment me again, or I'll take

196

you right here.' The darkness slipped away from him; he let Abbey's smile draw him back from desperation, let all of her draw him back from the blackness as he rose to his feet and took her hand.

Strawberry, silky curls burnished by the sunlight, her voice delicious, husky, as she whispered, 'It's not just sex I enjoy with you, Jake. You make me feel strong enough to handle anything. I don't know if I could have pulled myself together without your help.' At Jake's lack of response, she suggested, 'Will you show me where the art supplies shop is?'

'Hey, I'm warning you.' He opened the back gate, gestured her through, conscious that Abbey was asking in her own way for more of him than he wanted to give. 'I'm not that special.'

'Yes, you are!' She wrenched from him, faced him. 'You didn't have to do anything for me! You could have been here with Holly now. I don't *want* the only safe place to be with you, Jake – but it is!'

He pushed on his sunglasses, shaken. 'You've got the wrong idea about me, Abbey, I'm not some knight in shining armour.' He didn't want her to make him feel good about himself.

'Perhaps knights don't have to be wearing armour.'

'I'm not as good as you think I am, Abbey,' he said gently before letting the gate close, 'just remember that.'

'Well – ' she was determined to make something of this time with Jake '– perhaps, Jake Westaway, you are as good as I think you are.'

'I doubt that,' he said with certainty.

'What do you think, Monty?' Marianne washed the carrots, following the couple's progress through the back gate. 'She knows how to handle that brother of mine, or what?'

'Yeah, but I'm not convinced Jake knows how to handle Abbey.' Monty chuckled wryly. 'I think if he's not careful, he'll find out he's bitten off more than he can chew.'

'Rubbish!' She swatted him with a dish cloth. 'They're good together. You wait, Monty, you'll see I'm right – next year, he'll be bringing Abbey again. A woman knows these things.'

Monty thought about Zav and Miles Pendleton-Smythe and shook his head. 'I'm reserving judgment.'

'No need, you seen these?' Marianne pulled the previous evening's photographs from a cupboard, handed them to Monty.

'Cor blimey, maybe you're right.'

'Are you sure this is all you need?' Jake laughed as Abbey took the carrier of acrylics, wet palette, soft drawing pencils and heavy-duty paper, brushes and varnish from the shopkeeper.

'If there's anything else, I'll come back and get it.' She grimaced. 'But I do need some more clothes, if I'm staying.'

'Yeah, you need some more clothes.'

'Fancy a trip to a vineyard?' Jake asked as they stepped back out into the sunshine. 'One of the cousins who came to Marianne's party – his father, my uncle Ramon, owns it.'

'Yes!' She brimmed with enthusiasm. 'I'd love to. When?'

'Around mid-week?'

'That'd be perfect! I could get the outline drawn out by then.'

'He has horses. Do you ride?'

'About as well as I swim.'

'That bad?'

'No, not quite that bad.' She laughed. 'Miles disowned me when we went swimming. I think I cramped his style.'

Miles. Good. It reminded him what he was doing, kept his mind focused.

'Yeah, I wonder why?' He laughed when she punched his arm, 'But I'll tell you one place you're graceful, Roberts.'

'I'm not graceful at all,' she said, matter of factly.

He pulled her against a blank wall. 'In bed you are.' Jake meant it, but felt a bit ashamed when Abbey's cheeks turned pink on gold.

'Thank you.'

Damn! Did she have to be so polite?

'You're welcome. Talking about bed, I'd better take you to the *farmacia*.'

For the remainder of the day, Jake fought the urge to drag Abbey up to their room and lose himself in her. He tried to sit still whilst she began her preliminary sketches, then, sensing his restlessness, Abbey suggested, 'Shall we do something else for a while? Perhaps Monty has a camera I could use? It'd mean less time sitting still for you.

'Would it mean more time in bed?'

He shot her a sexy grin, broke into laughter when she responded, 'I hope so.'

'Yeah, sure,' Monty said, 'I'll get it. Talking about

photos, Marianne put these away for you.' He reached down the pictures from the cupboard, handed them over, then left in search of his camera.

Abbey was shocked at the blatant sensuality screaming from the photograph where Jake had her full attention, his hand lost beneath the hem of her short skirt, both their expressions hungry. 'It's beautiful, can I keep one?'

The other, more traditional photograph was – by accident – almost as telling; Abbey's eyes shining with laughter and Jake's intense, serious expression were pure photographic genius.

Jake knew he wouldn't keep his copy. If he did, he'd need her every time he looked at it. Miles would have been faxed his by now, he thought with grim satisfaction, he would know how it felt to be betrayed. And Jake hadn't done with the bastard yet. His fist began to clench around his copy; anger ripping through him anew when he thought of his trusted friend trying it on with Zav.

'Jake!' Abbey snatched it from him. 'You'll ruin it.'

'What?'

'The picture, you'll ruin it. What were you thinking?' Whilst she spoke, she straightened the photo.

He took a deep breath, schooled his anger. 'Nothing you'd want to know about.'

Sensing darkness in Jake again, Abbey distracted him. 'Tell me about Ramon's vineyard?'

He was a second relaxing, then said, 'It'll be the first time I've been there in a while. He's always wanting me to visit.'

'Will he mind me coming?'

'I don't think he intended me to go alone.' He was

relaxed again by the time Monty turned up with the Instamatic camera; Abbey had discreetly slipped the photographs into her art carry-bag, sensing they had for some reason brought on Jake's angry mood.

'Will this do you?' Monty handed her a bag with a couple of films in. 'Use these up, I can get some more.'

'Thank you. Jake, shall we do this down by your boat?'

'Great.'

'So I don't have to sit still any more?' Jake shot her a wry grin as Abbey packed away the camera and the instant photos. From the corner of his eye, he spotted last night's photographer, his presence at the end of the jetty nothing short of clumsy.

Determined the man would have plenty to report to Miles, Jake took the camera from Abbey with one hand, wrapped his other around her waist, drew her against him and kissed her.

The gesture puzzled Abbey, but she accepted it for what it was and smiled against his lips. 'You're crazy, Westaway.'

'Let's go on the boat, I'm hard as a rock.'

Abbey laughed deliciously as Jake kicked the cabin door closed, spun her around, his mouth swallowing the husky sound.

Clutched in Jake's powerful arms, Abbey gasped when he backed her against the work surface, whispered against her lips, 'I'm going to make you purr, Roberts.' He kissed her almost savagely, the rigid length of his arousal nudging through the fabric of her skirt. His hand kneaded her bottom, impatient, deft fingers tore away her silky briefs and a deep groan

201

broke in his throat. 'Lord, Abbey, you're so lush.' His mouth teased her nipples through thin cotton; he grazed gently with his teeth, whilst his ingenious fingers massaged her moist heat, toyed with the centre of her pleasure and increased the pressure when she bit his shoulder. Abbey then threw back her head and arched to his touch in the most submissive, feminine gesture Jake had ever seen. Fingers spread at his neck, she raised her leg, her instep stroking the back of his jeans-clad lower leg, her free hand unbuttoning the clinging T-shirt. As Abbey's full, voluptuous breasts escaped the fabric, Jake felt the rush of something he couldn't control. Shucking his restraining jeans, kicking them aside, he entered her swiftly, groaned with deep pleasure when Abbey's moist heat sheathed him tightly.

Primordial need rode Abbey as Jake's palms supported her buttocks and she wound her legs around his hips, an exquisite undulating rhythm too urgent for their stance. Without missing a beat, Jake lowered Abbey to the hard deck, plunged, harder, faster, until she tremored, squeezed, bucked wildly against his climax.

'Ah – ' Jake supported his weight on his elbows, the aftershocks quivering through Abbey gripping him.

Her green eyes were all but eclipsed by dilated pupils and soft curls spilled over his forearms. Abbey's slow, satisfied smile caught at something inside him, her lips swollen as they were from his savage kisses. Again, Jake was struck by the contrast of raw sensuality and freshness in Abbey. 'You're something else,' he whispered, gasping with disbelief when he grew hard again inside her. He grew harder still when she arched gently towards him, her words husky. 'I'm going on top this time, buster, it's my turn to torment you.'

Much later, after they returned to Monty's, Jake joined her beneath the brolly-shaded table on the back lawn where she worked.

Instinctively, Abbey looked up as he approached, smiled at him.

Damn it! Why did she have to smile at him like that – like she believed in him? And why did his bloody insides jolt at that lop-sided smile? Right at that moment, he had the greatest urge to get mad with her. Then he thought of Miles, all the feedback he'd be getting from his excuse for a private detective, and managed to crush the emotion. 'How's it going?' He pulled up a chair.

'Jake, do you like me?' Abbey had seen the most telling expression cross his features; it had chilled her to the marrow.

'Sure I do. Why else would I ask you to stay with me?'

'I don't know. Just then, you looked murderous.'

'You're imagining things.' Hell! He'd have to watch it. Abbey had him taped – what he hadn't realized until that moment was just how well. But what she'd read was his anger, not his feelings for her. 'I had something on my mind.'

'Don't tell me, it's something you don't want to share.'

'Yeah.' He pushed his fingers back through his hair. 'Look, do you mind if I shoot back over the boat for an hour? I need to look at the engine.'

'Let's get something straight, Jake.' Abbey shielded her eyes from the sun. 'You don't have to tell me where you're going or what you're doing. I don't expect you to spend every waking minute with me, I'm a grown woman, in case you hadn't noticed.'

He merely gave a single nod and left the garden by the back gate.

'You care about Jake, don't you, Abbey?' Marianne asked nonchalantly, joining Abbey beneath the brolly, setting down a pitcher of freshly squeezed orange juice.

'Yes, I do.'

'I thought so.' She raised her glass in Abbey's direction. 'I don't mind bettin' he's a soft spot for you. I ain't seen him this ruffled in years.'

Funny little shivers kept running down Abbey's skin, Marianne's words, 'I ain't seen him look this ruffled in years' ricocheting around inside her. Other words too, Jake's words – so certain when he promised she would be the one to walk away – echoed around in her mind. How could he be so certain when Abbey could literally feel the emotion growing between them?

CHAPTER 8

They arrived at Ramon's vineyard, Jake's attempt to introduce Abbey met with, 'Ah, Luis told me all about Abbey! You are an artist, *sí*?' Ramon squinted his eyes – eyes that held the light of mischief. 'You are putting my nephew here in the spin, I hear?' Ignoring Jake's scowl of disgust, the elder man continued, winking, 'You are the first lady-friend he's bringing to visit me in a long time. I hope it means something.'

Shaking Ramon's hand, Abbey smiled. 'I'm afraid not. We're friends, that's all.'

But the brow raised in response said Ramon wasn't convinced.

'Come – ' Ramon rubbed his hands together ' – I'll show you and your "friend" around, Jake. Luis is joining us for dinner this evening, before you leave.' Ramon winked again at Abbey. 'He insisted on joining us when he learnt you were visiting with Jake.'

'Oh, lovely.' Abbey smiled. 'I'll look forward to that.'

Abbey completely missed Jake's gloomy expression, his irritation because every male she came into contact with turned to putty when she smiled.

Well, it doesn't matter to you, Westaway, he reminded himself sharply, this is your show – you're

205

the one who'll shock her into walking away at the end of the week. You're the one who makes her sexually impatient. Miles's woman – and she can't keep away from you.

Within minutes, the three of them were on horse-back, Ramon leading them in a leisurely tour of his lush green and white-rock land.

Abbey was overwhelmed by the urge to sketch Jake on the frisky dark horse; he as relaxed in the saddle as she was tense. The slight breeze moulded his black T-shirt to his lean, muscular form, black jeans hugging long legs, feet angled in stirrups.

A small smile played on her lips. What woman in her right mind would 'walk away' from Jake Westaway? He was wrong – so wrong about that. Somehow, Jake had the power to keep at bay the nightmare side of her life; he made being with him more important than the forces that may have crushed her if she'd been alone.

Abbey found herself completely in awe of the luxuriant native beauty, storing mental images that would seep into paintings in the future. She relished every moment of the freedom spreading through her; freedom from fear – sweeter, because she knew it wouldn't last forever.

'Yes, I received the fax!' Miles reddened with anger. 'I also received the actual photograph this morning, Pedro.' The photograph trembled in his fingers. The fax hadn't been so hard to take because transmission made the photocopied picture grainy, but this crisp, night-shaded photograph was enough to raise his blood pressure by several black line notches. 'So where is Abbey now? On her way home?' He had never seen

Abbey dressed like that – her laced-front dress the most deliberately provocative he had seen. Westaway must have picked it out for her, the bastard. What was she doing, letting him put his hand up her skirt? And what aggravated him more than anything was the sensual expression on Abbey's features, the blatant insinuation of foreplay in the photograph.

What really peeved Miles was that she had never looked at him like that; never let him grope her in public, never revealed so much of herself to him in public as that trashy dress revealed to Jake. In public – or in private.

Abbey had no right to look so beautiful, so tempting for Jake Westaway, when all he got was her neck-to-toe elegance. And the way she had looked when she had visited him in hospital was appalling! Some old, tatty denim jacket, sizes too big, and that awful baggy sundress. God! She hadn't even combed her hair by the looks of her. A bag woman – she'd reminded him of a street dweller. Eyes too big, too wary, her fingers reaching out to touch him as if in awe of his male beauty.

Miles stared at the photograph, at the eroticism it portrayed and hated Jake Westaway more than he'd ever hated anyone. The man took on women as if they owed it to him!

'Well, not this woman, Westaway.' Miles fed his anger. 'Not this woman! I had to work – and I mean work – just to get introduced to her! And you're not getting with a crook of your bloody finger when I had to struggle for months to get nowhere!'

'Talking to yourself, son?' The door closed and Miles started.

'Ah – Father!' He let the photograph drop to the bedclothes and forced a sickly smile. 'I'm merely working out how to even the score with a double-crossing bastard I trusted.'

Miles's father, grey on blonde, tall, slender, sank into the comfort of the overstuffed visitors' chair and surveyed his son. 'Anyone I know?'

'Westaway.'

'Jake?' His father seemed genuinely surprised. 'Never. That chap's as solid as they come, dear boy.'

'That chap – ' Miles tossed the photograph in his father's general direction ' – is bonking my girlfriend!'

Elegantly, Miles's father rose from the chair and studied the photograph. 'I wonder, Miles, have you behaved with any more restraint?'

'Of course I have!'

'Really?' A droll tone to his reply. 'Maybe you could tell me then, son, why it is every time I have visited you thus far, there has been a flushed nurse "buttoning up", so to speak?'

He eyed his son, but Miles showed no shame, just stared straight back.

'And holding interviews in your sick-room – really, Miles, do you think I don't know what you've been getting up to these past weeks? I am footing the bloody bill for this charade.'

'Well, *she* didn't visit me! She's with him!' His beautiful, petulant mouth twisted. 'I refuse to let him steal her off me after my efforts!'

'I have the sensation, son, this is the first time a woman hasn't danced to your tune.' Miles's father shook his head. 'You are thirty-four, young man. I would have thought by now you would have learned

you cannot have the entire world dancing to your tune.'
He waved a dismissive hand. 'Have you clinched the
deal with Marrowbait Holdings?'

'I've been too busy,' was his sulky response.

'Doing what, exactly?'

Miles couldn't meet his father's eyes.

'You've been wasting your time sulking, haven't
you?'

'I have a private detective watching them. I want him
to bring Abbey home, away from that walking penis.'

The elder man tutted, shook his head, his patience
wearing thin with his only son. 'Your girlfriend, Miles,
may well prefer the company of Jake Westaway. Accept
it.'

Mottling, Miles jerked upward in his bed. 'Never!
She is mine, Father. Abbey would never succumb to
Westaway's crude advances – ' he jerked his finger in
the air ' – she was probably steaming drunk when that
photograph was taken and Westaway was taking advantage. Likely he spiked her bloody drink or something of the sort.'

Tiring of his son's attitude, Frederick pulled a
neglected, rolled-up fax from the machine. 'Have you
seen this?' he boomed.

'No – ' Miles gave a dismissive wave of his hand ' –
I've had other matters on my mind.'

'You've blown the deal with Marrowbait Holdings.'
Frederick flung the fax on to the bed, 'Lost yourself a
few hundred thou in the wrangle. You're a bloody idiot,
Miles.'

Miles was stung by the insult.

'Debauching the nurses is one matter! Sulking over
your inability to keep a decent girlfriend is another!

But – ' he tutted, shook his head ' – letting yourself become so emotionally derailed that you cannot finalize a simple deal like this!' He prodded the curled piece of thin paper. 'Makes me wonder whether you're the right man for the job.'

Angrier, redder, more impotent as his father continued, Miles centred all his hatred on Jake Westaway. He hadn't been able to concentrate at all well since Abbey's postcard. And his concentration had been shot to hell since receiving the photograph from Pedro.

'I will not let Westaway have her,' Miles said stubbornly. 'No!'

Frederick's mouth curled with distaste. 'You have never lost a conflict in your life, Miles. Deal with it!' His anger spilled over. 'Deal with it.'

'I intend to, Father.' Miles's manner was cool, offended.

'I don't mean with your private detectives! I mean you should keep your mind on your work, boy, and forget about what Abbey Roberts is doing with Jake Westaway!'

'Mmm.' Miles wasn't about to give up, but he made a poor attempt at responding to his father's suggestion. 'Yes, sir.'

'Why don't I believe you, Miles?'

'I don't know, Father,' he said, his pale blue eyes innocent.

Shaking his head, Frederick pointed his finger in Miles's direction. 'Work, Miles, is the only dependable thing in our lives, m'boy. When the Abbeys of this world have decided they can live without you, your money, your work is still there.'

'Quite, quite.' Miles just wanted his father to leave so

that he could contact Pedro again, so he could form a workable plan to get Abbey home – out of Westaway's reach.

Frederick sensed he was wasting his time with Miles, sensed also that perhaps the time and trouble he had taken to protect Miles from losing in the past had been a big mistake. The family name and honour had been preserved during Miles's army career, but at what cost? The boy didn't know how to lose because he had never lost.

'I'll sort it, Father.' Miles mentally walked his father to the door, opened it for him, showed him out, but his father stayed, staring at him.

'The business, or Westaway?'

'Both.'

'There's something you ought to know before you launch a vendetta against that man.'

As far as Miles was concerned, nothing he could learn would alter this knot of rage formed in his stomach.

'Mmm?' He gestured with his fingertips.

'Westaway could have beaten you in the pool, on the targets and at every stage of the physical combat comps.'

'Nonsense!' Miles pushed himself up slightly against the fat pillows. 'I won those trophies fair and square!'

'It did look that way, didn't it?'

'Of course it looked that way! That's how it was!' Then, as his father remained silent, 'What are you saying, Father?'

'Screws were turned. Wheels were oiled in order to keep certain traditional honours in the family.'

Miles's cheeks darkened with fury. 'You're saying you forced Westaway to throw the comps in my favour?' His words had a sinister hiss.

'I have said all I'm going to say on the matter. Now, will you still be here in a week? I'm busy until then.'

Suddenly, Miles didn't want his father to leave, he wanted him to explain his 'screws were turned' comment.

But whilst he grasped for the words to keep his father from leaving, Frederick raised his hand in farewell. 'Do sort yourself out before I come again.' And with that, he left.

And he left Miles to handle more inept rage than the man had ever known in his life. 'How *dare* he suggest I didn't win those trophies fair and square!' And 'I will have Abbey back! At any price, Westaway.'

Ramon rode off, leaving Jake and Abbey to enjoy the remnants of their picnic. 'I have business to attend to, nephew. Take your time, we have dinner when you return?'

'Hey, how're you doin'?' Jake tickled Abbey's nose with a stalk of corn, a smile curving his mouth as her eyes flickered open.

'Okay.' Abbey's voice soft, husky; she inhaled the sweet summer scents, let the birds and insects' symphony lull her.

Close by, one of their horses blew out his breath, a soft, lazily contented sound; just about how Abbey was feeling.

If anyone had told Jake weeks ago that he'd enjoy a picnic in the corner of a corn field, with an artist who knew exactly how to make him laugh, knew exactly how to infect him with something suspiciously close to happiness, he'd have scowled at them, told them to get a life, because his wasn't like that.

Neither of them had mentioned Miles or Holly for a while; the thought floated into his mind when a butterfly landed on Abbey's jeans-clad curves before flitting away.

A pang of unwanted guilt twisted in his gut. He was still determined – whatever the cost – to end this nirvana by telling Abbey exactly what he'd been playing at in seducing her. But there wasn't any need just yet.

'Do you ever wish you could stop time?' Abbey reached across, took the corn stalk from Jake's fingers, then raised herself on to her elbows to look straight into his eyes.

'No.' Except maybe when Zav –

'I'd like to stop it right now.' Abbey sat up, crossed her legs. 'And sketch all of this.'

Chuckling, Jake said, 'You had me worried for a minute there, Roberts, I thought you were going to get slushy.'

'I wouldn't dare.' She wrinkled her nose and her eyes sparkled with laughter. 'You'd be across this field in no time screaming "save me from this woman"!'

'Damn right.'

Abbey lay down again, closed her eyes and absorbed disappointment at Jake's reaction. No matter how much he made her laugh and made her body sing out for his touch, the only stirring words he spoke were sensual ones. There were no promises from his lips, no murmured words of love. Nothing about any kind of future. Abbey would've given her favourite sable paint-brush away to hear words of love from Jake, or even some kind of reference to the time beyond this week.

Because no matter which way she looked at him, no matter that he was incredibly, completely wrong for her, she had fallen in love with him.

Languid, light-headed through drinking Ramon's full-bodied wine, Abbey stretched on the checkered rug, a husky sigh escaping her.

'So what job is it you're going on at the end of the week?'

'I don't have the details yet.'

Abbey opened her eyes as she felt Jake's shadow moving over her, a slow smile turning to husky laughter when Jake asked,

'Ever make love in a corn field?'

'Have you?'

Pure male appreciation lit Jake's eyes when Abbey raised her mouth to his, then rose to her knees and pushed him flat to the rug and smiled that mindblowingly sensual smile of hers.

'Think I might be about to –' Jake's words were laced with laughter as he yanked her on top of him.

But Abbey shook her head, her palms catching his wrists and setting them beside his head. 'You have to see how long you can keep still.'

'Abbey,' he growled, 'it's not that easy – '

But his protest turned to a gasp of pleasure when she eased up his black T-shirt and her tumble of sunlit hair whispered over his torso; her lips made a soft, moist track downwards, delicate fingers unsnapped his jeans; and as she pleasured him with sweet kisses, Jake almost regretted showing Abbey the scintillating art of foreplay.

Abbey made love to every sensitive inch of Jake, revelling in the unexpected power of her femininity;

wanted him to become so aroused that he'd lose control. She didn't have long to wait.

'You're doing my head in – ' he yanked at her tight, sexy jeans ' – you might want it slow, Roberts, but I don't,' and after he'd lost himself in her, driven them both to a shattering zenith, Jake stared down at her, a perceptive light in his smouldering eyes. 'That was what you wanted, wasn't it, lady? To make me lose it?'

'Now you know how you make me feel, buster. Sometimes, it's sensational to lose control.'

'Sensational?' He weighed the word. 'Hell, that's putting it tame – something you ain't.'

As the sun drifted lower, they rode back to Ramon's white single-storey, red-roofed home. Abbey regretted the passing of time with every heartbeat; she wanted to savour every second, to keep time still.

'Ah!' Ramon greeted them at the verandah. 'Good! You are back. Luis is joining us for dinner. Jake, you and Abbey really must stay the night. There are two spare rooms – one over the garage, one upstairs. That way, you can enjoy the evening without worrying about the drive home.'

'Lovely!' Abbey enthused, grasping the hope of distraction with a whole heart. Jake had lapsed into one of his laconic moods again, and she knew that in order to protect herself emotionally, she needed to begin distancing herself from him. He was slipping away from her, losing interest; she could sense it.

'Luis is in the garage, Jake. He'd like to show off his new car – take a test run, if you want to go along and join him?'

'Sure.' Without so much as a nod in Abbey's direction, Jake took their horses round to the stables.

Abbey watched him go. They had spent the entire day steeped in intimacy and now he had deliberately cut her off.

'If you don't mind, Ramon –' Abbey dredged up her brave face ' – I would like to take a bath before dinner?'

'*Sí.*' His eyes followed Jake's tall, lean form for a spell, then snapped back to Abbey's elfin beauty. 'You and Jake fight?'

'No. He can only take so much female company before he feels stifled.'

Whether Ramon understood or not, he was unfailingly polite. 'He is still mourning, perhaps? And restless.'

'Perhaps,' Abbey returned with a smile.

'So all this effort's for Luis?' Jake queried as Abbey blotted her subtle lipstick and dabbed perfume behind her ankles.

Frowning, Abbey studied Jake's features in the reflection. Since Jake had returned to their room from the garage, he hadn't spoken a word.

'Whatever's wrong with you, Jake, save it until we're away from here.' The words surprised her as much as Jake, who drew a sharp breath. Abbey picked up the mascara brush and applied a thin layer to her lashes.

'I've got stuff on my mind.' He stoved long fingers back through his hair, looked away from Abbey's stunning figure.

'So tell me, if it'll help.' She zipped up her toiletries bag and stood, the simple, dark-blue silk dress she'd brought with her just in case they stayed to dinner, falling in soft folds to mid-calf.

'You wouldn't understand.'

With a pang, Abbey wondered if he thought of Zav, perhaps of a time when they'd shared a room, prepared to go down to dinner with his family. Whether, as Ramon suggested, he still mourned.

Instinctively, she touched his forearm, looked up at him. 'Perhaps I wouldn't, Jake, but you do me an injustice if you think I wouldn't try.'

Jake turned away, silently cursing Abbey for trusting him. Cursing her, because holding back, allowing himself serious misgivings over what he was doing, didn't help him feel any better. Jake had never intended to initiate such warmth in Abbey's forest-green eyes. Trusting eyes, damn her!

'We'd better go down.' He shrugged on his dark suit jacket and held the door wide for Abbey.

Luis's open admiration of Abbey didn't help Jake's mood at all. 'It's good to see you again, Abbey!' His English perfect, he gestured to her to sit beside him, 'Marianne's was a good party, yes?'

'Lovely.' Luis was a very handsome man, intelligent too, with dark eyes that followed Abbey's every gesture. She thought she recalled Marianne saying her cousin was a salesman; no doubt a very successful one.

Because Jake spoke at length with Ramon, Abbey found herself taken up by Luis. 'You should stay longer, I am staying for the weekend; a day isn't long enough.' He tipped his glass towards Abbey slightly. 'You are an artist? There is much beautiful scenery in the area, you could paint to your heart's content.'

'I know.' Abbey smiled, enjoyed the open appreciation in Luis's eyes. 'It is sensational here – and your father has a lovely home, Luis.'

'Then stay as our guest for a little longer?'

217

Tempted. Abbey was sorely tempted to allow Luis's flattery to envelop her; he was the kind of man who would cherish a woman, spoil her . . . It would help her ease out of Jake's life. That was what Jake wanted, she could tell by his coolness toward her. He had reached the point where 'enough was enough'.

'I will leave with Jake, but thank you for the offer, Luis, it's charming of you.'

'Not at all.' He smiled as if he knew he could convince her to stay. 'Now, tell me of your work?'

And whilst Abbey and Luis launched into a discussion of Abbey's work and the art world in general, Jake's mood darkened.

He slugged back a glass of wine, which Ramon quickly refilled. Jake's own conversation with Ramon flowed, yet all the while, Jake found himself eavesdropping on the other conversation taking place at the table.

'Your son wouldn't be trying it on with my girlfriend, would he, Uncle Ramon?' Jake finished another glass of wine, aware of some violent stirrings in his stomach.

Ramon laughed. 'Luis may try, but he will not succeed.'

Abbey laughed at that moment. Jake glanced around and knew a surge of something he hadn't felt in a long, long time.

Pure, unadulterated jealousy.

Her eyes were filled with laughter and warmth, her voice a husky whisper when Luis put his palm over her hand, and whatever he said to Abbey made her smile. That delicious, lop-sided smile that hit him straight in the guts, worse this time because she was smiling at Luis.

'So, if you could paint anyone, Abbey – ' Luis leant

back in his chair, arched his fingers on his stomach, his darkly lashed eyes trained on her ' – who would you choose as your subject?'

Immediately, Abbey's eyes slid to Jake; the darkness, the anger as his gaze met hers shocked her. She had been about to say 'Jake', but couldn't. Not in the face of all that hostility.

'It's hard to say,' was her non-committal reply.

'Ah – I wanted to know if anyone particular drew your artistic interest.'

'People in general draw my interest,' Abbey said evasively, 'but I paint other things as well.'

'Tell me – '

Jake scowled.

He kept a lid on his anger whilst Luis drew Abbey's easy chatter all through the liqueurs and coffee, provoking her soft, husky laughter, but when Luis caressed her fingers and smiled with practised sensuality, Jake sprang to his feet. 'Abbey – ' he put his hand to the back of her chair ' – we have an early start tomorrow, we should hit the hay.'

'It's been a wonderful evening, Ramon, Luis.' Abbey rose to her feet. 'Please let me return your hospitality should you ever visit Kent.'

Ramon smiled and nodded, walked with them to the dining room door. 'I might hold you to that.' Then, 'Luis will be in bed no doubt when you leave, but I will rise at six to see you on your way.'

Luis leant to kiss both Abbey's cheeks. 'I 'ope we meet again soon, Abbey.'

Feeling Jake tense as he cupped her elbow, Abbey merely smiled. 'Who knows?'

The second the bedroom door closed behind Jake, he

spun around to confront Abbey. 'What was that about?'

But Abbey was angry too, fists planted on her hips, green eyes alight with emotion. 'I would like to ask you the same thing!'

'All that crap about art! What does he bloody know about it?' He gritted his teeth. 'He was trying to get into your bed!'

'Don't be so coarse!' Abbey fought the urge to slap Jake. 'I'll tell you what's coarse – ' she took a step towards him, determined not to be intimidated by Jake's height, or the strength of his anger ' – what's coarse, Jake, is your imagination!'

'I wasn't imagining you smiling whilst Luis pawed you. I wasn't imagining you agreeing with everything he said like some mindless bimbo!'

'You were listening, were you?' Abbey defended herself. 'You seemed engrossed in conversation with Ramon to me, Jake.' She clenched her fists at her side. 'If you'd made any effort to speak to me in the past few hours, I would have responded – but you're too chicken to admit you've had enough of me – so you take the easy way out and ignore me!'

'I didn't ignore you. I told you, I had things on my mind!'

'Fine!' She trembled with rage. 'Did you think I'd sit and sulk through dinner because you weren't paying me enough attention? Well, tough, Westaway, I don't rely on you for tidbits!'

'You didn't have to spill all over Luis,' he retorted darkly.

'And what do you expect me to do? Ask him not to speak to me?'

'Speak? You were a hundred-miles-an-hour seducing

the man! Were you two setting up some sordid meeting for the middle of the night? Is that why you wanted to stay so bad?'

Abbey's rage erupted and her palm met with Jake's sculptured cheek. Her fingers stung and dropped to her side as she shook with emotion. 'How can you say that?' she gasped, 'You and I made love this afternoon, Jake.' Butterflies, sweet grass, the memory painful now because it had been so intrinsically beautiful.

Equally shaken by raw jealousy, Jake hit back. 'Correction, Abbey, we had sex this afternoon.'

His words reviled her. It had been so beautiful. so magical, and Jake was reducing all that beauty to 'just sex'.

Husky words caught in her throat. 'If that's all it was, why are you so angry with Luis for wanting the same thing?' She raised her chin, sun-kissed strawberry blonde curls shifted against her shoulders.

'I'm angry with you, not Luis. I'm angry with you because you acted like a tart and I thought you had more class.'

Shocked laughter escaped Abbey. 'That's rich, coming from a fully paid-up member of the "lay them and dump 'em" school of thought!'

'This isn't funny, Abbey,' Jake thundered. 'At least I had bloody good reason for seducing you – Luis wouldn't need one.'

'Pardon?' Night sounds: insects grew suddenly louder through the open window, the air oppressive. 'What reason?' Something treacly, heavy, churned in Abbey's stomach. At Jake's stunned silence, she insisted, 'What reason?'

Swallowing, Jake crossed to the open window, stared

out over lush green dusk-shaded vines. Today or tomorrow? What did it matter? It didn't alter the truth. He could wipe all that trust from her eyes, turn it to anger in a minute.

A cold chill raced down Abbey's spine. Jake turned very slowly, silhouetted against the darkening sky. Suddenly, what had happened that evening didn't matter any more because Abbey knew by his grave expression there was much worse to come.

'I wanted you when we were on the boat.' He loosened his collar, yanked away his dark red tie and let it hang. 'But I didn't come on to you because you were Miles's woman.'

'I know that.' A light frown touched Abbey's brow.

'I had no intention of making it with you, but Monty let something slip, something he thought I already knew.'

Abbey swallowed, her mouth dry. Her knees felt shaky, but she had to remain standing. Her dread increased as Jake rubbed his forehead and forced himself on.

'He told me Miles hit on someone real special to me.' Anger glittered in his dark eyes. 'Miles knew I loved her – but it didn't stop him trying to seduce her when they were posted in Germany.

'Are you talking about Zav?' The words escaped her – a bowling ball in the stomach couldn't have winded her more. Unable to keep her knees from trembling, Abbey grasped around for some support, found the overstuffed armchair and sank on to its arm.

'Yeah. I trusted Miles – and what really cuts is he was around when I found out Zav had been killed. Like the snake he is, he sympathized, pulled me up by the braces – ' his voice broke before he got himself under control ' – and all the time, the bastard had been trying it on with her.'

The reason? It danced just outside Abbey's grasp; she loved Jake, and although the truth hammered at her, denial barred its entrance into her shocked state.

'When I found out, the night of Marianne's party, it was off with the boxing gloves, stuff the rules, I wanted something that mattered to him. I wanted to seduce you and make damn sure he found out.' Jake shoved his hands deep into his dark trouser pockets. 'I wanted him to know how it feels to have someone you trust turn the spiked knife.'

'If you're relying on me to spread the word to Miles, forget it. Do your own dirty work.' Abbey wanted to fight, to scream and shout; and she wanted to crawl into the overstuffed chair and sob with pressing hysteria.

'He already knows. That photographer at Marianne's party – he's the guy who followed you from my boat. He was working for Miles.'

'How do you know?'

'Part of my trade's identifying the adversary, feeding them what I want them to know. It wasn't difficult; the man was hopelessly inexperienced.'

'You're a clever man, Jake.' Abbey knew there was pain awaiting her, anger too powerful to restrain, but she held on to the fuzzy edges of denial as her emotional buffer.

Prepared only for Abbey's anger, Jake knew a twist of acid guilt at her white-faced acceptance. He wanted her anger, her outrage at his betrayal of not only Miles's trust, but her own. If Abbey didn't give him that, he'd never be free of her haunting green eyes or her husky voice, or the way her body moved so sensuously against his.

'I thought you'd at least slug me one.' That's it, jerk, his conscience piped up, invite her to be angry!

'Why?' At all costs, Abbey had to deal with this when she was alone. There was too much to face with Jake around. 'You only made me one promise, Jake. It'll be fulfilled.'

Jake had feasted on her body, taken her love and shown her safety, security, laughter and pure happiness like she'd never known. But he wasn't going to strip her of her dignity and reduce her to a blubbering wreck right here in their room.

Solemnly, Jake nodded. 'I'll take the room above the garage.'

'If you don't mind, Jake, I'd rather be the one to move to a different room.'

Civil! Hell, she was so civil – Abbey was making the whole thing so easy. Why didn't she fight him?

Smoothly, Abbey collected her belongings. Her whispered, 'Goodnight, Jake,' could have been 'goodbye'.

But he wasn't sure. He was sure, though, that Abbey's unique, exquisite perfume lingered on the bedding and made him ache with remorse for what he'd done to her.

'If you'd been angry, Abbey, I wouldn't feel this crappy.' He punched the pillow, but her perfume rose from that too. Turning the pillow over, something like grief lodged in his throat, kept sleep at bay; Abbey's lop-sided smile, her vibrancy danced in tempting, nebulous images before him. 'Lighten up, Westaway, you'll be fine come morning – free to cruise with the

Hollys of this world.' But even to his own ears, Jake's voice was decidedly ragged, and as he finally began to slip towards sleep, a voice in his head said, 'Admit it. This revenge lark ain't all it's cracked up to be.'

The taxi journey to the airport was gruelling for Abbey. The foggy protection of denial had burned away like mists in the morning sun and she had a long way to go before she could free the emotions bubbling like some newly awakened volcano in her stomach. Focusing only on reaching home and the solitude of the beach house, Abbey made it intact by taxi to the airport and booked herself on the next flight home.

'Morning, Ramon.' Jake grinned. 'Abbey not down yet?' He'd come to a few decisions during his sleepless night and was ready to talk them through with Abbey – grovel – anything.

Ramon gestured graciously for Jake to sit down at the place set for him. 'No, not yet. Go ahead, eat, Jake.'

Jake took a bite of the warm croissant and a slurp of his coffee, 'I'll go and shake her up in a minute.' He glanced at his watch. 'Thought she'd be up and raring to go.' The strange emptiness he'd known, his first night without Abbey at close quarters, convinced Jake that they couldn't just say goodbye tomorrow and leave it at that. If he could talk Abbey into staying around for a while, they could sail back to England together when his job was finished.

Ramon disappeared into the kitchen.

'There wouldn't be any hurry, but I've to start a job later today and Monty's gotta run through the details.' He glanced at his watch again and pushed aside his empty plate, called to Ramon, 'I'll go 'n see what's keeping her.'

Jake tried the door of the room above Ramon's garage and found it locked. He frowned, shielded his eyes to look in through the glass, the frown deepening as he could make out nothing other than a tidy bed. He supposed she must be in the shower, and Jake tried the door again. It was definitely locked.

Shrugging, he sought out Ramon. 'Do you have a spare key to the annex, Ramon?'

Ramon tossed Jake a key, turned away immediately. 'More coffee in a minute, Jake?'

'Sure.'

'Abbey?' The annex room had an undisturbed atmosphere; dust motes hung in air, lit by early sunshine. Jake strode straight for the bathroom, but found it empty. Only then did uneasiness whirl in his stomach. There were no belongings, no sign that anyone had been in the room; even the shower cubicle was dry. He spoke her name again, shoved his fingers through his dark hair and wandered back into the bedroom. A neatly folded sheet of paper caught his eye from behind the ornate bedside light. A sense of dread churned his stomach when he saw his own name printed on the front.

Jake, it read, *when you said I'd walk away, I didn't believe you. In a way, I was right because I didn't walk, I ran. There doesn't seem a lot to say, so I'll make it easier on us both and say goodbye. Abbey.*

'Easier?' Disbelieving, Jake blinked and read the note again; he thought he must have eaten breakfast too quickly because there was an obstruction in his throat, and the blurring of his vision could only be because he hadn't slept much.

How long he stood there, holding the note, Jake didn't know, but Ramon's voice disturbed his contemplation.

'Is everything all right, Jake?' He tapped on the door, but remained outside.

'Yeah,' left him roughly, 'come on in.'

'Where is Abbey?'

'Gone.' It was really sinking in now. You said the words and it brought them to life. 'Did you know?'

Ramon shook his head. 'No, Jake.'

'So did she walk? How did she get away from here? We're miles from anywhere!'

'Abbey returned to the dining room last night and asked me if she could use the telephone to make an urgent call, but I thought little of it. I showed her to my study, said goodnight and left her to it.'

'Can I see?'

Shrugging, Ramon accompanied Jake to his study. There was a neatly folded note with 'Ramon' printed on the front; Ramon opened it immediately. Jake found a small card within Ramon's telephone index with the equivalent of an English cab firm's details written on it. So that was how she'd got away.

'It's odd.' Ramon frowned. 'I asked her if you'd fought and she said no.'

'What – what does your note say?' Jake was feeling sick, his sharp mind fraying around the edges.

'"Thanks for your hospitality."' He handed it to Jake. 'Read it, there's nothing personal.'

Ramon, it went, *these have been amongst the best days I've ever had, I'm sorry to leave so abruptly. I cannot*

227

explain my departure, save to say it's over between Jake and I, and I have to put some distance between us. My apologies and my warmest thanks for your hospitality. Abbey Roberts. And beside the note, she'd left money to pay for her phone call.

Ramon shook his head. 'Use the telephone, Jake, ring the taxi firm.'

He'd picked out the number before Ramon finished speaking. Jake spoke in rapid Spanish, waited silently, then responded, 'Thank you.' And replaced the receiver.

'Yeah. Name of Roberts, she was picked up from the main gates at three a.m., the driver's only just cleared his job after dropping her at the airfield.'

'Ah, what a shame. I wondered.' Ramon considered Jake. 'Sometimes, if we want to be caught, we go slowly. I don't think Abbey had any intentions of letting you catch up with her.'

'No – ' Jake cursed under his breath ' – she didn't.'

'Some things are not meant to be, my friend – ' Ramon sighed ' – but a lovelier young woman I haven't seen in a long time.'

'Guess I'll just load up my gear, Ramon, I've a job to get to. Thanks, it really has been great.'

'Until just now, yes?' A perceptive light shone in Ramon's dark eyes.

'Y'could say that, mate.'

Jake gunned the hire car away from Ramon's, waving until the man was a speck against his beautiful, luxuriant vineyard.

He had one thing on his mind. Putting Abbey out of his mind. But her perfume lingered in the vehicle, her husky laughter vibrated through his body. He turned on the radio for the distraction value, concentrated on the straight road ahead and shoved on his sunglasses. 'Just another lay, Westaway, don't get sentimental.' Yet he grimaced when he cleared the edge of the corn field where he and Abbey had picnicked, stepped a little harder on the accelerator, tried to close out the soft laughter, the closeness, both physical and mental, they had discovered that day. It'd scared the shit out of him. It was too much like something from a long time ago. Too much like he'd felt with Zav around.

Usually, Jake reflected, the amount of time he'd spent with Abbey would be enough – enough for him to have itchy feet and the need to move on. But, usually, he was the one to move on. And somehow, because he hadn't been the one to physically set Abbey down somewhere and take off for pastures new, he had a nagging, unfinished feeling.

'It'll pass.' Jake pulled on to the highway, turned up the music, forced Abbey from his mind. Trouble was, every damn love song that came on the radio had words like 'don't know what you had till it's gone'. In exasperation, he shoved in the complimentary classical tape, let it play over and over all the way back to the hire-car station near Monty's.

'Hey, Monty!' Jake strode into the restaurant. 'How's it going?'

'Are you alone?' Monty frowned into the sunlight, passed his friend a cup of coffee.

'Y'could say that.' Jake leant against the marble bar. 'I got dumped.'

Monty laughed. 'You're kidding, right?'

'Nope.' Jake shook his head.

229

'Jake!' It was Marianne. She rushed over and kissed Jake's cheeks. 'Where's Abbey?' Before he could reply, Marianne declared, 'I'm real glad you found her, Jake, Abbey put the twinkle back in your eyes.' She shook her head. 'Lord knows, it's been missing for long enough!'

'Er – Marry – ' Monty tried to shut Marianne up, but could only cringe as she continued.

'Abbey put the life back in you, brother. I said to Monty, I've not seen you so relaxed, so happy, since Zav was around.'

'Marianne!' Monty watched nervously as a frown creased Jake's brow. 'Abbey's dumped him!'

'No!' Marianne gasped. 'You shouldn't have let her, Jake. You are an idiot!'

'It was my fault,' Jake muttered. 'I used her to get back at Miles.'

'Oh, Christ.' Monty rubbed his chin. 'It's what I told you about Miles seducing Zav, ain't it, Jake?'

'Yeah.'

'And now you're sorry.' Marianne frowned at Jake; there was no laughter in his dark blue eyes as he nodded slowly.

'You could say that.'

'I have the perfect excuse for you to visit with her.' Marianne turned about, returned with Abbey's portfolio, all the preparatory drawings and the unfinished painting of Jake neatly put away inside. 'Take this to her, you can make amends.'

'It's not that simple, Marianne.' Jake took the portfolio in any case. 'I told her the truth – why I'd seduced her.'

Marianne paled. 'You did not!'

Monty groaned.

'Uh-huh.'

Marianne grabbed the portfolio back from Jake. 'I'll post this! You don't deserve another chance.'

Jake was inclined to agree with Marianne, then he shrugged. 'What the hell. Let me take it, Marianne. If I'm passing by her way, I'll drop it in.'

'You'd better "pass her way",' Marianne threatened. 'Abbey cared about you, Jake.'

That got his full attention, dark blue eyes fixed on Marianne. 'How do you know that?'

'I asked her.'

'What did she say?'

Shrugging, Marianne said, 'She cares for you, but I knew that without asking. I could see it in the sketches – in her eyes. And you care for her, Jake. You won't admit it, though, will you?' Jake frowned as Marianne stared at him. 'What are you afraid of, Jake? Being hurt?'

He stared at the dregs in his coffee cup. 'Yeah, maybe.'

'Well, I hate to bring you back down to earth, mate – ' Monty pulled a file out from beneath the bar ' – but you need to be making tracks within the hour. You're meeting your client for dinner this evening, and you're on the job from then on.'

Jake closed his eyes, drew a deep breath. He had to focus on the upcoming assignment. Abbey would be okay, she had her voice back now. He recalled those big, tear-drenched green eyes and the fear he'd helped to send scurrying. Lord, she'd made him feel good. So good. Better than he had in a long, long time.

'Jake?'

'Yeah.' He flipped open the folder and studied the details. The client needed a bilingual bodyguard for a

231

minimum of a week; he also wanted a bodyguard who packed. 'I'll need to sign for a weapon, Monty.'

'It's all arranged.'

'Mind if I take a quick shower?'

'Not at all, Jake.' Marianne rested her palm on Jake's shoulder. 'I'll make you some lunch before you go, darlin'.'

'Thanks, sweetheart. Monty, will you check on *Free Spirit* for me before you leave for Sitges tomorrow?'

'No probs, man.' Monty took the small wad of notes from Jake. 'The old guy down at the pier's pretty keen, he'll be even keener for this.' He laughed and pocketed the money. 'You get sorted for that job.'

CHAPTER 9

Familiar, safe. Abbey felt the beach house's embrace as she entered its beloved solitude. Here, she could be herself and no sooner had she closed the door behind her than the tears rushed down her cheeks.

There was comfort too because no one knew she was home yet and wouldn't – until she chose to let anyone know.

Abbey had the overwhelming urge to set up her equipment and begin sketching, let the pain inside her come out on to canvas. All she could think of was Jake. The way he'd used her to have his revenge on Miles. Part of her wished he'd lied by omission. Abbey was too sickened, too upset yet to be angry, but the anger lurked and she knew it would be a long time surfacing. It was always the way for her; but when it did, it would be awful. If there was some way she could force out the anger and have done with it, some way she could have shouted, cried and fought with Jake. But, she reminded herself, the only thing she'd had left when he'd done with her not twenty-four hours before – the only thing she could hang on to – was her dignity.

Miles. Abbey supposed she would visit him in a few days and see how he was. But how would he greet her?

Was he in possession, as Jake had said, of a copy of the photograph of Jake and herself?

Remembering the photograph, Abbey had to find it amongst her luggage. Had to study his expression – was Jake really so good an actor she had been completely taken in?

Yes. The answer was yes. Those dark, sensual eyes of Jake's held nothing more than lust. Unexpectedly, the anger she feared ripped through her. She ripped up the photograph and threw it down the waste disposal, the satisfying sound of gravelling machinery destroying his mockery. That's what it was. He'd been playing with her all along.

Suddenly the house began to stifle her. Angry tears streamed down her cheeks now as she swiped at everything in her path. 'I'm such a fool!'

Startlingly, the telephone Abbey had never used began to ring. But she was running for the front door, for an attempt at freedom from pain, so picked up the telephone in passing and smashed it feebly against the wall. Weakly, it rang on and on, but Abbey kept on and on too, down the cliff path, on to the beach, toward the sea.

Jake slammed his palm against the wall. There was still no reply from Abbey's telephone. He only had time to try once more – he'd to join Mr Ernest Wood for dinner in five minutes.

Impatiently, he tapped out the number again; the flight Abbey would have caught should have seen her home long ago . . . A dreadful gut feeling that she could be in jeopardy lodged inside him. 'C'mon, sweetheart, answer the bloody phone.' Then it occurred to him. She might not answer, because he was the only one who

knew the number. No one else knew she had a telephone.

'Pig!' She slammed her fist down on the water, fought
with it. 'I'm not going to waste my tears on a no-good
jerk like you!' Abbey tilted back her head to stare at the
clear sky, the tears she didn't want to waste pouring
freely, wetly down her cheeks. 'I love you,' she shouted
hoarsely. 'I want to hate you, but I love you, you – you
bastard!'

By the time she'd done railing at the sea, at the sky,
only the circling gulls paying her any mind, Abbey
dragged herself, exhausted, from the lapping waves.

She thought she could hear the telephone ringing
through the open door of the beach house, decided the
minute she returned to the beach house, it was going in
the bin – or somewhere she couldn't hear it. If it had a
ringer that could be turned off, it was getting turned off.

One thing she treasured above anything was the
privacy, the lack of a telephone, the way she could
literally cut herself off from the world, and work. Like
the old adage, Abbey knew she just needed time to
absorb and rise above her affair with Jake. Time to lose
herself in her work and find her equilibrium.

Ernest Wood was a mild-mannered, slightly nervous
gentleman who needed Jake's interpretation skills when
it came to the finer points of his transaction. The man
had a suite next door to Jake's room in the hotel; they
ate together, played chess, and Jake checked for intru-
ders regularly.

But there was never anything in the slightest bit
threatening connected with Mr Wood.

'Who do you think poses a threat to your security, Mr Wood?' Jake asked him whilst they shared a beer and a game of chess in Mr Wood's lounge room.

'My partner was injured trying to pull off this same deal last year,' he replied, his finger trembling slightly on the queen as he pondered his next move. 'Having a bodyguard who could double up as an interpreter was my partner's idea. He's not had the nerve to move in business circles since his face was – er – altered.'

A cold chill slithered up Jake's spine. 'Sounds rough.'

'I'd rather not go into detail.'

'Okay.' Jake was tempted to ask if he could use the phone to try Abbey's number again, but resisted. The daytimes, filled with business meetings and the smoky conference rooms, translations and negotiations, kept him distracted. But come the evening, Abbey's perfume seemed to rise up and surround him, haunt the bloody life out of him. 'I wouldn't move that, Mr Wood,' Jake warned, the man about to put his Queen in jeopardy. 'The game'll be over if you do.' He'd use the phone in his own room once Mr Wood was settled for the night.

'Ah! Thanks, Jake.' The man drained his glass of beer. 'I'm bushed tonight, think I'll turn in early if you just want to check around for me?'

It was a routine Ernest Wood insisted on. Each night before he retired to bed, Jake had to check every corner inside and outside, the corridor and the wide balcony of their tenth-floor hotel room. It didn't matter to Jake. He was being paid for taking good care of Mr Wood. But something felt wrong about the whole set-up. Jake couldn't put his finger on what it was. Just a gut feeling. Maybe it was the way other business men treated Ernest Wood. With respect, affably, almost as if he were their friend. Jake could sense bad feeling a mile off, and there just didn't seem to be any in the air around this man.

Maybe, he counterbalanced the thought, his last six-month stint with his Far Eastern gentleman had been one so suffused with tension and antagonism, his responses on full alert the entire time that the money he was earning this time seemed almost too easy by comparison.

Yet he could identify no threat to Mr Wood.

By the end of a week filled more with visions of any danger Abbey might be facing than the man he protected, a week during which he'd tried to telephone her every evening and during afternoon recess – for an hour at a time – Jake was becoming jumpy, imagining something had happened to her. He had to keep reminding himself that she wouldn't answer the telephone, would she? But he couldn't stop trying to get through to her. He knew something for sure. He'd made one of the biggest mistakes of his life taking Abbey as his lover. Not so much the taking her, more the reason. He shouldn't have done it; and for the first time in his life, Jake regretted a relationship with a woman. Regretted it ending.

The following day, he was due to return to Monty's, pick up *Free Spirit* and sail back to England.

He punched out Abbey's number on his room phone and pulled open the door to step on to his balcony. The monotonous ring-ring sound echoed lonely in his ear. 'C'mon, answer it, darlin',' he growled.

There was a sharp knock on the adjoining door. 'Jake! I saw something move outside!'

Flinging the phone on to his bed, Jake dashed through the door, his fingers instinctively on the gun nestled in his underarm holster.

'I checked it a couple of minutes ago, Ernest.' Jake waved the man to go into the bathroom. 'Lock the door, just in case.' Jake could feel the danger rather than see it. He turned off the internal light and slowly edged toward the open balcony door, heard the bathroom door close behind Ernest Wood.

The phone was ringing again, but Abbey had turned the volume right down. Every night, about the time she washed her brushes, the little red light signalling someone was trying to reach her flashed. On impulse, she took it from the kitchen windowsill and flicked the switch. 'Hello?' But there was no response. 'Is anyone there? Will you stop trying to ring me, you creep!' Still no response. A soft moan escaped her. Abbey had toyed with the idea it might be Jake. But it wasn't. It was just some bloody crank caller. She hesitated, listened and there was nothing, so she snapped off the 'ringer' switch and tossed it back on to the windowsill, covered it with a couple of flannel tea towels. Then she shivered. It could be him. Could her stalker be tormenting her?

For the first time since returning to the beach house a week ago, Abbey allowed herself to consider the danger lurking behind the back drop of her life. She hadn't told anyone she was back. Hadn't wanted to speak to anyone. She wanted to paint to ease the pain in her soul. The pain had consumed her to the point that the dangers almost hadn't existed, they had taken a step back into the shadows.

Longing to push the telephone down the waste

disposal, Abbey held it through the tea towels for a moment, held it above the gaping hole. But what if she needed it? What if there was an emergency? Shuddering, she shoved it to the back of the windowsill and left it there. Tomorrow, or the next day, she'd have a phone properly installed – one with a different number and an ansaphone attached . . .

Nothing, there was nothing on Ernest Wood's balcony, but Jake still had the lurking sensation that all wasn't as it should be. 'Okay, Ernest – ' he knocked on the bathroom door ' – all clear.'

The following day the big sign-up was taking place and Ernest looked ragged. A week of tough negotiations had taken their toll on him. 'We ought to exchange rooms, you and I.' Ernest seemed more nervous than ever. 'I can't sleep in here, Jake.'

'Sure, if that's what you want,' Jake agreed without hesitation. 'If not, I'll ring downstairs, see what else they've got available.'

'I'll feel safe enough in your room.' Ernest removed his glasses, rubbed his eyes. 'Maybe I'll sleep if I have your room.'

'Don't worry, Ernest, I'll stay awake. You'll be okay.'

'How will you manage that?'

'Plenty of training, plenty of coffee.'

'Thanks.' Visibly relieved, Ernest moved into Jake's room, called back, 'Is this phone meant to be off the hook?'

'Shit!' Jake strode in and lifted the receiver from his bed. The phone was dead. It wasn't ringing. Had Abbey picked it up and put it down again? Nothing he could do about it now. He replaced the phone by the bed and said goodnight. 'The phone in my room isn't working.' Ernest yawned. 'I reported it, someone's going to fix it tomorrow.'

Ten minutes later, Ernest snored, slept the sleep of the innocent and Jake was disturbed from his position in a chair by the darkened windows by a sensation of movement outside. Automatically, he stole out on to the balcony to investigate.

Trees rustled down below, the dotted lights of other hotel rooms in the area gave an incomplete, patchwork feel to the night. And it was there, danger, he could smell it.

There was barely time to scan the surrounding area; a faint hissing sound, a thud-like impact in Jake's shoulder, warmth spilling downward, a savage curse from his lips.

Gripping the wound, Jake stumbled through the balcony doors, locked them and reeled toward the bathroom. He dragged a towel around his upper arm and held it there, then staggered to the chair and slumped into it, his gun in his lap.

'Ernest!' he tried to call, but the word came out in a harsh whisper, not enough to disturb the snoring man.

Sick, disoriented, Jake fought the sleepiness pervading his senses. Shock was creeping through him like a cold upward chill and he couldn't clear his head; blood spread across his shirt, warm, wet on his chest. He tried to get up from the chair, but was disoriented. Abbey's image filled his mind; the thought that he might never see her again. He fought the blackness, using Abbey's soft, husky voice, playing it over in his mind. The afternoon in the corn field . . . remembered his own anger. Anger because he'd wanted to reach out and take the whole of her. Not just the physical side of their relationship, but the whole woman. Anger because she'd made love to him so exquisitely, Abbey had given him so much more than he'd given her. Anger because she always gave more than he wanted to take. And because she trusted him and she shouldn't have. He'd used her. For his revenge. He bent double, the shock receded – pain screamed from the bullet wound and Jake slumped from the chair to the floor.

She was back. Had told no one yet. The fool and her tied-up fortune was back home . . . a sitting duck. Did she think if she didn't tell anyone then he wouldn't know? Naïve, so frighteningly trusting, it'd be so easy to steal her away and demand a ransom. So easy, but too easy just now. She had to suffer a while yet. And when she least expected it . . . when she was ready to go out of her mind . . .

'Rick?' A grey veil of hopelessness had settled around her. Visiting her mother at Misty Hills and finding her blank and completely unresponsive had pulled Abbey down another notch.

'Abbey? Great! You've got your voice back.'

'I've been busy. Do you want to come over for lunch? I've done the preliminaries on some new work.'

'Are you okay?' He frowned, rubbed his forehead with his gold pen. 'You sound a bit – I don't know – subdued.'

'I'm all right. I've just been to visit my mother, she isn't so good.'

'Be there at twelve, okay?'

'Sure.'

As soon as Abbey laid down the phone, she regretted breaking her silence with the outside world. It'd been safe, private without anyone knowing she was home. One attempt to reach her father had resulted in her hesitating whether to leave a message on his ansaphone, but in the end, she didn't. There wasn't any point, he was out of the country. Just as Lynn was – she was back on a series of long-haul flights and wouldn't be home for another week.

Two weeks hadn't done much to put Jake from her thoughts and his presence was in evidence in each of her new paintings. All of them featured the sea, boats, a Spanish fishing village, Jake lurking somewhere in the three paintings. It wasn't that she'd planned to have him there, he just appeared. Long, lean, moody, dark eyes glinting with sensuality.

'So who's this character?' Rick sipped his juice, enjoyed the shade from hazy sunshine on Abbey's verandah, watched her closely as he waited for her hesitant reply.

'Just someone I met.' Someone who hadn't contacted her, hadn't really wanted her, had pushed her out of his life. Someone she should hate, but couldn't.

'You look tired, Abb.'

'Do I?'

'You're supposed to be resting, not working.'

'I had a holiday – ' she picked at her pasta, smiled ' – a couple of weeks was as long as I could stay away.'

'When did your voice come back?' Rick tucked into the pasta, his tone concerned.

'Took about four days.' Looking out to sea, Abbey felt the familiar pain welling up in her. And it was familiar now, she could co-habit with it, but sometimes it rushed upward, shook her. She ached inside for Jake to hold her; despised the traitorous emotions that wouldn't budge.

'Have you seen Miles since you made it home?'

Grimacing, Abbey shook her head. 'No, Rick. I keep saying I'll visit him tomorrow – but somehow, when tomorrow comes, I can't bring myself to go.'

'He's in a private hospital now.' Rick waved his fork. 'Apparently he wanted to set up office and his father found him somewhere they'd bend the rules a tad.'

'That sounds about right,' Abbey observed wryly. 'Do you know where?'

'I've got a note of it – ' Rick flipped open his fat leather organizer ' – here, Abbey.'

'I'll visit him tomorrow.' She fingered the card. 'I owe him an explanation.' Again, her gaze drifted over the ocean.

'Abbey, have you been working night and day on these preliminaries?'

She shrugged, 'I've been working on them . . . you know how I lose track of time, Rick.'

'I do.' He smiled, rose to his feet. 'And speaking of time, I've just time for a quick coffee, then I'll have to split – I've a meeting in a half-hour.' Rick picked up his plate and followed Abbey indoors. 'I want you to promise me you'll rest, Abbey. You're not looking any better than you did after that fracas at your exhibition.'

'Gee, thanks!' She laughed and it sounded strange. Like she hadn't done it for a long time. 'I sleep when I'm tired, Rick, you know how I am.' Then, shrugging, she disappeared into her daylight studio. 'I've a finished painting here, only a small one . . .' her voice drifting as she moved away.

'You've really got the bit in your teeth.' He frowned as the tea-towel muffled telephone fought to be heard.

Locating the pathetically ringing phone, Rick flicked its switch. 'Hello, Abbey Roberts's residence? Yes, she's here. Just a moment.'

As Abbey reappeared with the small, A5-size portrait, Rick handed her the telephone.

Flinching, inwardly cursing herself for not dumping the thing in the waste disposal, Abbey whispered, 'Who is it?'

'Marion?' He shrugged. 'Couldn't tell properly.'

'Hello?'

'Abbey, at last!' Marianne's tones reached her and Abbey relaxed into the dining chair. She sounded so fraught, Abbey was compelled to ask, 'Is something the matter?'

'Jake's missing you, Abbey. He needs to see you.'

'I don't think so. There's nothing for us to say, Marianne.'

'But he's unhappy, he made a big mistake sending you away.'

'I don't know what he told you, Marianne, but it was a mistake us getting together in the first place.'

'Are you happy?' Marianne demanded. 'Wouldn't you rather be with Jake?'

'It's not an option, Marianne. I've been trying hard to forget him.'

'It hasn't worked?' Her tone hopeful.

'I'm still working on it.' Abbey bit her cheeks to keep the rising pain at bay.

'It isn't working for Jake, either, he told me not to ring you, told me you wouldn't answer the phone.'

'He couldn't know that.'

'Jake said he's the only one who knows the number, so you wouldn't answer. He tried to reach you every night when you first left.'

Every night, the telephone had burbled away from beneath a wad of tea towels . . .

Rick cleared his throat, distracting Abbey. 'Marianne, I'm in a meeting with my agent. I'm sorry, but I don't want to see Jake.'

'I can't hear you properly. I'll phone back this evening, Abbey – give me your decision then?' And the line went dead.

Tactfully, Rick had wandered back out onto the verandah. 'I'll have to make tracks, Abbey.' He glanced at his watch. 'The sketches are amazing, but listen, I don't want you wrecking yourself getting these paintings finished.'

'And what do you think of the portrait?'

Rick held the small painting, studied it, nodded. 'It's the best you've ever done. Who is he?'

'Jake Westaway.' She bit at her bottom lip. Jake had missed her? The words had hovered around her, now they sank right in. The thought of seeing him again sent bubbles of anticipation racing through her. 'Rick, could you drop me off to see Miles, please? I might be going away again and I really must visit him and explain a few things.'

'Sure, we'll have to leave right away, though.'

'Right.' She pushed her feet into scuffed trainers, tucked her plain white T-shirt into the waistband of her jeans, and caught back her hair into a scrunchie.

Whilst Rick made the short detour to the Plumegate Private Hospital, he told her about her father's visit to his office. 'He was convinced I'd sent you away as part of a publicity exercise. Then you could've knocked me down with a feather – Miles telephoned me – *he* wanted to know where you were, and I thought you were with him!'

She chuckled wryly. 'I'm sorry if you got it in the ear. Despite my age, my father worries if he doesn't know where I am. I sent him a postcard.'

'Will you be okay here?' Rick pulled up outside the plush Georgian building.

'Course.' Somehow, hearing from Marianne had warmed her, evoked fresh memories of Jake; the rare brilliance of his smile.

The reception desk was thick walnut. A beautiful nurse smiled a measured smile at Abbey. 'Can I help you, dear?'

Cringing inwardly, she replied, 'Could you direct me to Miles Pendleton-Smythe's room, please?'

The nurse studied her for a second. 'Mr Pendleton-Smythe? And you are?'

'Abbey Roberts. A friend.'

'I think he may be in physio, I'll check for you.' She lifted a telephone and Abbey turned away, picked up a glossy magazine and perched on the edge of a deeply upholstered chair.

'He's just finished, Miss Roberts, his nurse is coming to collect you.'

Miles's nurse looked more like a model. She patted her red hair, gestured for Abbey to join her. 'I'm Miles's day nurse, Miss Roberts.' Abbey wondered if there was some kind of accolade attached to that title, as the woman looked so smug about it.

He was sweating, dishevelled, when Abbey followed Miles's day nurse into his vast room. 'We're going to go outside today, aren't we?' The nurse smiled, her eyes widening when Miles boomed,

'Abbey!' He wiped his wrist across his forehead, grabbed her hand as she neared his bed and yanked her toward him. 'Sweetheart, how wonderful to see you! What have you been up to?' And to the nurse, 'That'll be all for now, Francesca.'

Puzzled at his demonstrative gesture, Abbey settled in the seat at the side of his bed. Physio? She didn't think so – Miles had the look of a man who'd just had sex.

'What's the matter?' Abbey began to feel uncomfortable under Miles's scrutiny. Uncomfortable with the knowledge that she didn't really know this man at all.

'Darling, why haven't you been to see me before this?'

'I wrote to explain.' Abbey slid her fingers from his.

'I presume your affair with Westaway is over?'

'Jake?' She gasped, wishing she'd gone straight to Spain and visited Jake, rather than Miles.

'Westaway cannot sustain a relationship, Abbey, I knew you'd be back, darling.' He smiled, his most charming smile, his fingers toying with her strawberry curls, 'Besides, he can't afford a woman like you, you're out of his league.'

'Is that what you think?' Abbey wanted to wipe the smug expression off Miles's features. 'He told me you'd have a photograph of us together.'

In an instant, Miles produced the sensual photograph. 'This.'

Calmly, Abbey looked at the picture, then dropped it to the bed. 'Yes.'

'Do you want to tell me what's been going on?'

247

'You might not believe this, Miles, but all the time we were on Jake's boat, he never touched me.'

'Oh, do come on!' Miles pushed himself upward, would have shaken Abbey if he could get close enough. 'Westaway cracks on to anything in a skirt!'

'Apparently not "Miles's woman".'

Miles laughed at that, which shocked Abbey. 'Why is that funny, Miles?'

'I believe you could resist him – but don't ask me to believe Westaway could keep his hands off you!' He jerked his thumb at the photograph, the photograph Abbey loved and hated all at once. 'You look like you can't wait to get inside one another's clothes.' New anger surged through Miles, his gaze fixed on Jake's hand settled on Abbey's thigh, 'If you're trying to say Jake Westaway didn't touch you, Abbey, I have to tell you, I know differently.' He tossed down the picture. 'But, I'm willing to forgive you, darling, because I adore you.'

'Why did you have me followed?' Abbey was seething. She didn't want Miles's forgiveness – not for something she'd wanted.

'When I received your postcard, I had to have someone check you were all right, darling.' He shrugged. 'I knew you'd be at Jake's sister's.'

'You should have known I was all right – I was with your friend!'

'Darling!' He reached out to caress her curls. 'I trust you implicitly, it's Westaway – his brains have always been in his jeans. When he was our self-defence instructor in the army, he screwed anything remotely female.'

'Am I supposed to be flattered, Miles?'

'No, no, darling, but with hindsight, you can see what kind of man he is?' He smiled and Abbey had the greatest urge to bolt from the room screaming obscenities at him. 'If something did go on between you, I want you to know I don't blame you, Abbey. I know women find Westaway hard to resist.'

'Let me tell you something, Miles. Jake Westaway is a better friend to you than you deserve. He never denied he was attracted to me, but he didn't touch me until that night!' She picked up the photograph. 'And he wouldn't have touched me then, but he was raging, Miles – and do you know why?' She didn't wait for a reply from his shocked mouth. 'I'll tell you why – because he found out that night that you hit on Zav every chance you got!' She rose to her feet, trembling with anger. 'He trusted you, Miles, really trusted you! Jake wanted you to know how it felt to be betrayed by someone close. He loved Zav!'

'So he deliberately seduced you? I rest my case.' Miles was so flippant, Abbey almost choked.

'No, Miles, we seduced one another.' Her eyes were steady as she said, 'There's a world of difference.'

As though the whole matter was of no importance, Miles batted his hand under his chin. 'You're back now, darling, that's all that really matters. We can salvage our relationship.'

'I came back, "darling",' Abbey whispered, 'to let you know exactly where you and I stood. There's no future for us, Miles.'

'You're frustrated! I am still capable of having sex, you know! Kick a man when he's down, why don't you?'

'It has nothing to do with sex, Miles.' Briefly, she felt sympathy for his shallowness. 'If I really loved you, wild horses couldn't have chased me into Jake's arms – '

'Where is he now, then?' Miles retorted. 'On the job with some other woman?' He wagged his finger at her. 'Any woman can have sex with Westaway, Abbey, but no one gets to keep him.'

'Zav got to keep him.' Abbey shook her head. 'You knew he loved her, but you didn't care, did you? It didn't stop you trying to win her away from him?'

Miles raised a single brow. 'Zav was a beautiful woman, but she missed Jake when they were posted apart.'

'What's that supposed to mean?'

'Sometimes, she needed – company.'

'She probably needed to talk, Miles, nothing else.'

'Perhaps.' He sighed. 'But she liked me.'

'That doesn't mean she would have left Jake for you!'

'Ah – but we'll never know, will we?'

Disgusted, Abbey shook her head. 'You didn't deserve Jake's friendship, Miles. They were going to be married – you should have respected their relationship.'

'Really? And you're presuming Westaway was faithful to Zav? I'll not deny he loved the woman,' Miles replied callously, 'but the man's a perfidious jerk!'

Her pulses jumped. Abbey had never imagined Jake would be unfaithful to Zav . . . never. She could feel the blood draining sickly from her cheeks.

'Darling, why are you raking over something that has nothing to do with you? It's all in the past, for pity's sake, leave it there.'

'Seeing that I was Jake's mode of revenge, Miles, it has everything to do with me. It's the only reason Jake Westaway had sex with me!'

A laugh broke from Miles, 'So he'd like you to

believe. Jake is nothing if not clever, Abbey. Giving it a label – revenge – gave him all the excuse he needed.'

'It doesn't make any difference.' Abbey glanced up as Francesca entered the room and smiled at Miles. 'It's over between you and me. I don't know whether it's because of Jake – it might be, or it might have ended this way in any case.'

'If you're going to go running after Westaway, Abbey, I'd advise you not to – he won't have wasted any time finding a replacement.' Miles couldn't believe it, Abbey was about to dump him! 'Don't forget I've seen him in action.'

'So have I.' Abbey battled with her confusion. 'Goodbye, Miles.'

'Abbey!' He jerked his whole body trying to reach out to her, and groaned with pain. 'Come back here! We can work this out!'

She closed her eyes and turned at the door. 'Miles, I don't want to work it out.' She took a deep, regretful breath. 'We can keep in touch as friends. You're still my financial advisor, I'm happy for you to handle my money affairs, but that's all.'

'Abbey! Abbey!' Miles's shouts followed her exit from the hospital. Somehow, the whole scenario with Jake had held an iota of decency, because Abbey had never believed Jake would be unfaithful to Zav. But had he even trashed that relationship? The woman he trembled just to speak about years after her death?

Sickened, disillusioned, Abbey caught a taxi to town, called in to visit 'Mr Helpful Sweat-a-Lot' at the police station, to let him know she was home; then bought in some shopping and ordered a telephone before returning home. She couldn't explain the feeling inside that

251

somehow, Jake had betrayed her not once, but twice. And the disgust churned on and on. Jake's words echoed in her mind: 'Remember, I'm not as good as you think I am . . .'

Somehow, though, Miles's words had helped with a difficult decision; she wouldn't visit Jake. Not now. She felt as though she was five years old and someone had told her Father Christmas didn't exist.

'Hello, Mum.' Jake tried to drag himself from sleep, focus on the small figure at the side of his bed. 'How're you doin'?' But the words were faint inside the oxygen mask.

'Ah! So you know who I am this time?' Concern sharpened her voice. 'All we've heard from you for days is "Abbey this – Abbey that"!' Jake's vision cleared to see his mother shaking her head. 'If I ever get my hands on that woman, I'll shake her! Leaving you in this mess! Trollop! *Puta!*' Barely pausing for breath, Ana Westaway wagged her finger. 'You're too soft with the women, Jake! They use you for the good time. You should find a proper woman – like Zav!'

Monitors, bleeps, a transfusion pack high on a metal pole. His head swam. He took a breath to defend Abbey, but could only manage, 'It was my fault . . .' and that so quietly that Ana Westaway didn't hear; she continued with her lecture as Jake sank back into darkness.

It was a week later before Jake could stay awake for any length of time.

'Jake!' Marianne pinched a grape from his fruit bowl. 'What a bloody relief to see you without all those wires attached! You're looking better, darlin'.'

252

'Liar.'

'Yes, but you will feel better when I tell you who I've spoken to, brother.' She kissed his soft dark hair.

Jake grimaced as the nurse adjusted a pillow behind his injured shoulder. 'You can have some painkillers, Mr Westaway,' she offered.

'Thanks, I'd rather stay awake.' He smiled, but it didn't reach his eyes. 'If it get's tough, I'll have something later.' He turned to Marianne. 'Who've you spoken to? My bank manager?'

'Abbey.'

Thunder filled Jake's eyes. 'You shouldn't have – '

'She was concerned about you, Jake.'

'That's the way she is.' He shoved his fingers back through his hair. 'I don't want to see her again, Marianne.'

'Now who's the liar?'

Jake shook his head. It was a lie, but it was for the best.

Undaunted, Marianne continued. 'I am speaking to her again this evening; she is deciding whether to visit you or not.'

'Tell her not to come.' Jake whitened with agony. 'It wouldn't be right.'

'For who?'

'For either of us, Marianne.'

'If Abbey wants to come and see you, I'm not going to dissuade her.' Marianne shot back airily. 'And I think she will.' She rose to leave then. 'By the way, Monty got sick of Ma slagging Abbey off. He told her the truth.' She half-grinned, half-grimaced. 'Poor Ma, she's a bit sheepish now.' With a wave, 'Monty'll be over to see you later; I'll send your nurse over with a painkiller. I'll

253

bring your nieces tomorrow, now you've stopped snarling at everyone!'

'Thanks, sweetheart.' Something like hope swelled inside him, lightened his mood for the first time since he'd been moved to the general ward, four days ago. He let his mind linger on that sexy laugh of Abbey's, her lopsided smile, the way something moved inside him every time she spoke. The way she made him feel so good. If she came to see him, he'd damn sure make it up to her. Fear – yes, he'd known fear because of the way Abbey made him feel. But no amount of pretending she didn't matter had helped. And no amount of countering the loss of her with the promise of other beautiful women had helped, either. She was another – like Zav – another rarity. A woman who'd reached right down inside him and yanked his heart right out from under his nose.

Right at that moment, fear of his feelings wasn't so bad as being without her.

From the moment Abbey entered the beach house, something didn't feel right. Maybe, she told herself, it was just that she dreaded Marianne's call; because she couldn't go and see Jake. Not now. Discovering that he couldn't even be faithful to a woman he'd professed to love – it had taken the solid ground from under her.

The telephone began ringing as soon as she set down her shopping on the kitchen work top. Taking a deep breath, Abbey retrieved it from the windowsill, at least it would all be over with in a moment.

'Hello?'

'There's something for you in your bedroom,' a rasping, monotone voice taunted. 'Something for you.' Then the line went dead.

That ghastly voice from her past, unearthly, cold, the voice that made blood curdle in her veins. The phone slipped through her fingers to the tiled floor and bounced.

Fear, sharp like knives, hacked at her nerves. Adrenaline surged through her, bade her run for the door, run, leave the beach house . . . but anger that she'd let herself be intimidated held her where she was. Her thoughts whirled. Who knew she was home? Only Miles and Rick and Marianne, of course . . . Bile rose in her throat and she forced herself through her bedroom door. A pale yellow sheet of paper was folded on her patchwork quilt, held in place with a long, sharp nail.

Ugly, dark writing leapt from the unfolding paper.

See what happens to those in your life who get too close . . . No one can help you. Two so far in hospital through my industriousness. Sleep well, Daddy's little princess. Soon you will sleep the sleep of the distraught.

'Hospital?' Miles was in hospital – she dashed back to the kitchen and rescued the telephone, tapped out Miles's number.

'Miles?'

'Ah! Abbey! I've been expecting your call, darling.'

'I need to ask you something.'

'Fire away, darling, anything.'

'That night, the night of my exhibition, when you had your accident?'

'Yes?' He sounded puzzled. 'What about it?'

'What exactly happened? Was something wrong with your car?'

'Yes, the blasted brakes failed. Apparently, the fluid escaped somewhere.'

'From a brake pipe? Could it have been cut?'

'Damned if I know, darling. All I know is the insurers wrote off my Porsche. Someone mentioned "tampering", but I was out of it for days – Father dealt with it. I have a new one lined up.'

'Thanks, Miles.'

Frantically, Abbey telephoned her father – he wasn't home, so she left a brief message on his ansaphone, then telephoned his long-time secretary. 'Is he well?'

'Yes, dear. Spoke to him just ten minutes ago.'

'That's all I wanted to know,' she finished. 'Give him my love?'

Then Rick. His appointment from lunch time had been extended, but his secretary assured Abbey that he was in fine health.

For an hour, Abbey telephoned everyone remotely connected with her during the past year, but apart from an exploratory and an appendix, there was no one in hospital.

All the while, the thought of Jake nagged at the back of her mind . . . But Marianne would have said something? Or maybe not. She plunged through her luggage, found a book of matches with Monty and Marianne's phone number on.

'Monty?'

'Yo!'

'It's Abbey.'

'Great! When are you coming?'

'I'm not phoning about that, Monty, I just want to know if Jake's all right.'

There was a pause at the other end of the line.

'Monty?'

'I'll get Marianne.'

'Monty – I just want to know if Jake's all right – '

But he'd already gone. A chill rose from her feet up. It was Jake. The other one in hospital was Jake. Deep inside, she'd known it all along.

'Abbey, I can't stay on long, can I telephone you later? Like we arranged?'

'Yes, just tell me, is Jake all right?'

That silent pause again.

'Is he in hospital?'

'He was shot.'

'N-no!' Then whispered, 'Is he – ?'

'He's alive.'

Suddenly, Abbey began to weep silently, bit the inside of her lips to keep any noise from escaping. When she could control the riot in her mind, she asked huskily, 'Is he badly hurt?'

'He's out of danger.' Pausing for a moment, Marianne added, 'He didn't want you to know.'

Frowning, Abbey gasped, 'Marianne, what happened?'

Briefly, Marianne explained, 'The job was supposed to be simple – ' Whilst she spoke, Abbey remained silent. 'The man Jake was guarding disappeared into thin air; terrified, we think – we heard nothing else from him. Jake was left to bleed to death; he and his client had exchanged rooms, it's obvious the bullet was meant for his client.'

'Oh, Marianne – '

'He'll short-circuit if he knows I've spoken about this to you. But, Abbey, you should come and see him. Talk with him? Jake won't admit it to me, but he's made a big mistake with you.'

'Marianne,' Abbey managed past the constriction in her throat, 'we're not right for one another.'

'Because he used you to hurt Miles?' Marianne's frank words seared Abbey. 'His motives were bad, but Abbey, Jake's unhappy, you don't sound too great – there must be a way you can work something out.'

Abbey sighed. 'I'd come straight over if Jake asked me – but can you understand? I believed in him and he used me. Will he recover? Where was he shot?'

'Would it make any difference, Abbey, if I told you he said your name over and over when he was unconscious?'

Staring at the phone, Abbey put her free hand to her stomach to steady the lurch of emotion there. It made all the difference in the world. 'Can we speak later? I need time to think this through, Marianne.'

'But will you answer the phone?'

'Yes. I'll answer it.' And Abbey waited for the quiet click at the far end of the line.

CHAPTER 10

Abbey tried to come to terms with Jake's shooting. Come to terms with the latest note and its devastating inference.

Somehow, her tormentor was claiming credit for Miles's accident, showing her Miles could have been killed. What she felt for Miles wasn't love, nothing remotely like it, but he could have been killed – just for being her boyfriend.

Facing Jake's shooting was a little harder.

A lot harder. He'd helped her dodge the shadow from her past and stolen her away to his boat, to his sister's home, then to his uncle's beautiful vineyard, its lush surroundings.

Letting her thoughts roam where they would, she thought of their picnic, the corn field, the laughter, then she ached inside when she recalled how Jake seemed to surrender himself, suddenly, briefly. He no longer hid behind the mask he'd developed over the years . . .

'Hey, Abbey, do you want to come back here again sometime?' He looked surprised at his own words, as if they'd slipped out when he wasn't concentrating.

She laughed. 'If I thought you meant that – ' she leant her elbows on his stomach, watched him wince ' – I'd say yes. But I don't think you meant to say it.'

'Damn! You're getting to know me too well, Roberts.'

Let it go . . . She let the question go, didn't try and pin him down. There wasn't any point. Instead of trying to extract a date, a time when they'd return together, she lay across him and covered his mouth with hers.

Jake laughed against her mouth. 'You've a good line in conversation stoppers, Roberts.'

She tugged gently at his bottom lip with her teeth. 'I've a bagful. If you lie really still, I'll show you the best one.'

'Lie still?' A sexy grin curved his mouth.

'Yep, if you move, I won't show you.'

He raised a brow, a sensual light in his dark eyes. 'I won't move.'

She stemmed her own thoughts there. The rest she would bring out another time. Abbey shook her head. 'Jake, there was something between us . . .' There was, but Jake didn't want it. 'For me there was,' she amended, 'you were playing games.' Even as she tried to convince herself of that, Abbey recalled Miles's accusation that Jake had betrayed even Zav. That being faithful was some kind of unnatural act for Jake.

Falling in love was like rolling in warm treacle, Abbey thought, you couldn't just flick it off when you felt like it; it stuck. What you found out about someone didn't alter what you felt, it just meant that, in spite of everything, you still loved them. If one person fell in love and the other didn't, it was, in Jake's words, 'tough'.

Staring at the latest note, Abbey dialled the main police station – the sub-station had closed for the day, so she left a message with someone else. 'If you could just tell Sergeant Wise I've received another note? My name is Abbey Roberts. Yes, I'll leave my number. Yes, I'm fine, I'll keep the note.' Abbey left the number of the mobile telephone, and the one she was due to have installed the following day.

After locking all the doors and windows, Abbey bathed and pulled on a terry robe. There was a silence about the house she was uncomfortable with; she knew it was the fault of the note. That horrendous realization that someone had invaded her privacy with such ease whilst she was away for a few hours. The horrendous suspicions that flew in and out of her thoughts. Rick? Could it be him? He'd been at her home . . . 'No.' She hated the thought for even entering her mind. Yet it had. 'It couldn't be,' she reasoned out loud because she needed to hear a voice, 'it couldn't be, he's too close to my age.' Just how old he was, she wasn't sure, but it couldn't be him. But it was someone. There was someone who meant her harm. Someone who would harm anyone who might protect her. Someone who wanted to isolate her to such a degree, by threats to the well-being of her friends, that her sanity would slip, slip away.

'No!' Abbey ran into her studio, slammed the door closed behind her. 'You'll not have my mind. It's mine!'

Her studio was brightly lit, no dark shadows there; it was the room in which Abbey felt safest, the room she took the little telephone into. Sun-yellow blinds were drawn and the dying light outside was offset by daylight bulbs. Pulling a massive bean bag into the centre of the room, she propped a sketch pad against her knees and let a pencil move in slow, soothing strokes over the slightly rough surface. She knew what the face would look like, knew she was trying to create some security

261

for herself by drawing Jake's likeness. Only in his arms had she known freedom from this constant fear.

'Jake, I want to see you again. I want to see you so much.' The awful vision, of a bullet hitting him, of him staggering, bleeding, filled her mind. And the awful truth. If she went anywhere near Jake again, he might be killed the next time. Her tormentor was posturing, showing her how clever he was, how ingenious. How easy it was to find her – find anyone connected with her.

The phone shrilled.

'Ah!' Abbey leapt from the bean bag, heart pumping; she flicked the switch and waited for the caller to speak. If it was that rasping, distorted voice . . .

'Abbey?'

'Marianne!' she gasped. 'Thank goodness.'

'What's wrong?'

'Nothing, really, I just gave myself a fright, that's all.'

'Are you going to come here? Monty will drive to the airfield to collect you.'

A vision swept through her mind of Jake being peppered with bullets – her mouth dried, her tongue stuck to the roof of her mouth. Or his car might be tampered with – he might be killed.

'Are you still there?'

'Yes, yes.' She couldn't concentrate because she had to convince Marianne of something she could barely come to terms with herself.

'When are you flying out?'

'I'm not coming, Marianne.' Abbey's husky voice broke on the other woman's name. 'I'm sorry, but it's not practical, I've too much work.'

Marianne responded sharply, in Spanish; Abbey thought it was probably a colourful curse.

'Pardon?' Abbey said, hoped her tone was nonchalant.

'Are you telling me you don't care about Jake?'

'I care that he was shot, Marianne, but that's all.' The harshness she tried for was feeble. She cringed at herself, then hurriedly continued, 'If he needs any money, I'll send some, but I can't spare the time.'

'I was wrong about you, Abbey Roberts,' Marianne burst out. 'I thought you loved Jake!'

'Oh, Marianne, of course not, he's not my type, surely you realized that.'

There was a tiny, shocked silence. 'Then I will not bother you again. Goodbye.'

'Goodbye.' Abbey said the solitary word to the dead line, sank into the bean bag clutching the phone, misery swamping her.

Time ebbed and flowed, pain and fear, loneliness and heartache taking turns with her emotions. Desperation clawed at her and squeezed; sleep and its shadows hovered just beyond the tossing emotional tide, swallowed her when she couldn't fight it any longer.

'Hey, Monty, how's it going?' Even to the casual observer, Monty thought Jake looked a whole barrow more cheerful.

'Okay, how's that gaping hole in your shoulder?'

'I'll live.'

'Yeah. Guess you will.' Monty scratched his head, 'Look, there's no easy way to tell you this, so I'll spit it out. Abbey's not coming.'

'Okay.' Jake looked down at the bedcover, a muscle twitching in his cheek the only outward sign of emotion. 'Guess she's too busy making up with Miles.'

'She said she's got too much work on, mate.'

Jake nodded, looked Monty in the eyes. 'Just so long as Marianne didn't tell her I caught a bullet. I didn't want her coming with a bagful of sympathy.'

'Marianne did tell her.' He scratched his head again. 'Funny that, we got a weird phone call from Abbey this afternoon, all she wanted to know was if you were all right – and were you in hospital?'

'What?' Jake's eyes darkened. 'Hell, I spent too long with her, she's got psychic on me.'

'Well, Marianne said she sounded freaked.'

Jake's thoughts slammed around, muzzed by pain-killers, met with shut doors. He rubbed his temples between finger and thumb.

'Then cool as you like, when Marianne spoke to her this evening, Abbey says she ain't coming to see you, she cared you'd been hit, but that was all. Oh, yeah, and if you need any money, she'd send some.'

'Man, I've blown something so good, I daren't even think about it.'

'Yeah. Good fun, gorgeous, a body like a goddess. And they don't come wrapped like that – and with money – that often, do they, mate?'

'I don't give a damn about her money.'

'Okay.' Monty grimaced, held up his palms. 'So what are you going to do?'

'Do?' Jake frowned, 'What the fudge can I do?'

Monty winked, pulled the curtain around Jake's bed and slipped a small telephone from his pocket, 'Call her. This afternoon, she said if you asked her yourself, she'd come.'

A smile twitched at the edges of Jake's lips. 'You want to get yourself a coffee?'

It seemed to ring forever. But he'd let it ring until she answered it.

It was a cycle bell, ringing, louder and louder, the cycle huge, its wheels bigger than she was with treads you could lose a shoe in. It was coming straight at her, the shadowy tormentor ready to run her down, flatten her, and Abbey couldn't move. Blood pumped loudly in her head, but not loudly enough to drown out the bell. She could feel its vibration through her body, tried to run, couldn't move.

Sweat turned cold on her skin, leaving her clothes damp, as Abbey jerked awake, the telephone ringing against her stomach. Disoriented, the nightmare still fresh in her mind, Abbey pressed the switch, held the phone to her ear.

'Abbey? Abbey, are you there?'

'*Jake?* Yes,' she eventually gasped, 'I'm here.'

A cold chill swept over Jake; he forced himself to slow down, 'Were you asleep?'

'Yes, yes, I was.' She rubbed her swollen eyes, snatched up a tissue from the studio floor and blew her nose, only one question needing an answer. 'Were you badly hurt?' Her voice broke with anxiety.

'Could've been worse.'

'No – don't say that.' She dropped her forehead to her palm, her mind serving up a scenario of Jake falling backwards at the impact of a bullet.

'You sound upset,' Jake chanced. 'Have you been crying?'

'No, I've got a cold, it always happens when I've been abroad.' She scolded herself to get her act together – and quickly. Marianne she'd fooled, but Jake was something else.

265

'Abbey, I made a big mistake throwing what we had at the wall. I'm sorry. I want you back – for real, I mean.'

She remained silent, fought the ache that lodged in her throat. If Jake thought for one minute she was in danger, if he thought for one minute that she cared for him, he'd put himself in grave danger to help her. Perhaps more danger than she herself was in.

She dragged air into her lungs and searched for the words to put Jake off forever. Words that would keep him alive. 'We all make mistakes.' She looked up to the ceiling, needing the support of some invisible force. 'You and I becoming involved was a huge one.' Knowing she had to be brilliantly convincing, she added for good measure, 'Fortunately, Miles is happy to overlook our encounter, Jake, and carry on as if nothing happened. I can't tell you what a relief it is.'

There was silence, then, 'That's big of him,' Jake growled.

'I thought so, too,' Abbey responded brightly, 'so no harm's done.'

'Just answer me one thing, Abbey – ' Jake could barely control the jealousy gathering, knotting, wrenching in his stomach ' – what we had, did it mean anything to you?'

'No, of course not!' She laughed callously for effect, blinked the tears from her eyes. 'No offence, Jake, but you're hardly my ideal man.'

'And Miles is?'

She stumbled there. To join forces with Miles to push Jake away – it was the ultimate blow to that sweet, unexpected love. 'Miles comes close enough.' The words ripped her in two. 'Like you said, he has enough "dosh" to keep me interested.'

But she had to hang on to her reasoning, push Jake away . . .

Closing his eyes against the pain, Jake growled, 'You didn't give Miles a second thought when we were making love.'

A sob rose up, which Abbey converted to a sharp laugh. 'Don't be obtuse, Jake. You said yourself, it was sex, we didn't make love. It didn't mean anything, it was a holiday romance.'

'Maybe it didn't mean anything to you, Abbey.' The catch in Jake's voice had Abbey ready to swim across the channel to be with him.

She coughed to cover a rush of emotion, recovered her composure sufficiently to end their conversation. 'Well, thanks again for all your help, Jake, I wish you a speedy recovery.'

Dropping the telephone, crazed with anguish, Abbey sprang to her feet. 'You've got what you wanted!' she yelled at the walls. 'There's no knight in shining armour going to save me now! Why don't you come and get me and get this whole thing over with?' She hugged herself, her throat hurting with emotion, with loss and creeping fear. 'Oh, Jake, I'm so sorry. I love you. If there was any way –' But the great, dry sobs shook her again. 'I could handle all this with you around . . . Without you, I don't know – '

Her deepest fear, of madness, crept closer.

'Abbey!' It was Rick.

She turned off the ansaphone and picked up the receiver. 'Rick?'

'I haven't heard from you since we had lunch, Abb, thought I'd swing by and bring lunch for us this time. You can show me how your work's coming on.'

'Sure.' She forced enthusiasm into her voice. 'Father's coming over around lunchtime, too; he got back from a trip a couple of days ago.'

'Shall I come another time, then?'

'No – please, come today. He can be hard work so it'll help if you're here.'

'Okay.'

'Don't worry about bringing lunch, I'm cooking.'

'See you between twelve and one?'

Normally, Abbey would have revelled in the uninterrupted peace she'd known, but she'd seen menace in every corner, known nights of torment that left her trembling, shocked; laced with visions of a man who would make everything all right – the man she couldn't have.

Last night, she'd heard the stalker when he wasn't there, used her panic button twice to bring the closest police patrol vehicle dashing to her aid.

Police Constable Stapleton had been polite, assured her that other people with panic buttons had false alarms too. 'I just feel so stupid.' Abbey batted a moth away from her on the floodlit verandah. 'I heard something – someone walking across here – I know I did.'

'There's no one around, Miss Roberts. I've looked everywhere. Perhaps it was a cat?'

The constable had been gone maybe twenty minutes and Abbey heard it again. The footfalls outside her studio window, pacing the wooden verandah. Fear like flashing lights in her head, like madness, like hell. The wood creaked outside; he was walking up and down, taunting her.

She pressed the alarm in her pocket, sank to the bean bag which she'd relocated in the corner and curled up on it, eyes fixed on the locked studio door. 'You'll not have my mind,' she whispered, over and over. A vision of her mother, when she'd visited her at Misty Hills Hospital, rose in her mind's eye. Rebecca – her beautiful, tragic mother – so alone in her torment; the woman, once so vital, so vivacious, now unresponsive, staring, lost in her private limbo . . . Limbo? Was it better there? Abbey gripped the cushion as the boarding outside creaked again. Was it better in a world where panic was dulled by medication? No! She shook her head. No.

Bang bang! A loud knock on the door.

A scream ripped from her.

'Miss Roberts, it's PC Stapleton! Are you all right?'

'I'm not going crazy!' she shouted at him. 'I heard him out there! He was there!'

Stapleton stayed for half an hour, his partner searching around whilst he made tea for the three of them.

'Are you sure you're okay?' they asked when a call came through. 'We have to attend an RTA.'

'Yes.' Maybe she had imagined the stalker, maybe it *was* a cat . . . It was almost dawn and Abbey felt her panic receding.

Jake hadn't tried to contact her again and Abbey was relieved about that. It was sad relief, though, because he'd given her up so easily. Her tormentor, after toying with her, became strangely silent – and that was the difficulty; she never knew when or where he would strike at her next . . . Or if, the next time, she would be taken to that dark, suffocating hell.

But she didn't think so. Not yet. He was biding his time, wearing her down, making certain she was so close to cracking that she would be an irretrievable wreck . . .

just as her mother was. A psychological weakness that her tormentor knew about, played upon. Because always lurking was the threat of insanity, the silent world where day and night had no meaning; decisions had no meaning.

Absently, Abbey tidied the kitchen and lounge, showered and pulled on her jeans and a huge white T-shirt; she took her sketch pad out onto the verandah to await her visitors.

'Rick, it's great to see you.' Abbey poured him a coffee and they stayed out on the verandah. 'I'm glad you got here first.'

'Why's that, then, Abb?' He grinned. 'Afraid you'll get a lecture from your dad for not getting enough sleep?'

'No.' Abbey chuckled and realized how much she'd missed the outside world. 'It's just sometimes he still smothers me, you know? It's hard to explain, maybe it's because he's not Pop – ' Her words drifted, her attention snapped when Nedwell Roberts's car drew up behind her home.

'Is there anything else worrying you, Abb?' Rick asked tentatively. 'You seem a bit tense.'

'I'm fine. Let me show you what I've been working on.'

'These are beyond incredible.' Rick whistled at the progress Abbey had made on the paintings that had only been pencil outlines the last time he'd visited. The detail was minuscule, fantastic. 'You just get better and better.' He glanced up at Abbey, couldn't ignore the mauve smudges beneath her eyes any longer. 'You should get out and have some fun, Abb.'

'Lynn's coming to visit tomorrow. Remember you met her at the exhibition?'

'Great. Get out and spoil yourself a bit, it'll do you good.'

She merely nodded. Nedwell Roberts waved from the path and approached the verandah.

'Darling,' he said as he stooped to kiss Abbey's cheek, then shot Rick a piercing glance. 'You've been working Abigail too hard. She looks dreadful.'

Abbey rolled her eyes as she poured another cup of coffee. 'Rick doesn't stand over me with a whip, Father, I work at a pace I set myself.'

'Thank you.' He took the coffee cup from Abbey. 'It's not as if you need to work, is it?' He sipped the scalding coffee. 'You've enough money in trust – you needn't lift a finger for the rest of your life.'

She frowned at Nedwell. 'I don't paint for the money, I do it because I need to.'

Rick looked vaguely uncomfortable whilst they ate; as soon as they finished, he pushed up his sweater sleeve and glanced at his watch. 'I'll have to shoot off in half an hour, Abbey. How about I take these in for you?' He gathered up their plates and nodded at her to follow him inside.

'I've a mega-cheque for you in my pocket, Abbey, but I didn't want to discuss business in front of your dad.'

'Thanks.' She took the money from him. 'I don't know when I'll have these paintings finished, there's still a lot to do on them.'

'Hey, whenever you're ready. I didn't expect you to have done as much as you have, Abb. Listen, I think you should take off again, have another break – the world can wait for your work for a couple of months.'

'Do you really have to dash off?'

'Tactical exit – I don't think your dad approves of me.'

Abbey couldn't deny that. But she couldn't fathom a reason for the animosity she sensed. '*I* approve of you.'

Rick laughed. 'I'll make the coffee, you go and have a chinwag with Nedwell.'

'Cheers.' Abbey joined her father. 'I didn't appreciate you discussing my finances in front of Rick.' The words shocked her as much as they did her father.

'Only because it's true,' he shot back. 'You should paint as a hobby, not this – you look like you're killing yourself. You simply must take better care of yourself, or you'll end up like your mother.'

'I'm not strung out. And I'm not looking worn out because of my painting.'

'Oh?' He lit a cigar, blew the smoke out slowly. 'Why then? Are you not well?'

'I had an affair and it didn't work out.' She grasped that as an excuse, because it was only part of the reason.

'Is it over now?'

'Yes.'

'Miles.' Nedwell tapped a wodge of ash from his fat cigar. 'I heard from his father he was entertaining several of the nurses. I'm surprised you let that upset you.'

Somehow, Abbey didn't want to talk about Jake, she wanted to keep it all close, private. Jake. He flitted so often in and out of her thoughts that he was part of her life now. Even knowing she couldn't contact him again, he'd become part of her.

'And I'm surprised Miles was indiscreet after all the trouble he took getting introduced to you.'

272

Shrugging, Abbey stood to take the coffee tray from Rick. 'It surprised me too.'

'I'll have to leave shortly.' Nedwell flicked through his diary. 'I'm *en route* to the city; I'm calling in on your mother first. Have you visited her lately?'

'I'll come with you,' Abbey said on impulse, frowned when her father looked displeased.

'Go another day, she can't cope with two visitors at once.'

Abbey glanced at Rick, who raised his brows slightly. 'Fair enough.' She drained her coffee cup. 'I'm having a car delivered tomorrow, I'll drive there later in the week.'

'A much better idea, darling.' He patted the back of her hand and smiled. 'I'll just use the little boy's room, then I must take my leave, Abigail.'

The three of them walked up the hill to where the cars were parked and Rick gave Abbey a hug. 'Now, you ring me if you want to talk, okay?'

'Thanks.' She squeezed his hand. 'I will.'

Her father hovered whilst she waved Rick on his way. She recalled another time, so clearly, when she'd waved Jake away from this very spot; when she'd known there was something special between them. His words: 'You know, Abbey, if we'd spent any longer together, I don't think you'd need that note pad of yours.'

'Abigail?'

'Yes?'

'I said, are you sure there's nothing else bothering you besides the upset with Miles?'

Confused for a second, because she didn't remember her truth-bending exercise, Abbey looked at him vaguely. Then she clicked into gear. 'Don't worry about

273

me. Everything's fine.' She walked him to his car. 'Will you take some flowers to Mum for me? Tell her I'll visit her soon?'

'I'll do better than that.' Nedwell smiled. 'Let's drive into town and you can pick out a bunch.'

'I haven't got my purse – '

'Really, Abbey, as if I'd worry about a few pounds.' Shrugging, smiling, she climbed into the luxurious car. 'I haven't locked up.' She frowned down at the beach house.

'We'll only be half an hour, I'll drive you straight back.'

'Okay, no one ever comes this way, do they?'

'Very few, Abigail.' He signalled and pulled out on to the bending road.

'How was your business abroad?' Abbey sank into the plush upholstery.

'Not good.' He kept his gaze straight ahead, 'We lost an acquisition I wanted to add to the company portfolio.'

'Where was it?'

'It was in Australia.' He leant forward slightly, flicked on his CD player. 'Your friend Lynn was impressed with this little gadget.'

'She would be – ' Abbey laughed ' – she loves her music.'

'It's the top of the range,' he returned proudly.

And the music set aside the need to talk, much to Abbey's relief.

She nipped out of the car at the flower shop, Nedwell's tenner in her hand, and returned with a colourful bunch of flowers.

'Rick suggested I go away again.' Abbey flicked on the seat belt. 'If I decide to, I'll send you a postcard.'

'I'd appreciate knowing where you were before the arrival of a damned postcard, Abbey. I worry, you know.'

She frowned at that, buried her nose in the scented flowers. 'Well, I probably won't go anywhere.'

'No.' Nedwell leant forward and flicked on the console again, several speakers springing into symphonic life.

As they neared the beach house, he turned the volume down. 'I want you to be honest with me, Abbey. Is there anything else bothering you besides your disastrous love affair?'

'No.' Her reply came too quickly, but Abbey had made the decision weeks ago to deal with her tormentor herself; there was nothing to be gained from having her father worry, and she certainly didn't want to put anyone else in danger. That thought alone brought Jake into her mind. Was he still in hospital? Had he recovered? What did his latest woman look like?

'Are you certain?'

'I fell in love, Father, it's just taking some getting over, that's all.'

'I could have a word with Frederick Pendleton-Smythe, see if we can't get you and Miles back together?'

Sickly, Abbey shook her head. 'No.' The idea that her father thought her so in love with Miles that she was mooning over him was repulsive, but it stemmed questions she didn't want to answer. 'I'm coping, okay?'

'If you say so, Abigail.' He slowed to a halt on the road above her home.

'Do you want me to come inside with you?' Nedwell climbed out of the car.

His offer surprised Abbey. She shook her head. 'Thanks, but I'll be fine.'

Either he didn't hear her or he ignored her reply, because he followed her down the winding little path.

'Do you want a coffee before you go?' Her eyes darted around the house; it had a violated feeling again. There would be a note somewhere – Abbey could sense it. But she didn't want her father to see it. There would be too many claustrophobic questions, too much raking over the coals.

'Ah – ' he looked around ' – no, I'll make a move.' He glanced at the kitchen clock. 'Do get some rest, darling.' He kissed her briefly on the cheek and strode to the door. 'There's no need to see me off.'

Abbey didn't argue, raised her fingers in a wave.

It was in her bedroom, pinned to the quilt with another long nail.

Anger surged through her. Rick! He'd been here each time she'd got one of these. It had to be him. 'No.' She stared at the missive, too churned up to unfold it, shook her head. 'Rick, not you, please – ' she sank to her knees ' – I thought we cared about one another.' Denial held the full impact at bay. 'No.' She replayed the whole lunchtime through her mind, but couldn't recall if she'd left Rick on his own at all.

Angrily, on impulse, she grabbed up the telephone and dialled Rick's number. She got his secretary, 'Rick's at an afternoon appointment, Abbey. If it's urgent, I can give you a number to reach him.'

'It's urgent.'

'Okay.'

* * *

276

'Rick?'

'Abbey, what is it?'

'Did you go in my bedroom today?'

'What?' He sounded completely shocked. 'Abbey, what are you talking about?'

'Did you leave a letter nailed to my quilt?'

'What! Of course I didn't! I gave you the cheque in an envelope. The closest I went to your bedroom was the kitchen.' He paused. 'Abbey, has something happened? Do you want me to come over?'

'No!' She began to tremble. 'No, I don't want to see anyone.'

'Okay, let's get this straight – someone left you a note?'

'Mmm.' She stared at it through her open bedroom door.

'It wasn't me. What does it say, Abbey?'

'I haven't looked.'

'Get it while I'm on the phone. I'll stay on the line while you look, Abbey.'

When she didn't reply, Rick pushed her. 'Abbey, you can have the police check me out – anything – I swear I didn't go in your room.'

'Wait there.'

Her pulse pounded when Abbey pulled the note from her bed. The obscenely ugly writing glared up at her: *Soon you will sleep the sleep of the distraught forever. All that is yours will be mine.*

'Abbey?'

She grabbed the phone, dropped it and picked it up. 'I'm here.'

'Shall I call the police?'

She shook her head. 'I'll do it.'

'I'll come and stay with you, Abbey.'

'You mustn't! Just believe me, Rick, you mustn't do that.'

'I'll be there in half an hour, you sound like you need company.'

'No, Rick – don't!'

But the line was dead.

She tried to ring him back, but he'd turned off his phone; she rang his secretary's number, but the line was engaged.

'Tell him not to come here, please!' she beseeched the heavens. 'He'll only get hurt!' And the other, horrible suspicion: if it was Rick, if he was her tormentor, he'd have her cornered.

On impulse, she tried Lynn's number.

'Hey! Abbey!' Lynn enthused. 'I've just filled up' with petrol ready for the drive to your house tomorrow.

'Could you come now? I wouldn't ask, but I need to see you.'

'Now? I guess so, but I need a kip before I set off, give the Friday traffic time to clear out of the way?'

'Oh, thanks, Lynn.'

'No probs, I'll be there around midnight.'

Abbey shivered. She hoped she was right. If there were two people around her at the same time, there was no danger to her friends and associates. And somehow, she sensed it was just men who drew out her tormentor's ire.

She heard a car screech to a halt on the top road, put on the outside lights.

'Abbey?' It was Rick's voice.

She called back to him.

'This is why you're looking so rough, isn't it?' He

held the note, the shock in his expression so real that Abbey doubted Rick was her tormentor.

'It happened after your last visit, too. That's why I thought – I'm sorry.'

'Can I use your phone? I need to cancel an appointment for this evening.'

'Course.'

During the following couple of hours, Abbey told Rick everything, how the torment had begun on the night of her exhibition.

'I asked Lynn to drive up tonight, Rick. There's something else – the last note implied that any man involved with me, or helping me, would be in danger too.'

'I don't know how you stay here on your own, Abb. Wouldn't you be better taking off for a while?'

'I could. But he knows everywhere I go. The only place I feel safe is in my studio. I've been sleeping in there.'

'Have you contacted the police about this latest threat?'

'They'll send someone over when they've got the time, probably tomorrow morning.' She frowned. 'What could they do? We're talking about a monster who took me right out from under the noses of my parents, Rick.'

'Okay, look, if you and Lynn are crashing in your studio, I'll stay the night in your room.'

'I'd be scared for you.'

'The lounge, then? I'll crash on the settee.'

'Rick, you don't have to do that.'

'And before I leave you girls to it in the morning, we'll go over this whole place together to check for notes, okay?'

The panic was receding a little in Abbey, relief that

her isolated attempts to deal with the situation had at last been shared. 'Rick, thanks.'

'Abb!' Lynn got there a little before midnight. 'Find me a bed, I'm bushwackered!'

Lynn's arrival brought light into the place and lifted Abbey's spirits; she hustled her friend into the studio. 'It's put-me-up's, I'll explain tomorrow.'

'Honey, it could be a washing line and I'd sleep like a log.'

True to his word, Rick checked over every inch of the beach house with Abbey at his side before he left the following morning. Lynn followed them, a piece of thick-cut toast in one hand, a coffee in her other, picking up snatches of what had been taking place, gasping with horror as she learnt more.

After Rick left, Lynn shook her head. 'Sweetheart, I need to get you out of this place for a while. What have you been doing to yourself? You look shot! Have you given up eating or something? Boy, that exhibition of yours was great, wasn't it? How's Miles?'

Kept busy answering Lynn's questions for a couple of hours, Abbey finally let her friend convince her they should go out for lunch. 'I'm staying for a couple of days, Abb, and I'm not leaving this place until you start looking better. And you can tell me all about your boat hunk and the stuff you got up to.'

But Abbey told Lynn only the barest facts about Jake, 'I finished with Miles when I got back. It didn't feel right any longer.'

'Happens like that.'

* * *

'I love this place.' Lynn parked close to the marina, then they headed for, and slumped into seats at, the pavement café. 'The seafood is lush.' Within seconds, the waiter brought them menus. The normality of Lynn's bright chatter soon began to chase away the shadows. 'Let's get rolling drunk and stay in town here tonight.'

Laughing, Abbey placed her order and relaxed back in her chair. 'That sounds like fun.'

'No "sounds like" about it, mate. We can eat, drink, spend, drink, get dolled up, dance – '

'And drink?' Abbey shot back wryly.

Plans for the rest of the day grew more and more ridiculous whilst they ate and Lynn knocked back her fourth large glass of wine before setting the empty vessel down.

Her eyes fixed on something behind Abbey. 'Oh, God, Abbey, I'm in love . . .'

Curious, Abbey twisted around; her wine glass jerked from her fingers, crashed to the pavement. Jake! The tall, powerful figure walking toward the restaurant was Jake.

'Oh, heavens,' her husky voice catching. Shocked by the impact he had on her after so many weeks apart, Abbey slapped her hand over her mouth to keep from calling to him and turned her back to him.

'I saw him first,' Lynn joked, then, 'Abb, you look like you've seen a ghost. Wassup?'

'Shh – ' Abbey picked up the discarded menu and opened it around her face ' – that's him.'

'Jake?' Lynn said too loudly, and Abbey cringed.

'Shh!'

A shadow fell across their table. 'Don't blame your

friend, Abbey, I'd already seen you.' His tone was rough; slowly, Abbey let the menu slide to the table.

'Introduce us, then, Abb!' Lynn piped. 'Where's your manners?'

Abbey could barely draw breath; she was caught in Jake's dark gaze as he searched her face.

His expression hardened. 'Miles let you out of his sight, then?'

She swallowed past the lump in her throat. Grabbed hold of a serviette to keep herself from leaping up and crushing herself against him.

Lynn pulled a face. 'Miles? He's history, mate, she dumped him soon as she got back home!'

'Is that right?' Blue eyes plunged into Abbey, shook her insides.

'Yes,' Lynn blurted out, refilled her glass and slurped on some more wine, oblivious to the turmoil she was causing Abbey.

'I can understand why you gave me the flick, Abbey, but why bother lying?'

'I didn't want to see you again.'

'That was all you had to say. You didn't need to dream up a bloody soap opera.'

'I had my reasons,' she countered, looking away from his intense gaze. 'Leave it, Jake, we've nothing to discuss.'

Lynn crossed her legs and settled back in her seat, nursing her freshly filled glass of wine.

'Look me in the eyes and say that, and maybe I'll believe you.'

Closing her eyes briefly, head down, her voice husky, Abbey whispered, 'It's over – you had what you wanted – just go away, Jake.'

He folded his arms, scrutinized her averted face.

'No.' Jake knew Abbey would look up at him, and when she did, he repeated, 'Tell me you don't care about me to my face, Abbey, tell me to get lost – but look me in the eyes when you do it.'

'Go – away.' She forced her eyes to his, but her focus blurred.

Jake nodded, his stance unmoved, his beautiful, powerful body rigid.

'I said go away.' To her horror, Abbey realized her vision was blurred with tears, and Jake hadn't moved a rock-hard muscle.

'No.'

'You have to – '

'I'm not going anywhere, Abbey. Not until you answer some questions.'

'S'cuse me, gotta go!' Lynn eased from her seat, grimaced in Jake's direction as she hurried indoors.

Pulling a chair across from a nearby table, Jake sat, tugged Abbey's palm from her eyes.

'What's going on?' He held her fingers tightly.

'You used me!' She cast around for the means to push Jake away. 'I don't want you, you're a pig!' She jerked her hand away from his, jarring his shoulder.

He grimaced, rubbed his shoulder. 'Take it easy, that's where I took the bullet.'

'I'm sorry.' New pain twisted inside her. 'You don't understand!'

'Try me. You said you could tell me anything.'

'Jake, don't do this. I hate what you did to me – to Zav – you two-timing devious bastard! If you'd been faithful to *her* I might still believe in you, but you said you loved her and – '

'What?' His voice was steely, his eyes glittering. 'I *never* cheated on Zav, Abbey.'

'Yes, you did! Miles said – '

His jaw tensed. 'Miles said? That means it's true?' Jake's thumb brushed the wetness from Abbey's cheek, and when she shook her head, moved away, his warm tones filled her. 'I used you to get at Miles because I was hurting so bad.'

Abbey looked down at the table, Jake stumbled on, everything was coming out wrong, clumsy; in a second she'd get up and walk away, and he didn't blame her. 'I'm sorry, Abbey,' he faltered and Abbey looked up to see Jake struggling. 'Whether you believe me or not, I didn't mean to hurt you – it was Miles I was gunning for.' Because Abbey listened, yet didn't respond, Jake fumbled on. 'For what it's worth, I've never cheated on a woman.' He shrugged to cover his mounting nervousness. 'I – er – I guess you believe Miles.'

'Why would Miles lie?'

'I reckon he figured if he couldn't have you, Abbey, he didn't want me in the running.' Jake spread his fingers around the back of his neck, unable to tell from Abbey's expression whether he was gaining ground or blowing it completely.

'So what are you saying, Jake? That you're sorry?' That husky voice of hers hit him straight in the guts, made him even more nervous, but defensively so.

'I'm saying I made a big mistake and, yeah, I'm sorry. But I'm not going to spend the rest of my bloody life paying for it. If you want me half as much as I want you, give me a chance, Abbey.'

'If you care for me at all, Jake, don't come anywhere

near me again.' Abbey sprang to her feet and hurried toward the inside of the restaurant.

'No!' He caught Abbey's wrist, spun her round, his arm clamping around her waist. Instantly, his mouth found hers, enticing, offering her the world. The warmth of his body against hers drew a small moan to live and die in Abbey's throat.

So many emotions crashed and whirled inside her; the bittersweet memories of their time together gripped her. Abbey wanted to laugh and cry at the same time because there had never been anyone who could instantly make her feel so safe, so strong, yet so feminine and sensual. And she had never loved anyone so much.

But it hammered away inside her mind that surrendering to Jake's potent, single-minded need would be as good as signing his death certificate.

'Abbey, I've missed you.' His dark eyes searched hers; his fingers splayed along her jaw. 'I couldn't get you out of my head.'

Being cold wouldn't do it now, only the truth would do it. 'A lot has happened, Jake. We can't go back to how we were.'

She felt his muscles tense beneath her fingertips. 'Have you got someone else?'

'No.'

'It's nothing we can't deal with then.'

'Jake, it's something I can't deal with – just being near me is putting your own life in danger.' She shook her head slightly; her burnished, sunlit curls fell over his fingers. 'The bullet that landed you in hospital, it was because we'd been together.' She caught at her bottom lip. 'Next time he'll kill you and I don't want you dying for me!' Trying to pull away from Jake was useless.

His expression was implacable, his arms like bands of steel around her waist. 'What gives you the right to make that decision for me? Have you stopped to think how I'd feel if something happened to you?'

'You'd find someone else, Jake. I don't need anyone else, but I need to know you're safe!'

He frowned at her. 'It's not the first time I've been shot at, Abbey, and it won't be the last – that bullet was meant for my client.'

'No, it wasn't! That's how it was supposed to look to everyone else.'

Jake guided Abbey back to the table, where Lynn sipped merrily on her wine, raising her glass in their direction; he drew a chair close up to Abbey, listened carefully whilst she explained about the latest notes, about Miles's accident and the suspicion his Porsche had been tampered with, about the fact that her tormentor knew the two men she had been involved with were in hospital – and the inference was that he'd put them both there.

'Why didn't you tell this before?'

'If I'd come to see you, I'd have put you in danger. You wouldn't be alive now.' She added quietly, 'I've lost enough, Jake. I lost Pop when I was eight – it all stemmed from that bastard meddling in my life. My mother remarried, but she never recovered from Pop's death. She had a breakdown not long ago.'

'Have you seen her lately?'

'Not very recently – ' Abbey's words a whisper ' – I'm going to visit her in two days.'

'Do you guys mind if I go and do some shopping? My wages are burning a big hole in this pocket.' Lynn tapped her hip.

'We'll be here or – ' Jake glanced at Abbey ' – we'll be on my boat, *Free Spirit*, first one down at the jetty, Lynn.'

'Magic.' Lynn gave a little wave, 'See you in a bit!'

'I don't want anything else to happen.' Abbey's voice was husky as they watched Lynn stroll away. Her eyes met his. 'It was hard enough facing up to the fact that you'd been shot because of me.'

'Getting shot was the easy part – you stonewalling me was the tough bit.' His eyes were dark, intense. 'Abbey, you can't make this decision for me.'

'I won't have you in my life, Jake.' Her tone soft, yet insistent. 'The price is too high.'

'Why?'

'Because I care about you.' Her green eyes captivated Jake. 'I hate what you did, but I don't hate you. It'd be easier if I did.' Regret flickered in her eyes. 'Things are never that simple though, are they?'

'If you care, don't cut me out, Abbey.'

'I have to. Imagine, Jake, if you'd felt in any way responsible for Zav's death – wouldn't it have been a thousand times worse?' She touched the back of his hand with her fingertips. 'Besides, we're wrong for each other, we both know that.'

Jake leant back in his chair, ran his fingers through his hair. 'You're asking me to walk away and leave you to face this creep on your own? Because you think we're wrong for each other? Because you're afraid of losing someone else? No way.'

'It's not your choice, it's mine. We don't have a future.'

'No, Abbey, you don't understand.' Jake leant to-wards her, rested his elbow on his knee. 'I'm not going

287

anywhere. You can't say you care about me and expect me to leave.'

'Admitting I care doesn't mean you have to stay, Jake. I thought you'd be running the three-minute mile about now.'

'However this thing between us started, Abbey, it isn't going to end with me running the three-minute mile in the opposite direction.'

Despite the seriousness of their conversation, a smile twitched at the corner of Abbey's lips. 'That's not too encouraging, Westaway, not after the last promise you made me.'

His words, 'You'll be the one to walk away', moved tangibly in the air between them.

Jake grimaced. 'I want you back.'

'It doesn't change anything, Jake,' Yet even as she spoke, the simple honesty of Jake's words moved her.

'Hell! Abbey, how many bloody ways do I have to try and say I need you?'

'*Without* swearing?' The wry humour in her soft, husky voice gave him a glint of hope, but he knew he'd have to give like he hadn't in a long time. Sincerity in romantic relationships was something he'd sacrificed a long, long time ago; sacrificed to stop feeling the pain . . .

'I care.' Jake looked uneasy. 'I wish I could turn back the clock, start again, wipe out the rotten things I did to you. I want your trust back – I need you.'

'I can trust you as a friend, Jake, but I don't want to get involved with you again.' Heat rose to pinken her pale cheeks as she remembered Jake's lovemaking genius. 'I'm not prepared to be just another conquest. Not for any man, not even you.'

Jake literally felt her slipping out of reach. He'd

288

forgotten just how hard Abbey could dig in her heels. Just because she said it quietly, didn't mean she meant it any less. 'I really screwed up, I'm sorry, Abbey.' For a long moment, he stared at her, burning inside with regret, no one to blame but himself.

Jake knew he should just get up and walk away, but he couldn't. Abbey couldn't put it any plainer, no second chance. He wanted to give her something – like himself, with as many strings attached as she wanted to tie on; like his boat – or the moon – anything Abbey wanted, he'd give her. But how the hell did he say something like that? If he didn't care, it'd be easy. That was the pig of it, it was only hard to say because he *did* care.

'If you ever need anything, Abbey – '

The answering smile was faint, but it was still Abbey's unique, knee-buckling, crooked smile, letting him off the hook. 'Thanks, Jake.'

'Hope you guys ain't driving back tonight?' He glanced at the empty wine bottles amidst the coffee cups.

'No. We booked in here.' She gestured to the Tudor-fronted seafood restaurant behind her, sensing Jake's reluctance to go.

The sensual glint in Jake's eyes stole Abbey's breath. How many times had she imagined seeing him again with that exact expression? More than once a minute.

'I'll be here for a while; I've some work to do on the boat.' He spotted Lynn approaching the restaurant and rested his hand on Abbey's forearm. 'I mean it, Abbey, if you need anything – just ask.'

Abbey committed every detail of his face, his body, to memory as he leant towards her, she thought just to peck her cheek, but his mouth covered her lips in a hard, brief kiss. And in an instant, Jake was gone as suddenly as he'd arrived.

'Wo-ow! Abbey, when you said he was hunky, I never thought he'd be that gorgeous!' Lynn dropped her shiny carrier bags to the pavement. 'You two sort out your problems?'

Abbey's eyes were brighter than they'd been since – forever; her cheeks were flushed. 'Yes, we're just friends.'

'Dangerous!' Lynn pulled a white blouse from one carrier. 'I don't kiss my "friends" like that!'

'What can I do, Lynn? He'll be putting himself in danger if we get together.' Briefly, Abbey went on to explain, 'It's not worth it for something that'll fizzle out in no time.'

'A rock and a hard place.' Lynn gathered up her bags. 'Come on, Abb, let's get togged up for a night out, that'll cheer you up.'

Strangely, though, there was comfort for Abbey in her unexpected meeting with Jake. She instinctively knew however many women there were in Jake's past, he wouldn't tell any of them he cared unless he meant it. He might tell them he loved them to get them into bed – but 'caring' – that was something different altogether.

Jake would be on the seas within days – restless, the threat of being tied down driving him where she'd never see him again.

But he'd be safe. He would be safe. Nothing else mattered. It was the right thing to do – and she'd done it.

'Why?' she whispered to the mirror whilst Lynn showered in her own room next door. 'Why does doing the right thing have to be so – so bloody *awful*?'

CHAPTER 11

The club was noisy; flashing, coloured lights and the crush of revellers saw Abbey and Lynn escape a little before midnight.

The fresh air outside a relief. Lynn said a cheerful goodnight to the burly doorman, Abbey rubbed her eyes to rid them of flashes; the night was faintly misty, deliciously quiet. But only for a second. Sharp rat-tat explosions split the air, then shouts, screams, confusion.

'What the hell? It's in the marina!' The doorman pointed down the hill, pulled a cellular phone from his pocket. 'Police! Gunfire!' he snapped out, then, 'Better send an ambulance – !'

'No!' Abbey grabbed Lynn's sleeve. 'Jake's down there!' Whilst she yanked off her high-heel shoes and dashed straight down the dangerously steep grassy hill, emergency vehicle sirens wailed in the distance. Amongst neat rows of masted vessels, a boat hissed and creaked its last. Flashing blue lights neared, casting their intermittent beams across a pale hull as it subsided.

Shouting, instructions, confusion littered the night. And Abbey knew without any doubt that it was Jake's boat that hissed, flashed like some glowing funeral pyre, then died.

A sense of unreality surrounded Abbey as she dashed towards the jetty. Numb with horror, Abbey became part of a panicked press of helpless onlookers trying to get to someone; only able to watch whilst the emergency services kicked into action. Somewhere, she registered powerful beams of light centred on the marina; but it wasn't real. It was something she was in amongst that couldn't be real.

'Move back, please.' A figure in a white helmet held Abbey back. 'There's nothing to see.'

Everyone stepped back, but no one could tear themselves from the scene.

'Go home, folks, there's nothing you can do.'

'Excuse me – ' Lynn caught the man's arm ' – we've a friend with a boat here. Can we find out if he's okay?'

'We're waiting for Todd, the manager. He keeps a log of owners' movements.'

Todd. The name permeated Abbey's shock, made it all real.

'Come on, folks, move back. If any boats go up, you'll all be in danger from flying debris.'

'But – ' Abbey grabbed the fire-chief's arm ' – what about – ?'

'Come back in the morning, love. It'll take a bit to get sorted here.' Then to a dazed PC, 'Can we get these access streets sealed off?'

Lynn tugged Abbey from the frenzied scene, from the shouts and crush, from the onlookers moving reluctantly back as the police cordoned off the area.

'We'll come back later, Abbey.' Lynn linked her arm

through Abbey's and firmly led her up the winding path to the restaurant-cum-hotel.

'Not Jake, Lynn,' croaked Abbey. 'It can't be Jake's boat.'

'We don't know whose it is.' Lynn had sobered instantly, and when she glanced up the path, she saw a familiar figure running in their direction; he wore jeans, a dark T-shirt, his anguished features stark in the harsh street lights.

'Abbey!'

Her head jerked up, then she was lifted clean off her feet and crushed in Jake's arms.

'I thought you might be down there,' he growled clutching at her. 'Dear God, Abbey – ' intense darkness glittered in Jake's eyes as he pulled away from her to look at her ' – thank God you're okay.'

Abbey clung around his neck, gasped, 'Jake! I love you, God, how I love you.'

Jake's harsh breathing, the power in his arms held the horror at bay; but the flashing lights casting their eerie blue glow, together with the helicopter's throbbing engines and its wide, bright, cone-like beam, kept the horror hovering, kept it alive, brought every shuddering second in Jake's arms into sharp relief.

'What if it's *Free Spirit*?' Abbey whispered. 'Jake – you love that boat.'

'I can replace it.'

Lights were blinking on and curtains were pulled aside all around the bay; like eyes opening sleepily, then being shocked and couldn't close again.

'Guys, I hate to break this up,' Lynn interjected, 'but maybe we'd better get up to our rooms – ?'

Jake glanced down the hill and Abbey caught the rage

293

in his eyes. 'I'm sorry, Jake.' His boat, if it was his, was the one thing he valued.

He frowned at Abbey, a muscle jerking in his cheek. 'I'll worry about it tomorrow.'

The three of them shared a nightcap in the restaurant, drank in stunned silence whilst the rest of the bay opened its eyes and gawked.

Both Jake and Lynn stared in horror at Abbey when she spoke. 'Jake, I can cope with this whole mess, but only if you get right out of my life. If I have to worry about you every second, about what he'll do to you, I'll go insane.'

'You can cut that crap out right away,' Jake shot back harshly.

'But – '

'I heard what you said, Abbey.' His eyes challenged her. 'You ain't taking it back now.'

Lynn yawned. 'Oops, sorry, got to get to my pit, guys. I'll leave you to it.'

Rising to his feet, Jake held out his hand to Abbey. 'That's where we're going.'

As soon as Jake closed the door behind them, he challenged Abbey.

'What are you playing at? You tell me you love me – then you tell me to get out of your life! You'll have to help me out here, Abbey. I'm damn sure you meant it 'cos a woman like you just doesn't bandy words like "I love you" around.'

'I meant it.' Abbey hugged her arms. 'I just wish I didn't.'

Jake leant on the windowsill and looked down on the activity in the bay.

'Where do we go from here?'

'Our own separate ways.' She looked him straight in the eyes; things would never be simple with Jake, they'd never be tranquil. They were worlds apart and always would be.

But Jake was badly off kilter. He'd been waiting outside the hotel for Abbey to return from her night out, unable to accept there was nothing left but 'friendship' between them.

'Is that what you want?'

'No. But it's what I'm going to do.'

'Hell.' Jake raked his fingers through his hair. 'I get shot at, some jerk tries to shoot ten kinds of glory out of me and I still don't get the girl. That's not supposed to happen.'

Despite everything, Abbey laughed softly, her fingers splayed over Jake's firm, shadowed cheek. 'It doesn't have to happen till morning.'

'That's one hell of a tempting offer, Roberts.' His lips hovered close to hers; if they touched, he'd stay. Abbey wanted him so badly, she threaded her fingers around his neck, rose on her tip-toes and brought his mouth down on hers.

Any other woman, Jake thought as he deepened their kiss, his hands running hungrily over her curves, any other woman, and I'd be running that three-minute mile . . .

Jake stirred first, Abbey's soft moan the first sound he heard. A shaft of sunlight fell across her hair, burnished it, made him touch the soft curls.

She'd lost some weight since they'd last made love, not much, but enough to notice, yet she was still lush, exciting, an unforgettable lover; somehow, she sprang to life in his arms. And she loved him. And she made him feel so damn good.

Slowly, Abbey's eyes fluttered open. 'You still here?' That voice huskier, sexier than the memory, the lopsided smile ten times more potent.

'Yeah.'

'Are you waiting for an encore before you leave?' Whilst she spoke, her fingers closed around him, tantalized him until he groaned with need.

'Abbey – ' He frowned lightly, gave up when she wriggled over him, swallowed his objections, then, 'I'm not going anywhere.'

'Good.' She kissed him, explored him, loved him until Jake thought he'd explode; he'd have agreed to anything to keep her.

'Can I ask you something?' Abbey's breathing finally slowed – their lovemaking had been incredible, undeniably so.

'S'long as it isn't a proposal.'

'No.' She laughed, leant over him. 'I won't propose – that evening at your uncle's?'

'Yeah?'

'You were so mean. Why?'

'I was ticked off with myself for caring about you.'

'That's all?' She pushed a lock of hair from Jake's forehead.

A sheepish smile curved his mouth. 'I was jealous of the way you flirted with Luis.'

'He asked me to stay.'

'I was ticked off about that, too.'

'Did you think I would?'

Jake shook his head. 'No.'

'You shouldn't have ignored me, jerk.' She nestled

her leg between Jake's, savoured the lightly furred heat of his skin.

'I don't know what it is about you, Roberts – ' he pushed her gently on to her back, trapped her wrists with his palms ' – but you torment the hell out of my body.'

'I bet you say that to all the girls,' she whispered against his lips as he drove into her.

Jake didn't consider Abbey's words until they showered together and his hands soaped her curves. 'I don't say that to every woman. They usually say it to me.'

She just smiled, that beautiful, vibrant, lop-sided smile, soaped her hands and lathered Jake's lightly furred chest. 'Like I said, you're a macho sex-machine, Westaway.'

'Gee, thanks.' He laughed as Abbey's hands teased him. 'Not now, Roberts, I'm wrung out!' But, unbelievably, he responded.

'Tell that to your body.'

She rinsed the soap from her skin and stepped from the shower.

'Roberts!' His arm snaked out, pulled her back beneath the rods of water. 'You can't do that to me and waltz off!'

'Not my problem.' She rose on her tip-toes and kissed his chin, made to leave the shower again.

'It is.' His arm trapped her waist. 'Don't start what you're not about to finish.' He raised her off her feet.

It was almost lunchtime before they left the room; Lynn had left a message with the receptionist to say she'd gone to have her hair styled – she'd catch them later.

'I'll come to the marina with you, Jake.' Abbey drained her coffee cup. 'You might need a friend.'

'Back to the real world.'

'I prefer ours to the real one.'

Jake gave a single nod. 'Let's get this done with.'

'Hey, Todd.' Jake kept hold of Abbey's hand as he approached the boat-house office.

'Jake.' Todd rubbed his eyes. 'What a bloody night.'

'What happened?'

'Some galoo crept in here and set off a series of tiny explosions around the hull of *Free Spirit*.' He blew a breath. 'No one saw a damn thing.' Todd rubbed his palm against his cheek. 'We've craned her up, Jake; she's a mess, but repairable.

'The police said it was a good thing you'd taken off for the night. Every explosion penetrated clean into the cabin.'

'Oh, God.' Abbey closed her eyes, leant against Jake's shoulder.

'Is she safe to go on?'

'Well, she's got a flotation collar on. The police are on board, better ask them, mate.'

'Sure.'

Todd rubbed his red-rimmed eyes, 'There'll be a night-security guard on the job from now on. Insurance company'll likely insist on it – and probably a video camera.'

'Guess I won't be going anywhere for a while.' Jake grimaced, 'Any idea how long repairs'll take?'

'Couple of weeks.' Todd shrugged. 'Soon as the insurers give the go-ahead, I'll know more. They're coming over any time now.' He filled the kettle. 'Do you two want some coffee?'

'Thanks.' After filling in some forms for Todd, Jake

wandered out of the office and stood beside Abbey, who stared at *Free Spirit* from the jetty.

'What do you think?' Abbey asked.

'Vandals.'

'You sleep on your boat overnight, don't you?'

'Usually.'

'It was him, flexing his muscles.'

Jake dropped his arm along her shoulder. 'We'll never know, Abbey.'

'No. Where will you stay?'

'A hotel.' Jake shrugged, 'Unless you want to return my hospitality for a couple of weeks.'

'Careful, Jake, this could start to sound like commitment.'

'I ain't going to marry you, Abbey, so cut it out.'

She laughed. 'Relax, Jake. If you're really worried about it, you can have your own room. Come and stay for as long as you want.'

'Just two weeks – max.'

'Until your boat's fixed up.'

'Yeah, thanks.' He looked up when a head popped out of the cabin door.

'Mr Westaway? Good, could we ask you a few questions?'

'Can I give them your phone number as a contact, Abbey?'

'Of course.' She recited it.

'Will you be okay with Todd for a while?' Jake kissed her. It would take a while because he had a few questions of his own.

And a few suggestions – none of which he wanted Abbey to hear.

* * *

Lynn stayed with Abbey for another couple of days; the three of them laughed and talked, swam and talked and laughed some more; but Lynn was due to fly out on the long-hauls again and 'had to do some serious sleeping'.

'Now you're looking good, I'm off.' She hiked her bag on to her shoulder. 'And, Jake – !' She prodded Jake's chest. 'When you get sick of trying to figure Abbey here out – ' she gave her pal a cuddle ' – I'm in the phone book – I'll give you the lowdown.'

Rolling her eyes heavenwards as if she'd heard it all before, Abbey grimaced. 'I'll just check around, Lynn. You're bound to have left something behind – a man or something.'

As Abbey disappeared, Lynn elaborated. 'Men get crabby with Abb, because she never plans more than a couple of hours ahead.' They walked slowly along the path to the road. 'Don't book any holidays with her' – Lynn ticked off on her fingers – 'she'll have dumped you by the time it arrives; don't ask her to go out to dinner with you in a month's time – you won't be going around with her then.' Lynn paused. 'And whatever you do, don't for one minute imagine Abbey's your ideal girlfriend – she'd rather paint than have a serious relationship!'

Disbelieving, Jake shook his head. 'So how come she went out with Miles for close on six months?'

'Jake, she went out with him maybe twice a month just to keep him sweet – he had to bulldoze her into it every time. He's crazy about her. Still bugs her, even now – along with every other bloke she's been out with. Difference is, she can't avoid Miles because he's her financial advisor.

'When you get bored, have a listen to her ansaphone

tape.' Lynn fanned her face. 'Since she got that machine, it hasn't stopped buzzing! Men used to phone her agent and piss him off – her father – even Miles!'

'Are you winding me up?'

'Nope. It's not that there've been that many men – well, it depends what you class as many – they just kind of hang in there, hoping for more.'

'You're putting me on.' Abbey? *A femme fatale*?

Abbey ran up behind them, slapped a colourful hairbrush in Lynn's palm. 'Will you come and visit me next time you're home, Lynn?'

'Why don't you bowl up and stay with me for a day or two?' Lynn cocked a brow, glanced at Jake. 'You could come along, Jake – in two or three weeks. I'll have to check my schedules.'

'No, I don't think so.' Abbey's words drew Jake's shocked reaction – he'd been about to say 'okay'.

'Go on – ' Lynn opened her car door 'I'm always coming here. We can go to the theatre, you could show Jake where your father works, do all the tourist stuff.'

'Maybe.' Abbey, Jake noticed, did look distinctly uncomfortable. 'Could we talk about this some other time?'

'Getting you to make plans, Abbey – ' Lynn grimaced comically ' – it's like getting a stone to bleed.'

'I just prefer not to.' She shrugged. 'You know me well enough by now, Lynn.'

'It's been great meeting you, Jake.' Lynn rose on her tip-toes, kissed Jake's cheek. 'Maybe we'll meet again some time.'

'Yeah.' Puzzlement grew inside him. He'd never noticed Abbey's failure to commit to any kind of plan. But he had the strangest sensation that Lynn had being trying to warn *him* from becoming involved with Abbey. Because she didn't want to see him hurt? That's what it felt like. And it was weird. He thought he knew Abbey. She was the one who loved *him*.

Once they'd waved Lynn along the road, Jake tackled her.

'What's the longest you've gone out with a man?'

She shrugged non-comittally. 'Not long.'

'Six months?'

'If you're talking about Miles, it was about that.'

'Does he still contact you?'

'Sometimes.'

'And how many others are there?'

'Other what?'

'Exes – how many of those still "bug" you?'

'A few.'

'How many men have there been?'

'Can you count how many women there've been in your life, Jake?'

'Hell, no.'

'Exactly, and I wouldn't ask you.' She slipped off her trainers. 'Beat you to the sea!'

Jake towelled his hair, pulled on his jeans. When Abbey stepped into the shower, he slipped from the bedroom, making the excuse that he needed a coffee.

Switching on the ansaphone tape in the hall, he rewound it, let it play. He wasn't bored. Just damnably curious.

There were seven messages from Miles, two from her father, one from Rick . . . And all were interspaced with messages from men. Exes. He grew tense as one well-spoken voice said: 'Abbey, I can't get you out of my thoughts. Have dinner with me? Still love you, darling.'

'What are you doing?' Abbey's voice rose behind him as her arm slid around his waist.

'Who was that?'

'Grant Rossington. We went out together a couple of times.'

'The man sounds besotted! He made me want to heave.'

Abbey shrugged. 'It's just the way he talks. He's insincere.'

'Miles is on that thing seven times.' His tone accusory.

'So?'

'You said you'd finished it with him.'

'I have.' Abbey frowned. 'Jake, what business of yours is my ansaphone?'

'Do you do this with all your men, Abbey?' Jake's eyes challenged her. 'Get them on the hook, then ignore them?'

'I have both men and women as friends, Jake. They're being affectionate, nothing more.'

'Sounds like you've slept with the lot of them.'

'Don't be ridiculous! They're friends!'

Jake grasped the scant fabric of Abbey's short black jersey dress, held her at arm's length. 'Including Miles?'

'Miles can't accept I've finished it.' She covered Jake's fist with her hands. 'He'll stop ringing soon.'

'And when I'm on that thing – ' he jerked his thumb ' – trying to get hold of you, will you say the same thing to some other turkey?'

A shocked laugh rose from her – a confused light shone in her eyes. 'Jake, no other man would get away with replaying my tape for his amusement.'

'I'm not bloody well amused.'

Abbey planted her hands on her hips. 'There's nothing to be jealous of on that tape!'

'I'm not – ' Jake drew back from the lie. 'I am jealous. I don't want other men sniffing round you, touching you, I don't even want them on your ansaphone.'

The buttons on her dress popped, scattered on the wooden floor as she yanked from his grip, pulled the telephone plug from the wall. 'Fine! Don't trust me!'

'Abbey!' Jake yelled after her as she ran through the front door, her bare feet making no sound as she fled down the path and along the beach.

'What's happening to me?' Jake rubbed his forehead, stopped himself from running after her, turned back into the kitchen and made himself a coffee, which he took out on the steps. Whatever it was, he didn't like it. It was too intense. He was sounding like a jealous jerk, sounding like he hated to hear women sound. Possessive. 'Time to back-pedal, Westaway.' From the cliff edge, he scanned the beach for Abbey, tried to believe these gushing admirers of hers were only friends.

When she walked leisurely back towards the house, Jake rose to his feet, met her at the top of the path. 'I'm a jerk.'

His words sprang a laugh from Abbey, which surprised him. 'Jake, we're just different. My friends say they love me – yours say, hey, man, you're all right. It all means the same thing.'

'Abbey.' His expression serious as her forest-green eyes met steadily with his. 'You're all right.'

A slow, crooked smile curved Abbey's lips. 'Don't

look at me like that, I've got a painting to work on.' But whilst she spoke, Abbey threaded her fingers around his neck. Laughing, Jake raised her on to the bottom step and kissed her, his fingers touching her naked skin where her torn dress fell open. 'Give me an hour, Abbey, then you can paint all you like.'

Frissons racing over her skin, she closed her eyes briefly as Jake unfastened the remaining two buttons down the front of her dress. His tanned, strong hands stood out against the paler gold of her skin; his smouldering blue eyes were so potent.

'How private is this place?' his lips whispered against her sensitive skin. Abbey's unique perfume filled Jake's senses, her skin soft as warm golden satin beneath his calloused hands.

'There's no one around.'

Pure sensuality darkened Jake's eyes. 'Just an hour.'

Far from distracting Abbey from painting, she found Jake's presence inspired her; and ever aware that danger might lurk in the next minute, Abbey more than ever enjoyed the moment, thought no further ahead. She couldn't afford to let the dark shadows destroy the fling with happiness fate had handed her a second time. Jake – as rough as a dug-up diamond, a lover so skilled he could bring her to her knees; so jealous it frightened and thrilled her. And his moods, so intense; yet his spirit so easy for her to lift.

'If you want a change of scenery – ' Abbey bit into an apple as she stretched out on the verandah swing seat ' – I'd a car delivered a couple of days ago.'

'Thanks.' Jake, though, felt none of his usual restlessness; he kept expecting it to snap at his heels.

Somehow, Abbey replaced the disquiet in his soul with her easy laughter and that husky, sexy voice. Her lack of demands on his future had a strangely opposite effect on him – it ignited a smouldering unease in his stomach that if he didn't stick around, he'd never find this magic again.

And he was relieved that Abbey had stopped trying to push him away.

'I'm going out tomorrow morning.' She swung her legs off the seat, settled down beside Jake on the top step.

'Where?'

'To visit my mother, about twenty miles along the coast.'

'D'you want company?' Jake stretched out his legs, then leant his forearm across one of his knees. 'We could eat out on the way back.'

'Do you know where my mother is?'

He shook his head.

'She's in Misty Hills, a private psychiatric hospital. It's a beautiful place, Jake, but she doesn't talk much. She doesn't seem to want to.'

Jake's eyes reflected the tragedy, but they didn't shy away. 'What's her name?'

'Rebecca.' A wistful look crossed Abbey's features. 'The doctors always thought she'd make a full recovery, but she never has.'

'Was her breakdown connected with your kidnapping?'

'I don't know, it was so long ago. She tried so hard to bring her life around for my sake. Neither Mum or Pop mentioned what had happened. I couldn't – it was all a blank to me. I imagine they didn't want to talk about it in case it triggered off my memory.'

'Your Pop? What exactly happened to him?'

'Pop's heart was weak and he died eighteen months after the kidnap. Those who knew him before I was kidnapped said it changed him.'

'So Nedwell's your stepfather?'

Abbey nodded. 'I think, for my sake, Mum remarried quickly, tried to fill the gap in both our lives; Nedwell had worked closely with Pop for years, he'd always been around, like an adopted uncle.'

'Filling gaps doesn't work.' Jake sighed. 'It must have been hell for your mum. Since Zav died, I tried plugging the gap – that was after just a couple of years together. It's tough.' He covered Abbey's hand. 'For you, too.'

After a moment's silence, Abbey pulled herself back. 'I take her a painting every time I visit.' She smiled at Jake and Jake thought his guts had been ripped right out. 'Sometimes she speaks. Sometimes she smiles. Sometimes she does neither.' Abbey hooked her elbow around Jake's neck. 'I'm going to give her a portrait of you this time.'

'I want to come with you.'

'I've always gone alone.' Abbey slid into Jake's lap. 'It's too private to share my mum's illness with anyone.'

A frown knotted Jake's brow. He couldn't tell whether this would be one of those times when Abbey would dig in her heels, or give in suddenly, with a smile.

'Do I get to see the painting?'

'Sure.' She sprang from his lap, tugged his hand and pulled him towards her studio. 'You are highly honoured, Westaway – ' she held the door for him ' – no man has stepped foot through this door until now.'

Jake looked around the light, airy room, the lighting

307

natural, capitalizing on the tall windows and pale walls. A humongous bean bag sat in the dead centre of the white ceramic floor. The atmosphere was wonderful. Pure Abbey at her best – without the shadows.

'Here.' She handed him the small acrylic portrait. 'Is he gorgeous, or what?'

Jake laughed. 'Outstanding.' It was brilliant. 'Did you do this from memory?'

'Yes, I shoved the photograph of you and I down the waste disposal in a temper.'

'Shame, that was some picture.'

'I know, but I didn't appreciate the reason for it.'

'I think I'd just as soon forget it, too.' Jake grimaced. 'I ain't too proud of myself.'

Shrugging, Abbey rose on to her tip-toes and kissed him hard before moving away. 'It's past, forget it.' She gathered up a sketch pad and pencil, a small box of water colours and pushed on her sunglasses, perched a white peak cap on top of her swirling curls. 'I'm going on the beach for a while. Just make yourself at home, help yourself to whatever you want.'

Jake chuckled at that. 'If I did that, you wouldn't get much painting done.'

He expected her to move out of her studio door, but Abbey turned on the spot, that slow smile lighting her features. 'Ever made love on a bean bag, Westaway?'

CHAPTER 12

'Let me pay for those, Abbey.' Jake pulled a note from his black jeans and threw it on to the flower-shop counter.

'You'll have to give them to Mum, then.' She passed him the delicately scented freesias. 'She'll love you forever, they're her favourites.'

'I can tell you one thing, Abbey, I've never been "loved" by a girlfriend's mum. I'm the kind of jerk they lock up their daughters against.'

Laughing, Abbey picked up a bottle of carbonated water, spotted a huge container of the same and heaved it to the counter of the greengrocers. 'This should last Mum a while, she polishes off a whole bottle every time I go.'

They climbed into Jake's Land Rover, more fun, Abbey said, than her showroom-new car.

'Are you nervous about today?' Abbey asked as Jake pulled out into the road.

'Yeah, a bit. It's not knowing what to expect.'

'Just be yourself, Jake. She's just lovely.' Abbey bubbled with excitement. 'I'm really glad you're with me.'

Jake shot Abbey an uncertain smile. 'How often do you see her?'

'A couple of times a month. My father goes a lot more.'

'How come?'

'I spent a long time discussing visiting regimes with the head honcho; apparently, any more would be stressful for her. It's me. She only gets upset after my visits.' Sadness stabbed through her, 'I'd go every day if I had my way.'

'There's nothing to stop you from asking about that when we're there.'

'I do, I always ask. But the chief psychiatrist's adamant.'

'Hell, if I wanted to see someone, I wouldn't listen to that crap.'

'You would, Jake, if it was for their good, you'd do anything.'

'If you'd got your own way, we wouldn't be together right now.' He changed down gear around a sharp bend and Abbey thought how sexy he made that simple man-oeuvre appear. And Jake was right, his words struck a deep, deep chord as he added with uncharacteristic brev-ity, 'I'll take what we've got right now every time, Abbey.'

'Even given the danger?'

He shrugged, kept his eyes on the road, 'It doesn't make any difference. Life was the pits without you.'

'Poetic you're not,' Abbey laughed huskily, deeply touched, 'but that's the nicest thing you've ever said to me.'

'I'm working on it.'

'Don't.' She wriggled round to watch him better, buried her nose in the freesias. 'I like the way you mean things. It wouldn't sound right coming from you if you dressed it up.'

He slowed at a large black and white Tudor-style sign. 'This it?'

'Yes.'

Rebecca Roberts's cheerful black nurse greeted them, 'You're looking well, Abbey!' Her beautiful soft brown eyes lit on Jake. 'Oh, and who's your friend?'

'Callie, this is Jake.' They shook hands and Jake visibly relaxed.

'Ooh, nice!' She winked at Abbey. 'Sweetheart, Rebecca's been off her food for a couple of days; the doctor took a good look over her, she's not sick or anytin', but he stopped all her medication because she's not eatin'. We got her on liquid vitamins and plenty of drinks. We been encitin' her wid tasty food, but she's not interested.'

'Where is she?' Abbey looked so upset, Jake put his arm along her shoulder, squeezed her.

'Bin expectin' you, down by the river.'

Abbey bolted from them, ran down the gentle slope.

'You look like a coffee man to me, Mr Westaway. I'll bring out some?'

'That'd be great.' Jake felt vaguely uncomfortable. 'Shall I leave them to it for a while?'

Callie chuckled richly. 'That girl, got no manners stranding you here! Come on, I'll take you down there. She worries too much about her mum. I tell her, I take good care of your mama, girl, don't worry!'

'How often does Nedwell visit?' Jake kicked a small stone with his toe, looked down sideways at Callie's kind, round face.

'Three or four times a week. Spends an hour with the staff, checking every detail, then he talks to Rebecca for an hour, leaves again.' She grinned broadly, pointed to

Abbey. 'Now, that girl, when she comes for her two visits a month, she's here from breakfast time till sundown!'

Jake could hear Abbey's deliciously husky tones; she sat facing her mum. As Jake and Callie approached, Abbey rose to her feet, took Jake's hand and gave him a smile that made him feel about fifteen feet tall.

'Coffee, everyone?' Callie beamed. 'I'll bring one for myself! We'll have a party!' Winking at Jake, she moved off up the gentle, grassy slope.

'Mum, this is Jake Westaway.'

Jake almost crumpled to the thick, check rug; Rebecca Roberts wasn't some poor, wizened form in a wheelchair; she was ethereal, beautiful, so like Abbey. Older but stunning. She didn't wear an old brushed nylon nightgown and pasty-coloured slippers, but navy blue tailored slacks and jumper.

The small portrait was in her lap; either she stared at that, or the ground, Jake couldn't tell; he almost dreaded Rebecca looking up in case she instantly hated him. He felt strangely nervous. 'We brought you some flowers, Mrs Roberts.'

'Rebecca.' Abbey tugged Jake's arm to sit beside her on the rug. 'Mum likes to be called Rebecca.'

Slowly, very slowly, Rebecca moved her gaze from the portrait in her lap to the staggeringly handsome man beside her daughter. Even more slowly, she extended her hand towards Jake.

Carefully, he took her hand and smiled. 'Pleased to meet you, Rebecca.'

For long seconds, Jake fell under Rebecca's scrutiny. He sensed that she, like Abbey, could see things others missed, possessed a heightened knowledge of good and

312

bad, of things that mattered. He hoped Rebecca Roberts realized just how much he cared for her daughter.

And he remained silent, because he didn't make a habit of engaging in inane chatter.

'Shall I tell you how we met?' Abbey talked as if her mother was replying, reading barely perceptible facial expressions. 'I'll tell you everything, soon as Callie comes with the coffee. It's a great story.'

Jake frowned as Abbey looked up at him. She laughed huskily. 'Don't worry, I won't go into detail about our love life.

Groaning, Jake put his face in his palm. 'You're a nightmare, Roberts.' He grimaced. 'I thought this would be painless – you know – what paintings you've done, where you've been! I thought we'd be genteel and drink tea, for heaven's sake!'

Abbey was in hysterics as he dropped his hand from his face. 'I didn't think you'd put me under a microscope!'

'That's something I'll never need to do,' she teased him. 'There's too much of you.' Regardless of her mother's presence, Abbey kissed him as naturally as if they were alone.

Abbey amazed Jake with her candour as she related the details of her exhibition, her loss of speech, how Jake had been about to spend a couple of weeks with his 'luscious girlfriend', but instead had become entangled in Abbey's life. The way her voice had eventually returned. Callie interjected with plenty of 'Oh! Lowdy's' and laughed when Abbey related how the big box of condoms had spilt from Jake's locker, seemed to shout their presence even as she threw them back

313

inside and closed the door on them. She looked tearful when Abbey told of Jake's shooting, how she'd tried to hold him out of her life.

Rebecca's attention was riveted on Abbey; every now and again, her gaze slid slowly to Jake, and she studied him. Unlike Abbey, he couldn't tell what Rebecca was thinking; he assumed it was likely she wished Abbey had never laid eyes on him. He'd been chased away from more than one girlfriend with anything from a yard brush to a tyre wrench.

But when Rebecca sought his gaze, Jake didn't look away – he found himself willing her to understand. He really did care. More than he wanted to admit to Abbey, but if a mother could sense those things, then she would. She would sense that he'd die himself before he let anyone harm Abbey.

'Sounds to me like you two been through some big ups and downs together.' Callie wiped beads of sweat from her forehead. 'How about some lunch? I'm exhausted just hearing about it!'

Jake rose to his feet. 'Abbey packed a picnic, Callie, I'll get it from the Land Rover.'

'I don't hold out too much hope that Rebecca will eat anything, but you never know, Abbey's picnics are the highlight.'

Walking beside Jake to the car park, Callie chatted easily. 'I've looked after Rebecca for the last eighteen months; she's barely changed physically.'

'She and Abbey are remarkably alike.'

'In looks, yes.' Callie took the huge bottle of spring water and a flask from Jake. 'But Abbey's spirit is much stronger. When you think about it, she'd have to be strong with all she's been through.'

314

'The kidnapping?' Jake's dark brow raised slightly in question.

'It didn't end there, though.' Callie waited whilst Jake hoisted out the wicker picnic basket. 'I mean, that girl was kidnapped, lost her pop and got a stepdad all in the space of a couple of years. I've always supposed it was a good thing he was a friend of the family and not a total stranger, and he cares so deeply about Rebecca.'

Jake raked his fingers back through his hair with his free hand. 'Must've been tough for him – a what, nine, ten-year-old girl to take on?'

'Mmm.' Callie responded non-comittally. 'You know one thing that would make me really happy? To see Rebecca make that full recovery the doctor says she's capable of.' She sighed, looked down at the practically identical women on the plaid rug, Abbey talking animatedly; her mother still.

She shook her head. 'All that money Abbey pays me – I'd give it up in a minute to see Rebecca talk and laugh.'

'Doesn't Nedwell provide for Rebecca?' A frown touched Jake's brow.

'He pays for the basics. In the early days, Abbey was here nearly all the time. Rebecca put her foot down, wrote out a note. She does that sometimes. Said she wanted Abbey to get on with her life, wouldn't let her come here every day. After a year, Nedwell's buddy on the staff, some renowned shrink, said Abbey should cut her visits to twice a month. They argued for hours! But that girl stopped arguing dead when she was told it'd help Rebecca recover if she cut back – on account of her getting distressed after every visit. Abbey insisted her mum should have someone of her own – a friend, had to be a qualified nurse. Poor kid, she was devastated.'

315

'Guess you get attached to someone when you work with them every day.'

'I took one look at Rebecca and I had to be her nurse, Jake. She was terrified, all locked in.' She chuckled. 'Call me daft, but I didn't want no one else looking after her. What I'd call a bond formed the moment we met.'

'I can relate to that, Callie. Something very similar happened to me with Abbey.'

They were nearing Abbey and Rebecca, so Callie lowered her voice.

'You know, Abbey is terrified of losing her mind. She thinks she's exactly like her mother, but you get the chance, Jake, you tell her, she's stronger.' A plump brown hand rested briefly on Jake's forearm, 'You tell her, she inherited her mother's beauty but her pop's strength. She don't listen to me.'

'Rebecca!' Callie rolled her eyes heavenwards. 'You just scoffing all that food to make a liar out of me!' The woman chuckled happily. 'Boy! It's good to see you eat.'

Callie's enthusiasm and Abbey's soft, husky laughter mingled with the bird song and ripple of the river over stones. There was a small, wooden ornamental bridge over the shallow river, lush green woods on the far side that hosted a myriad of bird song.

Clearing away the serviettes and chicken bones, strawberry stalks and paper cups, Abbey's gaze moved up to Jake when he spoke. 'This is some beautiful place, Abbey.'

She smiled at Jake, her eyes filled with all she felt for him; strangely, a lump rose in her throat. Abbey loved him so much it hurt.

'Don't look at me like that, Roberts – ' his own words

caught in his throat unexpectedly ' – you'll have me turning my back on a life of playing around.'

She managed a laugh. 'I doubt that.'

All the while, Rebecca watched them silently.

Time moved so quickly, the three of them entertaining Rebecca, whilst she remained virtually silent. Only her unexpected 'yes' or 'no' peppered their conversations.

'The doctor'll be real pleased you got your appetite back, Rebecca.' Callie chattered happily as they strolled slowly toward Jake's Land Rover.

'Back in a minute – ' Abbey had caught sight of Mr Ruddley, the head psychiatric doctor, striding from the car park towards the hospital. She dashed to intercept the tall, sprig-haired man.

'Doctor Ruddley,' she gasped.

'Ah! My word, Miss Roberts!' He stretched out his hand, his manner cordial. 'How is your mother today?'

'Improved – I still don't agree that I should be allowed to see my mother only twice a month.' Because he was listening, looking genuinely sympathetic, Abbey tempered her tone. 'I'd like to come here at least three times a week, like Nedwell Roberts – my father.'

A beeper went off in the doctor's pocket he slipped in his hand, read a code, turned it off.

'The case meetings are in the morning, Miss Roberts – '

'Abbey,' she interrupted him. 'Call me Abbey.'

'As I said, the case meetings are tomorrow.' He tilted his head to one side. 'You are aware we have problems with Rebecca after your visits?' His pace quickened in the direction of the neo-Georgian-style hospital; Abbey hung in there at his side.

'Yes – but perhaps she's upset because I don't come more often.'

'I have to go, Miss Roberts, there's an emergency. Come tomorrow, I've a scheduled meeting – all morning. I'll consult with the team, ask some questions, then meet with you?'

'I'm coming again tomorrow morning.' Abbey raced back to join the others. 'Daniel Ruddley says it's okay.'

Jake took hold of Abbey's hand and studied Rebecca's features for a reaction. There was a glimmer of a smile in her eyes; slowly, it spread to her mouth. 'Come tomorrow, Gaily?' Expectation raised her tone to almost childlike.

Unexpectedly, Rebecca's hand reached for Jake's, a silent question sat in her eyes.

'Yeah. I'll come too.'

For a moment, Rebecca looked frightened; both Abbey and Jake caught the look, and Jake steered her to a bench at the edge of the car park. 'What is it?'

'Don't tell him.' Rebecca formed the words slowly. 'He'll be mad.'

'We won't tell anyone,' Abbey reassured Rebecca, but had no way to know who 'he' was – or even if he existed.

A wistful smile crossed Rebecca's features as Callie performed the evening rituals. 'I'll just collect supper from the kitchen, Rebecca, won't be a jiffy.'

Rebecca knew there was something for her to look forward to, but she couldn't bring it into focus. Then it came to her as the soft evening breeze carried the fragrance of freesias to her: Gaily . . . Her smile was brilliant, but there was no one in the room to witness it.

318

Yes. Gaily was coming tomorrow. Must remember that – hold on to it.

The thready thoughts almost broke when Callie returned with her sing-song, 'Supper, Rebecca!'

The aroma of warm rock cakes mingled with freesias and hot chocolate; the small plastic container holding her nightly medication beside a plastic beaker of water.

Rebecca hesitated before raising the cake to her mouth. There was something she should be doing, or shouldn't be doing. Something she'd been trying to do without telling anyone; but those scents, aromas, they were the safe ones. Freesias meant Gaily had made everything all right. And there was only Callie with her, smiling, encouraging her to eat to 'help the tablets down'.

It made everyone happy when she ate. Tomorrow, she'd be happy, even better than today.

Whilst Rebecca ate, Callie chuntered around, chattering whilst she picked out an outfit for the following day. 'This, Rebecca?'

'Yes,' Rebecca managed to say. Tomorrow would be even better than today!

Callie hung the deep lavender jumper and matching trousers on the outside of the wardrobe door. 'Uh-huh, you look good in this.'

A small smile curved Rebecca's mouth as she swallowed a mouthful of the rock cake. Strawberry jam on it – strawberries . . . Gaily. The thoughts were easier, more lucid; her smile broadened. Almost at the end of it – I must be almost at the end of it.

She was still managing some thoughts, albeit sleepy ones, once Callie had gone and Rebecca enjoyed the softness of deep pillows. She pulled the string to turn on the bedside light and reached for a beaker of water, but

319

her hand trembled badly, unexpectedly, sent the delicate china vase to the floor, scattered the freesias. Shards of colour turned to writhing nest of snakes, stinging, turning red as she tried to fling them, kick them away. 'No! No!' For a brief second, she stilled, liquid warmth drenching her hands and feet; a flash of lucidity reminded her what she'd done wrong. Why she was like this. 'No! No! I forgot!' she screamed, and struggled when hands stronger than her own finally restrained her; firm, kind voices, they tried to help, but couldn't – they wouldn't listen.

On the way back to Fasthead, Jake pulled into a restaurant car-park beside gardens, vast oak trees and couples sitting at picnic benches eating; children running, shouting.

'I've got a horrible feeling something's going on, Jake, and I don't know what.'

'I got the same drift.'

'Mum's never lost her appetite before. And who doesn't she want us to tell we're going again tomorrow?'

Jake rubbed his hand around the back of his neck. 'A doctor? Who knows? Whatever the reason, something was frightening her.'

'Maybe we could find out more tomorrow.'

They ate salad; Jake raised his alcohol-free beer toward Abbey, 'I'll have something stronger when we get home.'

Home. It sounded so good to hear Jake say that; but she merely raised her own glass in return, fully aware he meant nothing by it.

'You ought to contact Todd, get a progress check on *Free Spirit*, Jake.'

'Tiring of my company already, Roberts?'

She slid her sunglasses down her nose and studied him. The day Jake left her life, that would be the day she would mourn like a fool. 'No. Apart from your moods, you're good company.'

'Moods? What moods?' He frowned, fork suspended half-way to his mouth.

Laughing, Abbey wriggled along the picnic bench and moved into the seat beside him. 'The ones you get any time a male friend telephones me.'

Jake nodded, a slow smile curving his mouth. 'Those moods. I didn't think you noticed.'

'It's like having a possessive bear around, Westaway.'

'You complaining?'

'Not yet. I only said you ought to ask Todd how the repairs are going, I didn't say I want you to leave.'

'Yeah.' Jake finished eating in silence. Now he understood what Abbey meant when she'd asked him if he ever wanted to stop time. Stay with Abbey, open-ended, free to take off whenever he chose. Not when *Free Spirit* was fixed, not when Abbey tired of him in favour of some 'lovey', but when he was ready.

Purely out of habit, Abbey pressed the replay button on her ansaphone when she walked into the spacious hall. She shot Jake an amused glance because he hovered, listening.

A stream of messages played whilst she kicked off her trainers and unfastened the top knot of hair, shook it free to tumble around her shoulders.

Her father – how was she? How did she find Rebecca's mood? Lynn – she was busy for a couple of weeks, but would contact Abbey then. Miles, his obvious joy at securing a couple of tickets to an invitation-only Summer Ball – would she come with him? He'd be in a wheelchair, but they could still have fun – strictly as friends. And Rick – was she all right? Would she telephone him to let him know everything was okay?

Grant – would she return his calls?

Abbey watched Jake as he tried to control his tight expression.

'Jake.' She raised up on her tip-toes, threaded her fingers around his neck. 'You're here with me, they aren't.'

Despite Grant's oozing voice in the background setting his teeth on edge, Jake let Abbey cajole his mood around while their mouths met and crushed in a feverish embrace.

Then a voice stayed all movement from them both.

'I'm trying to contact Jake Westaway – name's David Waterman.' The caller gave a local number, then added, 'If you'd get in touch soon – '

Jake's eyes were dark, searching as he raised his mouth from Abbey's.

The loud beeper sounded the end of the telephone messages.

'Who?' Abbey whispered.

Jake shrugged, saw confusion dance briefly in Abbey's eyes.

'I should've told you, I gave Todd your number in case anyone came looking for me.'

A sense that the outside world was about to intrude on them rippled through Abbey. 'How about some coffee?' Her husky whisper broke the looming silence. 'I'll get it while you return that call.'

'Sure.' Jake released her, watched her as she carted the empty picnic basket into the kitchen.

Abbey could hear Jake's deep voice, but not the words; she let it wash over her as she emptied out the basket and made a jug of coffee.

This time next year, would she still be carrying the memory of Jake around with her like something she'd won but had no right to keep?

Served her right for making plans – even a day ahead. It never worked.

Jake smiled when he entered the kitchen, it was one of those 'sorry – gotta go' smiles. And he looked on edge.

'When are you leaving?'

'Day after tomorrow. The good news, is it's for regular clients – I've worked for them before.'

'Oh.' Was she supposed to be thrilled that he was going?

He grabbed up a stool and slung it down opposite Abbey. 'You always knew this wasn't forever, Abbey.'

'It should be. You know this is special, Jake, you're just too chicken to admit it.'

He couldn't meet those incredible eyes; if he did, he'd admit everything and right now, anything was too much.

'Maybe you could go to the Summer Ball with Miles?' Damn, that left a bad taste.

'I will not!' Abbey sprang to her feet. 'How can you say that?' Barefoot, she moved to the front door, searched deep inside herself for the dignity to let Jake go. She didn't want to become just another shrilling discard; yet felt with every molecule of her being an angry need to lash out.

Jake took a deep breath as he watched Abbey slip through the front door; on a scale of one to ten, this shot off the clapometer of tough things to do. He ran his hand around the back of his neck. There must be another way, he tormented himself, knowing there wasn't. If there was, they'd be doing it.

Abbey stared at the lace-edged sea below; recalling vividly the night when *Free Spirit* had been peppered with explosions – the way Jake held her so tightly – too tightly for someone who didn't care. Even if Jake drifted like a cork at sea for the rest of his life, she had to believe he would come back. It was the only way she could cope now, this minute, with him leaving. He *would* come back.

'This is the last time –' Jake jammed his hands into his jeans pockets and strolled out onto the verandah ' – the last freaking time I do something this damn difficult.' She stood at the edge of the cliff, the sea-breeze catching and tossing her golden curls, moulding her plain white T-shirt against lush curves. Jake let his eyes feast on her trim hips, the length of her shapely thighs, bare feet lost in short, spiky grass.

'Yeah, this is the last time,' he muttered under his breath, moving towards her.

That slow, beautiful smile curved Abbey's lips as she turned, sensing Jake's presence. 'Hi' – that single word giving Jake all the freedom he needed.

'Are you okay, Abbey?' He took hold of her out-stretched fingers, the breath all but leaving his body when she kissed his knuckles, the gesture so gentle, he felt something wrench inside.

'I'm okay.'

'Abbey –' Jake pushed the windswept hair back from her forehead.

'I'm okay, Jake, really.'

Leave it, Westaway, his inner voice warned, you'll

blow this if you don't quit this emotional crap.

'Right.' He answered both the voice and Abbey, then walked behind her as she took the sloping path to the beach.

'Will you ring me some time, let me know you're all right?'

'No way. I ain't talking into that thing.' He jerked a thumb over his shoulder towards the beach house.

Abbey laughed, realizing today at least was safe, it was theirs – and tomorrow. It was further than she thought most of the time.

'Maybe we ought to get an early night.' A sexy smile spread across Jake's features.

'It's only eight!' She glanced at the dying sun, a smile beginning at one corner of her mouth.

'Gives us plenty of time.' As he spoke, Jake's arms closed around her.

'I hope Mum talks again today.' Abbey packed the basket with chicken and salad, strawberries and a can of squirty cream.

'Doesn't it happen often?'

She shook her head. 'It's only ever a few words, I think the medication she has makes her too sleepy to respond. I wish they wouldn't give her anything. I wish they'd just let her body mend itself.'

'Yeah.' Jake rubbed his hand around the back of his neck, 'Sometimes people need a bit of help, Abbey.'

'For how long, Jake? It's been so long.' Her words caught as she remembered the vitality her mother exuded – a memory she was frightened would fade too soon.

'Hey –' Jake put his arm along her shoulder ' – Rebecca

325

will recover, Abbey, it just takes some people longer than others.'

'I keep wondering whether I'd be better bringing her here to the beach house, along with Callie.'

'Have a talk with that Ruddley dude, he seems reasonable. He'd know best.' Jake lifted up the basket. 'Come on, let's get going, the weather looks a bit dodgy.'

Thick, ominous dark clouds gathered over the sea; the air was oppressively hot. Her mind in turmoil over her mother, Abbey set aside her sorrow that Jake would be going the following day.

Jake scanned the spot by the river where they'd spent the previous day; raised his hand in a salute when Callie waved to him.

'They're over there.'

'Oh, no.' Abbey's spirits plummeted. 'Mum's been wheeled out – that means she's having a rough day.'

'Maybe seeing you will improve it.'

'Thanks.'

'Hello, Mum.' Abbey leant down to give Rebecca a hug, but met only with the empty expression in her mum's eyes. She fought to keep the shock from her voice as her eyes lit on her mother's bandaged hands. 'What happened to you? Did you fall?' Whilst Abbey unrolled a thick woollen rug over the grass, she continued talking to Rebecca. 'I'm going to have a chat with Daniel Ruddley when he comes to see you today.'

'Callie?' Jake's voice lowered. 'Does Rebecca get many days like this?'

'Not too many this bad. It's the medication, Jake. Apparently, she was very agitated late last night – after I'd gone off duty. The duty doctor reckoned it was a build-up, Rebecca not having been sedated whilst she was off her food.' She shrugged ample shoulders. 'In their wisdom, they likely gave her a syringe full of sedative.' At Jake's frown, she added, 'Sometimes it's the only way, Jake. I couldn't look at the drugs list this morning, Mr Ruddley takes all the notes to case meetings.'

'Will Rebecca even know Abbey's here?'

'I guess, but she won't be responding today – I'd my high hopes up yesterday – ' Callie sighed heavily ' – I really did. There was something inside her fighting back.'

Even the birdsong from the small forest over the river seemed to dim in the incredible heat; perspiration poured down Abbey's face as she kept up her one-sided conversation, pausing now and then for a non-existent reaction from Rebecca. Her voice grew husky after a while, and Jake handed Abbey a bottle of water. 'Here, I'll tell Rebecca about *Free Spirit*. Do you like boats, Rebecca?'

She didn't answer, didn't even look at him; it was too much effort to keep her head up on her neck. There was so many things she should tell them – both – but she couldn't remember any of them. She couldn't remember getting out of bed this morning, couldn't raise a lead-weighted limb. Callie must have lifted her into the chair.

Aware only that her daughter was here with a man who seemed familiar; had she seen him before? But even that silent question was too difficult. It joined the discord in her mind, whirled outward away from the centre of thought and shattered into a million pieces – became as irretrievable as all those other important things.

327

'Miss Roberts?' It was around mid-day and Dr Ruddley's voice silenced the conversation Abbey had taken up with her mother.

Pushing the hair from her eyes, Abbey rose to her feet. 'Hello again.' She extended her hand. 'Mum's not so good today.'

'I'll take a look at her, Miss Roberts – ah – Abbey, then we'll have that chat, eh?'

'Okay.'

Jake took hold of Abbey's hand. 'Let's take a walk on the bridge while the doc does his bit?'

'Callie said they had to sedate your mother during the night.' Jake's expression was serious as he searched Abbey's features for a response. 'Apparently, she was agitated.'

'Yesterday, though, Jake – there seemed to be hope of getting her back. I had this sensation she was coming back.'

He covered Abbey's hand where it rested on the rail of the bridge. 'It'll work out.'

Turning, Abbey wrapped her arms around Jake's waist, helplessness twisting in her stomach; his masculine scent escaped his black T-shirt as his strong arms around her helped to restore her equilibrium.

'I want Mum to have her life back.'

Jake nodded, looked down into Abbey's eyes. 'Yeah, I know.' Strong gentle fingers entwined with her hair. 'But when you've done all you can, you owe it to Rebecca to get on with your life.'

'When I've done all I can.' She rose on her toes to kiss Jake's chin. His mouth found hers and the strength of his almost-savage embrace left her breathless.

Her cheeks were flushed when Daniel Ruddley strode

over to the bridge; his hands were shoved into his trouser pockets, head down.

Jake made to move away, but Abbey caught his hand.

'Physically, Rebecca is fine.' Ruddley clipped open his notes and gestured to a white table and chairs at the side of the bridge.

'Why is Mum kept so sedated?' Abbey frowned, 'Yesterday, she spoke, smiled, there was a huge improvement, Mr Ruddley. All these drugs are wrong – I know she would be better without them – '

Daniel Ruddley held up his palm, 'If I may interject, Miss Roberts? The reason we sedated Rebecca last night was because we believe she tried to kill herself.' As Abbey drew a shocked gasp and crushed Jake's fingers, the doctor paused, then continued gently.

'I had an extended meeting with the night sister over every aspect of your mother's care. It appears from the records that her periods of agitation always coincide with your visits, but there's no evidence of upset following your father's visits. The 'episodes' haven't occurred at any other time.'

The words clawed at Abbey's insides; the oppressive heat scratched at her skin, ripping open pores that drenched her. She could hear Ruddley speaking so calmly, had to force herself to listen.

'I'm afraid I've had to reinforce our earlier decision to keep your visits to a minimum. Try and understand, there's no other common factor – I wish there was.'

'How did she try to kill herself?' Abbey's words a stunned whisper.

'She tried to slash her wrists.'

'No! That's crazy!' Abbey shot back. 'Mum wouldn't do that!'

'Miss Roberts, I know it's a shock. What you have to remember is your mother is here because she's mentally ill. Depression, mood swings are all part of the instability.'

'I don't believe she tried to kill herself.'

'This kind of thing is never easy to accept, Miss Roberts. I read the written report on the incident when we had our meeting earlier.'

'Then whoever wrote it must be wrong!'

Ruddley's patience strained at Abbey's obstinate response. 'Miss Roberts, the night doctor on call out, the night sister – all the staff are highly qualified. There was no deviation in their accounts.'

'Tell me, then – what did their accounts say?'

'Abbey – ' Jake grimaced, he could see she wasn't going to let go of this one ' – what happened isn't Ruddley's fault.'

Daniel blinked his thanks at Jake, but didn't avoid the question. 'In a nutshell, the night sister found Rebecca jumping and screaming at a broken vase, her hands bleeding. She waved a piece of broken china and slashed at her arms. It took the sister and three orderlies to subdue her until the duty doctor arrived. He found lacerations consistent with a suicide attempt.' He paused for breath. 'Fortunately, the blood loss was minimal. Ironically, her agitation lessened the damage.'

Her mother's delicate hands held fragile champagne flutes; they weren't hands that destroyed; they weren't hands that gave up. 'Who gave her china? She shouldn't have been given china!'

Daniel Ruddley looked uncomfortable, cleared his throat. 'Ah – it was the vase you put her flowers in yesterday.'

330

All the while, Callie had remained silent, taking in the details. 'Wish I'd been there,' she whispered to Abbey as Ruddley paced close by, 'but I can't work night and day, I've a family.'

'You don't believe it's true, do you?' Abbey wiped the perspiration from her forehead.

'I only know what the night sister told me when she handed over; Rebecca was sleeping like a baby by then.' She rubbed Abbey's upper arm, glanced at Jake. 'I'll fetch us all a tray of coffee.'

'Mr Ruddley – ' Abbey sighed ' – I just wish I knew why my visits upset Mum; I had the feeling she was happy to see me – and especially yesterday.'

Callie returned with the coffee tray, set it down on the table. 'I'll take Rebecca and me a cup each, leave you with the tray.'

'Sometimes,' Dr Ruddley continued, accepting a coffee cup from Abbey, 'we find it difficult to differentiate between what we want to feel and the signals that are actually being sent to us. What I'm saying, is, you would expect Rebecca to be happy to see you, therefore, that's what you believe.'

'I do believe it,' Abbey said stubbornly. 'You've only known my mother since she came here, Dr Ruddley, I've known her all my life.'

'You knew her, Miss Roberts. Whatever happened to trigger your mother's breakdown changed her. As I've explained before, there's every chance of a full recovery, but there's no time scale for these things. Every patient is different.'

'What would your advice be? That I never visit my mother?'

'Not at all, Miss Roberts, not at all. In the light of last

night's episode, we'll monitor your mother very closely, perhaps slowly lighten her medication. There's every chance you could continue your bi-monthly visits.'

'But not increase them?'

'That's something to aim for in the future, when Rebecca responds more successfully to treatment.'

'Have you spoken to my father? Does he know what happened last night?'

'Yes, we contacted him first thing this morning. He was understandably upset, wanted to come straight over, but we told him there's nothing he can do today.'

Abbey dropped her forehead to her palm. 'I had plans.' Her voice was thick with emotion. 'I thought her so much better – I was convinced it was because she'd been taken off medication. I was going to discuss the possibility of Mum and Callie coming to stay with me for a while.'

Silence hung in the hot air for a second, then Daniel Ruddley supplied, 'Again, that's something to consider in the future, Abbey. If your optimism could cure your mother, she'd be away from here by now.'

A small smile curved Abbey's mouth. 'Perhaps I'm guilty of expecting too much too soon.'

'It's understandable, completely understandable. The situation for the next of kin is often far more gruelling than it is for the patient – the patient exists for a time on another plane. Even simple decisions, like whether to drink tea or coffee, are beyond them.

'Once there's an improvement, we'll keep the question of visiting more flexible. The situation can be reviewed regularly. Rebecca was, after all, a very sociable character before her breakdown, never out of the limelight.'

'Okay.' Abbey looked from Ruddley to Jake.

Daniel Ruddley rubbed his chin, 'I'm thinking of your mother, I'm afraid, sacrificing your feelings for her well-being.'

When he put it that way, Abbey was helpless. She'd do anything for her mother's well-being. Do anything to glimpse the spark she'd seen in her mother's eyes the previous day. 'I should like to be able to speak to Callie or yourself in the meantime, Dr Ruddley.'

'Of course, Miss Roberts, feel free to contact us any time.' Daniel Ruddley rose to his feet. 'If you'll excuse me, Miss Roberts – ' he corrected himself 'Abbey – I have others to see.'

'Yes, of course.' She nodded, numbed by the revelations, feeling that she had taken a hopeful leap forward, then a hundred paces back. 'I'll keep in contact.'

Their picnic was as subdued as the previous day's had been content. Still, things didn't make sense to Abbey; surely she couldn't be so wrong?

She wasn't wrong! Daniel Ruddley didn't know Rebecca Farraday-Roberts better than she. Beneath that lacklustre figure in the wheelchair was her mum. Her laughing, loving mother.

Jake and Callie's lively banter helped fill the oppressively still day's silence, helped keep Abbey's spirits from flagging. Thoughts niggled away – Rebecca *had* been pleased to see her yesterday. She *wouldn't* try to kill herself.

Whilst Callie helped Jake carry the picnic tackle back to his Land Rover, Abbey knelt before her mother, took hold of her hands. 'Mum . . .' She paused, held her breath, awaited some flicker of recognition from Rebecca. 'I know you didn't try to kill yourself. I know they're wrong.'

Abbey thought she could have imagined the slight movement of her mother's fingers in her own. 'I love you.' She hugged Rebecca, closed her eyes, imagined the embrace was returned.

'Got to make tracks, Abbey.' Jake touched her shoulder. 'It's getting late.'

Slowly, reluctantly, Abbey stood back from her mother, then pushed her wheelchair towards the car park. 'Don't look so down, Abbey.' Callie smiled. 'Tomorrow's another day – might be a better one.'

'I know,' was Abbey's response, but she didn't know. Tomorrow, Jake was leaving to work away; tomorrow, her mother might be just the same. For a second, there was nothing to hang on to.

'I'll phone you, Callie.' Abbey hugged the woman as they said their goodbyes.

Silently, Abbey stared out of the window at the heavy clouds. Even the open window didn't do anything to dissipate the heat – the breeze was hot against her cheeks. There was so much confusion inside her, she didn't dare begin to face the pain caused by her mother's silent hell – not knowing what would happen next – and Jake's imminent departure – not knowing if he would ever come back.

CHAPTER 13

Jake opened the Land Rover door for Abbey, helped her down the large drop to the sandy floor.

'Abbey?'

'Mmm?'

He couldn't just walk out, not like this. 'I'll cancel the job and stay.'

'Cancel?' Automatically, without thinking, she shook her head; something told her to let go. 'I'm fine, Jake. No one will ever convince me that Mum tried to kill herself.'

They drank tea in Abbey's vast kitchen, silent until Jake spoke. 'I'm making an early start, guess I'd better get my gear together – so long as you're sure you don't want me to stay.'

'I'll paint for a while.' She slid from the stool, needing creative solace because it was the only thing in her life that was constant.

'Now?'

'Yes, now.' Her tone husky, fragile.

'Abbey, I'm going away tomorrow – can't you give me tonight?' That she preferred to paint was inconceivable to Jake. 'Don't I mean anything to you?'

She pushed the hair back from her forehead, stared at

him for a long, heavy moment, then turned to move towards her studio; as she walked away, she gasped, 'Yes, you do, but right now I need something I can depend on.'

He grabbed her shoulder, spun her around.

Thunder filled Jake's blue eyes, turned them grey; he let his hand fall to his side. 'Don't you mean you want to hide away?'

'No.' She considered for a second, then, 'Maybe. I'm confused, Jake, I can't make sense of anything that happened today.'

'Talk to me, don't keep it all inside.'

'It won't help.' She stepped back, shook her head.

'Yes, it will.' He touched her cheek with a single finger. 'Hell, if it was me struggling to deal with today, you'd be on overdrive trying to help me out.'

A smile crossed Abbey's lips. She moved into Jake's arms, held him, realized just how short time was.

'Stay there.' Jake gently pushed Abbey's naked shoulder back against the pillows.

Groggily, she registered Jake's darkly dressed form, his hair still damp from the shower.

He leant over her, kissed her, then she sank away. Jake spoke, but she couldn't capture his words in her sleepy mind.

Whilst Abbey slept, Jake drove towards the marina, where his meeting was to take place. He rolled his shoulders as he drove, Abbey's image strong in his mind – the way she'd taken him right to the limits of his restraint with her silky hands, her warm, full mouth, her entire body; somehow, she had redirected her creativity to their lovemaking. Jake had purposely left the beach house before Abbey woke; he wasn't certain he could leave if she'd opened her eyes and smiled that sexy, lop-sided smile at him, or whispered his name in that appealing, husky tone of hers.

Just thinking about her brought a smile to his face. Unconsciously, he slowed his Land Rover, had to fight the urge to turn around. But he'd arrived at the marina.

Todd stuck his thumb in the air to acknowledge his arrival – gestured towards his office. The others had arrived, too.

'Maybe you could call later, Abbey,' Callie suggested. 'Rebecca's still sleeping.'

'Did she have a peaceful night?'

'I think so, love. There's nothing on her chart – no extra medication recorded.'

'I guess that's something.' Abbey chewed at her bottom lip. 'Did the night nurse say anything to you when she handed over?'

'Just that – ' Callie hesitated, changed her mind. 'Nothing to worry about – ring me around lunch-time, Abbey, I'll know better then how she's doing.'

'I'll do that, thanks, Callie.'

Relieved, Callie replaced the receiver. She'd been about to blurt out that Rebecca had been given so much sedative the previous night that the night nurse had mentioned it would be a miracle if they heard anything from her for the next forty-eight hours.

Instead of her usual one hundred per cent concentration, Abbey's thoughts constantly drifted to last night, and Jake's sexy, all-male grin as she had explored his beautifully muscled body, his deep laughter when he had insisted 'enough was enough' and practically thrown her on her back, entering her warmth in one swift movement. She shivered deliciously at the vivid recollection, frowned down at her poised brush. 'Must have it bad, girl,' she whispered, washing out the acrylic-laden brush in a jar of water, automatically reshaping the brush to a fine point. With an apologetic grimace at the painting propped on her easel, Abbey left her studio and wandered out of the beach house on to the verandah.

Thoughts of her mother haunted her, too, together with the familiar helplessness that the phone call to Callie had done nothing to diminish. Without consciously doing so, Abbey wandered down the path, on to the beach, the oppressive heat of the previous day even thicker. So many questions pressed in her mind: Had her mother tried to commit suicide? No! Then she tried to imagine what each single day of the past two years must have been like for Rebecca. Wished for the millionth time she had been in the country when her mother's breakdown had occurred.

She kicked up droplets of water from a thin wave reaching up the sand. Nedwell Roberts's words as clear to her now as the day he'd spoken them: 'Abbey, darling, you know I would never have put her into a psychiatric hospital if I'd any other choice.' He'd looked harassed, tired, shaken as he'd run his fingers back through his straight steel-grey hair. 'I just couldn't cope, darling, try to understand. She completely flipped – drifted around the house in her nightdress all day, babbling nonsense.' Then he'd added confidingly, 'I didn't tell the doctors the full extent of this, but she came at me with a knife.' The colour had drained from his features as he recalled, 'Her eyes were wild, Abbey – crazed. I didn't know her. I have to tell you, I was frightened for Rebecca's life,' he'd added, 'and mine.'

As all the details unfolded, it came to light that Nedwell had struggled with Rebecca's care for a month before eventually taking the advice of a doctor friend of his, Daniel Ruddley. Nedwell was at his wits' end after finding his wife had overdosed with secreted tranquillizers and alcohol. Consultations took place with a team of doctors, and within the week, Rebecca was committed to the Misty Hill Hospital for treatment.

Always, the sensation of guilt dogged Abbey. If she hadn't been in America on an extended holiday with Lynn . . . If she'd been closer to home – maybe she could have done something to protect her mother's health. Perhaps she would have seen the signs, been able to halt the decline into limbo, into the lonely hell her mother lived. A small wave broke over her feet and drew her thoughts back to Jake. He was the least talkative man she'd ever known; yet Abbey could sense his moods, his restlessness, his inner battles. There was something so pure, so honest about him beneath his casual manner.

A hot breeze whispered around Abbey's loose sundress; she shivered with apprehension – thickening dark clouds pushed down heat. She spun around, aware of a presence before any words were spoken.

'Hello, Father.' A slight laugh broke the words; her father's suit trousers were rolled up above his ankles and he carried shiny black shoes, socks balled inside them, 'I wasn't expecting visitors.'

'I was down this way, and I felt we ought to discuss Rebecca.'

He walked beside her, Abbey walking in the edge of the waves, Nedwell on the drier sand.

'I spoke to Callie this morning, sounded as though Mum had a reasonable night.' Abbey was about to add that she was calling back a little later, but Nedwell shouted:

'Reasonable? What's reasonable about being pumped full of drugs and not knowing whether it's night or day? What's reasonable about your mother trying to kill herself?

Abbey frowned. 'I forget sometimes – ' she turned from his angry features to look out to the grey cast sea ' – that Mum being in hospital upsets you too.' And suddenly, unexpectedly, she felt compassion toward her stepfather.

'Upsets me?' He gritted his teeth. 'What kind of life do you think I've had these past two years?'

She rubbed her arms, shivered despite the oppressive heat, then shook her head slightly.

'There's no improvement, no flicker of life in her! Two damned years, Abigail!' His anger bordered on the irrational, as if he, too, were so close to the edge he could tip over at any moment.

Then Abbey grasped at some hope. 'There was an improvement – a couple of days ago when I visited her, she spoke, she smiled.'

'What did she say?'

'Just a few words.'

'Hah! Babble you could make no sense of!'

Nedwell's anger frightened her, but she persevered. 'She will recover – we'll get her back.'

For a split second, he looked annoyed, then halted in his steps. 'I'm sorry, Abigail. Sometimes, I get so very frustrated.' His strained expression softened as he asked, 'When Rebecca spoke, could you make sense of it?'

'Yes. But it was strange.' Abbey brought the words into her mind. 'I'd arranged to visit again the following day and she looked happy, then concerned – no, more frightened. She said, "Don't tell him."'

He rubbed his chin. 'Don't tell who, I wonder?' He paused. 'Did she say anything else?'

'No. I wonder if there's anything else we can do.'

'There's nothing more I could do, my time and finances are stretched as it is.'

'But Mum's wealthy.' Abbey frowned. 'It hasn't all gone?'

Nedwell stiffened, turned away, faced the shore. 'Self-respect, Abigail, demands that I pay for her treatment with my own money.'

'But there must be a joint account?' Rebecca had always been generous to a fault, no reason not to be. Money, lack of it, had never been a family concern.

Abbey followed Nedwell's slump-shouldered form back up the beach, sat down beside him on an outcrop of rock. 'Mum would hate you to be this unhappy.' She felt guilty for suggesting they do more for Rebecca. 'When she's better, she'll appreciate everything you've done.'

He rested his elbows on his knees, exhaustion etched in his features as he stared out to sea.

'Your father – '

'Pop?' Abbey gasped. 'What has any of this to do with Pop?' Just saying his name plucked a familiar chord.

'Before he died, he altered his will with your mother's blessing.' He wrung his hands as he continued, 'Both of them acknowledged his impending death would make your mother a very wealthy widow. He wanted to protect Rebecca from the kind of anxiety your kidnap caused them both.'

Abbey frowned.

'Protect her from fortune hunters. He felt leaving all his money without condition to Rebecca would increase her vulnerability.'

'Are you telling me Mum is broke?'

'No, no.' He laughed grimly. 'Your mother has a very sizeable fortune. But the bulk of their joint wealth was put into your Trust fund.'

Abbey grimaced. 'I knew that. I imagine Pop thought I'd be settled by my mid-twenties.' She sighed. 'If Mum still has a sizeable fortune of her own, how come you're struggling?'

'There was a codicil. If anything untoward, or un-expected, happened to your mother, her assets were to be frozen, to remain untouched – even by her spouse.' He added sharply, 'This "breakdown" of hers appar-ently comes into the bracket of "untoward".'

'Did you know that when you married?'

Nedwell fell silent for a second, then turned to face Abbey, his smile a tad frozen. 'Of course.' His eyes darted back out to the sea. 'I married her for love, not money. If anyone tells you differently, they're lying.' He was almost too emphatic about that, but Abbey sensed the whole situation with her mother was taking a dreadful toll on Nedwell's tight command.

'In some ways, the fortune has been a curse.'

Nedwell's mouth straightened into a thin line, as he stared blankly out to sea. 'You never have to concern yourself with money matters now, though, do you?'

'I'd rather have my family intact than the wealth. As for the money, it's relatively untouched – Miles Pendleton-Smythe handles my finances. I live off my own earnings.'

Nedwell raised his brow. 'Probably wise.'

Abbey shuddered. Out over the sea, lightning arched from cloud to cloud. 'The kidnapping was a long time ago – I thought it was over.' Her voice caught as she added, 'But it isn't over, not the nightmares.'

Almost absently, he asked, 'I thought you didn't remember anything?'

'Not until – ' She hadn't meant to discuss the exhibition, the threatening letters, the shadows on her existence since then – but Nedwell's expression invited confidence. And strangely, his purge of emotion made everything easy.

'There was no warning, nothing, and it all began again at my exhibition . . .' She went on to tell him of Jake, of Miles, how they had both been endangered because of their involvement with her. And the poisonous letters after her exhibition and since her return from Spain. 'It seems that anyone whose life I touch is in danger.' Abbey dropped her forehead into her palm. 'It all sounds so weird that, sometimes, I think I'm going crazy. I've even suspected Rick, of all people!' She winced at the horrible suspicions. 'And when Jake took me on board *Free Spirit*, I suspected him. Whoever he is, he knows all about me – everything I do – who I see – everything!'

Nedwell's eyes darkened. Briefly, his hand rested on hers. 'You suspected Rick?' He squinted. 'There's something about that man I don't trust, never have.'

'He's too young.'

343

'How old is he? Do you know?'

'No, but – '

'You should tell the police.'

Revolted, Abbey lurched to her feet, her mind spinning sickly. It couldn't be Rick.

'Darling, I didn't mean to upset you.' He walked beside her towards the beach house. 'I'm only thinking of your safety. God knows, I've all but lost your mother, I don't want anything else to happen to this family!'

The lightning out at sea moved in closer; loud cracks punctuated the thick heat. Large drops of rain thumped onto the sand.

The genuine concern in Nedwell's voice broke through to Abbey. 'One of the letters said I should tell my father to free up his assets, to be ready for his demands.'

'Then the perpetrator doesn't know everything about our family, Abbey.'

In answer to her questioning glance, he continued, 'If he's assuming I could raise any kind of ransom, he's wrong.'

They hurried towards the beach house. Stinging rain fell heavily, the thunder and lightning almost constant now, crackling through the air.

Once inside, Abbey grabbed a couple of towels from the downstairs bathroom and threw one to Nedwell. 'He is wrong.' A moment of hope rose in her, that if her tormentor could be wrong about Nedwell's financial position, then he may not be so clever. 'He is assuming you and Mum share the wealth.'

His voice was muffled, still covered with the towel, his words slightly thickened. 'Wrongly.'

Abbey shuddered. 'He may be wrong, but he's biding

his time. He's going to kidnap me.' Her tone more distressed, she threw her towel to the floor. 'And he will harm me if he doesn't get a ransom.'

'What can I do? If I had assets, I would use them, but my capital has been drained with Rebecca's care.'

'I suppose you'd have to contact Miles.'

'Dear God, surely it won't come to that!' He groaned. 'What are the police doing? Anything?'

Abbey wished she hadn't confided in Nedwell. He was apt to fire questions so hard and fast, it made her anxiety mount. 'They've installed a panic alarm; it doesn't make any sound I can hear, but it sets off a – ' she struggled to remember the term ' – flash-graded call.'

Because Nedwell had seemed so shocked at her revelations, Abbey found herself playing up the part of the police in her life. 'They come straight round and scour the premises, all the surrounding area.'

'Well, that's some comfort, I imagine.'

'It keeps me sane.'

'You know, I'm surprised you haven't got a body-guard or a private detective working for you.'

'I have enough protection with the police.' She added for good measure, 'They keep watch on me,' whilst crossing her fingers behind her back.

'It sounds so. But if you change your mind, dear, I know an extremely discreet chap. I've used his services myself in the past.'

'Thanks.' Abbey disappeared into her bedroom to change, left the door open a little so Nedwell could continue speaking.

'This Jake character, when are you expecting him back?'

'Jake?' She snapped her attention from the dry jeans

345

and huge black T-shirt Jake had left behind. 'He isn't coming back.'

'But you'd like him to?'

'Yes, but Mister Westaway isn't the steady type.'

'You never told me what he does for a living?'

'He was a martial-arts instructor for the Army, around the time Miles went through Sandhurst; they were at college together before that. Now he's a minder.'

'On one of his "minding" jobs at the moment, is he?' Nedwell glanced in the hall mirror, rearranged his thick grey hair.

'Yes, for someone he's worked with before.'

'Abroad?'

Abbey didn't know, but she improvised as she emerged from the bedroom. 'As far as I know.'

They were quiet for a while, then Nedwell prompted, 'Do you still hear from Miles?'

'Yes, of course.' Abbey took the soaked towel from Nedwell. 'That reminds me, I owe him a call at the moment.'

'Ah, I see.'

He asked then about her paintings and Abbey responded, 'I took a small one for Mum a couple of days ago. I think she liked it.'

'Good, good, I'm sure she does. About Rebecca – I think we should leave her care as it is, they know her at Misty Hills. If you think of anything else we can do, we'll discuss it?'

'Yes.' Abbey was heartened by that.

'This business with the man who's threatening you – I still think you should involve the police more, Abigail.'

'I've involved them enough.' She smiled wryly. 'The

346

amount of false alarms I've called them out on, I think they've decided I'm paranoid.'

Nedwell digested her words, then, 'Would you like me to stay for a while? I don't have a meeting until this evening.'

'Thanks, but I'm fine. I want to try and get some painting done. Will you have time for a cuppa before you go?'

'Splendid! If it's not too much trouble, a cup of real coffee would hit the mark.'

Whilst Abbey balanced a coffee filter in one hand and the aromatic grounds in her other, the telephone rang several times. 'Would you get that? The answering machine must be turned off. I won't be a tick . . .'

Hurriedly, she set up the coffee filter and rinsed her fingers, made her way to the hallway.

Nedwell was just replacing the telephone.

'It was that Jake fellow.'

'Jake? Why didn't he hang on?'

'Strapped for time – it was a message, where to meet him.' He leant towards the low telephone table, picked up a pen. 'Let me write it down before I forget.'

Standing over Nedwell, she watched whilst he wrote: *7.00 tomorrow evening, meet Jake at Bluff Cove Lake.*'

'Did he say anything else?' Abbey couldn't keep the smile from spreading across her features.

Nedwell shook his head. 'No, just that.' He tapped the note with the pen. 'I think he was on a public phone.'

'Ah – right.' Abbey's non-committal answer disguised elation at hearing from Jake; and surprise at the romantic location Jake had chosen. Bluff Cove Lake was a secluded beauty spot – so secluded, very few knew

347

it existed; and if they did, even fewer knew how to find the entrance.

'Now are you certain you'll be all right?' Nedwell asked as he made to leave. 'I'll telephone you when I get home, shall I?'

'Okay.' She touched his elbow. 'Drive safely.'

Only when Abbey returned indoors from waving her father on his way did she remember that she'd been supposed to call Callie around mid-day. She glanced at the clock – she might just catch her before she left work for the day.

'Callie?' It was the direct number straight to her mother's private room. 'Thank goodness I caught you.' Abbey went on to explain how she'd been tied up with her father all day.

'I'm just about to leave, Abbey.'

'How is Mum? Is there any improvement?'

Callie cast a sorrowful glance at the slight form in the bed. 'She isn't any worse, Abbey.'

Abbey closed her eyes. 'Is she eating?'

'A little. They're reluctant to cut back on her medication because of the outcome last time.'

'The so-called "suicide attempt"?'

'Uh-huh. Listen, honey, call me first thing in the morning. Happen a good night's sleep will see Rebecca improve.'

'Okay.'

The day began with hopeful, weak sunlight; Abbey's call to Callie bought even more hope.

'I'd say – with caution, mind – your mum's looking brighter, Abbey.'

It was something – and with a promise to call again

the following morning, Abbey began painting with renewed vigour.

Such was her involvement, that Abbey didn't notice the passage of time until her stomach growled in protest.

Standing back, she identified the location in the painting: Bluff Cove Lake, the fantasized beauty spot coming to life on the canvas, the outline of ethereal lovers barely discernible amongst the trees.

It was already six o'clock. Abbey showered quickly and pulled on a fitted cotton jersey dress. The sunshine yellow suited her mood, her insides warming as she imagined Jake's masculine grin of appreciation. She brushed her hair until it shone in warm strawberry waves on blonde. Delicious anticipation raced through her veins as she recalled Jake's words the last time she'd worn the dress: 'Roberts, you look as sexy enough to eat in that dress, how the hell'm I supposed to keep my hands to myself?' She grabbed her handbag; her sto-mach protested again as she hurried past the fruit bowl, so she grabbed a banana and let the excitement of seeing Jake within the hour fizzle through her. 'Just promise me' – he'd pulled her close – 'you won't wear it for anyone else.'

'Just for you,' she'd whispered against his sensual lips before they tumbled to the kitchen floor.

The phone shrilled as she reached the front door. 'Hello?' Whilst she spoke, she turned on the answering machine. 'Aunt Rosemary, I was on my way out – '

'I won't keep you, dear.'

To Abbey's ears, the aunt spoke even more slowly than usual – she rocked from one lemon high-heeled shoe to the other. 'That's okay, what can I do for you?'

'Always so sweet.' She sounded as if she was eating. 'Darling, could I impose on you this evening? You're so much closer to Misty Hills than I am. I'm planning to visit Rebecca.' Rosemary swallowed. 'Nedwell, bless him, he's taking me along – just a short visit.'

'You want to call in and see me?' Abbey gasped in surprise.

'Yes, dear, well, freshen up before the visit.'

'I – er – that should be okay, Aunt Rosemary. Could you give me an idea what time? I don't know how long I'll be out, I'm meeting someone.'

'I think Nedwell said tonight – or was it tomorrow night? Oh, dear – you know what my memory's like – '

'I have to leave, Aunt Rosemary. I'll be late. Listen, if I'm not back from my walk, Father has a key.'

'Yes, dear. Off you go, don't be late.'

'Weird.' Abbey whispered as she set down the receiver. But she had other things to think about . . . more exciting things.

Even finding her car with a flat tyre didn't raise more than a 'damn' from her lips. Bluff Cove wasn't far – twenty minutes' walk if she hurried.

'Pendleton-Smythe!' Miles's crisp tone shot back at the caller.

'I want to talk to you.'

'You've got a bloody nerve, Westaway.'

'Can it, Miles. Talking about "nerve", you've got a barrowload, telling Abbey lies about me.'

'Lies? What lies?' There was a slight 'cornered' edge to Miles's voice and Jake smiled sardonically.

'Yeah, those lies.'

350

Miles cleared his throat. 'All's fair in love and war, old boy!'

'We'll discuss that. I'll be over in an hour.' He glanced at his watch: it was six-thirty.

'You can't! It's not visiting hours!'

Jake shook his head. What did Miles think he was going to do? Pound him in his bed? 'Hang loose, Miles, there's a way you can help repair the damage.'

'Ah – ' He tried for a confident remark, but it didn't come off. 'So pleased, old chap.'

'Miles might come up with something we don't know.' Jake turned to the others. 'What do you think, David?'

'Go for it. There's sweet Fanny Adams happening at the moment. It could be like this for days yet.'

'This is a waste of time.' Jake raked his fingers back through his hair. 'She ain't stepped an inch from that panic button.'

David lit a cigarette, studied Jake through narrowed eyes, 'Don't you blow it all by contacting her. You do that – we lose out. You'll be the first to see her, you have my word. She won't get hurt.' He offered Jake a cigarette, but Jake shook his head, just paced up and down in the cabin.

'Jake, get out of here – jump on that bike, go see Miles – at least you'll be doing something.'

'Yeah.' Jake pulled on the helmet before stepping into clear air, his frustration transmitted to the motorbike as he sped to Plumegate Private Hospital; and as he drove, Jake wished harder with every second that he'd stayed well out of it all, stayed with Abbey.

Abbey dipped in through the bush-concealed entrance to Bluff Cove Lake and inhaled the rain-sweetened air;

she was alone, instantly awed by the natural beauty around her. Secret and beautiful, a small hideaway – the thought curved her lips into a smile as she strolled beneath overhanging, breeze-rustled branches. The last rays of pink foliage-filtered sunlight turned the pale lakeside path to dark gold and sharpened the shadows; a squirrel raced full pelt up a wide tree trunk. Tomorrow, she'd put the squirrel in her painting . . . 'Ah!' She grimaced as her ankle jarred over in the high-heeled sandals and limped toward the bench at the far side of the lake, muttering, 'What kind of an idiot wears high heels for a two-mile walk?' Then laughed, too happy to care.

'Ouch!' She stumbled to the bench, glanced at her watch – it was almost seven fifteen. She kicked one of her shoes into the deep grass beneath the bench and rubbed her ankle.

Dusk's light breeze rustled through the trees and Abbey fancied Jake's footfalls moved through the long scrub grass behind her. Perversely prolonging her anticipation, she kept facing frontward. A bird skimmed the marble-smooth surface of the lake, caused a tiny wash of ripples before rising to an over-head branch; then its wings slapped before its abrupt departure left the thin limb quivering.

Abbey frowned, her head jerking up. A cold shiver of dread coursed through her, burst in her head. A dreadful, medicinal smell seized her nose, mouth, throat, her eyes watered, evoking flashes of memory from childhood. The same confusion, sense of drifting, being unable to fight, react or hold on to consciousness, dropping into darkness. Thick . . . hot . . . darkness.

* * *

Sweat created a layer, causing the thick smothering cloth to cling to her skin; Abbey wriggled her legs, her ankles restricted, bare toes striking hardness.

'At last, you are awake.' The monotone, surreal voice dipped into her shroud.

Abbey clamped her lips closed with her teeth to stifle a gasp. 'You don't cry like you did as a child – ' his taunt so eerily even ' – I have already contacted your daddy, little princess . . .'

The same taunts as those in her past. Heartbeat slamming against her ribs – too fast – any faster, she'd short-out, her senses would shut down, her mind would fragment.

Lie still, breathe slowly, use your heartbeat to block him out. Dragging air in through the stifling, damp shroud, the sweat on her body turned cold when he rasped:

'I asked him for a message, taped it for you, princess.'

There was a whirring sound of rewinding tape, then a click: 'Sweetheart, Mummy and I will have you home soon, I promise.'

A strangled sob stuck in Abbey's throat. Pop's voice . . . The same message her kidnapper had played her all those years ago.

'I promise you, we'll have you home safe very soon; we love you, princess.' The rich timbre of Pop's voice wrenched at Abbey; she trembled with anger, with agony, made a great, jerking movement against the bonds at her wrists and ankles.

A click halted the tape, then there was that sinister, hissy laughter. 'So sorry, Daddy's little princess, I mixed up your fathers. This is the tape I meant to play for you.'

'Abigail – I'll contact Miles immediately, and the pol – '

A snapping noise halted the tape. His menacing voice pushed at her ears. 'I advised him not to involve the police at this stage, my dear, nor anyone else – unless he wants to receive a souvenir in his morning mail.'

Real or imagined, Abbey heard sharp shears opening and closing. Her psyche reeled in terror, careened, spun towards the abyss.

Miles paled visibly when Jake entered the room. The borrowed white doctor's coat made him appear bigger than ever. And he felt small, tucked in his bed for the evening, like a baby faced with a giant gorilla.

'How're you doin', Miles?'

Trying to sink into the pillows, Miles grabbed the red 'call' string above his head. 'Lay one finger on me, Westaway, I'll have you turned into mincemeat.'

Jake shook his head, flicked the string out of Miles's fingers and tossed it over the curtain rail.

Two white palms raised towards Jake, 'Now, Jake, think what you're doing – '

'Don't ever – I mean *ever* – tell lies to any woman I'm with again, Miles. Your nasty little lies caused a lot of grief. Right?'

Sweat popped on Miles's brow. 'Jake, I'm sorry, I won't, I swear!' He pushed himself up a little against the pillow as the threat of physical violence receded. 'But Abbey's my biggest client – ' He paled again. 'You're not asking me to give up her business?'

'So long as you keep it "business".'

An audible sigh of relief broke from Miles Pendleton-Smythe. 'Certainly, old chap.'

Jake pulled up a chair at the side of Miles's bed. 'Now that's out of the way, I need some information.'

'That's it?' Miles frowned. 'You're not going to beat my brains out?'

'You sound disappointed, man. I'll tap you around if you're really desperate,' Jake shot back wryly.

'So everything's all right between us?'

Miles's relief was so tangible, Jake laughed. 'Man, I ain't so keen I'd ask for your hand in marriage. Let's just say our taste in women collided twice – and neither of us came out of it too well.'

A glimmer of a smile moved around Miles's petulant mouth. He knew a glow of perverse satisfaction that at least Jake obviously hadn't succeeded in holding on to Abbey. He made a pyramid of his fingers. 'So what do you want to know? I'll ring for coffee. We might as well be comfortable, aye?'

'Nedwell Roberts?' Miles slurped his coffee, 'Oh, he's a man of hidden talents, unfortunately, holding on to money isn't one of them. He was a brilliant chemist – and what he doesn't know about electronics isn't worth knowing.' Miles tapped his cheek with a manicured fingernail. 'In fact, I recall Nedwell telling me it was Charles Farraday – Abbey's pater – who bought out Nedwell's electronics firm when it had money problems.' Miles dusted an imaginary fleck of dust from his maroon dressing-gown. 'Charles Farraday.' Miles sighed with admiration. 'Now, he could spot a diamond opportunity a mile away.'

Jake didn't know if any of this would help, but he listened as Miles expounded, 'Any man who can turn around the fate of a third-rate electronics company and use it to build his fortune has my vote.' He stuffed a rich shortbread biscuit into his cheek. 'Charles had the capacity to make more friends than enemies – brought out the best in people. I've read his biography – ' he chewed ' – I'll dig it out for you some time. Charles kept Nedwell on, you know, when he took Nedwell's firm over and Nedwell became a close family friend.' He chewed, drank, swallowed. 'I recall Abbey telling me Nedwell was like an uncle to her before he married Rebecca.' He filled his mouth with more rich biscuit. 'Gorgeous woman – gorgeous! What a hostess!'

'Yeah.' Jake moved the biscuits out of Miles's reach. 'So, Nedwell – apart from his brilliance as an electronics boff and his spell as a chemist – he's pretty unremarkable? No skeletons?' Miles shook his head. 'Unless you can call those twin stick insects he has for sisters "skeletons", Nedwell's pretty straight, far as I know.'

'Has he got anyone looking out for Abbey?'

'Not sure, old chap, haven't spoken to him for a couple of weeks.'

'What do you know about Richard Bloomsbury?'

'Abbey's agent?'

'Uh-huh.'

'Do you know how much money he makes out of Abbey?'

'More than you?' Jake countered.

'I'll ignore that. He's well established, knows his clients and he knows what sells.'

'That's all you know?'

'Well . . .' Miles worked his mouth for a moment, dislodging biscuit crumbs from his perfect crowns before continuing, 'A lot of people don't care for him. He's upset a couple of my clients in the past.'

Giving up with his tongue, Miles washed out his mouth around a glass of water. 'I've heard some scandal, but it might be sour grapes.'

Jake shrugged. 'Shoot. Start with your clients.'

'Well, one of them told me – and I don't want you repeating this – one of them told me Bloomsbury refused ten K for a commission by Abbey.'

'Maybe she was busy.'

'So he said. But something else I heard – he buys Abbey's paintings himself, doesn't tell her, and ships them out to collectors all over the world.'

'Enterprising.' Jake shrugged non-comittally, glanced at his watch. 'Anything else?'

'Someone heard him say, and I quote, "The only way you'd be worth more, Abbey, is if you were dead".'

'Who heard that?'

'Idle party gossip, can't recall the source, old chap.'

'Thanks, Miles, I've got to go.'

'Just a mo – ' Miles held up his palm. 'You've got to tell me why you wanted to know all this – '

'Miles, I was never here. You never told me any of this.'

'Oh!' broke out from Miles in a mixture of disappointment and curiosity.

Jake turned and stared darkly at Miles.

'You can trust me – I – I won't cross you again,' then blew out a sigh of relief when Jake closed the door behind him and earned a breathy 'Good night, doctor,' from Miles's night nurse.

Jake pulled straight off the slip road and into the boat yard. The newly installed security guard waved him through the police cordon.

357

Once inside the boat shed, he parked the motorbike, took off the helmet and climbed on to *Free Spirit*.

'Here.' Jake pulled the small tape recorder from his inside pocket and tossed it to David Waterman. 'I don't know if there's anything helpful on there.'

'Thanks, I'll have a listen.' David connected a small earpiece to the chunky little tape recorder, popped it in his ear.

'Anything happening?'

The older man shook his head, scratched his thinning crown. 'Doesn't she ever shop? I've never known a woman stay around home so much! If my wife had her dosh, she'd shop till she dropped every day. Never mind going for walks.'

Jake reflected he'd never known a woman like Abbey – full stop. 'She paints, loses track of time.'

'Loses her sense of hearing, too, that ansaphone's tape's been buzzing for hours.'

Frowning, Jake jerked a thumb at the remote recording equipment. 'Anything special?' Something prickled up his spine, something felt wrong. Abbey did take breaks – she returned calls eventually – if she was home.

'Help yourself, it's all grindingly ordinary.'

'Abbey's definitely home?' Jake flipped the replay button, David's grey-white cigarette smoke looking lighter in the dimness.

'Yep – she went for a walk around 6.50, arrived back home – ' he checked his note of the relayed message ' – 8.40.'

'Was she alone?' Jake almost choked on the question, but he had to know.

'Yep – I'll save your ears over what Bill, the look-out guy, said when she went out.'

Jake fixed David Waterman with a glower; David Waterman wished he'd kept his big mouth shut. He grimaced, shrugged. 'He said he'd never seen a babe in a yellow dress look so sexy.' He rubbed his nose, conscious that he'd cleaned up the lewd remark. 'Nothing bad.'

'I can imagine,' Jake snapped, visualizing Abbey's unbelievably luscious curves in that yellow dress – hell, it drove him crazy just thinking about it.

'We think she came back minus shoes – carrying them, apparently.'

'That's not unusual, she walks down on the beach barefoot all the time.'

Exhausted but too wound up to sleep, Jake listened to the usual cast of callers on Abbey's ansaphone. Callie, Richard, Miles – needed to discuss finances . . . 'Aunt Rosemary? Never heard of that one.' He drummed his fingers against his leg. 'Where did Abbey go walking?'

'Ah – ' David sucked hard on his cigarette. 'We're not sure. One minute she was in view – the next – gone.'

'Which direction?'

Pulling a map across the small table, David indicated Abbey's route with a pencil. 'Last seen here.'

'Bluff Cove Lake.' Jake frowned. 'So she was meeting someone at Bluff Cove. Why didn't she drive there?'

'Bluff what?' David squinted through the smoke at the map. 'It's not on here.'

'Yeah, well, it's one of those places you only meet for one thing.' Jake's tone was grim. 'Locals don't want it on any freaking map.'

'She's forgotten you already, then?' David teased.

'Maybe.' He shook his head. 'But that's not her style. The one bloke she might meet can't – he's laid up.'

And Miles wouldn't appreciate that yellow dress.

Jake rubbed his hand round the back of his neck. Miles went for 'demure' every time – that dress was special to Jake. She wore it to excite him – no one else. Abbey's words hit him. 'I'll wear it just for you,' she'd said, those green eyes of hers promising.

Then there was another message from Callie: 'Abbey, soon as you get in, call? I've some news.'

'Send someone to the beach house.' The sense that something was very wrong prickled at Jake. Abbey might ignore all the other messages, but she'd be on to anything concerning her mother like a shot.

Coughing, David fanned the smoke from before his face. 'Are you off your rocker?'

'If you don't – ' Jake made for the cabin door.

'Hold it, man.' David stubbed out his cigarette. 'Look, what's eating you? She went out, came back – alone. I'm not blowing this wide open because you're having an attack of jealousy!'

'Something's wrong, Dave.' Jake grimaced. 'Something doesn't feel right.' And it wasn't just jealousy, it was gut instinct.

'You're knackered – imagining things – crash out for a few hours, Jake.'

'Yeah, I'm shot, but I was the last time I knew something was wrong – man, I turned back from a two-week trip to heaven because I knew something was wrong with her.'

David raised a disbelieving brow. 'And?'

'The jerk'd filled her bedroom with smoke, torched her verandah. I've a hunch she was drugged. I can't explain how I know something's wrong – I just know.' Briefly, Jake explained how Abbey did let things ride – but not when they concerned her mother.

For a long moment, David Waterman considered Jake's words. 'Okay.' He pressed a button on the portable console. 'Bill?'

'Bill here.'

'Anything happening?'

'Hang on, a car's drawn up. It's been too bloody dark to see much for hours here, mate. Security light's going on. I think it's Nedwell Roberts. Yes, it is.'

'Alone?'

'Affirmative.'

Jake stood behind David Waterman, willing Bill to catch sight of Abbey as she answered the door, yet unable to quell the sick sensation churning in his guts.

'What's he doing?'

'Letting himself in the front door.'

'Any sign of Miss Roberts?'

'Not since 8.40.'

David glanced at Jake's troubled expression. 'Will you reassure Jake Miss Roberts was in one piece? He's worried.'

Jake scowled. Worried didn't touch it.

'Well, it was getting dark, but that yellow dress is eye-catching. 8.40 – returned home.'

'See?' David spun from the console. 'Everything's cool.'

'Yeah.'

'Gov?' Bill summoned David on the console.

'Go.'

'Someone else on the scene. Hang on, looks like Richard Bloomsbury.'

Jake relaxed a bit; maybe now there'd be sight of Abbey.

Bill took up the commentary. 'Bloomsbury's stood at

the door, talking to Nedwell. Nedwell's shaking his head. Hang on. Bloomsbury's leaving, he looks pissed off.'

David scratched his head.

'Gov, I'm croaking for a coffee.'

'Yeah, yeah.'

Grabbing the excuse to do something, Jake made up a flask. He had to get out of here, had to do something. 'See ya.' Jake waved the flask.

'Wait!' The detective stood, his bulk filling the galley area. 'You don't go anywhere near that beach house.'

'I'm not that stupid.' Jake pulled on the helmet. 'I'm taking this to Bill – ' he tucked the flask inside his jacket ' – then I'm swinging over to Bluff Cove Lake.'

'You won't see a bloody thing there – there's no moon tonight. And don't let anyone see you!'

'They won't. There's no moon!' Within seconds, Jake's motorbike roared out of the boatyard.

'Gov?'

'Go.'

'Nedwell Roberts is leaving the beach house. He's carrying a small bag – everything's quiet. Looks like our girl's hit the sack for the night.'

'Thanks, Bill.' Dave chuckled. 'If Miss Roberts runs true to form, she'll be pushing that panic alarm pretty soon.' He lit another cigarette, 'By the way, there's coffee on its way over. ETA fifteen minutes.'

On impulse, Jake drove straight to Bluff Cove. He parked the bike in the narrow bush-concealed entrance, walked slowly around the lake. His guts churned. 'Shit, I'm imagining things,' he muttered as her unmistakable fragrance hung in the night-damp air.

Jake pulled the torch from inside his jacket and crouched, searching through the coarse grass beneath the trees. 'Why did you come here, darlin'?'

But the grass gave up no clues; he slumped on to the bench, distraught, closed his eyes and leant back. He drew her image into his mind – when he'd left her, pushed her soft, cool skin down against the bed; the way her eyes had barely flickered open, her slow, somnolent smile just beginning before she fell back to sleep. 'I shouldn't have left you, Abbey.'

Suddenly, her smile twisted, she grabbed his forearms. 'Help me!'

'Christ!' The torch bounced to the path as Jake sprang to his feet, the aberration echoing through him.

He stooped to pick up the torch, its powerful beam reflected something pale.

Jake had found what he'd been looking for. He wished he hadn't.

'Your stepfather is having difficulty getting money together.' The electronic voice was almost charming, then scraped over her, like the hot, shrouding blanket. 'Mister Pendleton "Smooth" isn't taking this seriously. You should have arranged things more efficiently . . .' he paused '. . . princess.' The scissors again, opening, closing; a violent yank against her scalp. 'They will all take me seriously.' Another tug, snip. Abbey tried to struggle, to scream, but her body lay traitorous, unresponsive, whilst her mind remained horribly aware.

Memories whirled, images in strobe lights; seconds before the nightmare began . . .

* * *

363

Hidden behind the coat stand on the stairs, laughter warming, tempting her to peep. The strange voice whispered in her ear. It sounded unearthly, yet the words held no menace. 'I went to your room and you weren't there, princess; I have a present for you.' She reasoned he must be Pop's friend because Pop called her princess, and giggled with anticipation . . . A present?

'You mustn't see.' He slid something over her eyes. 'And you mustn't speak, you don't want to get into trouble for spying, do you?'

Abbey shook her head, longing to turn around but somehow unable; too used to obeying adults to consider doing anything else, and too used to being cherished to suspect danger.

'Don't make a sound, little princess . . .'

Still. She stayed so still whilst he put something heavy, hot over her face, tried to wriggle free when the dreadful smell hit her senses; mouth opened to protest, but no words came out; confusion, bump-bump of her pulse, panic like an electric shock . . .

'Gov?'

'Yes – ?' His reply broken on a yawn, David rubbed his eyes.

'Thought you said there was some coffee on the way.'

'Shoot! Where is he?'

'Gov? He's just pulling into the run-off.'

'Find out where he's bloody been and get back to me!'

The pull-off, across the road from Abbey's home, was shielded from view by an outcrop of rock.

'Where've you been?' Bill whispered. 'Gov's doing his nut.'

Crouching down beside Bill, Jake pulled the lemon

high-heeled sandal from inside his jacket. 'This is Abbey's. Tell me why she'd carry one home and leave the other?'

Bill was on the mike in an instant. 'We got a problem, Gov.'

David rolled his eyes heavenwards. At that exact second, the recording of Abbey's ansaphone started up. 'Quiet.'

'Abigail, darling, forgot to remind you, meet me at Misty Hills tomorrow evening, about six? Ruddley wants a discussion with us both. Damn! I've left my wallet at the beach house, I'll have to come over and collect it; I'll try not to disturb you.'

David relayed the message to Bill and Jake.

'She wouldn't need reminding,' Jake ground out.

Some of Jake's anxiety had rubbed off on David Waterman; Abbey's lack of verbal response to important messages was making the fine hairs on the back of his neck stand up.

'I'm setting up a "false alarm" as soon as Nedwell reaches Miss Roberts's home.' David's words music to Jake's ears.

'She won't be there.' Jake's harsh whisper.

'Stay right there, Jake. Bill – get that uniform out of your back pack. I'll send a GPV to pick you up – go in with . . .' he paused '. . . Michael Stapleton, he's been to Miss Roberts's home before.'

Nedwell blinked – hard. 'Yes?' Was his response to the two smart young police constables on the beach house doorstep. 'What can I do for you?'

'This is Miss Roberts's home?' the taller one of them asked politely.

'Yes, Abigail lives here.'

'Sorry, sir, you are – ?' Bill took a step forward, but Nedwell blocked the doorframe.

'Nedwell Roberts. Abigail's father.'

'Could we come in and have a word with your daughter, sir?'

'Not until I see some identification.'

Bill stiffened, rooted in his back pocket for the ID card. The taller of the two produced his ID swiftly. 'You're right to be cautious, sir.'

'Here it is.' Bill flipped open his wallet, 'Now, sir, your daughter?'

'She's been in bed for a couple of hours, constables.' He gestured them into the hallway. 'If you'll wait here, I'll see if she's sleeping.' As he walked away, Nedwell continued, 'If she is, we shouldn't disturb her, she's taken some sleeping tablets – wasn't feeling well.'

'We do need to see her, sir. She put out a panic alarm.'

Nedwell paused on the stairs. 'I'll try to waken her.'

The constables could hear Nedwell moving around in the room above them, could hear too, the increasing volume of his summons. 'Abbey – Abbey! Wake up! The police are here to see you!' Then more loudly, 'Abbey!'

Cringing, Bill nodded to his partner, jerked his head towards the stairs. 'We'll go on up,' he whispered.

'Mr Roberts?' Bill tapped on the bedroom door, pushed it open. The taller of the two PCs moved into the doorway, frowned into the darkened room, stared down at the still form in the bed. As Jake's eyes grew accustomed to the shadows, he made out strands of Abbey's long, bright hair escaping over the patchwork cover; her yellow dress hung outside the wardrobe door.

'Completely flaked out.' Nedwell shrugged, his palms upward. 'But you can see, she's safe.'

'Wonder how come she put out a panic call?' Jake narrowed his eyes, absorbed the atmosphere of Abbey's bedroom. The fragrance, the ambience was all wrong.

'Maybe she hit the button by accident?' Bill supplied, smiling at Nedwell.

'Maybe.' Nedwell moved from Abbey's room, pulling the door closed behind him.

'Okay, well, now we know she's okay, we just need to re-set the alarm before we leave,' Jake put in, drawing a look of incredulity from Bill behind Nedwell's back.

'I think she keeps it beneath her pillow.' Smartly, he re-entered Abbey's room, then led them down the stairs, gestured them into the kitchen.

'What are you playing at?' Bill mouthed.

'Stall him.' Jake jerked his thumb toward the kitchen.

'Here!' Nedwell spun around when Bill entered the kitchen, whistling, and passed him the panic button which Bill made a show of 're-setting'.

'Be a good idea to put this back under Miss Roberts's pillow,' said Bill as he handed it back. 'Thanks, Mr Roberts. You know your daughter always makes us a cup of coffee when we come out to her.'

Nedwell looked annoyed for a moment, then recovered. 'Any other time, officer, I'd oblige, but I only came over to collect my wallet.' He looked at his watch. 'I've an early start tomorrow – travelling, you know.'

'Could I have a glass of water then, please?' Bill nodded understandingly. 'I'm parched.'

'You must be concerned about your daughter and

this "stalker" business. It's making her very nervous.'

'Of course.' Nedwell handed Bill a glass. 'But Abigail's problem is her overactive imagination. And she's very highly strung – like her mother.'

'Yes.' Bill gulped the water, supposed Jake hadn't finished what he was doing and sought to prolong the diversion. 'We've noticed.' Then, as Nedwell drummed his fingers on the work top and looked at his watch, Bill tried again. 'But she wasn't imagining things. We've had someone in for questioning.'

That got him. 'Really?' He edged on to the stool. 'Who?'

'I can't divulge that, Mr Roberts, much as I'd like to. You do understand.'

'Of course.'

'All I can tell you is it's a strong possibility we're on track.'

'That, constable, is wonderful.' Nedwell smiled. 'I'm sure my daughter wouldn't have needed her sleeping pills if we'd known earlier.'

'We were planning to phone her in the morning.' Hurry up, Jake! Bill sipped the water, his bladder chock full.

'Bill!' Jake boomed from the front door. 'We've got to get to an RTA, it's just come over the radio!'

'Thanks again, sir.' Bill spun around and charged from the kitchen.

'How in hell did you get away with the "ID" bit?' Bill ran to join Jake in the patrol car after disappearing into the nearest bush.

'It was Stapleton's.' Jake fired up the engine and headed the car towards the outcrop. 'He wasn't interested in ID, he was playing for time.'

368

'Shit! You took a chance!'

'Yeah, and you nearly blew it, fumblin' around like that.'

'Thought I'd left it in me plain clothes – I was brickin' it.'

'Jake! Where're you going?' Bill twisted around as Jake accelerated past the outcrop, where Stapleton remained concealed. 'You've seen her – what's the problem?'

'It wasn't Abbey – ' Jake gritted his teeth, flung the car down the dangerous cliff road ' – it was an older woman – those bits of hair weren't attached.'

'Shit.'

'I knocked, asked her if she was okay. If there was any chance it was Abbey, she'd have known my voice.'

'What about the sleeping pills?'

'I heard her moving around in the room. Abbey never touches them.'

'I still don't see how you knew.'

'There's things you notice about a woman when you spend a lot of time together. Abbey never hangs up something she's already worn – that was put there to cover the mirror.'

'What're you doing now?'

'Dropping you off.' He pulled on to the side of the road. 'Tell Waterman everything, I'll leave the car down at the marina, and pick up the bike.'

'Gov'll go apeshit!'

'I don't give one.' Jake prayed his instincts were right, that Nedwell Roberts would spend some time tidying up his act before leaving the beach house; but before Jake reached the boat yard, Nedwell was speeding inland, swearing vilely because everything had to be rushed now; because Rosemary had just called him stupid. 'I'll show you, you bitch!'

'Pendleton-Smythe?'

Miles's breath was short from his early morning exercise; he sat bolt upright in the grey pre-dawn light, his night nurse slid from the bed, wriggled into her uniform.

'What the – ?'

'I received this.' The visitor threw down a thick, wavy lock of Abbey's unmistakable strawberry-blonde hair, and a scrawly written note on cream paper.

'Oh, my God.' Ghastly white in the poor light, Miles held the lock of hair in his palm, hands trembling as he read the note: *Three million by noon, no police. No tricks. Conceal in 'painting for shipment' package. Locker, airport. Deviate – she dies.*

'I can raise one by noon, Miles, but three? No chance.' Richard slumped on the visitor's chair. 'What the hell do we do?'

'I can raise the rest, but you'll have to do the running around, old chap. Was there a key with this?'

Richard Bloomsbury nodded. 'I've got it safe.' He stood, then paced. 'I'd no idea she was missing – I called round at the beach house because she'd returned none of my calls – '

'Richard – tell me later – we don't have much time.'

CHAPTER 14

Nedwell Roberts hit the grassy road bank as he drove at breakneck speed, his eyes on his rear-view mirror as much as the road. Didn't look as if he was being followed – he slowed slightly and forced himself to try and relax – as if he could. He'd lost practically a whole night.

'I'm too old for this,' he muttered, glancing in his mirrors again; nothing – only a bike. 'I don't like changing plans!' In an effort to calm himself, he thought what he'd achieved. He'd spent hours in the beach house garage, working on Westaway's army colour Land Rover. The adversary he'd never met would have a wonderful surprise. He should have stayed away from Abigail. Nedwell sighed – some folk never learned. He wiped the back of his gloved hand along his forehead, hated the dampness there.

Those policemen! Looking for Abbey – couldn't have happened at a worse time. His knuckles turned white as he imagined what their interference could cost . . . the time they had already cost him.

Abbey's mind was clearer. The thirst that conjured dreams of long cool drinks drove her to wriggle ceaselessly against her tape bonds. She was alone, and had been for some time. The bonds stretched as the tape heated – unexpectedly, those around her wrists gave just enough to pull out a hand.

After pushing the thick woollen material from her head and taking a deep breath, she drew up her legs and dug her nail into the tape around her ankle to split it, then tore it free. It was dark, a dense kind of darkness – like a windowless basement. The air was thick and putrid with the stench of fish.

She sat up too quickly, became dizzy, her head thumping. 'Ugh – ' She stopped herself from reeling over, let the blood flow around her system, then squinted into the darkness and eased off the wooden platform she was on.

Hands held out before her in the darkness, she edged toward a crack of light at the far end of the vast building.

Her ears pricked – was that a car approaching? Mindless of what obstacles might lay in her path, she ran towards the strand of light, bare feet slapping on damp concrete, breathing sharp, fast.

She made it to the side of the door an instant before it swung open towards her, wished for some kind of weapon, but the thought was brief, the light blinding her as she struggled to focus on the tall figure spilling in with the light.

'Father, thank God!' she gasped, relief so great she slumped against the sweating brick wall, let her eyes close, her heart pumping a crazy, uneven beat.

Illuminated in the square spotlight of sunshine, Nedwell turned towards her. A rough sound erupted from him and his palm clutched his throat, speechless.

Abbey swayed through grogginess. The heat, the stench and the unbelievable relief of seeing her step-father brought a half-hysterical sound from her. She pushed herself away from the wall. Time seemed to slow as she took a shaky step into the light, shielded her eyes from the brightness. 'Take me home,' her choked whisper as she reached for his forearm to steady herself.

'Don't go anywhere with him!'

'Jake!' Abbey caught hold of the edge of the door for support as Jake yanked her father backwards, his arm locked around the older man's neck. 'Jake, stop it!'

She dragged at Jake's forearm, gasping for breath, whilst Nedwell turned white, eyes bulging.

'Jake! Stop it! He came here to rescue me!' Reeling, exploding thoughts wouldn't connect in her residually drugged mind. 'Let him go!' She kept pulling ineffectually at Jake's imprisoning arm. 'You're strangling him!'

'He wants strangling,' Jake hissed, jerking Nedwell backwards, away from Abbey. 'Tell her, Nedwell, tell Abbey how it was you who kidnapped her. Both times. Tell her!'

'No! Jake!' Repulsed, Abbey screamed the words.

Nedwell's eyes were closing, his oxygen supply severely limited. 'He came here to get me out! Let him go! He can't breathe!' Horrified, she launched herself at Jake. 'He's older than you! Stop it! You'll kill him!'

'Abbey, listen to me – ' Jake caught her flailing wrist in one large hand. 'Listen to me.' His voice low, menacing, his hand tightening around her wrist. 'He may be older, but he's dangerous. And he's a clever man, aren't you, Nedwell?'

Nedwell Roberts scowled. Still he didn't speak.

Unable to bear the accusation, Abbey exploded. 'Father! Tell Jake! It's not you – you came to save me . . .'

Feeling Abbey's confusion, torn between needing to hold her and needing to make her see the truth, Jake tamped down his own emotions. Staring at Nedwell with a glinting, impenetrable gaze, Jake forced out the words he instinctively knew would appeal to Nedwell's ego, 'You had me fooled, Mr Roberts.' At the same time, he released his hold on Nedwell Roberts but stayed by his side.

Blood froze in Abbey's veins at her father's unearthly laughter. Unearthly like – like distorted. It was the first audible sound he had made since entering the warehouse. But again, her mind refused to accept that he – that he – 'No!' Was she going insane? Was this how it felt? This swinging, sickening sensation, this darkness that loomed, where all sensations shorted out? A dense shadow lurked at the edge of her thoughts, a revelation, but Jake's voice brought her back into the present.

'Yeah, you really had me fooled. You know, I never would have had you down as a chemist.'

Slumping back against the open door, Abbey shook her head. What the hell was Jake talking about?

'And an electronics wizard?' Jake glanced at Abbey, hated what he was doing to her, but there was no other way.

'You couldn't keep on fooling Rebecca though, could you?' There was a slight taunt in Jake's tone. 'You just couldn't believe it when you found out Abbey's father – her real father – had protected the family fortune against scavengers like you. You didn't like that, did you, Nedwell?'

Sweat broke from all Abbey's pores. The ground swayed beneath her, but she fought the blackness inviting her, grasped the edge of the door more tightly for support.

Nedwell Robert's features twisted evilly. 'Never would have married the bitch if I'd known!'

That voice surrounded her. *That* voice. That unreal, hissing travesty of a voice. Distorted into a monotone nightmare . . . Darkness beckoned to her more strongly than ever – waited with the sweet, shimmering promise of relief. But Abbey dragged foul air into her lungs, fought with every nerve end to stay upright, those nerves dancing chaotically in every direction.

'So Rebecca destroyed your dreams of becoming a rich man, Nedwell?' Jake shook his head with feigned sympathy. 'After you went to all that trouble of marrying her. You must'a been damned mad.'

'Mad?' Nedwell trembled. 'Mad?' Dreadful laughter broke from him. 'I wanted what was always mine! Charles took everything – everything I had! What man in his right mind wouldn't try to get it back!'

'You're talking about your electronics company?' Jake supplied, glancing at Abbey. He shot her a look that said: Just hold on, it's nearly over.

'Charles Farraday was a pauper until he took my company over!'

'Life's a bitch.' Jake leant back in a deceptively casual movement. 'Guess that fortune should have been yours.'

'Exactly. And now it is.'

'Yeah,' Jake scratched his cheek, moved across the doorway slightly. 'You thought of everything this time, Nedwell.' Puzzlement shone in Jake's eyes. 'But I still don't understand how you managed to get a message to Abbey – you know, to meet me?'

Gesturing outward with his fingers, Nedwell smiled smugly, tapped his chest pocket. 'Easy. Mobile telephones are a wonderful invention.' Eager to show just how clever he was, Nedwell expanded. 'I'd already established how attached Abbey had become to you, so I phoned her number – took the message – wrote it down – and *voilà*! The message never made it to the ansaphone.'

'While I made coffee!' A rush of anger fought the thick malaise; the truth finally seeped through. 'You bastard!' She lurched towards Nedwell, brought her fists down heavily on his nose.

Jake's arm clamped around her waist. He dragged her to his side, held her there, stilling her, silencing her with a glance.

'Something else I don't understand, Nedwell. I guess you kept Rebecca drugged.' Jake shook his head. 'How in hell did you manage that?'

'Clever, wasn't it?' He rubbed his nose with a long, white finger. 'My dear – ' the word 'dear' he loaded with sarcasm ' – sister, Cynthia, refused at first to take a menial post in the kitchens at Misty Hills. Refused! Point blank! I mean at first – I had to visit dear Rebecca every single day to fix up her food myself – take her rock cakes and homemade chocolates.'

'Fix up? With drugs?' Jake interjected.

'Yes.' Nedwell batted his hand as though annoyed Jake had interrupted his flow of conversation. 'Cynthia eventually came around when I promised her a life of wealth. She was shocked, mind you, that I insisted she work for it!'

'Boy – ' Jake shook his head as though suitably impressed, his entire being tense with keeping up this dialogue that had to be – praying like he'd never done in his life that Abbey would understand. Tilting his head to one side, Jake whispered in awe, 'Does this mean Rebecca didn't really have a nervous breakdown? You even staged that?'

Picking an imaginary fleck from his crisp suit, Nedwell smiled abhorrently. 'Clever, wasn't it?' The smile broke into a laugh, a horrible, hissy laugh. 'The hallucinogens were a godsend. Best part of it is, everyone believed she was as mad as hatter! Even Rebecca herself began to believe it.' Nedwell reached out to hold Abbey's chin between his clammy finger and thumb. 'And you, my dear, dear Abbey, even you convinced yourself you were going insane, didn't you?'

Jake held her back when she would have lunged again, Abbey's bunched fist meeting with his forearm. Lies on lies! Like a bath full of snakes, squirming in her mind, poisoning everything they touched. 'Jake! Do something! You can't let him get away with this!'

'Hey,' he tried to convey more than his words with a look, 'you're safe, Abbey, be grateful. What the hell does money matter?'

Gasping, held upright by Jake and the massive release of adrenaline into her blood, Abbey could barely hear for the pounding in her ears.

'Guess a few mill ain't bad going for a few years' work.' Jake asked casually, 'You'll be meeting with your sisters, then?'

Whilst Jake spoke, Nedwell removed the small, electronic device from beneath his shirt collar. 'Both of them.' He cleaned the collar thoroughly on a snowy white handkerchief, then cast the device to the damp concrete.

Jake glanced at Abbey again as she trembled with rage, her green eyes burning in her white face, her anger directed at him as much as at Nedwell.

What was Jake doing? Letting Nedwell walk away? Was she supposed to just stand here and let this happen?

As though they had concluded a business meeting, Nedwell pushed back his cuff and looked at his watch. 'I must be going. You know, I shouldn't talk about this to anyone – either of you.' He smiled with false kindness at Abbey. 'I've left your boyfriend here securely in the frame, Abigail . . . Residue of the drugs I've used, some hair, and several other souvenirs are in his Land Rover.' At Abbey's shocked gasp, Nedwell elaborated. 'Rick was my first choice, but I really need you to keep schtum. I can only be certain of that by pressuring your lover.' His expression hardened. 'Tell the police and Westaway here will be gaoled for a very long time. You see, everything points to him. Plus, the fool impersonated a police officer, didn't you, Mr Westaway? Stupid, very stupid – and I thought we hadn't met.'

Briskly, he straightened his suit sleeves whilst the brunt of his words sank in. 'I have a car waiting to take me to the airport. Got my eye on a villa. When Cynthia and Rosemary see what I can provide, they won't call me stupid any more.' He turned to walk into the blinding sunlight, muttering, 'They shouldn't call me stupid! They're the stupid ones!'

Horrified, Abbey pushed at Jake's encompassing arms. 'Stop him!' She strained to break from Jake, but could only watch as Nedwell Robert's tall figure eased into a waiting limousine.

Briefly, Abbey caught sight of Nedwell's twin sisters

in the opulent interior; they were smiling, exuded excitement like youngsters off on a mystery tour, welcoming Nedwell like some conquering hero.

'Oh, God!' She watched, transfixed, horrified as the vehicle drew away, like a nightmare she had no control over. He was driving away – he'd *ruined* her mother's life . . . 'No! He can't do what he did and – ' She looked at Jake's exhausted features, her husky voice breaking, then fell silent. If she did anything, Jake would pay. This beautiful, honest, sexy man would lose his freedom. To him, that would be hell. As much hell as her abduction, her mother's incarceration.

'I won't tell anyone about any of this – ' her thoughts jumbled, confused ' – leave as soon as you can – I won't tell the police – '

He covered her lips with his finger, a light of amusement entering his sexy, dark blue eyes. A familiar shiver raced over her skin as, incredibly, the horror sank away. 'Do you want to make love before you go?' she whispered past his finger. 'I could massage – '

Swearing, Jake covered her mouth with his before she came out with any more lewd suggestions.

Someone cleared their throat. 'Miss – I'm Detective Waterman.' A well-built man appeared suddenly in the doorway. Briefly, he shook Abbey's hand, then turned his attention to Jake. 'That was great, Mr Westaway.' He gestured for Jake to lift up his black T-shirt. 'We'll take off the wire now?'

'Sure.'

Abbey spun around, watched with dawning realization as the plain-clothed officer removed the taped wire and tiny microphone from Jake's chest. 'Get everything you needed?'

'And more.'

The whole conversation had been recorded? Abbey shook her head to try and sift her thoughts. 'What happens now?' her husky voice cracked. 'Is someone following my – Mr Roberts?'

A broad, conspiratorial grin passed between David and Jake. 'He ain't going to be at the airport long, ma'am – that was one of our drivers. Nedwell and his sisters are getting a courtesy ride to the left-luggage locker, then straight back to the station.' Whilst he spoke, Detective Waterman gestured at the two of them to move out of the doorway, pulled the door closed and put a strip of striped 'Police – Do Not Cross' tape over the outside of the door. 'Within the hour, they'll be getting cautioned. The Soco guys will be here shortly.' He waved to a uniformed officer. 'Stapleton, could you stay here? No one goes in until scene of crimes has cleaned up.'

'Did you eat or drink anything whilst you were in the warehouse, Miss Rob – ?'

'Abbey, call me Abbey. I think so, everything's muddled in my mind. I think I drank something – flavoured water.'

'Judging by your eyes, there's a good chance you've been drugged, miss. The statement can wait, but would you mind taking a blood test? And we'll need your clothes for evidence.'

'Right.' Then she whispered, 'Is it really all over?'

'All bar the shouting.' David held open the car door. 'The police doctor is meeting us at the station.' Waterman chatted amicably on the short drive. 'We'll leave you alone until tomorrow after this. Can we reach you both at the beach house?'

Jake looked down at Abbey where she rested sleepily against him. 'That kinda depends on Abbey.'

'I thought you'd be taking off on your boat.' Jake heard a catch in her voice; sensed her trying to hold up. 'I didn't think I'd see you again.' She looked down, but not before Jake glimpsed the tears on her cheeks, 'I didn't know – you should have told me.'

'We'll talk about it later.'

David Waterman glanced in his rear-view mirror, saw Jake wasn't about to blow his own trumpet and plunged in. 'Jake had to drop out of sight, Miss – Abbey, else we might never have blown this open.' He indicated, turned into the police station car-park. 'Never known a guy fight sleep so long – didn't think we could do the job without him.' Then he chuckled and turned off the engine. 'Bloody right he was, too.'

'Waterman, shut up.' Jake growled. 'Miles had enough to do with it working, so did Rick, I didn't do it alone.' For Abbey's ears, he elaborated. 'Miles freaked right out when Rick came up with a lock of your hair – and the ransom note "he'd received".'

Abbey was still trying to grasp that Jake hadn't been away at all. All the time, he'd been around? Helping her?

Her thoughts buzzed relentlessly. She slipped behind a screen and threw off the prickly blanket. Her responses were perfunctory as the police doctor took a blood sample for analysis and, some time later, advised, 'Soon as I have the results of the blood test, I'll contact you. If Nedwell Roberts used the same drug on you as he used on your mother, you'll very likely sleep it off during the next forty-eight hours. It clears the system very quickly.'

'My mother? Is she all right?' The man nodded. 'There's some accumulation taken place in your mother's system, so we need to take things more slowly. There shouldn't be any long-lasting effects, for either of you.'

'Maybe not physically,' Abbey said drily, at which the doctor nodded gravely.

Abbey emerged from the medical room; her eyes immediately lit on Jake. His head drooped forward, his legs were propped on a low table; yet, as though sensing her presence, he blinked himself awake, rose to his feet. 'How're you doing?'

'I'm okay.' Feeling vague, dazed, as if her mind had thrown up a barrier and would only let the enormity of what had happened seep through a bit at a time. If Jake held her close, she would adjust when her world finally stopped pitching and settled. But if he didn't – she couldn't think of that.

Not certain of anything any more, Abbey hesitated; it struck her in that moment, as she stared silently up into Jake's masculine beauty, that she was the one who had to start giving. Jake had given more than she'd ever had a right to expect, sacrificed his beloved freedom on her account for too long. In some kind of fuzzed, off-centre logic, she thought the greatest thing she could offer him was that precious freedom. Tomorrow. Tomorrow would be soon enough for that – tonight she wanted to be with him.

A small smile curved her mouth. She extended her hands to him and took a couple of steps across the tiled floor, found herself in a ferocious bear-hug.w >   'For a minute there, my darling, I thought you were going to come out with some crap like, "I'll see you around".'

A husky laugh broke from her, with his heart pumping hard against her cheek. Then she leant back against his arms and looked up into his ocean-dark eyes. 'What would you have said?'

His smouldering eyes half closed. 'I'd have said you're having a joke, lady.'

A mildly puzzled light shone in Abbey's eyes. He responded to that with, 'Abbey, I ain't going nowhere. What does it take to get through to you?'

Her cheeks heated with the growing awareness that officers behind the counter had stopped talking and were watching them. Jake, on the other hand, seemed oblivious. In the silence, Abbey heard some keys rattle, then stop, as though clasped to muteness in the palm of someone's hand.

'You're not going anywhere?' she repeated vaguely, feeling elated, unreal, cautious all at the same time.

That really did it. A lock of hair fell down on to Jake's forehead with the force of his exasperated reply. 'I love you, Abbey – not "I want to have sex with you" – I love you like I don't wanna live without you!'

She flung her arms around his neck and stood on her tip-toes to kiss Jake's soft, firm mouth; he caught her up so her feet left the ground.

It was Jake who eventually raised his mouth from hers, let her slide down his body as he whispered close to her ear, 'We should finish this at home, Detective Waterman's waiting to give us a lift.' Completely untroubled that their audience was still gripped, Jake put his arm around her, grinned down at her with a smile that moved things inside Abbey she didn't know existed.

During the drive to Fasthead beach house, the detective glanced in the rear-view mirror, saw Abbey sleepily leaning against Jake's shoulder.

'Don't think old Nedwell'll see this side of the bars again in this life. We've got two conspiracy to murder's along with the double kidnapping. He's guilty and seems proud of it – his sisters are looking at a fair old stretch, too. You know, Nedwell's been bragging how he had you shot when you were on a job, Jake, and how he had Miles Pendleton-Smythe's car tampered with before some exhibition. That guy's some piece of work.'

'I'm wondering how he engineered that business at Abbey's exhibition.' Jake rubbed his chin, repositioned his shoulder slightly to cradle Abbey's head against his neck. 'I'm damn sure Abbey said he'd already left when the lights went awol.'

'Camera, mate. Linda, a pal of Abbey's, was taking a ride with him. He lifted the camera when they left; they went back to the exhibition to "pick it up" for her. Linda said Nedwell told her he'd just nipped in quick – she was sleeping at the time, been at the bevvy from what we can gather. All hell broke loose after that.' The detective slowed on the high beach road and indicated into the pull-off. 'Abbey sleeping?'

'Yeah.'

'She could be that way most of the time for the next few days from what the doc said.'

'Yeah, well, we'll get through it. I might do some catching up m'self.'

'Someone'll be over to look at your Land Rover, don't go near it meantime.' The detective waved before pulling away. 'Be in touch.'

EPILOGUE

One month later.

'You're a damned coward, Westaway, you should 'ave done it by now.' He grimaced at the approaching coastline of masts and fishing boats; the movement of people in front of Marianne and Monty's white home clearly visible through the thin morning mist.

'Hi.' Abbey emerged from the cabin, her hair tumbled down over his rugby top, skin dewy, green eyes sparkling. She smiled that crooked smile that twisted his guts and Jake automatically pulled the levers into neutral, pulled Abbey into the space between his legs. 'Woman, you're doing my head in, we're never going to make it to Marianne's at this rate.'

Husky laughter filled Jake's senses as he squeezed her tight. 'All I said was "hi".' She squirmed deliciously as Jake's mouth found hers, his reply delayed until he carried her roughly into the cabin.

'Yeah, well, you never did have to say much to get me going.' Unceremoniously, Jake dumped her on the bed. 'Stay there, I can't think straight when you're too close.' She frowned when he yanked open the locker door, leaned right inside, his voice muffled. 'There's somethin' I keep meanin' to ask you.'

'Ask away.' She smiled, sighed, closed her eyes. The past weeks with Jake had been outrageous, intense, sexy. He hadn't told her those precious words, 'I love you', again; but he didn't need to. He showed her; her skin rippled with warmth just thinking about his smouldering eyes, the way he tried to say nice things, the way they just came out all wrong.

Abbey sat up on the edge of the berth, dragging her fingers through mussed hair as Jake uprighted himself. For a moment, she saw panic in Jake's dark blue eyes. 'Ask away,' she repeated.

'Er – ' He shoved his fingers back through his dark hair, his gaze dropping to the deck. 'I was wonderin' – '

Abbey rose and moved towards him. Jake raised his palm, seemed almost desperate. 'Stay there!'

Shrugging, she dropped back down on to the edge of the berth. 'Okay.'

'I was wonderin' if maybe you'd like to . . .' he hesitated.

Abbey prompted him gently, 'Yes?'

'Hell!' He looked edgy, sounded almost abrupt. 'Now Nedwell and the ugly sisters are banged away, I was wonderin' if you'd like to – change your name?' His knuckles were turning white on the edge of the open locker door, sweat broke on his brow and Jake looked so unsure, so nervous; Abbey loved him more than ever.

'Change it back to Farraday, like my mother has?'

'Fu–dge, no, I mean to Westaway – ' he exploded ' – like my wife.'

'Yes,' Abbey whispered. She wanted to leap up, throw her arms around Jake, but her legs wouldn't hold her. And he seemed so – reluctant? Was this really what he wanted?

'Oh, God . . .' he moaned, his forehead dropping to the edge of the locker door, 'that came out all wrong.' He took a deep breath. 'I love you, Abbey, I'm just no good at this sh– stuff any more.'

Abbey couldn't sit back and witness his torment any longer. She leapt up, took his hands from the locker edge. 'Yes, I want to.' She pressed her mouth to his, loving the honest relief in his bear-hug response, a hug that raised her right off her feet.

What stunned Abbey more than anything was that Jake's eyes were wet when he eventually raised his head. 'I'm sorry, I'm no good at this – '

Abbey put a finger to his lips. 'It doesn't matter how you say it, Jake. I love the way you mean it.'

'I mean it.' A sexy grin curved his mouth. 'I'd show you how much, but it'll have to wait till after.'

'After what?' Abbey kissed him again, determined whatever Jake had in mind could wait.

'Er – till after the wedding.'

She laughed. 'You're kidding? Today?'

'Yep. In a couple of hours.'

'In your rugby shirt?'

'Well – ' his eyes lingered over her ' – I wouldn't object, but our guests might.'

'Guests?'

He led her onto the deck, handed her the binoculars. 'Those guests. Rebecca thought you'd like to wear the dress she wore to marry your pop.'

'Oh, yes!' Through the binoculars, Abbey could just make out her mother, a smiling Callie at her side, Lynn, Miles, Rick, Monty, Marianne and two children. Uncle Ramon and his sons . . . all Jake's cousins. 'Your mother's there, Jake.' She grimaced a little nervously.

'She'll start out by apologizing! She wanted to talk to you on the phone, but no one would let her – she'd have given the whole thing away.'

'Did you arrange all this?' Abbey shook her head in awe.

'Yeah, with Rebecca's help.'

'And you waited till now to ask me to marry you?'

Jake looked sheepish. 'I was scared.'

'Of me?' Abbey shook her head. 'You're not afraid of anyone.'

'I'm afraid of blowin' it with you. That's all I'm afraid of.'

'Don't be.' Abbey smiled that slow, sexy smile. 'I'm Gypsy Rose Abbey, remember? We're going to be friends forever. I know these things.'

Jake laughed at that, his tenseness evaporating, 'Seems like a long time ago you said something like that.'

'I meant it then, Jake, I mean it now . . .'

Jake swung a laughing Abbey round, kissed her, stuck his thumb in the air, could just make out the cheering response on land. 'I ain't never been this happy, darlin'.'

'It just gets better from now on, Jake . . .'

QUESTIONNAIRE

Please tick the appropriate boxes to indicate your answers

1 **Where did you get this Scarlet title?**
Bought in supermarket ☐
Bought at my local bookstore ☐ Bought at chain bookstore ☐
Bought at book exchange or used bookstore ☐
Borrowed from a friend ☐
Other (please indicate) _____

2 **Did you enjoy reading it?**
A lot ☐   A little ☐   Not at all ☐

3 **What did you particularly like about this book?**
Believable characters ☐   Easy to read ☐
Good value for money ☐   Enjoyable locations ☐
Interesting story ☐   Modern setting ☐
Other _____

4 **What did you particularly dislike about this book?**
_____

5 **Would you buy another Scarlet book?**
Yes ☐   No ☐

6 **What other kinds of book do you enjoy reading?**
Horror ☐   Puzzle books ☐   Historical fiction ☐
General fiction ☐   Crime/Detective ☐   Cookery ☐
Other (please indicate) _____

7 **Which magazines do you enjoy reading?**
1. _____
2. _____
3. _____

And now a little about you –
8 **How old are you?**
Under 25 ☐   25–34 ☐   35–44 ☐
45–54 ☐   55–64 ☐   over 65 ☐

cont.

9 What is your marital status?
Single ☐   Married/living with partner ☐
Widowed ☐   Separated/divorced ☐

10 What is your current occupation?
Employed full-time ☐   Employed part-time ☐
Student ☐   Housewife full-time ☐
Unemployed ☐   Retired ☐

11 Do you have children? If so, how many and how old are they?
_____
_____

12 What is your annual household income?

under $15,000	☐	or	£10,000	☐
$15–25,000	☐	or	£10–20,000	☐
$25–35,000	☐	or	£20–30,000	☐
$35–50,000	☐	or	£30–40,000	☐
over $50,000	☐	or	£40,000	☐

Miss/Mrs/Ms _____
Address _____
_____
_____

Thank you for completing this questionnaire. Now tear it out – put it in an envelope and send it, before 31 December 1997, to:

Sally Cooper, Editor-in-Chief

USA/Can. address	*UK address/No stamp required*
SCARLET c/o London Bridge	SCARLET
85 River Rock Drive	FREEPOST LON 3335
Suite 202	LONDON W8 4BR
Buffalo	*Please use block capitals for*
NY 14207	*address*
USA	

DACAN/6/97

Scarlet **titles coming next month:**

SWEET SEDUCTION Stella Whitelaw
Giles Earl believes that Kira Reed is an important executive. She isn't! She's been involved in a serious road traffic accident and is in Barbados to recover. While she's there she decides to seek out the grandfather who's never shown the slightest interest in her. Trouble is – he's Giles's sworn enemy!

HIS FATHER'S WIFE Kay Gregory
Phaedra Pendelly has always loved Iain. But Iain hasn't been home for years. Last time he quarrelled with his father, Iain married unwisely. Now he's back to discover not only has Phaedra turned into a beauty . . . she's also his father's wife.

BETRAYED Angela Drake
Business woman Jocasta Shand is travelling with her rebellious neice. Sightseeing, Jocasta meets famous soap star Maxwell Swift – just the man to help her get even with Alexander Rivers. But Maxwell already has a connection with Alexander . . . and now Jocasta is in love with Maxwell.

OUT OF CONTROL Judy Jackson
Zara Lindsey stands to inherit a million dollars for the charity of her choice, *if* she is prepared to work with Randall Tremayne for three months. Zara can't turn down the chance to help others, but she thinks Randall's a control freak, just like the grandfather who drove her away from home ten years ago. So *how* can she have fallen in love with Randall?